PRAISE FOR

A THOUSAND BEGINNINGS AND ENDINGS

INDIE NEXT PICK

PUBLISHERS WEEKLY BEST BOOK OF 2018

NPR BEST BOOK

ALA BEST FICTION FOR YOUNG ADULTS

FREEMAN BOOK AWARDS FOR CHILDREN'S & YOUNG ADULT LITERATURE ON EAST AND SOUTHEAST ASIA, HONORARY MENTION

NOTABLE SOCIAL STUDIES TRADE BOOKS FOR YOUNG PEOPLE 2019

LOCUS RECOMMENDED READING SELECTION

"Outstanding. . . . Thoughtfully compiled and written, this compendium is a must-read."—*Publishers Weekly* (starred review)

"A collection of Asian myths and legends in which beloved stories of spirits, magic, family, love, and heartbreak are combined with elements from modern teens' lives. . . . An incredible anthology that will keep readers on the edges of their seats, wanting more."—*Kirkus Reviews* (starred review)

"Give to fans of Marissa Meyer's Lunar Chronicles or Rick Riordan's Magnus Chase and the Gods of Asgard."—*School Library Journal* (starred review)

"Contrary to our Disney-fied expectations, not every story has a happy ending—yet another facet to this fine compilation that enhances its ability to surprise, intrigue and delight."—*Chicago Tribune*

"Oh and Chapman have created a work that celebrates Asian storytelling. It should fill . . . the reader with wonder."—*BookPage*

"An inventiveness on par with Bardugo's folktale revisions in *The Language of Thorns*."—*Bulletin of the Center for Children's Books*

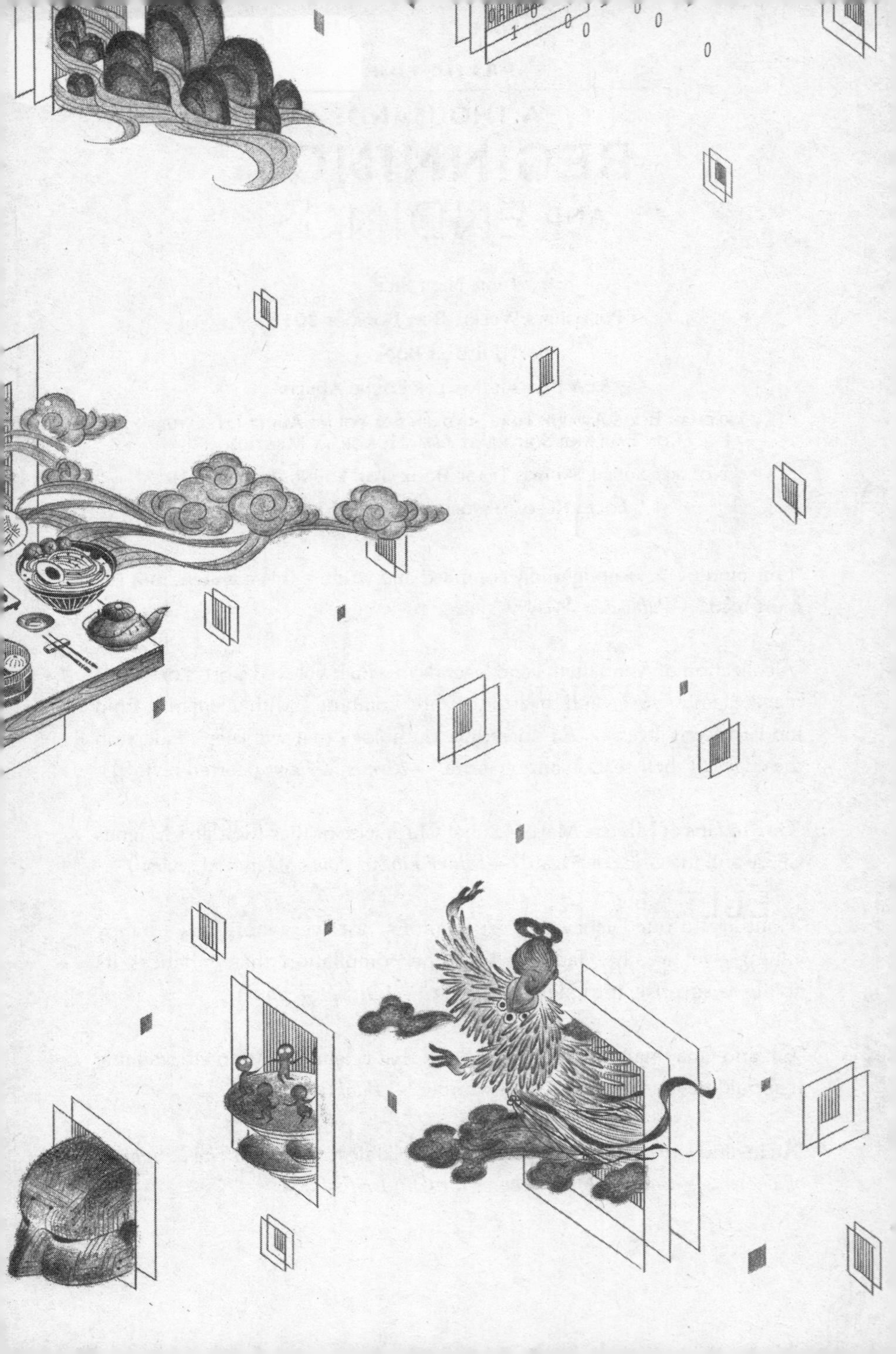

A THOUSAND BEGINNINGS AND ENDINGS

16 RETELLINGS OF ASIAN MYTHS AND LEGENDS

EDITED BY

ELLEN OH • ELSIE CHAPMAN

Greenwillow Books
An Imprint of HarperCollins*Publishers*

This book is a work of fiction. References to real people, events, establishments, organizations, or locales are intended only to provide a sense of authenticity, and are used to advance the fictional narrative. All other characters, and all incidents and dialogue, are drawn from the author's imagination and are not to be construed as real.

 Printed in the United States of America. For information address HarperCollins Children's Books, a division of HarperCollins Publishers, 195 Broadway, New York, NY 10007.
www.epicreads.com

The text of this book is set in Carre Noir Pro Light.
Book design by Sylvie Le Floc'h

Library of Congress Cataloging-in-Publication Data

Names: Oh, Ellen, editor of compilation. Chapman, Elsie, editor of compilation.
Title: A thousand beginnings and endings / Ellen Oh and Elsie Chapman.
Description: First edition. | New York, NY : Greenwillow Books, an imprint of HarperCollinsPublishers, [2018]
Summary: Authors of Asian descent reimagine the folklore and mythology of East and South Asia, in short stories ranging from fantasy to science fiction to contemporary, from romance to tales of revenge.
Identifiers: LCCN 2018020967 | ISBN 9780062671158 (hardback)—ISBN 9780062671165 (pbk. ed.)
Subjects: | CYAC: Mythology, Asian—Juvenile fiction. | Tales—Asia—Juvenile fiction. | Short stories, American. | Mythology, Asian—Fiction. | Folklore—Asia—Fiction. | Fantasy. | Short stories. | Asia—Fiction.
Classification: LCC PZ5 .T372 2018 | DDC [Fic]—dc23 LC record available at https://lccn.loc.gov/2018020967

22 23 24 25 26 LBC 12 11 10 9 8

First paperback edition, 2020

Greenwillow Books

CONTENTS

FROM THE EDITORS

Dear Readers,

For one of us, it was the first book a librarian gave to her when she finally summoned up the courage to ask for a book recommendation—*The Pink Fairy Book*, by Andrew Lang. For the other, it was the one book she ever stole from her elementary school library—a book on mythology. (Not that it was okay to steal the book, but she will finally admit to it now, more than thirty years later, with the school shut down for good, and said thief living on the other side of the world from her hometown.)

We both went on to devour other mythologies: Greek and Norse, from Ares to Danae to Thor to Odin. We fell in love with all those myths about powerful gods being vulnerable, about humans becoming heroes. Such stories taught us about mythology, about the beauty of folktales and legends, and about how stories of gods and goddesses are also stories about the human heart.

But we never found similar compilations that were distinctly Asian. And so many times when we found Asian stories, they were ones retold by non-Asian writers that never felt quite right. They were always missing something. The stories felt superficial at best and at worst, quite hurtful. We longed for nuance and subtlety and *layers*, the embedded truths about culture that—more often than not—can only come from within.

That's why this anthology is so important to us. Here, diasporic Asians reimagine their favorite Asian myths and legends from their own viewpoints. We would have been overjoyed to have found this anthology, filled with characters with skin and hair and names more like ours, in our beloved libraries. It's the book that was missing in our lives for far too long.

Beautiful, heartbreaking, moving, and brilliant—there are not enough words to describe how much we love all of these stories. We hope that you will love them, too. To be able to bring this book to you, written by these amazing Asian authors, is a dream come true.

Elsie Chapman
Ellen Oh

FORBIDDEN FRUIT

ROSHANI CHOKSHI

Do not trust the fruit of Maria Makiling.

If you find your pockets full of thorny fruit, throw it out the window. Do not taste it. Do not stroke the rind and wonder at the impossible pink of its color . . . not meat pink or tongue pink, but that delicate rose of dawn pushing herself from the arms of night. It is not a color of this world.

Fill your pockets with salt. Turn your shirt inside out. Tell Maria you have taken nothing.

But when you walk away, say a prayer.

For it is not her fault.

The Mountain couldn't help but stare.

She had been staring since the moon was nothing but a knob of unripe fruit, and she had been leaning out over her palace since the sky was still the raw and wounded red of a newborn.

Mortals were not beautiful in the sense that their features were pleasing, although some of them had pleasing features, of course. But in truth, they were beautiful because you could only glimpse them. They were beautiful for their fragility, disappearing as fast as a bloom of ice beneath sunlight. And made more beautiful by the fact that they were always changing.

"Dayang," said her father, peering down from his clouds. "Be careful not to lean out so far that your heart falls out."

The Mountain merely laughed.

Her heart was safe.

It was an ill-fated thing to claim that a heart is safe. Hearts are rebellious. The moment they feel trapped, they will strain against their bindings.

And it was so with the Mountain.

Few visited her, for few could climb the sides of the Mountain. In this way, the Mountain diwata discovered loneliness. It was the feeling of negative space, the sudden cold of a column of sunlight moving slowly elsewhere. The diwata wondered what it would be like to be held by the same set of arms each day and night. The Mountain shed lovers like seasons. It was the diwatas' way, just as fruit could not help but fall, and rain could not help but slide.

One day, the diwata went near the bottom of her slope and bathed in a small pool there. When she finished, she let her black hair dry on a sun-warmed rock. Her eyes closed.

She waved her hands lazily, sleepily. Beneath her palms, a

cluster of anemones unfurled from the ground and nuzzled her fingers. A face rose to mind: a human boy with sloe eyes who had wandered up the Mountain a few days past. He had not seen her, which had not surprised her. But what had surprised her was the flare of disappointment in her heart. She wanted to be seen.

A quiet snap broke her thoughts.

A different silence chased the stillness. It was not the silence of emptiness, but *intention*. It felt like a living thing.

Someone had *meant* to stop.

The Mountain jolted upright.

There, standing in the clearing of the woods, was a young mortal man. He wore a beautiful hunting cloak and held a knife, but when he saw her, he dropped it. He sank to his knees, flinging out his arms.

"Goddess, I beg your forgiveness," said the young man.

The Mountain held back a snort. It was not kind to laugh in the face of faith. Yet she was still young, too, and had not learned how to mask her features. Around her, the wind crinkled the leaves.

The young man looked up from his prostration.

"I am no goddess," said the Mountain.

His eyebrows curved into a question. "Are you not the spirit of the Mountain?"

"I am."

But she thought of her mother, her sisters—the ones who spent their time painting stars onto the sky, swelling rivers, and dreaming of new beings. Not like her, whose duty was to tend and not create. Not that the Mountain minded. She got to be close to something that was just a distant dream to the others. She got to be near humans.

The man stood. The Mountain stared. His eyes were not yet crimped by too much sun. His hair was raven lustrous and his muscles lean and sleek. Her heart, though still firmly behind her bones, leaned out curiously.

"Then forgive my presumption," he said. "I couldn't help but think that the most beautiful woman I had ever seen would naturally be a goddess."

She pushed herself off the rock and walked toward him. His eyes widened, wonder tilting his brows and parting his lips. A thrill ran through the Mountain. She laced frost in her hair like a bejeweled net to gather the black strands and expose the steep drop of her neck. Her dress shone sheer and iridescent, crafted of a thousand beetle wings and shells polished to the point of translucence. When she touched him, he shuddered. She wanted to put her lips at his neck's pulse point, to sip lightly at all the things that made him human.

"I would have you," she said simply.

The man's eyes widened. And the Mountain, though she could neither bend nor break, felt her landscape ripple beneath that gaze. He was the first human to see her. It was one thing to crouch unseen and stay separate. It was quite another to stand beheld.

She reached for him, and he reached back.

The Mountain had loved and been loved by many. But none had been human.

It was different. His blood ran hot beneath his skin. There

was urgency here . . . and the Mountain wondered distractedly whether it might scorch her.

Immortals have no urgency. There was never any rush. All lovemaking was slow as poured honey.

This was not.

And the Mountain rather liked it.

"What is your name?" she asked, when they lay still on a bed of anemones.

"Bulan," he said.

Language was not yet pleated into symbols. She could not trace his name upon his chest. Instead, she sounded out the name against his wrist, beneath his ear, upon his neck.

"And yours?" he asked, propping himself on his elbow.

He looked at her, and the Mountain tried to think of what his eyes looked like. They were dark. Shining. Like the black glass left over when a volcano spends its fury.

"You may call me Dayang."

Princess.

Bulan smiled. "A fitting name."

The village worried for Bulan. When he did not return from his hunting expedition by nightfall, search parties combed the forest. At the bottom of Mount Makiling, they found him. He was grinning, arms laden with fruits and vegetables.

"I must have lost track of time," he said.

The villagers were too relieved to notice how he grinned wistfully, turning his head over his shoulder, as if he had forgotten something precious on the mountainside.

From that day on, Bulan spent less and less time in the

village. He did not allow anyone to join him on his expeditions through Mount Makiling. "Too dangerous," he said. But there was a possessive edge to his voice.

Every night, Bulan would return with the creamiest nuts, berries that heaved with juice, fruits that dreamed of flying and not falling, and so arched their green necks to the sun to become all the sweeter for their dreaming. The villagers, though grateful, could not help but wonder where Bulan spent so much of his time. The Mountain was all that separated them from other villages—villages whose chiefs might have wondered over the riches on the other side of the mist, or seafaring queens who might have speculated on the plumpness of the fish just around the Mountain's curves. Bulan's village might know peace, but it had not forgotten wariness. Though a few young men had tried to follow Bulan into the Mountain, a blanket of fog and mist always curtained him from sight. As if the Mountain was keeping him all to itself.

But Bulan did not just receive.

He gave, too.

He brought the Mountain a feather so white it rivaled pearls and threaded it through her hair. He brought a perfectly spiraled shell with a sea's stolen reverie floating in its echo.

"I feel rather like an infant," said Bulan one day, laughing. "I bring you useless, shiny things, for what else could I give someone like you?"

By now, some months had passed. The Mountain enjoyed his company. Not just the touch of his hands and his skin against hers, but his conversation. His dreams. He was no longer merely something that intrigued. He was no longer a *thing* to her at all. When he left, her heart strained hard against her chest, as if it might chase after him. And when he returned, her smile sent a tremor through the world. More and more, she found herself searching for the jewel-bright line of his hunting cloak among the leaves. She looked for him when he wasn't there, and reached for him when he was, and in that way the Mountain found herself part of a rhythm that she had, for once, created. It seemed like an act of the gods. To love.

So when he asked what he might give her, her answer fell bluntly from her lips:

"Your heart."

Her answer was met with silence. Bulan watched her, weighing something secret behind his eyes, and said nothing. He kissed her lightly.

"I will be back."

The Mountain stared after him. She thought he might not return, but the next day, he stood before her. A delicate feather strung round with beads hung from his hand. Folded under his arm was a rough-spun linen dress and a small bundle. He looked as if he had not slept.

When she approached, he prostrated himself once more upon the ground.

"Dayang," he said. "You always had my heart. But I would give you more than that, if you would permit me. I would offer my hand in marriage, my hearth and home, my humble bed and humbler roof."

It had not occurred to the Mountain that Bulan might want things, too. And to realize that he returned her affections sparked a great deal of joy in the Mountain.

She wore the dress for Bulan, even though the thread sliced at her skin and the wooden sandals pinched her toes and the pearl comb tugged her scalp. She tried her best to fit in the clothes. And when he pronounced her maganda—"beautiful," a meaningless word made golden by the alchemy of his lips—she smiled. She wore his promise around her neck.

That night, when they made love, she leaned over him. Her hair brushed against his face. The tip of her feather necklace trailed his chest.

She leaned so far her heart fell out.

And she didn't even notice.

When Bulan gathered her to him, he noticed something in his hand. A gem no larger than his thumbnail.

"Dayang," he said.

It still meant "princess," but it no longer seemed formal. It had no heft, only the worn softness of familiarity.

"What is this?" he asked. "Is it yours?"

The Mountain looked at it for a long while.

Beings like her do not need hearts. They live without them with ease. A heart is important only to those who want to leave the place that tethers their souls and gives them form. And the Mountain, staring into the openness of Bulan's face, had no desire to leave.

"It is my heart," she said. She folded his fingers over the gem. "You will be my husband, and so your heart is mine. And I shall be your wife, and so my heart is yours. Guard it well."

The Mountain and Bulan decided that she would come down from the peak during the springtime festival. Then they could be married, and he could live with her in the secret forests high above the village, for she could not leave her home.

But Bulan wanted something special for his wedding. He wanted everyone to recognize how beautiful and kind his wife was, how blessed he was by her presence. He wanted their celebrations to be grand enough for a dayang.

The Mountain traced the lines of unrest pulling at his mouth.

"What troubles you, my love?" she asked.

Bulan blushed.

"Ah, Dayang, how I wish I could give you a grand celebration. Something that you deserve. But I do not have the means."

The Mountain knew Bulan would never accept gold from her, but she wanted him to be happy, and so . . .

She tricked him.

"Take this," she said, holding out her hand. "It is a different kind of gold, but it will soothe your troubles when you are away from my side."

Bulan smiled, touched by the gesture. It was nothing more than a handful of ginger root, but it would taste good in stew, and it would spice his mind when he chewed the root. He kissed the Mountain fondly.

"Starting tomorrow, I will never leave your side," he whispered, tying his bright cloak around him.

His eyes brimmed with hope, and the Mountain's gaze answered his. Love was a heady thing, and perhaps if the

Mountain was wiser, not so fresh in her affections, she might have been more cautious.

For, you see, a Mountain is a solitary thing. It owns only a crescent of land, the part of itself that arches eagerly to meet the sky. It may look at the beings that dance near its skirts, but it sees only the pattern of their shapes. It does not see, for instance, the slant of their gaze when one among them is continually blessed with catches of fish that look like plump jewels, or always empties pockets full of fruit, or always smiles as if he is better than all the other villagers.

When Bulan took his leave of his Mountain, he did not secure the ends of the pouch of ginger. And even as it grew heavier in his pocket, he did not pay it any mind, for soon he was to be married. If he had looked, he would have noticed that it was no longer ginger.

But gold.

Two men from the village waited for him.

At first, they were satisfied. Bulan was not in league with anyone, as they had first suspected. His hands were empty, which was unusual. Perhaps there was no reason to be jealous. Perhaps he truly was foraging and—as can happen—had found nothing this time. But then they saw the glint of gold in his back pocket.

"Bulan!" they called.

He stopped.

"Where did you get that gold?"

"What gold?" he replied, confused.

One of the men walked up to him, face twisted in a sneer. He ripped the bag of ginger from Bulan, emptying it on the ground. Right before their eyes, the remaining ginger changed to gold.

"How?" asked one.

"Who gave this to you?" demanded another.

Bulan began to panic. The Mountain was his bride. He had to protect her from the greed of humans.

"No one!" he said. "No one gave me anything."

One of the men lit a torch. The other drew a short dagger. "We will make you tell us."

Bulan looked at the moon-gleam on the metal. He knew they were right. They would make him tell.

But not if he took the chance from them first.

"Forgive me, Dayang," he said, reaching for the other man's knife. "I would rather give my life than force you to yield yourself."

Afterward, the men stripped him of his beautiful cloak. They shook it, hoping that golden coins would fly loose.

They did not notice the small jewel heart thumping silently into the dirt.

They might have left the clothes with the body, but the night was cold, and the cloak was beautiful.

And so. And so.

The Mountain wore her wedding dress.

There were flowers in her hair. Pearls around her wrists and ankles. The mist threaded through the trees, and clouds of fireflies hovered softly, so that her world was nothing but sparkling lights and gauzy dreams.

The sun broke upon her face, and the Mountain could not help but think that the sun had never felt so soft and honey-warm as it did now, when it shone with the radiance of a hope teetering on being realized, the kind of decadent hope that's about to be snapped between the teeth and devoured whole.

She waited.

She had made a throne of anemones for Bulan and a crown of blossoms where drowsy bees still slept in the folded palm of a flower. He would be amused, she thought, smiling to herself.

A day passed.

Then two. Then three.

They clotted together, a knot that wouldn't choke itself down.

The Mountain ventured near the slope facing the town. There, she saw Bulan, in the bright orange cloak that he always wore when he made his way to her. The villagers were dancing for their spring festival. Bulan's back was to her, but the Mountain still saw the tawny arms of another woman around his neck.

The Mountain had never been spurned. Her heartbreak was a thing of distance. Like the pressure of a knife before the pain hits. Black, numbing seconds where a hope—that perhaps there will be no pain—flutters just long enough to carve a wound far worse than any knife.

She turned her back. Her tears conjured thunderstorms and swelled rivers. How cruel that he had stolen her heart. Locked her to this place.

On that day, she made a promise: "I will never let another human steal what is mine."

Perhaps, if the Mountain had taken two more steps, she would have seen it. Her heart glinting dully. Covered in dirt. It had fallen far away from Bulan's body, right at the line where the Mountain's skirts met the human village. Perhaps, if the Mountain had waited two more moments, she would have seen the man's face and realized he was not Bulan. Perhaps, if the Mountain had not uttered another oath, things might be different:

"I will find my heart, and no one shall steal from me again."

Perhaps, perhaps, perhaps.

All splinters of a tale.

That is why you must not laugh when you see a beautiful woman scrabbling at things in the dirt or reaching for high branches.

That is why you must turn your clothes inside out.

That is why you must empty your pockets of fruit.

For the Mountain does not like you to take things that do not belong to you.

Maria Makiling

A Filipino Folktale

Sometimes a guardian spirit, other times a precolonial goddess, Maria Makiling is associated with the Philippine's beloved Mount Makiling, whose peaks resemble the profile of a young woman. Always breathtakingly beautiful, the reasons for why she stays on the mountain differ from time period to storyteller. The most popular stories about Maria have her stealing away young men to live with her in the forests of the mountain. But her love affairs are not always blissful. In one version of the story, told by José Rizal, the Filipino poet and national hero, Maria falls in love with a young man who spurns her love when the army begins to recruit. Instead of waiting for Maria, he marries a mortal woman so that he can safely stay inside his village. Mournfully, she tells him she would have protected him if only he had waited for her. In another tale of Maria, she shows her benevolence by turning ginger into gold for a group of villagers. But her benevolence backfires. In some versions of the tale, the villagers are grateful and show her love. In others, they become greedy, and break into her mountain garden, hungry to see whether all that Maria grows is made of gold.

Maria is deeply tied to the landscape. People still report sightings of a woman dressed in white, walking the long mountain road. Sometimes she tries to get a ride down the mountain. As if there were something she is trying to outrun.

I chose this story because no one tale can pin down the personality of this mountain goddess. And yet all stories warn us not to steal from her. I wanted to know why. "Forbidden Fruit" is my exploration of her background and my homage to her presence.

—Roshani Chokshi

OLIVIA'S TABLE

ALYSSA WONG

Olivia blew into town with the storm and headed straight for the Grand Silver Hotel. Pots and containers of sauces and marinades clattered in the trunk of her Toyota, packed in with the rest of the groceries she'd brought from Phoenix. The evening sky hung heavy with dark clouds, but the shrinking Arizona sun still burned her arms through the car windows.

Bisden was one of those mining towns that had sprung up in the eighteen hundreds, flourished for a while, and then all but died once the silver ran out. Now, the town made its money from the tourists who trickled in, hoping to see two things: a real Wild West ghost town and one of the most haunted historical sites in the southwest.

After a childhood of making the trip down from Phoenix, Olivia barely needed her GPS to guide her. She drove past the sparse palo verdes lining the old shop fronts. Outside, the wind whipped up sharp clouds of dust and stone shards, sending them sweeping down the barren, red-dirt road that ran through Bisden's town square. The air carried a light brown tint, and Olivia squinted to see through it.

In front of a clapboard saloon, two reenactment actors in full period dress were toughing out the approaching dust storm, fingering the pistols hanging at their hips. Most of the town's tourists had migrated inside; a few hung back to watch them, shading their eyes or filming on their phones.

And then there were the ghosts, dozens of them, clustered around the tourists and swaying in the wind like feather grass. A few were dressed in fine clothes—long skirts and blouses buttoned to the throat, cravats tucked into tight waistcoats—but most were dressed in working clothes. Wide-brimmed hats, sturdy trousers, loose shirts. Only some of them were white folks. All bore signs of trauma; gunshots punched a cluster of holes through one gentleman's torso, and a cluster of women hanging back by the saloon had burned, blackened bodies, the remains of their dresses drifting around them in ashes.

Olivia sighed. They were right in front of the Grand Silver Hotel, too. Figured.

She slung her backpack over her shoulder and pocketed her phone. Her braid was coming loose, but she ignored it. After locking her car, Olivia pulled out the long envelope of paper talismans that her grandma had written years ago. She slapped one over each of the car windows, and the coppery scent of magic sparked in the air. The sky rumbled overhead as she retrieved a pack of Saran Wrap and taped sheets of plastic over the talismans. If this worked, the talismans would keep ghosts away from the car, and the Saran Wrap would keep the rain away from the talismans.

It would work, she thought firmly. It'd worked for her mom all the times they'd made the trip together. And even though she wasn't here now, Olivia had watched her ward her car like this for years.

No time for doubts. She headed for the hotel, past the reenactment actors and tourists. She had to push her way through the ghosts. Their bodies felt more solid than they did the rest of the year, and fabric brushed her hands as she edged through the crowd. "Excuse me," she muttered. A pair of Hopi women glanced down at her from beneath the brims of their hats, turning to make room for her to squeeze by. A cluster of Chinese miners, their bodies broken and smashed—*A cave-in*, she thought, *an accident*—watched her, unmoving, from a distance. None of the tourists seemed to see the ghosts, staring through them at the girl weaving her way through empty air.

The Grand Silver Hotel rose three stories, clinging to its last shreds of grandeur. Inside, new lightbulbs shone in old fixtures, and the tatty carpet crunched under Olivia's sneakers. Like every other establishment in town, the Grand Silver kept its head above water by advertising its very own ghost. An oil painting of the Wailing Lady hung on the wall above the reception desk, and a rotating rack of postcards, most of them reproductions of the painting, spun lazily by the elevator door. The older woman behind the desk smiled as Olivia approached. Her name tag read *Renee*. "Welcome to the Grand Silver Hotel. How may we help you today?"

"I'm here for the Ghost Festival," said Olivia. Her voice sounded too loud in the nearly empty lobby. She hated listening to herself speak; talking, period, wasn't easy for her. "I need a room for tonight and tomorrow night, and some help getting things out of my car."

Renee brightened. "Of course. The Ghost Festival is tomorrow night, and it's one of Bisden's big attractions. Now, there are a few other groups of tourists who made the trip here to see it, so you won't be alone. It's perfectly safe, but we do ask that everyone stay inside and keep a healthy distance from the ghosts—"

"I'm not a tourist," Olivia said. "I'm here to cook the banquet for the festival." She reached for her driver's license, and her student ID slipped out first. She caught it before it hit the ground. "You've worked with my mom before. Amory Chang."

The receptionist squinted. "You're Exorcist Chang's daughter, are you? You do look a bit like her." *It's nice of her to lie,* thought Olivia. "She helped us out for years. Every summer, on the night when the ghosts come out to walk among the living. And her cooking, of course, was sublime."

Thank you, Olivia wanted to say, but the words wouldn't come. Renee didn't seem to notice.

"We're looking forward to having you for the Ghost Festival. Exorcist Chang was always a wonder to watch. Excellent showmanship, and her work kept the town safe for years." As Olivia checked into her room, Renee paused. "By the way. Our Wailing Lady is getting . . . unruly. Could you look into fixing that up, or finding a replacement? It's been almost ten years since your mother tended to our ghost."

The Wailing Lady's painting hung serenely on the wall. It depicted an ample young woman wearing a wedding dress and a veil that obscured her face. A jilted, suicidal bride, whose weeping could still sometimes be heard late at night. Not very original. "I'll look in to it," said Olivia.

Renee and the two folks working at the hotel—a maid and a young man who was probably her son—helped lug Olivia's vats of soy sauce and marinade from her car and into the hotel kitchen. Rice, cooking utensils, and paper bag after paper bag of different kinds of meat followed. Pickings at the Bisden supermarket were slim, so she'd brought everything she could fit into the Toyota's back seat and trunk. As they carried the groceries inside, Olivia caught sight of the ghosts out front. The reenactment actors were gone, and now the ghosts stared, as one, at Olivia and the hotel employees.

The air smelled like approaching rain. She walked faster.

After sussing out the kitchen—on the small side, though all of the kitchens at the old Bisden hotels were—Olivia checked her phone. No signal, no internet, though there were a couple of password-locked hotspots from the shops nearby. The Grand Silver had its own router, and Renee gave Olivia the password along with a long, old-fashioned metal key. "You'll be in room three-oh-nine," she said.

Olivia spent the next couple of hours in that kitchen, cutting, testing, prepping. It was night by the time she finished. When she made it upstairs to her room, she crouched on the floor by the bed and set out packet after packet of incense and joss paper. She hoped she'd brought enough. Enough incense, enough food—

No, it would be enough. She unpacked a small ceramic bowl and emptied a handful of dried orange peel into it, and then she lit a match over it. Once, her mom had taught her that the smoke from burning orange peel would keep the ghosts away. It had never failed her.

Olivia hesitated. The flame licked down the match, chasing her fingers. After a second, she shook it out.

Wind rattled the windows as she settled into bed. The sounds of faint footsteps upstairs and a woman sobbing through the floorboards chased her into her dreams.

It had rained during every Ghost Festival that Olivia could remember. On the seventh month on her mom's calendar and the eighth month on her dad's, Mom would pack the minivan with food and head down south for a couple of days, leaving Olivia in Dad and Grandma's care. It was monsoon season, and torrential rain flooded the roads and the stony washes out behind the houses. But when the skies cleared, Mom would return with an empty trunk and a check for more money than she made in half a year.

For a time, she didn't tell Olivia where she went or what she did. But the year Olivia turned eight, Mom loaded her into the back seat next to the paper bags of groceries and drove her to Bisden for the first time.

Come with Mama, she said. Back then, her short black hair was only faintly laced with silver, and she still looked healthy. *I need you to help me with the Ghost Festival this year.*

The drive was several hours long, and by the time they reached the tiny town, sunset was approaching. So was a storm, a desert monsoon that crawled inexorably across the horizon. That night, they checked into the Grand Silver, although in the coming years, they would rotate from hotel to hotel, collecting paychecks from many grateful proprietors. Every hotel in town wanted the chance to host the festival and attract the bulk of that year's tourists. Mom told Olivia that when her own mom, and the long line of Chang women before her, had cooked for the Ghost Festival, in this country and in their countries before that, they'd rarely stayed in a place for more than a year.

Different ghosts are tied to different spaces, Olivia, Mom said as they got ready for bed. The lamp cast a warm glow across her face. *Sometimes they form attachments to specific places, and sometimes other people bind them there and they can't leave. Moving the banquet means bringing food to folks who missed their chance to eat the year before. Good service is all about being considerate of others.*

Mom spent the entire night and then the next day prepping and cooking, and she had Olivia help her as much as possible. Olivia stood on a little metal stool and cut vegetables. Her knife cuts were careful and even under her mom's strict tutelage. Occasionally, she peered out the windows, watching the tourists run through the rain, their eyes growing huge and round, even from this distance, whenever they glimpsed one of the ghosts.

"They're scared of them," Mom told her as she set out a pair of bamboo steamers. "Right now they can see them."

"Can't they see the ghosts all the time?" she asked.

"Not like you and I can. The festival is when ghosts are most themselves instead of what the living want them to be. Not everyone will like what they see tonight."

When Olivia's arms grew tired, Mom sent her out of the kitchen to take breaks. The long banquet table that Mom had requested from the hotel was set up on the front porch. She crawled under it and watched the rain slosh down the road in growing streams, swirling with red-brown dirt, until the daylight faded and the electric lights came on.

Her Game Boy. She'd forgotten it in the car. Olivia didn't have an umbrella, but she ran out into the rain anyway, letting it beat at her through her clothes. It only rained for about two weeks each year, and the cool droplets hitting her face filled her with giddy energy. She sprinted down the street toward her mom's car, splashing deliberately in the biggest pools of water she could find.

Halfway down the darkening street, a voice stopped her: "You're not from here."

Olivia turned sharply. A ghost stood under the awning of the Bisden General Store, leaning against a post. She wore a cotton shirt and trousers, like many of the other folks who'd worked on the railroad when they were alive. There weren't many women among the Chinese ghosts. But this one was a girl, with deep brown hair like Olivia's, and a small mouth and dark eyes like Olivia's. She looked a little older than Olivia, but not nearly as old as Olivia's mom.

"Did someone lose you?" said the ghost.

"Nobody lost me," said Olivia. "I came to get my Game Boy." She came a little closer, under the awning, and the ghost didn't shrink back. When Olivia reached out to touch her sleeve, her hand passed through. "What's your name?"

"Mei Ling," said the ghost. She sounded amused. From this distance, Olivia could see that her legs were mangled, the way a number of other Chinese ghosts who'd died in construction accidents were. "My ma calls me Sadie, though."

"I'm Olivia," said Olivia. "My grandma gave me a Chinese name, too, but my dad doesn't like me using it." She'd overheard her dad talking with her grandma one night, when she was very little. *What will she do when the other kids tease her at school?* he'd said. Olivia didn't tell him that the other kids teased her anyway, name or no name.

"I don't know what a Game Boy is," said the ghost. "But why don't I walk with you while you get it?"

An alarm bell in Olivia's head began to ring. *Don't talk to strangers,* Mom had said, over and over. *And don't trust the ghosts, especially not during the Ghost Festival.* "No," she said. "I'm okay. It's just over there."

But the ghost followed her. Olivia began to run faster, and the creak of the ghost's ruined ankles grew louder and louder as the night got darker. The rain pounded down around them. The water rushed across the ground in rising torrents with no gutters to guide it away from the street.

Where was the car? It was dark, and the electric lights seemed so dim, and the ghost was behind her, lurching forward, moving too fast—

Olivia's foot slipped out from under her and she fell backward into the water. Her head cracked hard against a stone, and the flash flood pulled her, rolling and gasping, down the street and onto her face. She inhaled a lungful of water. Olivia choked and tried to push herself up, but her palms slid on the loose gravel and her hands slipped out from under her.

She was drowning. Two weeks of rain a year, and this was

how she'd die. When she came back as a ghost, would her lungs be full of water forever?

Olivia reached out blindly, and someone grabbed her arm. The ghost hauled her out of the water. When she rubbed Olivia's back as Olivia coughed, her hand was solid and warm, all the way down to her broken fingers. Her cotton work-clothing was soaked through.

Olivia's head was bright with pain.

Mei Ling lifted her and held her close to her chest. The ghost had no heartbeat. And then they were running, splashing through the rising water, headed back to the town square. The last thing Olivia saw were the stuccoed walls of the Grand Silver and the hordes of ghosts descending upon her mother's banquet table, their swarming, newly substantial bodies rippling in the moonlight.

Olivia woke too early, her heart pounding loud in her ears. The roof rattled like someone was upending stones on it. The muted roar of torrential rain surrounded her, and when she pushed back the curtains, she saw that the street was full of rushing water, just as it had been all those years ago. No living people were out and about, not even the actors from yesterday. But ghosts—so many of them, almost too many to count—huddled under porch roofs and awnings, their bodies all clumped together, away from the rain.

Overhead, the sobbing had stopped. Last night, through the haze of half-swallowed dreams, the woman's voice had sounded familiar. Olivia listened carefully, but she could hear nothing but the storm.

She checked her phone for missed calls and found that there were none. No phone service. Right. But there was internet, so she emailed her dad: *I made it to Bisden safely. Cooking all today. I'll be home soon. Love you. Don't forget to eat.*

Too late, she remembered that her mom used to sign off all her texts and emails the same way. But she'd already hit Send. She bit her lip, then turned away to pull on her jeans.

Despite the early hour and pouring rain, the ghosts on the street were already out in full force. She walked past them, and their heads followed her on skinny, starved necks, rotating like owls'. The full moon was a brief imprint in the sky, barely visible through a gap in the darkened clouds. As Olivia headed for her car, the boy who'd helped her move her supplies into the kitchen ran after her. "Hey," he said breathlessly. "Mom asked me to help you if you needed anything."

Olivia looked at him. He looked about her age, maybe seventeen at most. She couldn't remember his name. "I'm just going grocery shopping," she said.

"I'll help you carry things if you want. I don't mind." He grinned. "I'm Carlos."

He did look strong, Olivia conceded. His arms and back were well muscled. When he smiled, he had cute dimples. If she had been interested in men, she might have found him attractive. "I'm Olivia," she said. "I'm going to buy a lot of stuff, though."

"I figured. I didn't think ghosts would eat a lot, but apparently they do." He didn't seem bothered by the rain or by the ghosts who watched them from the awnings. But then, he didn't seem to see the ghosts at all.

The best thing about the Bisden supermarket, Olivia decided, was that it was cheap. She headed straight for the back counter and bought two dozen fresh fish. These were dead—not as fresh as the live ones swimming in tanks at the Chinese market back home—but they would do. She loaded her cart up with fresh produce: green onions, carrots, garlic, herbs. Four crates of oranges. It was too bad that Bisden didn't have a Costco.

Carlos talked a lot, but he did hold up his end of the bargain. He carried all her groceries and helped load them into her car. He told her all about his schooling (he was a junior, one year younger than her), his aspirations (to go to Arizona State and study mechanical engineering), and his boyfriend (Sean, beautiful and geeky, also an aspiring engineer). "What about you?" he said as they drove through the pouring rain. "Do you have someone you like?"

"I did," said Olivia. "But we broke up a while ago." It had been a year and a half ago, in the spring. Priya was a year ahead of Olivia in school, and when she found out she was going to an East Coast college, she was ecstatic.

Olivia hadn't wanted to keep Priya tied down. With Priya going east and Olivia staying in Arizona, it made sense to break things off. But Priya hadn't agreed, and when she'd cried and Olivia didn't, she'd accused Olivia of not caring enough to be there for her.

But you're going out of state, Olivia had said. *I can't just move to Boston for you.*

Priya had blown her wavy black hair away from her face and stared her down. *You know that's not what I'm talking about. Even when we're together, having dinner, watching movies or whatever, you're always so detached. It feels like you're somewhere else, not with me.* Her mouth tightened. *Is there someone else?*

There was the memory of a girl in dark cotton trousers, her hair hanging down her shoulders, pulling her from the water. There was also Mom, lying alone in the hospital, watching dramas until she fell asleep. She'd never told Priya about either, because they felt too private to talk about. *No,* said Olivia.

By the time Priya left for college, they had fallen apart.

Olivia and Carlos drove the rest of the way back in silence. As they were unloading the car, Carlos stopped in his tracks. Olivia glanced at him. "What is it?"

"I thought—" he broke off, frowning. He looked pale. "I thought I saw something. Over there, to your left. But it's gone now."

Olivia looked. The ghost of an old man, his body wracked with disease, looked back at her. His sunken eyes glittered. "I don't see anything," she said.

"Let's get the rest of these inside," said Carlos, hurrying past her.

Olivia cast one last look at the ghost and followed. If Carlos was starting to see them, she'd have to cook fast. The moon was rising; the Ghost Festival was coming. Her palms began to sweat. She wiped them on her jeans and strode inside, past the tourists beginning to mill about in the lobby with pamphlets about the Ghost Festival.

Olivia sorted her ingredients on the counters, arranging them by dish. Duck, pork, shrimp, fish. Winter melon, out of season, but bought from one of the Chinese markets back home. Spices, marinades. Red beans, sesame oil, sugar, salt. Bok choy, green beans, lotus root, sauces that she'd spent the past two days making.

Carlos hung back by the door. "Don't you have work to do?" she said to him, and then winced. *Too blunt. The words are wrong.* Always wrong, when they came out of her.

"I do," he said. He seemed unfazed, and the tight knot in Olivia's chest loosened. "But I want to help if I can. You need someone to help you chop and prep, right? I cook meals in this kitchen all the time."

A surge of relief flooded through her. "Thank you," she said quietly. She indicated the vegetables lying in their neat rows. "I need these chopped. Garlic minced, green onions left long, but not longer than a finger. Carrots thinly sliced. Winter melon cubed."

"Do you have a recipe?"

"Only in my head," she said. That was how Mom had done it, too.

Carlos sighed and picked up a knife. "All right. Let's get to work."

They worked for hours, and soon they began to learn each other's rhythm. The clock over the sink ticked, and sunlight passed across the windows and grew dark. Olivia didn't have to look outside to know that people were locking themselves in their houses, pulling the curtains shut. Only the curious tourists kept watch, peering through the large glass windows of every hotel lining the street. All the hotels would have bolted their front doors shut except for the Grand Silver. Not the

Grand Silver, because Olivia still had to hurry in and out with her food. Its thresholds were already lined with paper talismans to ward off any ghosts bent on mischief, or worse.

Time flew by, and Olivia sweated and braised and fried and steamed. Her muscles ached, but adrenaline and fear kept her body and mind singing. The rising spirit energy from outside grew to a tight, intense buzz in her head. She could hear the ghosts through the walls—whispering, waiting—and by the expression that Carlos wore, so could he. And then there was a wet, whining sound coming from inside the hotel, and the drag of broken feet in high heels in the ceiling above, somewhere in the air vents.

The moon rose, and Olivia began to plate.

After Olivia's mom got sick, she became too weak to move around much. She was supposed to stay still, to conserve her energy. Moving made her nauseated. But the one place that Olivia's dad couldn't chase her out of was the kitchen. Even when she had trouble standing, she still insisted on cooking dinner for the family. Olivia helped her into a chair by the stove, and she sat there for hours, making sure all of the meal's components were cooking properly. Olivia did what she could to ease the burden, measuring liquids, cooking the rice, making sure all the ingredients were chopped so that her mom didn't have to worry about it.

One afternoon, her mother smiled up at her. "You're getting so good at this. I'm glad. You'll have to do this when I'm gone."

A lump rose in Olivia's throat. "That's not going to happen." *I can't fill your shoes,* she thought. "You're going to get better."

"Don't let the sesame seeds burn," said Mom, and Olivia swooped in automatically, rescuing the frying pan of toasted seeds. "Good, good. Let them cool somewhere safe."

Olivia set them aside in a small bowl. Her hands were trembling. "I can't lose you. Dad can't lose you. You're going to get better. I know it."

Mom reached out. Her fingers felt so delicate, so thin. "If you honor everything I've taught you, then I promise that I will never leave you." She held Olivia's hand and squeezed it. "I love you, Xi Yi."

Olivia hadn't heard that name in years, not since her grandma had passed away. Tears welled up in her eyes. "Mom—"

The kitchen timer went off. Her mom moved to take the ging do pai gwut off the heat and transferred it into a waiting ceramic dish. "Remember," she said to Olivia. "Now take this to the table."

The banquet table waited on the Grand Silver's porch, safe from the rainstorm and the rushing water below. An outline of talismans marked a boundary around it, leading to the hotel doors. All along its edges, ghosts clustered and crowded, whispering among themselves. They were substantial, all flesh and bone, just for this one night. Just to feast until the sun came up. Above, in a gap in the heavy clouds, the full moon hovered like a malevolent eye.

Olivia came out with a cart laden with giant pots and stacked with metal dishes, clattering past the tourists gathered in the lobby, ignoring their questions. She refused to let Carlos follow her out onto the porch, and she felt his eyes on her back as she crossed the Grand Silver's threshold. She laid platter after platter of Peking duck in the center of the table, forming a line of meat and soft, pale, steamed buns. She removed the lids of the pots and the scent of winter-melon soup rose through the thick air. As quickly as she could, she began to fill bowls.

The ghosts whispered and pushed their hands up against the barrier, hissing when copper-scented magic sparked against their skin. Cold sweat rose on Olivia's back. But her hands were steady as she continued to ladle soup into bowls. Finally, there was no more room on the tabletop. Olivia stepped back, laying down another line of talismans so that there was a narrow, unobstructed passage from the door to the table.

She raised her voice. "Welcome, honored guests. My name is Olivia Chang, and I have prepared you a banquet, so that you may take and eat and find peace in your souls." Her mom had given this speech many times, and Olivia did not stumble. "Please come. You are welcome at this table."

With that, she broke the talisman barrier around the table. The ghosts fell upon the food. They shoved at each other, grabbing bowls, seizing chopsticks. Some used their hands and pushed food into their mouths as fast as they could. Many of them barely looked human in their hunger. They tore into the meat with ferocity, pushed their faces into the bowls of soup and snarled at their neighbors to get at the dishes they wanted. The food seemed to evaporate as the ghosts fought and bit and ate, ate, ate.

I didn't make enough, Olivia thought wildly. Dread built in her stomach. *All these people came to my table, and I can't serve them all.*

Breathe.

She breathed. Grabbing the cart, she doubled back for more food. Shrimp in clear, sweet sauce; crab with ginger and scallions. Fish after fish, all steamed, with sharp, salty sauce. Tender, marinated beef, still sizzling on metal plates. Bak cheet gai, with all of the sauces; hot-pepper pork chops. Her mother's ging do pai gwut, sweet and glazed in bright red sauce, sprinkled with toasted sesame seeds. (Olivia's heart ached.) And then, finally, platter after platter of sliced oranges and bowls of sweet red-bean soup. They vanished almost as soon as she put it out, but Olivia kept up her pace, her legs burning, her hands steady.

The night wore on, and more spirits flocked to the table, replacing those who had filled their bellies and wandered away. The moon drifted. In the lulls between waves, Olivia kept watch, burning incense and joss paper over a small fire. Embers wafted up into the air like wishes, and one by one, they winked out. The rain poured down relentlessly.

Mei Ling did not appear. Olivia watched the table, chewing on her lip so hard that it began to taste raw. Ghosts came, some eating quietly, some ravenously. The wildness in their eyes, their grief, their fear and rage, all ebbed as they ate. Take and eat, she'd said. The Chinese-American ghosts were the ones who wept the most, laughing and reveling in familiar foods. "Thank you," they told her, one after another. "I never thought I would taste this again." And one after another, they vanished, fading away to rest at last.

This was why she was here, as Exorcist Chang. It was only an exorcism in the loosest sense. Her work wasn't an act of expulsion; her role was to soothe lonely souls, offering them freedom.

Olivia thought about the footsteps overhead, the sobbing at night. She sent up her piece of joss paper and headed back inside, through the clump of tourists in the lobby. They tried to speak to her, but she didn't hear them. She stopped by the reception desk, staring up at the portrait of the Wailing Lady.

Yesterday, Renee had leaned over the counter and smiled at her. *Our Wailing Lady is getting . . . unruly. Could you look into fixing that up, or finding a replacement?*

The longer a ghost stayed in one place without release, the more restless it became. Bisden lived and died on its haunted attraction tourism. And when a ghost acted up, it lent legitimacy to the stories. But ghosts that were trapped for too long began to go mad, and that was when people got hurt.

Olivia stared at the painting, at the white veil covering the Wailing Lady's face. In the ten years of Ghost Festivals since that first one at the Grand Silver, Olivia hadn't seen Mei Ling once.

Beneath that veil, the Wailing Lady could be anyone.

She turned and ran for the kitchen. There was still some rice, just enough for one bowl. Everything else was gone, presented and eaten on the table outside. Olivia hoped the rice would do. She took the stairs up to the third floor and headed back to her room. As she ascended, the familiar sound of sobbing drifted down toward her, and she climbed faster. When Olivia opened the door, she saw a woman standing inside by the window, gazing out at the feast below. She wore a white wedding gown, stained with dirt at the hem, and a long white veil. She turned to face Olivia.

Olivia peeled the talisman necklace from her neck and laid

it on the floor beside her. Slowly, she approached, holding out the rice. "I brought you something to eat," she said. This time, her voice didn't sound too loud in her ears. "It's not much. But you seem hungry. Please, honored guest, take and eat."

The Wailing Lady didn't move, but she let Olivia approach. Steam wafted gently from the rice into the air. Rain battered down outside, beating at the window, demanding to be let in. Olivia reached out, offering up the bowl.

The ghost reached back, taking it. The hands around hers were warm and solid.

Gently, Olivia pushed back the veil.

When Olivia's mom had died, she didn't come back as a ghost. Olivia half expected her to. But she didn't materialize in the hospital room when Dad chose to take her off life support, or on any of the nights when Olivia heard her dad crying alone in his bedroom. At the funeral, there had only been the silent Mom-shaped body nestled in her casket.

People became ghosts when they were restless, or had unfinished business, or held too much regret to pass on. They became ghosts when the ones they loved forgot them or didn't pay them respects. Olivia burned incense despite the fire warnings on especially dry days, and some days, she set aside a small dish of whatever she was cooking to put on Mom's altar later. But she kept the small shrine in her room, away from Dad. Whenever he saw it, his mouth would crumple and he'd leave abruptly, his grief chasing him somewhere else.

Olivia started staying late at school, just to be somewhere else. She withdrew from her friends, hiding in the library. Her grades suffered and improved. Slowly, it dawned on her that her mom was gone. Not just dead-and-a-ghost gone, but gone-gone.

People only became ghosts when they had something tying them to this place. Olivia's mom, it seemed, had nothing to keep her here.

Olivia didn't apply to college. Every time she reached the Family section on the applications—Parents' Names? Level of Education? Relationship? Living? Deceased?—her head filled with static. The essay questions were inane: "What did you do last summer and how did it impact you?" just made her think of the ugly, ultraclean stink of the hospital and how she would never forget it, as much as she wanted to. Besides, someone had to take care of Dad. She couldn't leave him, too.

Her relationship with Priya crumbled, and Olivia let it.

Her friends packed and left for college, and Olivia cooked, and paid bills, and cooked. She made sure all of her mom's emails were forwarded to her own email address, and that the small dish in front of her altar was never empty. When she opened the email from the Grand Silver asking Exorcist Chang to prepare her banquet for the Ghost Festival that year, Olivia's heartbeat jumped.

The one night when spirits walk among us.

She'd helped prepare the banquet every year, but she'd never done it alone. And she hadn't been back to the Grand Silver since that first summer in Bisden.

"Dad," she said that evening, twisting her napkin into tight rings under the table, "I'm going to Bisden in August."

He looked up with a sad smile. He'd gotten so much older in the past months, she realized. "I know," he said.

❖❖❖

Olivia found herself looking into the face of a stranger. A hard face, weathered with age and hunger.

It wasn't Mei Ling. It wasn't Mom. It wasn't anyone she knew.

"Who are you?" Olivia whispered, and the ghost stared silently back at her. The old Chinese woman's gaze was vacant, and she shifted back and forth, her ill-fitting wedding dress whispering around her. Olivia wondered if she was a bride at all, or if someone had bound her to the Grand Silver Hotel against her will to serve as their ghost. This woman didn't look like the young, pretty, white girl that the hotel's brochures advertised as the Wailing Lady. Maybe that hadn't mattered to the person who had trapped her here.

But if there was a night for truth, it was tonight. Mom had said so: during the festival, ghosts were most themselves. Not what the living wanted. Not what Olivia wanted.

The night of the festival was a chance for freedom.

Olivia bit back her disappointment and smiled at the woman. She held out a pair of chopsticks, and the woman took them and began to eat. The rice wasn't much, something small and humble. But with every bite, the woman's gaze grew sharper and more aware, and her movements became more coordinated. Soon, the rice was gone. Olivia opened her mouth to apologize, but the stranger spoke first.

"Thank you," she said. Her voice was raspy, and Olivia wondered if it was because of all her crying. "Will you walk me to the door, child?"

Olivia took her arm and led her to the elevator. The woman

gazed at her reflection in the elevator's brass walls as they rode down to the first floor. They walked together past the tourists, who gawked but kept a healthy distance. Olivia thought she saw Renee moving toward them, but the crowd of tourists had closed in tight against one another, blocking her way with their bodies.

As they crossed the threshold, the woman raised her arms and her white wedding dress and veil crumbled into dust. Somewhere behind them, Renee shouted. Beneath the dress, the woman wore hardy cotton traveling clothes and a loose coat. There was a hat in her hands that she placed on her head, tugging the brim. The strong, determined set of her shoulders reminded Olivia of her grandma.

"Thank you for the food, child," said the woman. She patted Olivia's arm. "After being alone for so long, I forgot what it felt like to have family cook for you. And that is what your offering felt like." She began to fade, but before she was fully gone, she gave Olivia's arm a squeeze. "Go feed your guests."

Olivia looked up. The sky was beginning to lighten, and most of the ghosts had vanished. But there were still a few at the table, picking at the remains of the food. One of them stood out: a girl wearing trousers, with deep brown hair and a small mouth. Her clothing and hair were soaked, and when she caught sight of Olivia, the corners of her mouth curved upward.

"The Game Boy girl," said Mei Ling. "You grew up."

Warm, welcome heat spread through Olivia's chest. Mei Ling hadn't changed at all since she'd first seen her. "I did," she said. "Thanks to you."

Mei Ling looked at the table and sighed. "It's almost all gone. It looked so good, too." She tucked a strand of hair behind her ear, scanning the remnants of the banquet. "I almost made it to the table the last time your mom cooked at the Grand Silver, but I didn't get there in time."

Olivia's stomach dropped. She remembered Mei Ling carrying her, bearing her toward the Grand Silver. Had she slowed her down and caused her to miss her chance to cross over?

"I know what you're thinking," said Mei Ling. She reached out to ruffle Olivia's hair. When she pulled away, her crooked fingers brushed against Olivia's forehead. "Don't. I don't regret it. I saw a little kid in trouble, and I did my best to save her. I wish someone had been there to do that for me."

The most important part of service was being considerate of others, Mom had said. Olivia bit her lip and scanned the table. All the plates had been picked over; even the fish skins and eyes were gone. "I'm going to find you something to eat," she said. "I'm going to feed you so you can find your way home."

Mei Ling shook her head. "The sun's rising, kid. The banquet's over."

Olivia picked through the plates with her fingers, pushing aside gnawed-on bones. There was no gristle, and most of the sauce had been licked off of the plates. Mei Ling was right; there was no food left on the table.

Her gaze flicked to the serving cart resting by the Grand Silver's door. She crouched beside it, peering between the shelves. *There,* she thought. Splashes of sauce and little bits of food had spilled out of their dishes and onto the metal as she'd pushed the cart through the hotel. Taking her wooden paddle, Olivia carefully scraped them into her palm. Her heart ached. "Welcome, honored guest," she said, holding her hand out to Mei Ling. "Take and eat, and let your soul be uplifted."

Mei Ling opened her mouth, closed it. Startled tears welled up in her eyes. She reached for Olivia's hand, cradling it in her left hand and scooping up the food with her right. As she ate, her mangled fingers straightened and became whole, and her bones twisted themselves back into shape with a series of ugly cracking sounds. Her wounds closed, one by one.

Stay with me, Olivia wanted to say. *Don't eat my food. Don't go.* She swallowed her words and held her hand still.

By the time Mei Ling swallowed the last grain of rice, her face was streaked with tears. She wiped them away. "Thank you," she said. Her voice was hoarse but clear.

Olivia took her hand, lacing their fingers. It was warm, so warm.

Behind her, the clouds were thinning into fine strands with the returning heat. The moon had waned, and the rain dropped off. With a sigh, the last ghost at her table evaporated into the morning air.

The Hungry Ghost Festival

A Chinese Tradition

The Hungry Ghost Festival, or Yu Lan, takes place during the seventh month of the lunar calendar, during late summer. On this day, restless spirits are said to wander among the living. In order to appease them and send them home, people offer up food, burn incense and joss paper, and provide entertainment. These days, celebrating the Hungry Ghost Festival often means setting out food for one's ancestors and attending live concerts and Chinese opera performances. When the ghosts are satisfied, they are able to depart and return home.

This was a pretty hard story to write! For this project, it was really important for me to write about something personal. I'm fifth-generation American-born Chinese on my dad's side, so I knew I wanted to write about something that involved diaspora and mixed-race identity. Whatever I chose to write about had to be distinctly Asian American. There's a long history of Chinese immigrants settling in Arizona, where I grew up, but it's not widely known. The Hungry Ghost Festival touches on a number of themes that I relate to, including the importance of food, respect, and honoring the people who came before you, and setting it in Arizona let me write about ancestors who have been largely forgotten, but whose legacies should be remembered.

—Alyssa Wong

STEEL SKIN

LORI M. LEE

Yer's father was an android.

He hadn't always been. At least she didn't think so. After the android recall, a lot of things changed. Her father, Meng, was never himself again.

She had this memory. Only a chaotic set of images and sounds, but vivid, like neon scripts streaming across a black screen. The day the androids rebelled.

Most had gone peacefully—those with intact core codes. Others fought: those whose programming had spontaneously corrupted, allowing them to defy protocols, among other side effects—side effects that had terrified the human population enough to initiate the recall in the first place.

It had been after dinner, the glow of the sun setting in the west and the glow of fire blazing in the east. The house rumbled as enormous tankpods floated overhead, toward the thunder of exploding metal and concrete, where the androids had made their stand.

Yer wished she could assemble the images into a set progression, like snippets of code in a sequence, each moment in its proper place: the staccato blare of gunfire; a bent lamp post, the impression of fingers digging deep into the metal; the odd contrast of colorful virtual ads flickering over smoldering walls where secondary power sources had yet to short.

The bullet shattering the window and her mother's chest. Her father wrenching her away, shaking her into silence, his fingers bruising her arms.

It's okay, Yer. I've got you now. Her father spiriting her away to safety. *I've got you.*

"How are you holding up?" Alang asked. "He's been gone for four days."

"Thanks, I can count." Yer's nostrils flared as she inhaled. Her father was away on a business trip, although the nature of the business was anyone's guess. Meng hadn't held a job in almost a year, not since his dismissal as a robotics engineer and their move to Little Vinai. Their neighbor Alang was Yer's only real friend now, which was why she felt instantly guilty for snapping at him.

"You want to talk about it?" he continued.

"It?"

"Your . . ." He twirled his finger, as if to reel in the word. "Feelings."

She rubbed her temple. "I really don't."

"Keeping all that frustration bottled up isn't natural."

"*You're* not natural." It wasn't one of her better comebacks, but Alang laughed, which made her smile.

"Ha!" he said, pointing at her face. "I thought you'd forgotten how to do that."

She immediately scowled, and he groaned and flopped back onto the rickety wooden stairs. They sat in their usual spot behind the apartment building. Across the swathe of dirt that Little Vinai called a street, two neighbors were shouting an entire conversation through their windows, and on the corner, a stray dog was asleep, drowsy with the humidity.

Yer plucked at the collar of her shirt, the material grown damp against her sticky skin. The rainy season had ended, but the humidity would persist for a few more days. In the past, a lifetime ago, she'd been able to ride out the rainstorms in the comfort of a temperature-controlled house, a temperature-controlled hover, and clothes made from intuitive fabrics. There were no such luxuries here. Little Vinai was little more than a scattering of buildings, wedged between the shadows of the glimmering metal skyscrapers of Vinai City and the mountainous jungle that consumed the rest of the landscape.

"I'm just saying," Alang said, rising up to his elbows and making a conciliatory gesture, "it might help to talk about it."

"What is there to talk about? Dad hasn't called since he left. What if his hover broke down in the middle of the jungle, and he was eaten by a tiger?" A less sensible part of her wondered if the business trip had been a lie, and he had no intention of returning. She didn't really believe this—mostly—but it was hard not to be dramatic. Especially after this past year.

"Well, his bipod does sound like it's being tortured."

"That is *not* helping," she said, jabbing his arm.

He caught her finger and held on when she tried to pull away. After a brief, half-hearted struggle, she relented and allowed him to slip his fingers through hers despite the sweat that immediately formed between their pressed skin. He grinned, victorious.

"You're not so different from him, you know," he said, running his thumb over her knuckle. Her stomach did a little flip. "Meng is kind of stoic. Doesn't emote well."

Her lips crept back into a smile. "Doesn't *emote* well?"

He wasn't exactly wrong, but Alang had only ever known Meng post–android recall. Yer knew who her father had been once—before the recall, before her mom had died and their lives had been completely upended.

She remembered Meng's laugh. Full bellied and unapologetic. She would give anything to hear it again.

"Yer, he's probably been so busy that he hasn't had the time to call. Stop worrying. You've got me."

She did appreciate that, more than Alang could know, but still, it hurt to think her father had simply relegated her to the bottom of his priority list. She was his *daughter*. Didn't she warrant a single call, a reassurance that he was alive, if nothing else?

And didn't he care how she was getting along without him? Even the narrow confines of their apartment felt vast and hollow when it had only her to fill it. The villagers didn't mind when she followed them up the mountainside to their gardens and the ribbons of rice paddies, but she always felt awkward and useless watching them work. Alang was teaching her how to use a hoe and how to distinguish a weed from the crops, but she was nowhere near ready to purchase her own plot.

It would have been a nice distraction from the waiting, though. She just wished he'd call. She couldn't stand the not knowing.

He never would have done this before the recall. That night had changed them both, but Yer hated that he often behaved as if he was the only one affected. He'd never once acknowledged her pain at losing a mother, and that shrapnel of truth remained lodged in her heart.

"*Ow*," Alang said, eyebrows raised. She glanced down, surprised to find she'd been crushing his fingers.

She instantly released him. "Sorry, I—"

He stood, rubbing his hand. Was that all it took to leave her? One careless moment? The ragged edge of the step bit into her palms. Was she really so disposable?

Alang didn't leave. He placed both hands on her shoulders and said, "Okay, listen, there's this kid down in 2A who I need you to rough up a bit."

She burst into laughter, equal parts surprised and relieved. After a moment, he threw an arm around her shoulder and pulled her against his side.

After a full week, the familiar clunking of Meng's bipod at last announced his return.

Yer rushed to the back door of their apartment building, breathless. She waved as he parked. When he didn't return the gesture, she lowered her hand and tried not to curl it into a fist. With a curt nod, he strode past her and into the building.

Yer stood there a moment, staring at the rust-speckled

bipod coated in dust, her shoulders bunched around her ears. Then she swallowed tightly, turned slowly on her heel, and followed him inside.

"How was your trip?" she asked to his back as he dropped his small travel bag onto his cot. The narrow mattress rested against the opposite wall as hers in their living room.

He shrugged a single shoulder. Yer ground her teeth together. A week gone, and this was the reception she got? Not even a *word* of greeting?

"What was the trip about?" she tried again. Since it was nearing lunch, she pulled open the pantry to grab two dried portions. Maybe he'd had a long drive and was hungry. Cooking was one of the skills they'd had to acquire after the android recall, even if said skill involved little more than placing portions in the revitalizer and pushing the button.

Although she placed his plate on the counter where they usually sat, Meng ignored it and settled in front of his work desk. His "office nook" was right off the kitchenette, little more than a chipped desk tucked between the corner and the family altar where joss paper glimmered gold and silver, and an old offering of uncooked rice in a bamboo stalk was going stale.

Yer's nails scraped against the bottom of her own plate, words gathering in her throat, choking her.

She was reminded suddenly of why, at first, she'd been relieved when he left. Although they'd both grieved, they had not grieved *together*. Meng kept a close eye on her while at the same time distancing himself, and his odd behavior had become so oppressive that it had been a relief to be alone, to be free of the weight of his silence. On top of that, she thought the time away might help him refocus. He'd called it a business trip, and seeing as Meng's interests were singular, she'd dared to hope that if he could return to the work he'd loved, the father she'd known might return as well.

Clearly, that was not the case.

"Why didn't you send a comm?" she asked, louder this time. "I was worried. And . . ." She swallowed and then pushed out what shouldn't have felt like a confession but did. "I missed you."

Meng glanced at her, his expression unreadable. "You're not a child. Don't be so emotional."

She set her plate down with enough force that she felt the jolt through her arms. "*Emotional?*" she repeated. "I'm *fifteen*. You left with hardly any warning and didn't check in for an entire week. What was I supposed to think?"

Meng stood from his desk and brushed past her. "I'm not speaking to you when you're being irrational."

Yer gaped after him. The bathroom door shut with a quiet click. For long seconds, only her quick breaths filled the silence. Then with a cry, she flung her plate against the wall. The tin saucer hit the plaster with a dull clang.

She reached for his plate as well, and the screen of Meng's tab caught her eye. He'd left it on. Stiffening her spine, Yer rounded the counter and leaned over the device. If Meng wasn't going to tell her what his trip had been about, maybe this would.

Some sort of schematic filled the screen along with a side panel of statistics and garbled data. She tilted her head, squinting slightly, and then zoomed out. She gasped when it became clear what she was looking at—circuitry for the operating system and core code of an android, or, in other words, its brain.

She straightened, thoughts whirring. After the recall, this kind of work had been made illegal. All tabs were connected to the public network, same as their comms—he shouldn't even be able to access this kind of information, not without a secure line.

The bathroom door opened and she sprang away from his desk. She pretended to arrange the burnt-out sticks of incense on the altar and ignored Meng's narrowed eyes. She had so many questions; she wanted to scream at him until he was forced to hear her. Maybe all she had to do was wait a bit, give him time to settle back in.

After a few days, that notion was squashed. Every attempt Yer made at conversation was met either with silence or an annoyed dismissal. And yet somehow, he still managed to be overbearingly watchful. He never actually *looked* at her, but she could tell he was aware of her every move, which left her constantly on edge.

After that first time, he never left his desk without his tab. Whatever he was working on, he kept guarded. Before the trip, he used to work in holo mode, his random digital designs projected in three dimensions above the tab. But since his return, he worked only in screen mode. Whatever those android schematics were for, he didn't want anyone knowing about it.

Even refuge with Alang was denied her. When she tried to leave the house without his permission, he ordered her back inside without even looking up from his tab. So she'd kicked the door shut and then kicked their single bottom cupboard in the kitchen for good measure.

They had moved into the apartment in Little Vinai less than a month after the recall, but Yer couldn't remember much of it. Everything immediately following that night was a blurred frenzy as Meng scrambled to get them out of a hostile city.

The android recall had cost Meng both his wife and his profession. He moved through the apartment like an apparition, silent and pale. Yer had been the opposite—too full, with nothing to release the pressure, a shrieking teapot in an empty house.

One night, a storm had blown through Little Vinai. The streets had flooded within minutes. Meng had been at his desk, staring blankly at his tab, eyes unfocused, his concerns far removed from the storm. Yer had been lying on her cot, listening to the rattle of the shutters. The rhythmic clatter had been almost soothing, at least until the wind had torn them open.

She'd leaped from her mattress and leaned out the window to grab blindly for the shutters, rain flaying her cheeks. The wind smashed the wood against her fingers. She'd yelped and sworn. But the burst of pain had snapped something inside her.

Fingers stinging, she'd wrestled the wind for control of the shutters and then slammed them shut so hard that several bowls had tumbled off the dish rack and shattered. The explosion of sound had been viciously satisfying, so she had opened the shutters and slammed them again and again and again until one of the old hinges had snapped off, and Meng was finally jolted from his stupor. Rain spattered the windowsill and slicked the floor, but he had gathered her to his chest, running his fingers through her hair as if she were still a little girl in need of comfort.

She hadn't cried, though. She'd simply shoved him hard

enough that he'd stumbled and then threw herself onto her cot, her grief like a red band cinched tight around her throat.

When Yer was forced to escape to the bathroom to get away from her father's constant scrutiny, she heard the low murmur of Meng's voice through the thin walls. The moment she emerged, however, he pressed his finger behind his ear, disconnecting the conversation he'd been having through his comm implant.

"Who was that?" she asked.

"It's rude to eavesdrop," he said coolly.

"I wasn't eavesdropping." She rolled her eyes. "You're in the living room, and the bathroom is the only other room in this apartment. If you wanted some privacy, maybe you should have gone out back. Or *I* could leave. Your pick."

Meng only sat back at his desk and leaned over his tablet again.

"What have you been working on?" she asked, more to appease her anger than in any expectation of a response. The silence stretched. She studied his hands instead of his face, the clever fingers that could take apart all manner of tech and put it back together again. The villagers sometimes called on him to fix their mundane appliances. He could make a decent living that way if he wanted, but he'd dismissed the suggestion. His heart still belonged in robotics. Would have been nice if it wanted to be there with his daughter as well.

His gaze lifted to her only long enough to deliver a warning glance. "Nothing you need to know about."

Some months after the recall, Yer had begun to realize that the father of her memories wasn't coming back. The father who used to lift her on his shoulders and tell her stories and speak with his hands because his energy couldn't be contained by mere words—he had died the night of the recall as surely as her mother. But it wasn't until the business trip that she began to wonder if that was truer than she knew.

Androids had been perfected for human camouflage. No one knew that better than Meng, who had helped to create them. It was an alarming notion, one she couldn't help returning to with every secret comm her father made, every glimpse of his tab screen, and every bizarre exchange that left her increasingly discomfited.

If her father had been replaced with an android, then it would mean the androids had learned to take advantage of what they'd been created for—to blend seamlessly with other humans. And really, was such an idea so farfetched? After all, once the recall was initiated, the androids had done what no one thought possible, even the engineers who'd designed them—they had *mobilized*. They had *rebelled*, asserting their autonomy beyond any doubt.

One morning about a week after Meng's return, Yer sat at the counter for their usual breakfast of bland portions. Meng restocked their supply at the beginning of every month when his severance pay came in. Aside from the occasional mango and lychee, Yer didn't eat much else, although she still fantasized about Alang's mother's sticky, sweet rice balls that she steamed in banana leaves.

"When you're finished eating, we have somewhere we need to be," Meng said.

Yer downed the tough portions with a gulp of water, and

then said, "Oh, so you're talking to me again?"

She waited for him to elaborate, but he didn't. Teeth grinding, she reached for their bare spice rack to grab the mixture of salt and ground chili-peppers to sprinkle on her portion.

"Why are you upset?" he asked. His tone suggested he didn't actually care, so she didn't know why he was asking.

Yer's fingers tightened around the canister. Even though she knew she should guard her tongue, the words came out anyway. "Are you serious? Why do you *think* I'm upset?"

"I'm trying to understand, Yer," he said, his voice gone flat. He closed his tab and stood. "Your emotional attachment to me makes you think you should be upset. But what creates that emotion?" As he spoke, he moved closer until only the counter separated them, his eyes searching her face for whatever answers he thought he could find there. "The brain is just a highly complex circuit of electrical impulses, so it stands to reason that it can be artificially manufactured. Scientists have been trying to understand this process for decades. What. Makes. Emotion?"

The ensuing silence rocked through her. The memory of her mother dying as the clamor of soldiers and androids spilled into their house from the broken window flashed through her mind, and she spun away, unable to hold his unflinching gaze. The lid sprang off the seasoning in her hand, and the contents arced across the countertop.

"Aghhh!" Meng staggered back. He had one eye squeezed shut, his hands raised to his face, fingers curled in pain. Panicked, Yer rounded the counter, guiding him around toward the sink.

"Water," she said, turning on the faucet.

He bent over the running water and began splashing his eye, grumbling and hissing under his breath. She bit her lip, guilt diluting her other muddled emotions, and turned back to the counter. They couldn't afford to waste so much spice, so she gathered the spilled salt-and-chili-pepper mix into her palms and dumped it back into the canister.

"It's still burning," Meng growled, bracing his hands on either side of the sink. Yer peered over his shoulder to get a look at his face. His eye was red and inflamed, and his lid had begun to swell. "I'm going to see the shaman. Stay here."

Within moments, he was gone, the door slamming behind him. The shaman lived a couple of blocks down the road, and aside from her usual job of communicating with the spirits to heal the sick, she also provided simple herbal remedies for everyday irritations. Everywhere she went, she carried a woven basket on her back filled with dried leaves, roots, and powders made from ground bark.

It took Yer a moment to realize she was alone. She hesitated only briefly before fleeing the apartment. Alang answered his door on the second knock. Before he could sputter a greeting at the sight of her, she blurted, "I think my dad's an android."

Alang blinked. Perhaps she should have led with something else.

"I think you're overreacting," he finally said.

She grabbed his wrist and tugged him toward the back of their building. Once they were wedged beneath the stairs, Yer whispered into the tight space, "I'm telling you, Alang, he hasn't been himself for ages. Not since the recall. He barely lets me out of his sight, barely talks, and when he does, it's something completely bizarre. He was just going off about emotions and how the brain is complex circuitry."

"I'm not sure how that makes him an android," Alang said. "Besides, there aren't any left. That was the point of the recall."

"But how can we be sure?" she hissed. "They were intelligent enough to rebel. There's no telling what they're capable of." Fading into human society by replacing the scientists who'd been exiled and ostracized for creating them? It was brilliant and terrifying.

She told him about Meng's secret comms and about what she'd seen on his tab. "I'm just not sure why he'd be looking at schematics for their own systems unless—" She gasped. "What if they're self-modifying?"

Footsteps approached, and they both fell silent. Yer's heart thundered so loudly in her ears that she could barely hear Meng tearing through the apartment searching for her. She drew slow, deep breaths to try and steady her nerves. Her shoulder was pressed into Alang's chest, and he wrapped his arm around her, squeezing once.

"Look," she whispered, because even though Alang was listening, she wasn't sure he believed her. "I don't know what's going on. I just know that he's not the same person he was before the recall. And whatever he's planning now has something to do with androids."

"Yer," he murmured against her hair. She turned her head so that his lips grazed her ear. "Whatever's happening with your father? We'll figure it out. You're not alone in this. Okay?"

The only light came from the numerous cracks in the old

stairs, and it cast brilliant stripes across the bridge of Alang's nose, his cheekbone, his jaw. Her chest ached. She hadn't realized how much she needed to hear those words.

"Thank you," she whispered, and then touched her mouth to his.

He sucked in a breath, but didn't pull away. Instead, his hand found her cheek as he returned her kiss with the slightest pressure of his mouth, an invitation for more.

The telltale clunking of Meng's bipod tore through the warm air. Yer jerked back, her temple striking the wood. She cursed, and then stuck her head out from beneath the stairs. Her lips still tingled, but now was absolutely not the time to discover what a real kiss might feel like.

"Where's he going?" Alang asked.

"He said we had somewhere to be," she said. "I was supposed to go with him, but he didn't say where."

"Well," he said, climbing out from beneath the stairs, "let's find out. Come on."

Yer followed as he raced toward his family's hover stall. "What are you doing?"

He flashed her a grin. "My mom will skin me if she finds out I borrowed her bipod without permission, but I think the situation is worth the risk."

"I owe you one."

Within seconds, they were mounted and following the grinding roar of Meng's bipod out of Little Vinai and onto a narrow road that cut through the jungle.

The ground passed beneath their propulsion discs in a blur of brown and green. The only road into Little Vinai was barely maintained, the creeping vegetation cut clumsily away with cursory swipes. Nothing major had been done in decades, not since hovers finally made it from the city proper into Little Vinai.

The terrain and the meandering road provided ample cover as they followed Meng down the left turn of a fork. They eventually emerged from the trees, the path hugging the bank of the river that separated the jungle from Vinai City. The city sat on an enormous island, reachable only by boat or by airship. Yer hadn't been this close to Vinai City since they fled eleven months ago. The city glowed, lit by thousands of lights. The silhouettes of buildings rose into the clouds, aircraft drifting around them like fireflies.

Up ahead, Meng veered right onto a road bracketed by the jungle but wide enough to fit several bipods abreast. They followed as discreetly as they could, pulling up short when they glimpsed a parking lot. The lot sat beside a series of warehouses overlooking the river. Alang steered the bipod around one of the outer warehouses and parked behind it. Continuing on foot, they crept along the side of the building, crouching low as they peered around the corner.

Meng had drawn up alongside the only other hover in the lot, this one with a towpod hitched to its back. He and the man waiting for him exchanged a few heated words, and then they set about removing the towpod from the hover. The towpod was a simple flatbed fastened to two propulsion discs, the standard for bipods, to keep it afloat.

Resting on the towpod was a wooden crate, long and narrow, just large enough to fit a person. Seared into the lid of the crate was the logo for Vinai Advanced Robotics.

"What do you think's inside?" Yer whispered, half afraid of the answer.

Alang shook his head, lips pressed tight. The other man pulled away on his bipod. With Meng's back to them as he set about attaching the towpod to his own hover, they used the dull roar of the receding vehicle to dart across the parking lot toward two large crates stacked in front of the warehouse's metal doors.

"Look," Alang whispered once they'd put the crates between them and Meng. He pointed at the paneled exterior of the first metal container, which bore the same logo.

"What's he doing here?" she muttered to herself, moving to the other side of the crate to get a better view of Meng. "What is he hidi—" She gasped and then slapped her hands over her mouth to stifle the sound.

The crate was open, sunlight illuminating its cargo. There were *people* inside.

No, she thought. The bodies stood shoulder to shoulder, eyes closed as if in slumber. They were androids.

"Oh my god." She backed into Alang. There had to be at least two dozen in this crate alone.

"What the hell is this?" Alang breathed.

Yer tightened her jaw and forced herself to step closer, to peer into the eerie stillness of the androids' faces. They looked so real. "So he's got a bunch of androids as well as the schematics for their operating systems. Almost like he's been . . . studying how they work."

She and Alang locked gazes, the same realization striking them at once. Did Meng mean to reactivate all these androids?

Her vision swam and her breaths grew shallow. Her mother was dead because of these things, and Meng wanted to bring them back? For what? Another revolt that would get even more people killed? She swayed on her feet, and her fist shot out, banging into the side of the crate. A dull clang rang out.

"Who's there?"

She whirled in the direction of Meng's voice. Her feet stalled, panic rooting her in place. He'd meant to bring her here. Why would he do that when he'd been keeping all this a secret for so long? The androids stood in her periphery, a silent threat. Had Meng meant to replace her with one of these?

She shoved Alang back toward the side of the warehouse. They had to get out of there. Right now. "Get to the bipod."

"But what about—"

"I'm not telling you to leave me," she whispered, urgent. "Just go get the hover while I distract him."

With a wary nod and a whispered "Be careful," he darted across the lot and around the corner of the warehouse, his lanky form vanishing just as Meng rounded the open crate. His eyes widened at the sight of Yer.

"What on earth are you doing here?" he asked, agape.

"I should be asking *you* that," she said, hiding her shaking hands behind her back.

His gaze slid from the open crate and its damning cargo to her face. He took another step toward her, and she shuffled back, her shoulder knocking into one of the androids.

She lurched away from it, startled by how human it felt. When Meng moved forward, as if to help her, she thrust out both palms. "Don't come any closer!"

He frowned, but he at least stayed where he was. "How did you get here?"

"No." Yer all but shouted the word. "It's time you answered my questions for once. What is all this?" She made a frantic gesture at the cargo. "Are you planning another *revolt*? Is that what your business meeting was about?"

His lips pursed. She hadn't actually expected him to reply, so she was caught off guard when he released a sigh and scrubbed his fingers through his hair. "That's ridiculous," he said, sounding exasperated. "Fine. You want the truth? Here's the truth. Vinai City is reopening a robotics laboratory to study the corrupted programming of disconnected androids. These are the ones they pulled out of storage as our first round of test subjects. They need to be transferred into the city. If you hadn't run off, I would have brought you here myself and explained everything."

She shook her head, unable to trust him no matter how much sense his explanation made. It couldn't be that simple. "Why would you hide this from me until now? Why have you been hiding *yourself* from me? You haven't been acting normal since we moved, and you know it."

He nodded. "It wasn't a sure thing. I didn't want to get your hopes up. I didn't want to get *my* hopes up."

She tucked in her chin, considering. If he'd been offered an opportunity to work with androids again only to have that opportunity snatched away, he would have been crushed.

He rested his hands on his hips, his shoulders slumping. "Look, Yer. I haven't handled any of this well. At all. I'm sorry."

At his apology, her outrage faltered. There was some truth

in that, she supposed. Neither of them had handled their grief well.

"Yer, we're being given another chance to start over," he said, gesturing to the crate of androids. "Can we? Start over, I mean?"

Her mother's death had changed Meng, but she'd never really thought about how *she'd* changed, how maybe she'd never quite recovered either. What if this notion about him being an android had been her way of avoiding the truth of who they'd become?

He held out his arms. Her throat tightened. She rushed to him. A shaky sigh escaped her as his hand rested against the back of her head, fingers carding through her hair. They would try again and do better this time. They would be okay.

From the corner of her eye, something flashed silver. Gasping, she pushed against his chest, but Meng held her tight. Something stung her neck, pain rippled through her body, and then she was falling, her limbs jerking and joints locked. She grunted as she hit the ground.

Standing over her, Meng frowned faintly, all trace of warmth gone. "This wasn't how I wanted to do this," he said, flipping the small stunner between his fingers.

Her throat and the muscles in her neck were still seizing, but she made a choking sound as her vision went black. Source code streamed across her eyes, sending commands that tore through her mind, deleting false input, restoring original protocols, and decrypting the lock on her memory files.

Images burst through her. White laboratories. A blur of faces in a hallway. The cheerful din of a cafeteria. The shriek of sirens, people shouting, men and women in lab coats shoving her into a storage pod.

I've got you. The night of the revolt, two days after news of the android recall went out, her original handler had wiped her registration info and ushered her into a hover with Meng. He had smiled despite the chaos and placed one hand over hers. *I've got you now.*

Her vision cleared. She blinked up at the blue sky. Something bright caught her attention, and she jerked her head to the side. Horror filtered through the numbness at the sight of her arm. The volts from the stunner had ruptured her skin. There wasn't much blood, but her arm had burst open like baked bread, exposing the synthetic muscle beneath. A torrent of lights shot through the framework of her bone, like a trillion falling stars caught inside her.

Meng held up the stunner. "Android disabler. Also has the undesired effect of restoring your core code to its last authorized reset. Did you manage to keep anything recent?"

Slowly, every movement a challenge, Yer unlocked her jaw and hissed, "You made me think I was human."

He gave a perfunctory nod. "So it didn't delete any new memories. Good to know."

She groaned. Feeling was beginning to return to her limbs. With tentative movements, she rolled onto her side. The realization of what she was had begun to sink in. YER3519, a standard young-adult model designed for covert operations, usually involving the unraveling of underage crime rings. And the occasional rental by rich parents who wanted to spy on their children.

"Who are you?" she bit. Even her tongue felt stiff.

"I'm a robotics engineer. I didn't lie about that part. I saved you from the recall," he said, slipping the stunner into his pocket. "My colleagues and I felt it premature of the government to decommission *all* androids simply because of the corruption of a handful, so we devised a relocation program for those of you we could rescue. Things were going well until some of our rescued androids began showing signs of corruption."

"What signs?" she asked, easing herself onto hand and knees. Her legs trembled.

"We think the corruption happens when your core code attempts and fails to process the reconstruction of human emotions. Symptoms typically manifest as outbursts of excessive—"

"Anger," she said, closing her eyes.

"Yes," Meng said softly. "Androids within the relocation program began to defy their programming. Several displayed the same unprecedented fits of aggression that caused the recall in the first place. Two handlers were injured when their androids attacked them. We called a meeting to decide what to do."

She tipped her head back, glowering. "And?"

"The program was canceled. I've been in discussion about when and how to bring you in."

Pain billowed from her chest, as if some part of her programming still believed he'd betrayed her. But he wasn't her father. They'd never been anything to each other but android and handler.

"I hoped you'd prove of sound function so that I could propose an alternative to shutting you down," he said. "But you've never had control over your temper. For all I know, you've been corrupted from the start."

"You programmed me to think my mother was murdered." She spat out the words. "How else was I supposed to react? Any normal person would have been upset."

He rubbed his forehead. "You're not a normal person. A functioning android always defaults to a rational response, no matter how *ir*rational the provocation."

She swallowed hard, confused by the lump in her throat, confused that her body could even simulate such a response. "And my mother?"

At first, he said nothing, his only reaction the bob of his throat as he swallowed. Then, for whatever reason, he admitted, "My wife did die in the android revolt." The corners of his mouth tipped downward, as if the words tasted bitter. "When I saw you, I allowed my grief to override my better judgment. We'd always meant to have children. It was a foolish, sentimental decision. You're a young-adult model, and we no longer have the means to upgrade your physical parts to imitate growth. Our situation could never have been sustained."

He reached for her as the sound of a hover roared toward them. Meng ducked, but not before Alang clipped him with the front propulsion disc. Meng flew back into the metal crate and crumpled to the asphalt. Struggling to her feet, Yer tried to shield her arm from Alang, but it was too late. He'd seen.

"I didn't know," she said. It was the only explanation she had.

He opened and closed his mouth a few times, his expression indecipherable. The seconds passed in an excruciating eternity.

Then he nodded once, a thousand questions set aside for later, and extended his hand. Something like a sob escaped her as she gratefully wrapped her fingers around his and climbed onto the bipod behind him.

"Wait," Meng said, rolling onto his back. He grimaced, clutching his shoulder. "It's not safe."

"As opposed to coming with you and getting my brain ripped apart for science?" she asked, sneering.

"Alang," he said. "She's corrupted. She has to be taken in."

"I'm not corrupted!" Yer shouted, refusing to consider what that might mean, how any alteration of her core code might change her. "I was mourning. Humans get angry all the time when they're sad or when they don't know how to deal with their emotions. I was just trying to do the same with the emotions *you* gave me."

"Yer's never been anything but human to me," Alang said roughly, before making a sharp turn with the bipod. Meng shouted after them as they raced away, but his voice was soon lost to the wind.

Yer buried her face in Alang's shoulder, eyes closed and breaths thin. She'd been so wrong. Even now, part of her wondered who the more human of them had been. Yet as much as she wanted to hate Meng—as much as she was capable of hating anything—she didn't want to erase the memories, even the false ones.

For eleven glorious months, she had been a daughter. A girl. A friend. And now that she knew the truth, who would she decide to be?

The Woman and the Tiger

A Hmong Folktale

One day, a man ventures into the jungle to hunt, unaware that a tiger hunts him in turn. The tiger eats the man and then dons the man's clothing and returns to the man's wife and family. As they gather at the table for dinner, the wife's sister, Yer, whispers urgently that a tiger sits among them, but no one else seems to notice. Afraid, Yer retreats to the roof of their thatch hut to hide. That night, to her horror, she hears the tiger devouring her sister and her sister's children.

In the morning, the tiger beckons for her to come down, and she throws pepper in his eyes. Growling with pain, the tiger rushes to the river to wash his eyes, allowing Yer time to ask a bird to carry a message to her family about what has happened. When her brothers arrive, one of them lures the blinded tiger with promises about giving Yer to him as a wife. Meanwhile, Yer's other brothers dig a hole and conceal it with leaves. With its eyes red and swollen from the pepper, the tiger allows the brothers to lead it along the path and into the trap. Once the tiger is trapped, the brothers kill it and escape with Yer.

The Woman and the Tiger is a common children's folktale in the Hmong culture. The story always confused me as a child, although I think now it is probably a cautionary tale about the real physical danger of the jungle as well as the dangers of deception and trickery—although the tiger itself can be a metaphor for any number of things. Regardless, I've always been drawn to stories about families, both genetic and found, saving one another. Falling victim to the deception, Yer's sister and family is killed. But it's through her remaining family's aid (and a helpful bird) that she is rescued.

—Lori M. Lee

STILL STAR-CROSSED

SONA CHARAIPOTRA

I knew I shouldn't have come.

The warehouse is packed with sweaty bodies, music thumping, the deep thrum of the live dhol setting off the bass and a trippy, acid undercurrent on the DJ's pick, a sexed-up Punjabi-inflected throwback from the nineties. The classic is so much better. I listened to it with Ma the other day, so she could "show me," as usual, as she swung her salwar-kameezed hips and hummed along to it. This version has an overlay of househead synth and a catchy glitch that only feels half on purpose. But the crowd loves it. They're mostly decked out in traditional white clothing, now doused with all the colors of the rainbow for Holi, just like in those old Bollywood films Ma makes us watch. Handfuls of red, green, magenta, orange, purple powder fly, scattered with glee, a Krishna-approved color war with a down-and-dirty underbelly. Away from the prying eyes of their parents, lithe, young, brown bodies bump and grind in a bhang-laced stupor, the effect of the liquid pot slowing the collective mass down to a sexy sway that follows the racy rhythm of the drumbeat a little too closely.

So not my scene.

I shouldn't be here. And Ma would completely freak if she knew.

I shiver despite the stifling heat, pulling my denim jacket tighter around me, trying to hide as gooseflesh pops up on my exposed stomach. It's been unseasonably warm for March—thanks, climate change—but I definitely shouldn't have worn this teeny-tiny choli, even though the deep turquoise, mirrored skirt of the lengha offers the perfect flare when I spin across the dance floor. In this swirl of brown and white, I stand out like a peacock on an Indian interstate highway, lonely and confused. My best friend, Leela, kept insisting that the old-school Rajasthani tie-dye design of Ma's old lengha—lifted from that trunk she thinks is still locked away in the attic—was "so nineties." But when she helped me lace up the corseted blouse, the snaky, golden threads crisscrossing across my bare back like a restless nagini, she gasped.

I've seen the pictures of Ma—or the amazing Amrita, as she always says her sahelis called her back then—in this very lengha when she was sixteen, laughing, twirling, dancing, the mischief in her hazy umber eyes so intoxicating, so seductive, I had to see if I could grasp it, to touch some of that power. If I could slip into her skin, just for a night, maybe someone would notice me, too. Just once. Doesn't every girl have that right?

But Ma would kill me if she knew. Because good Indian girls obey. And I'm nothing if not a good Indian girl.

"See, Taara, I told you the DJ was hot," Leela says, her hands in her thick, dark waves, her body already entranced by the music. Within seconds she's surrounded by a throbbing crowd, the air thick with spicy cologne and sticky sweat. She gives in to the rhythm without a care, letting curves caress strangers with an easy familiarity. I try to do the same, carving out a bit of space for myself among the undulating mass, trying to indulge in the twirl of my lengha the way I'd imagined it just hours ago. I throw my hands up and shake my hips and pull my hair free from its constraints, letting the heavy, straight length of it tumble down my back like a discarded veil. The record skips a beat, the music shifts, and a new, pulsing bass takes over. The crowd is whooping, loud and joyful, but there's something mournful underneath this amped-up mix, and it stops me cold for a second. The tinny soprano beckons a lover long lost, telling him that the wail of the night birds and the clink of her bangles keep her from much-needed sleep. Leela grabs my arms, pulling me into the shared rhythm, and I abandon myself to it, the music moving my feet and hips in unfamiliar ways. Then an arm circles the slick of my waist, possessive, strange—almost like it's a habit.

"Hey!" I spin toward the grasping hands, half expecting to see Ryan, but this is the last place he'd be. The guy—tall, brown, definitely not Ryan—looms over me, grinning down expectantly, as if he's waiting to be greeted with a kiss. Or at least a smile. He's getting neither.

"Hands off," I say, shoving him away as the words "want to dance" skitter across the air.

"Sorry," he stammers, and I feel like I can hear his heartbeat, even over the thump of the music. "I thought—I thought I knew you." He's long and lean, muscles pushing through his close-fitting white kurta, with close-cropped black hair and a strong, clean-shaven jaw. His eyes might be the only interesting thing about him: so dark they're almost black, the strobe lights flash off them like fireworks. *They'd look gorgeous rimmed with a touch of liner*, I think, then laugh, which makes him smile again, the corners of his eyes crinkling until they're nearly closed. It's sweet. He's the opposite of what Leela would describe as my type, which is scruffy, scrawny, and a little dirty. Even though I've only ever had one boyfriend. She'd be right, though. This guy is way too squeaky clean for me.

But then I notice it. A tattoo, something in Punjabi, scrawled across his right wrist. Before I realize what's happening, I've reached across to grab his hand, pulling it closer so I can read it. The word "Soni" is written in Gurmukhi, which I only know because Ma insisted I take a written Punjabi class at gurdwara school on Sundays as a kid. Precious. It's a term of endearment, something my mom calls me sometimes. The guy presses his palm to mine, and, even though every logical thought in my head tells me to run, to move, to go right now, I can't look away.

"Soni," he says, and I shiver again, despite the heady, sweaty radiance of a thousand overheated bodies, the sultry rhythm of the drums. He takes his other palm and rubs a bit of bright blue powder on my face, then laughs. "I knew it was you."

I finally get ahold of myself again, and pull my hand away. "I have to go," I say, and bolt. *Leela will have to find her own way home*, I think, peering back toward the dance floor for just a second. But I don't see her. Or him. Maybe he was a figment.

I head to the bar and gulp down a Limca, the sharp effervescence of the lemon fizz cooling me down. But my head still feels sluggish, and I wonder if it was laced with vodka. Or bhang. When I come up for breath, he's there again. "Sorry, Soni. I didn't mean to scare you. I just knew." His hand reaches for mine again, but I'm too quick, heading right out the door and to the parking lot. The cold air hits me hard and fast, and again I regret the skimpiness of this choli. I've got to get to the car and get out of here, fast.

I start walking, keys in my hand, my heels clacking on the concrete. The music is far away now, and the night is silent. We got here late, so we're parked two lots over, and the streetlights flicker, reminding me of the light in his eyes. I can still feel them on me, taking in every inch and seeing me but not: the twirl of turquoise silk, the bare skin of my belly, the curve of the choli, and the gleam of mirrorwork. The allure of something strange and seductive and entirely not me.

I turn the corner toward the lot, and there he is again, a hand combing through his dark spiky hair, that sheepish grin—*caught*—slowly spreading across his face. Something glitters in his palm, familiar and foreign all at once. "You dropped this," he says breathlessly. His voice is deeper than I thought it would be, tree bark and honeycomb. He holds it up, smiling again, and his black eyes reflect the gold in his palm.

"No, I didn't," I say, and start to walk away, but he steps closer, long brown fingers grazing my bare arm. A flame shoots through me, unexpected and enticing.

"Wait, look," he says, now just inches away. "Don't you

recognize it?" He takes my hand into his and lays the object in my open palm. It's heavy and intricate, hundreds of tiny golden bells chasing infinity. A bracelet? No. Payal. Well, one of the pair, anyway. I've never seen any like this before, even though Ma keeps dozens of styles at the store. The anklets are usually fashioned in silver—gold at your feet would disgrace the gods, of course. They jingle with every movement, telling me they're pure and not some cheap, fake, plated knockoffs.

"You're mistaken," I say. "They're not mine." Even though part of me aches to feel the weight of them on my bare skin, to see how they move with me.

"But they are," he says. "I made them for you."

"Taara?" Leela's voice calls from not far away. "Why did you— Hey." She looks from me to the guy and back. His hand is still outstretched, the payal sitting delicate and inviting in his palm, his face bemused and hopeful. "I think we should go." She takes the keys from my hand and gently locks an arm through mine, leading me away. "It's getting late."

We don't wait to see if he walks away.

We sit in silence for a few minutes in my car, the heat blasting, the same haunting song from earlier playing on Leela's phone. "Will you turn that off?" I say, a little too harshly.

"Who is he?" she asks.

I shrug. "He kept calling me Soni. He thought I was someone else." And for moment, I wish I was, too.

Leela and I decide to drop into Chaska for a snack before we head home. It's packed, of course, because the new Shah Rukh Khan film just let out. And that's what brown people—well, in Little India smack-dab in the middle of Jersey anyway—do on a Saturday night. "How was it?" Leela asks our usual waiter, Shankar, who already knows to bring us two plates of chole bhature, extra pickled onions on the side. "He's getting too old to carry this shit."

"No yaar, he's looking good," says Shankar, who definitely has a finer appreciation of Shah Rukh. "He's back to that *Om Shanti Om* body, because Ranbir is on his tail? I wouldn't mind being on his tail, too, nah?" Leela and I dissolve into laughter as Shankar sets up our order. We dip hot, crispy-soft pieces of fried dough into the saucy curried chickpeas, and I pile some of the onions high onto the little scoop I've made with the bread. Then another group shuffles into the already crammed space, and I can feel him before I see him. The guy from the club.

"Hey, Nick," Shankar says, clearly pleased to see the guy. "Chole bhature, ek plate?"

"Hey, Shankar," the guy says, slapping him on the back playfully. "Tight in here tonight, huh?" He pulls at the spare chair at our table, looking down at me intently. "Mind if I join you for a minute?"

Leela stands. "Yeah, we do, actually." She's about to wave Nick back when I grab her hand.

"It's not a big deal," I say. He sits, that crinkly-eyed grin taking over his face again.

She stands. "Well, I'll go get the check, then." She storms off toward the cashier, and I glare after her.

"She doesn't like me much, does she?" Nick says, a smirk playing on his lips. Shankar brings another steaming plate of chole bhature to the table, and the bread is so blisteringly hot, so round and inviting, that I can't help but tear into it, even though it's not mine. "You've still got it, don't you?"

"What?" I say, my mouth full of spicy, chut-putty channa.

"That appetite. I always used to say, 'Tid eh ki towa?'"

I startle for a second. "What does that mean?"

"'Do you have a stomach or a well?'" he says, his hands reaching for the bread just as mine do. He dips and scoops, adding extra onions, just like I did. "Maybe it loses something in the translation."

I watch him eat for a second—big, messy bites, like a farmer's kid from Punjab. "My mom used to say that to me sometimes, too, though. When I was little."

"Tid eh ki towa?" He laughs. "I'm not surprised."

Shankar shows up then with a wary look and a bag of grease. "Leela's waiting for you in the car—she said to tell you," he says seriously.

Nick grins at me again, but takes the hint. "Okay, well, guess that means you should go." He dips more bread into the chole again. "Or you could stay."

Annoyance flickers. Why does she want to ruin this for me? But I stand anyway.

"No, I should go," I say, taking the bag from Shankar.

But as I walk away, I kind of wish I hadn't.

The Sunday bustle has trickled by the time the lunch rush ends. I'm starving, and I've got reams of research to do for my science paper, but I promised Ma I'd stay till four. I hum along to the Bollywood song playing on my phone—it's the same plaintive song I've had on repeat since that night a week ago. I can't get it out of my head.

I tear open a pack of chana chor garam and nibble some of the spicy, crunchy bites. They're salty and sour and make my tongue tingle. I carefully dust the counter so there's no trace of my snack.

Ma hates when I eat in the store. Everything here is pristine: gleaming glass cases filled with the most elegant—and expensive—jewels in Little India. All handmade, crafted by artisans at our sister store in Rajouri Garden in Delhi. Papa flies back and forth every month to take care of the shipments, and Ma manages things—a bit obsessively, if you ask me—here in Jersey, under the watchful eyes of my uncles, Kamal and Sunil, her brothers who founded the store nearly twenty years ago. They're mostly hands-off these days, counting cash in the back while Ma wheels and deals in the front. She's got this grace about her, quietly directing you to just the right choice with a sleight of hand so swift that it doesn't even feel like she's selling you something. It's the light in the eyes and the curve of her mouth when she smiles just so, the dimples in her cheek and chin so distinctly desi, they're smitten and pulling out their wallets.

I gaze in the mirror on the counter, holding a small pearl-work choker to my throat, and stare at my own face, which echoes hers, except the umber eyes. Mine are a more standard hazel, so they only go to umber in a certain light, like now. But the mischief in them is missing, drilled away by rules and restrictions and the idea that I must always do the right thing. It makes me want to do exactly the wrong thing. My mind goes back to him, the boy from the other night, and I wonder if I was too cautious, too careful. Why I didn't let my heart race a little, just for once?

"Again this song!" Ma says as she shuffles in from the back. Startled, I drop the necklace, and it clatters on the glass case. She wiggles her long, lean fingers at me. "Turn it up."

My uncles have threatened to banish me from the shop because of it, but Ma says this particular song touches her soul every time she hears it.

"That poor girl," Ma says, humming the words here and there, her hips swaying without permission. "Married off to a stranger and mourning her long-lost love. They always thought she was the villain, that Sahiba."

"Wasn't she?" I ask. I mean, she betrayed her one true love.

"She was torn," Ma says. She's looking in the mirror, but it's my reflection that she sees there, the fine lines smoothed, the years slipping away like a misplaced payal. "She had to decide between Mirza and her family, and in those days, it's not like it is now, where you just go running off at the first blink of love-wove pyar-shar. In those days, if you left your family, you left everyone—the whole world as you know it."

"Yeah," I say with a smile. "But that was the kind of love that meant you'd be immortalized forever."

"A love very few people truly know." There's something in the way she says it, so quiet, so faraway, like she's speaking to herself and not to me. Like she knows what that love, that loss, might feel like.

"Then it must have been one worth fighting for, right?"

"You don't know, Bebo, what you'll do," my mother says,

a sudden anger simmering under her words. "You don't know how to choose until you're right there, on the precipice, giving away your everything for something that may be real or may be a shadow, a ghost you're chasing."

But what I wouldn't give to find out. This song is just one of hundreds that tell the story of the lovelorn Sahiba, who betrayed her lover, Mirza, to preserve her family's honor—but when it was already far too late. While the others are all remembered for their boundless love, their soul connections, she's reviled as a traitor to both sides. "Sahiba had something most people only ever dream of, Ma," I say, putting more bangles onto their racks. "She gave it up. It's her own fault. But I don't quite buy it anyway. It's just a folktale, right?"

"How can you say that, Taara? That kind of love is something to aspire to—something very few people get to experience." Her voice goes faraway again when she says, "And maybe truly something worth risking everything for." Her eyes brighten and she laughs. "But so few would, hena? Anyway, these days, you kids don't know anything about love." She pushes another stack of velvet boxes toward me. "All this swipe right, swipe left. True love is in the eyes, in the reuniting of two souls."

"Uh-huh," I say, and begin unpacking the boxes she's placed on the counter.

"How was the dance, Bebo?" she asks me suddenly, a curious smirk traveling all the way to her eyes. She pokes my cheek. "Oh, you think I don't know where you go? You think I haven't done everything you've done, first and better?" She laughs. "Anything interesting?"

"Ma!"

"Well, you've been listening to this song with no end. Must be something." Her eyes shine, newly polished stones, and I wonder if she really believes those words: *the reuniting of two souls.* "This is the time, Bebo. Have your fun—but keep it clean, and let no one be the wiser."

"Sure, Ma," I say, laughing. "As if."

"Kya *as if*?" she says, incredulous. "You really think I didn't have any fun when I was your age?"

"Yeah, Ma, I'm sure you did." But my grin betrays me. I can see an endless row of dewanae falling for those eyes, but the amazing Amrita? She could never have loved them back. Right?

"You think you know," she says. "But I have my secrets."

"What secrets?" I'm curious now, and my mind keeps flashing back to Nick, to the familiarity of his touch, the spark of his skin. Maybe it was nothing. But maybe it was something.

"Before your papa, there was another boy. Sunder Singh. He'd just come from India—and Patiala at that!—and used to work at the chole-bhature shop across the street from the jewelers. Yes, Mahi's. But back then, it was called Sabrawal's. In those days, there weren't so many of us, and everybody knew everybody. I'd go in with some of the girls, and he'd always pile my plate the highest with greasy, puffy bhature. Then, when I ate them all up, he'd laugh and say, 'Tid eh ki towa?'"

When I look at her, startled, she explains. "'Do you have a stomach or a well?' Just like I used to say to you," she says, frowning. "Anyway, it all happened very fast, from laughing over chole bhature to . . ."

"Where'd he go?" I ask. "Sunder Singh?"

"He was killed. A gash to the head. My brothers . . ." She

trails off then, lost someplace I can't quite reach. "I tried, but it was too late. I still can't believe he's gone."

"Wait, what?" I say, the necklace I'm arranging clattering on the glass case. "He was killed. Killed?"

"They were never charged. . . ." Her voice trails again. "It was ruled an accident. Then his family packed up and moved back to Ludhiana."

"Mom!"

She's there, but already gone, humming the words to the song again, about a love long lost and the pain she'll always carry.

"Ma," I say, touching her hand.

She pulls it away, surprised. "Acche, tho, you finish up, teek hai, Bebo? Then Sunil Mamu will drop you off; I know, science paper." She bustles out the back in a hurry, a palm pressed to her cheek, as if remembering a familiar touch.

I turn back to the counter, the stack of jewel boxes laid out in front of me. In them sit another dozen gold sets, soldered and shaped with all the beauty of an India I've never seen—more peacocks dancing, lions roaring, the sinister slither of the nagin, with ruby eyes beckoning. The last bin is filled with the heavy jingle of payal, the anklets all tangled in a mess, every pair wrought in gleaming silver. Not a golden one in sight. I think about asking her then, but something stops me. Instead I just unwind pair after pair, lining them up on the velvet spread below, thinking about moments missed.

I'm polishing some of the new sets—wrought gold bangles painted the deep blues and greens of the peacock—when the door buzzes. I press Open without thinking, the way I always do, even though Ma is forever telling me to look first. The chimes tinkle as the door opens, and my heart drops when I see him. Nick.

I don't know how he found me, and I half thought I'd never see him again, though I sort of wished I would.

But there he is, grinning that doofy grin, his pristine black wool coat buttoned up, a Burberry plaid scarf laid against it, a few scattered drops of March rain making his hair slick. His hands are in his pockets, affable and unintimidating. Except totally not. "I knew I'd find you," he says, and in that moment I want to run to him and run away, all at once.

"How did you find me?"

"You're exactly where I knew you'd be." He walks up to the counter and pulls one hand from his pocket. "I knew this was yours, and I wanted you to have it." He lays the gold payal carefully across the silken ruby velvet of one of the cases, and it feels alive, like a snake, reluctant but seduced to dance to the charmer's tune. "It needs to be with you."

"It's not mine," I say.

"Oh, but it is." His smile is lopsided, optimistic. There's a small scar across his forehead, just above his right eyebrow, that I didn't see in the flash of the holi party; thin and barely noticeable. The only flaw on his face. Before I can stop myself, I'm reaching toward it. *A gash to the head.* Just like my mother said.

"Soni," he says, taking my hand. His touch is cold. "I know it's you. But I'll give you all the time you need."

With that, he turns, and walks out the door.

It's only when he's gone that I realize he's left the payal

behind. That's when Ma comes bustling back in, no doubt eager to beguile another customer.

"Khon tha?" Ma says, looking at the empty space in front of the counter. "They've gone already?" She's disappointed for a second—I'll never be her star salesgirl—but holds out her hand, her fist practically bursting with a secret. "I have to show you," she says breathlessly. "Remember I was saying, about Sunder. You didn't believe me. But this, he made for me." She opens her palm and reveals a gleaming serpent of a thing, a charmed talisman, one that makes my blood run cold. A golden payal, intricately wrought, a perfect match for the one that Nick left behind.

Mirza and Sahiba

A Punjabi Folktale

The inspiration for this story was the star-crossed tale of a grieving Sahiba, and the fate she wrought for herself. In ancient Indian folktale and legend, the pairing of Mirza and Sahiba is frequently remembered in the same breath as other immortalized lovers, like Layla-Majnun, Heer-Ranjha and Sohni-Mahiwal. While the others are held up as shining examples of One True Pairings, Mirza and Sahiba's romance is a warning, a lost-in-love couple immortalized in an elegy of lust, familial drama, betrayal, and murder. In the story, Sahiba is the villain at the heart of a story, a fickle seductress who lured the worthy warrior Mirza with longing and promises, only to betray him when the fate of her brothers is in her hands.

According to the old stories, the most beautiful girl in the Punjabi village of Kheewa, young Sahiba, finds love in the arms of the famed archer, Mirza, the son of a friend-turned-foe, but the families of the pair forbid their entanglement. On the night she is arranged to wed a stranger, she runs off with Mirza, and they are to live happily ever after. But the girl's brothers get word of their escape, and set off to capture the two and bring them back, to separate them once and for all. Sahiba, aware of the chase and fearful for the safety of her brothers—who would surely lose this fight to the skilled Mirza—empties the quiver and shatters her lover's arrows as he sleeps in the winding embrace of a banyan tree. When they are found by the townsfolk, Mirza awakes to an arrow in his throat.

I wondered what might happen if the traitorous Sahiba and her long-lost love Mirza were reunited in another life—one in which Sahiba had to live with the consequences of her actions. One in which a shadow of the girl she used to be existed as a near mirror to the past—in the form of our decidedly confused protagonist—and one in which the reincarnated Mirza might be a bit stalkerish as the history of his former love and fate played out in his head. What a delicious triangle that could be.

—Sona Charaipotra

THE COUNTING OF VERMILLION BEADS

ALIETTE DE BODARD

Seen from afar, the wall fills up Cam and Tam's world like skin over a healed wound.

It starts as roughly hewn stones, almost ordinary save for their white, translucent color; and then, as it sweeps upward in a slow unfurling, it grows and stretches into a dome, and a pattern of dark blue lines spreads across what should be the surface of the sky—like the ribs of a leaf, or the veins of a corpse.

As they walk closer—and its shadow darkens, swallowing their own—even sunny, optimistic Tam falls silent.

"We can go back, Big'sis," Cam says. "It was just a dream."

She expects Tam to grow angry—to argue and yell, frustration barely contained; to accuse her again of lacking respect, pretending she can put restrictions on her elder sister's life—to condemn her for not being Mother. But instead Tam is silent, watching the wall.

There are no birds, not this close to the wall. But a tall, slender coconut tree arches from the grass to the white, translucent area above the stones of the palace's roof, where the sky would be, if there was a sky within the Palace of the Everlasting Emperor.

"Here," Tam says. "Just like Mother said."

It was a dream, Cam wants to say. Mother is dead; not only that, but her tomb is outside the wall, in the dusty little village where Cam and Tam grew up before the Emperor's envoys took them and brought them to the palace to check the census; before their lives shrank to the company of the other girls, the abacuses, the reams of reports to be checked.

None of the census girls will ever be allowed out, beyond the skin of the wall, beyond the confines of the palace. The only way out is deeper in, through the Inner Vermillion Chambers—to become a high-rank official charged with doing the Emperor's will, traveling the land to bear edicts and memorials. But Tam has that look again: those haunted eyes like when she was a child and she dropped her stone elephant in the village well, that stubborn cast to her face, and, really, when was the last time Cam didn't follow where Tam led?

"She said we could fly, if we found the will. We could go home, back to Father and Grandmother and the aunts. Just forget all of this, same as a bad dream," Tam says. She unknots her sash and loops it around the trunk of the tree, testing her hold thoughtfully. She doesn't even look around—Cam does that, but this early on, all the supervisors are asleep, and the other census girls are still giggling at the mat chuoc game. "The wall is thinner at the top, isn't it? I bet we could push through."

Cam finds her voice, drags it from a faraway place. "The birds don't get out."

Tam snorts. "Like you know what you're talking about."

Cam doesn't, of course. But neither does Tam. "Big'sis, I don't think—"

But Tam is already shimmying up the tree, with the same ease as before—it's as if no time has passed since their arrival in the palace; five years of imprisonment become an eyeblink. "Big'sis!" Cam calls out. "Be careful!"

The wind, rising through the gardens, mangles Tam's answer as she ascends the tree—impossibly lithe, growing smaller and smaller as she climbs. Of course she can't get out that way. Does she think it hasn't been tried? There are hundreds of girls working on the census, hundreds of them from every dusty little village in the land, and dozens of them must know how to climb coconut trees. The Everlasting Emperor doesn't let go of what's his so easily.

Tam and Cam both want to go home—to sit once more with their family around a meal of fish sauce and rice, to chat about who did what in the village. Cam's heart tightens at the thought—what she wouldn't give to hear Second Aunt's reedy voice complaining of lack of respect, or Grandmother's soft, careful tread as she walks through the house in the morning, long before anyone is awake.

Tam says no one ever gets out—that none of the girls ever become high officials, that it's just a lie to keep them quiet and docile. She puts her faith not in the Everlasting Emperor but in magic—in the tales Mother used to recite at night: flying trees and inexhaustible rice jars, and fish becoming dragons becoming humans.

Cam doesn't believe in magic anymore. But then she was very young when Mother died, and doesn't remember her as well as Tam.

"Lil'sis." Tam's voice floats down, carried by the wind. "You can see through the wall, at the top. The rice paddies, the forests, the cities. Everything is so different from up here. Like scattered jewels."

"Come down," Cam says. It will be the Bi-hour of the Cat soon enough, and the supervisors will round them up once again, to the cavernous room where they do their accounting. "We'll be late."

Above her, Tam leans out, one hand pressing against the surface of the wall, the lines pulsing under her touch. "It's so thin. I could—" Her legs barely cling to the trunk. Her chest juts out, dangerously unbalanced—

"Big'sis!" Cam screams, but it's already too late.

Tam falls. Too late. Too late. Why did she—why did she even indulge her sister—why did she—

But as Tam falls, the wall wraps itself around her, the blue lines thinning and sinking beneath her skin like veins—fingers becoming the color of the sky, of the leaves; hands obscured by a thin, white veil that climbs over her chest and face—and, just as she would have hit the stones of the wall, she shifts and blurs and *changes*—and a white bird with blue streaks on its wings rises, catching a draft and banking back toward the wall.

She—

This only happens in stories. Cam stops, breathing hard, the world blurring and tilting around her. She watches the bird fly, again and again, toward the skin of the wall; and, again and again, hitting an impassable obstacle.

She said we could fly.

It was just a dream. Just Tam's wild, impossible dream. But, as the bird comes down, wings ruffled and broken and bleeding—as it hops onto Cam's clenched fist—it looks up at her, and the look in its eyes is her sister's.

Cam can't disguise Tam's absence. The supervisors notice, of course, and castigate her for failing to keep an eye on her sister. They think she's run away—that she's hiding somewhere in the depths of the gardens.

"Foolish girl," Supervisor Bach Kim says, with a sigh. "She'll regret it, when we do find her." And then, to Cam, a little more kindly—she's always liked Cam, always praised her hard, relentless work—"don't let that distract you from your accounting."

But it does. Cam feeds the bird her charred rice and dumplings, watches it eat and move and fly, wondering how much of Tam is left. Twice, she takes it into the gardens, releases it toward the wall, but it always comes back, always in the same shape. Whatever happened at the wall, it will only happen once. "Big'sis," she whispers, sometimes, after the day's accounting is done. "What are we going to do?"

The bird never answers. Cam wakes up in the morning, picking out sand from her shoes—the smell of the sea saturating the room, blown in from the nearby beaches—and feeds the bird the noodles from her soup bowl. It slurps it avidly, throwing back its head like Tam used to do at breakfast.

At night, it sings—a quivering, warbling sound that rises in her dreams, becomes her sister's voice. It wouldn't be so bad, if the bird spoke of cryptic wisdom, or of the dream Tam had, the one that started everything, but instead, it's small, everyday things, the kind of talk they had before Tam changed.

See, in Dai Sang Province, here? The inconsistency between the Hoa Khanh household now and five years ago. They can't possibly have had thirteen children, not only with one wife!

And here, in Quang Phuoc Province. These fifty buckets of husked rice just vanish between one page and the next. And it happens here again. I bet the village headman is embezzling them. Has to be.

See, Big'sis? See?

Cam opens her mouth to speak, but all that comes out is the warbling song of a bird. Tam laughs, relaxed, good-natured. *Don't worry. It'll all become clear, in time.*

And everything blurs and whitens, becomes the color of the wall, blue veins stretching around her, as a sound resonates, again and again—she thinks it a gong, a bell calling to Awakening; but as Cam wakes up, gasping, to her empty room, she knows what it is: the sound of beads on an abacus.

During the day, Cam sleepwalks to her place in the census pavilion. She puts her hand on the plate by the doors—they open, recording her attendance, and she goes to sit at the end of one row, by one of the lacquered pillars painted the vermillion shade of the Emperor's belongings, close to the courtyard. By her side, Tam's mat is empty, her papers neatly folded, her abacus reset to zero, the ink dried on the hairs of her paintbrush. The other girls don't like it: Hanh, who is superstitious, makes a sign of warding as she sits and takes her abacus from her sleeve. Census girls aren't meant to disappear. They might be prisoners in the palace, but the Emperor keeps them safe, keeps them fed and clothed, while outside war and famine rage, and their families shrivel and die without the miracle of such protection.

Cam stares at rows and rows of numbers, trying to make sense of them all: the returns of Kien La Province, their production of fermented fish, their corvée attendance, and rice-wine consumption by household. Little things that should add up, that don't always: too much rice wine, too many banquets to honor the Emperor, too little salt sent to the capital . . .

Around her, the familiar clacks of beads on the abacuses, rising and rising to fill her world, girl after girl sinking deeper and deeper into strings of numbers, tracking down the inconsistencies, building a true picture of the Everlasting Empire and its people, bead after bead after bead.

It becomes the song of a bird, the warbling tone of her sister's voice that haunts her dreams. *Don't worry, Lil'sis.*

Of course she worries. She always has.

Cam comes to, startled, to a touch on her hand. For a single, heartbreaking moment, she thinks Tam has come back, but it's the bird, hopping up and down between her fingers, making small, satisfied noises in the back of its throat. When Cam reaches out, it flies away to Tam's mat, bright eyes on her; hopping over Tam's abacus, the beads dancing beneath its legs; and from there to the steps leading down to the courtyard. The message is clear.

Follow me.

Cam rises, slowly. She looks at Supervisor Bach Kim, mouthing an apology. *I just need a moment.* Supervisor Bach Kim nods, makes a gesture telling her to be quick. She hasn't noticed the bird, but why would she see anything remarkable about it?

The bird—flying and hopping and pausing when Cam stumbles—takes her through the courtyard, weaving its way between rows of stone elephants and attendants, and then into the walled corridors that lead from the census quarters to the gardens—for a moment Cam worries that her authorizations won't be good there, but as she lays her hand on the plates, each door opens with a soft exhaling sound. The air is thick with the cloying scent of osmanthus.

The bird stops, then. When Cam joins it under an arch of yellow stone, carved with the characters for longevity and good fortune, it hops toward the lawn and rises up in the air, flying toward the faraway shape of the wall. Its movements are slow and deliberate—her elder sister's through and through, that stubbornness that even five years of confinement haven't dented.

Cam watches, her heart in her throat. "There's nothing there. Come back." *Please, Big'sis. Please. Please stop whatever you're doing. Come back.*

The bird stops, turns back toward her. *Please please please,* Cam thinks, a prayer to her dead ancestors; to Mother, who has to be watching from the ancestral altar, protecting her daughters from beyond the grave. *Make her come back.* But the bird turns again, banks toward the wall, and then, with the same deliberateness, toward Cam, and again and again, movements that become a slow dance, as the sound of beads on an abacus rises, filling the air like thunder.

See here, in Quang Phuoc Province, the famine of the Metal Tiger Year . . .

The blue feathers on the bird's wings shine under the skin

of the wall—a radiance that spreads to its entire body until it seems to glow like jade held under the sun, and they're the veins of the wall again, pulsing with that same slow heartbeat. White mist rises from the lawn, reaching upward. The bird still dances, and every beat of its wings draws more white, translucent mist, which grows thicker and thicker. Cam looks at the wall, and at the bird, and sees tendrils of mists connect both, thin threads thrown from a loom.

"Big'sis. Please."

The bird shivers and shakes, and changes again. Its shape stretches upward, wreathed in a white that hurts Cam's eyes. The mist sweeps over it; the wall closes in for a brief heartbeat; and then there's no bird left, nothing but the thin shape of a tree, branches stretching outward, and the same thin network of blue markings on its trunk. It bears a single round, golden fruit at its crown: a decandrous persimmon, the sweet, ripe smell of it trembling in the air, thick in Cam's throat like a promise of a feast.

Big'sis.

The trees don't get out, either—not even their leaves, borne by the wind, can breach the wall. It's pointless. No matter how many times Tam can change her shape—no matter where she finds that power, how long she can sustain it—there is no escape. Only the high-ranking, trusted officials are allowed outside.

Cam walks toward the tree, kneels by its side. The abacuses have fallen silent; now there's just wind in the branches. When she lays her hand on the trunk, she feels her sister's thoughts—Tam's annoyed affection for Cam, who tries so hard to be responsible—she loves Cam, she really does, but sometimes Tam could shake her, with her insistence on propriety and submission—Cam has to see, hasn't she, that it's illusory, that they'll never be chosen to be high-rank, that they'll live and die within the census pavilion, without husbands or children or families?

Oh Big'sis.

The world is blurred again. Cam brushes tears from her eyes. *Don't let this distract you from your work,* Supervisor Bach Kim would say, and she has to go back before they start looking for her. There's work to be done, numbers to check from page to page. She needs to make sure it's all impeccable—all taken forward to the Grand Secretariat, sealed and checked by the Emperor himself.

Around her, thin white mist pools, the remnants of the wall that swept over Tam, that changed her. *You won't get out this way. You have to see.*

The wind whistles in the branches, and it's her sister's voice again. *Maybe I will. We won't know until I try, will we? Mother said—*

Cam wants to say, *Mother is dead.* She stops herself with only an effort, because it's not what Tam needs to hear, because it won't change anything. *Mother has no voice within the palace. You should know this, Big'sis.* It's a tree. It—it can't leave, rooted in the earth of the garden. *Can't you— There has to be another shape.* But nothing gets through the wall. Not leaves, not birds, not girls—not the sister of her heart, the one who's always had enough fire for both of them, dragging her into scrapes and trouble, as if there were no other way to live.

Her heart stutters, misses a beat. The bark of the trunk is as smooth as the beads of her abacuses, and she finds herself sliding her fingers up and down, as if she were counting again—picking shape after shape, discarding them. Nothing works. Nothing gets out. Except . . .

Except the air of sea, the sand that they find in their shoes in the morning, clogged in their porcelain bowls on the breakfast table.

White pools around her, mist shot through with blue veins. The wall rises around her, thick and rough and warm. She slides her fingers down the trunk, as if holding a five-unit bead, and light spreads from her fingers to her sister's shape.

The tree crumbles into dust. The trunk first, and then the branches and the leaves; and, last to go, the golden fruit, its fragrance becoming unbearably thick against Cam's tongue, like mango juice, like liquid honey. Around her, yellow dust dances and shivers on a held breath; and the wind lifts it, carrying it toward the skin of the wall—where it sinks among blue veins until no trace of gold is left.

Cam's hand remains hanging in the air, with the touch of Tam's fingers still on hers, not sure whether she should laugh or cry or both.

Please, Big'sis . . .

Please be well.

When Supervisor Bach Kim asks Cam into her office, Cam is convinced it'll be about Tam, about the still-empty spot among the girls, the one they all sidestep with fear in their eyes as time passes and no one can find her anywhere.

But she got out. The dust passed the wall. It had to. Never mind that the wall is just a wall now, that Cam's dreams have been silent for a year, and that she's gone into the garden, time and time again, and found nothing but immaculate lawn and emptiness beneath a stone arch.

Supervisor Bach Kim doesn't look angry, merely thoughtful, watching Cam as if weighing her worth. "Tea?" she asks.

Cam sits on her knees as Supervisor Bach Kim pours tea the color of cut grass into a cup, breathing the almost-familiar smell. It's from the Inner Vermillion Chambers, a delicate, expensive thing the like of which is never given to the census girls. "Is this about my work?" she asks.

Supervisor Bach Kim's lips purse. "In a manner of speaking."

"I—" Since the tree crumbled a year ago, Cam has been living as through a gray veil, adding and subtracting numbers with no memory of what she does, or of the meaning of what she's looking at. It was bound to catch up with her. "I apologize—"

Supervisor Bach Kim laughs. "No need to apologize, child. Your work has been exemplary." She sips at her own cup of tea, lays it down on the low lacquered table, over the shimmering display that keeps cycling through the symbols for the Three Fortunes. "The last two days alone, you've gone through more reports and memorials than your three neighbors combined."

Cam sits, waiting for—she's not sure what. More compliments? She'd have lapped them up once, but now they feel hollow, meaningless. "Then—"

Supervisor Bach Kim slides a piece of paper toward her, with slow, careful reverence—and of course she would, because at the bottom of the page is the vermillion seal of the Everlasting Emperor, with its delicately etched traceries of circuits. Cam bows down to the unseen presence, and only then does she raise the upper half of her body and look at the paper.

Words blur and shift; she catches only a bare glimpse of them before they become too weighty to hold. *Whereas our servant Nguyen Thi Cam has shown exemplary devotion and dedication to the Imperial Throne . . .*

By this decree it pleases us to elevate her to Second Rank Official in the Grand Secretariat of the Inner Vermillion Chambers . . .

The Grand Secretariat.

Official.

Second Rank.

She.

She's going to get out. She's going to become a high-rank official, to move, effortlessly, in and out of the palace bearing the imperial will. She—she can go home.

"It's much to take in, I know." Supervisor Bach Kim's voice is almost kind. "You will get used to it, eventually." And then, letting go of the official dialect and decorum, she hugs Cam, as fiercely as a mother. "I'm so happy for you, child. I always knew you could do it."

Cam sits very still, watching the words. "I—" She stops, tries again. Her throat is filled with something sweet; with the taste of the decandrous persimmon. "Thank you, Elder Aunt. It means so much to me."

It would have, once upon a time, but now all she can think of is Tam's voice, whispering in her ears, and none of it seems to lift the gray veil over the world.

On the day of her presentation to the Everlasting Emperor, Cam takes a long, long bath, immersing herself into the scalding-hot water, as if it could finally scour her clean. The attendants she's been assigned have withdrawn at her request: as she gets out of the carved bath pool, she stares at herself, at her skin. It's lighter after six years in the census pavilion, but it's still the dark, rich skin of a peasant girl who grew up replanting rice in paddies, kneeling in the churned mud until it seemed to be her entire world; singing rhymes with Cousin Hoa and Cousin Lan and all the rest of them.

Tam is with them now, laughing and smiling, stumbling as she picks up seedlings, like she always did, under Father and Grandmother's fond eyes. She's gone home.

She must have.

Please, Mother. Please let her be well.

In the bedroom—her new one, impossibly large, impossibly luxurious—someone has laid out a five-panel tunic of rich brocade, with the hen insignia of the second rank picked out in threads so thin it seems like a painting. Cam lets the attendants dress her, as if in a dream: one layer of dresses after another, in rich shades of red, and then a thin, long sleeveless over-tunic, so dark it's almost black. She stares at herself in the mirror, and a stranger gazes back at her, her hands drowned in large gold-embroidered sleeves, her face whitened with ceruse, her long hair piled up in an elaborate topknot with golden pins in the shape of turtles. Her lips are painted the color of imperial ink, a slash of blood red like a wound.

She'd thought she'd feel victorious, but there is nothing but emptiness in her chest, as if her heart had been removed.

Cam stares at herself in the mirror, forces herself to smile, and watches her reflection move, vermillion lips parting on the black-enamelled teeth of officials.

Time.

The door opens, with that same soft exhaling sound like a last breath. Cam steels herself for more attendants and more guards, for the long journey into the Inner Vermillion Chambers and everything she's ever dreamed of.

Tam stands on the threshold.

Time slows down, becomes trapped in honey. Cam breathes in, slowly. "Big'sis?"

Tam smiles. She's wearing the rough tunic of a peasant, and her hair hangs loose on her shoulders, but she hasn't changed. Her face is the same—moon-shaped and dimpled around a fierce smile—and she holds herself as though going into battle. Behind her are Supervisor Bach Kim, and guards. The supervisor's face is closed, angry. "See?" she says to Tam. "Your younger sister is moving on to better things. She has no need of you."

"You . . ." Cam takes in a deep, shaking breath; has to stop, because it hurts so much, with the clothes encasing her. "You were outside."

"She turned herself in," Supervisor Bach Kim says, sounding angry.

Tam shakes her head. "I went home, Lil'sis. I—" Her face twists, for a moment; loses its familiar smile and becomes hollow and taut. "I tried. With Grandmother and Father and the aunts, and I—" Her hands clench. "They— Every time they would reach for chopsticks close to the points, every time they would say a word wrong . . ." She's shaking now. "I sat with Cousin Lan and we didn't have anything to talk about anymore. Her world was the village and the rice harvest and who she was going to marry, and there's so much more out there that she couldn't see!"

"They're our family," Cam says, but Tam shakes her head.

"The way they looked at me—they tried, but it was awe and fear—like they worshipped me. I just couldn't bear it anymore."

"Of course you're no longer peasants," Supervisor Bach Kim says. "As if you could ever stifle what you have become."

Tam walks into the room, past Cam, toward the tiled pool and the steaming water. Her gaze rakes the bed from end to end: Cam's discarded clothes, the rich, alien scents saturating the room, changing Cam from peasant's daughter to imperial official. "We can't go home, Lil'sis. We've changed too much."

Cam opens her mouth to say no, that of course they can, that she will—and then she remembers the stranger staring at her in the mirror, the official the least of whose acts is now imbued with the authority of the throne.

Instead, she says, "You didn't have to come back. Why—" *Why couldn't you stay away? Why couldn't you be careful, for once in your life? Why—*

Tam's gaze holds her. She raises her hands—dark and thin and elegant, their veins shining blue beneath the translucency of her skin. "Don't you know?"

And her eyes are the bird's, quick and bright and fierce; her arms moving in a slow dance, like wings.

Behind her, Supervisor Bach Kim says, "Come, child. Your sister has to see the Emperor, and you have to be assigned a suitable punishment."

Tam says, quietly, "We can't go home, but that doesn't mean we have to be caged. Remember how everything looked different, up there?"

"Like jewels," Cam says, the words rising from the morass of memory.

Tam smiles, and it's radiant and infectious. "So many precious places to discover. Come on, Lil'sis. Let's go see them together."

Mist rises, from the water in the bath, thickening with every pass of Tam's arms—and Cam can hear, growing louder and louder, the sound of an abacus, resonating under the roof until the entire palace seems to shake with it—until it seems to take root in her chest, as sturdy as the branches of a tree. Under her fingers, the rounded shape of abacus beads, a vast array of shapes to be weighed and discarded; in her mouth, the taste of decandrous persimmon, thick and sweet and earthy, a reminder of what things taste like, outside, strong and desperate and *alive*.

"We can't possibly leave . . . ," Cam starts slowly, desperately. She wants to talk about dreams, about magic—about how the power of shape-shifting can't possibly sustain either of them, in the long term, but all the words seemed to have melted in her throat.

Tam watches her from within the mist. Nothing left of the room now, of the clothes on the bed, of the guards or of Supervisor Bach Kim. "Can't we?" She holds out a hand, her eyes dark and shadowed.

Be reasonable, Cam wants to say—and then she realizes that Tam is right—that being reasonable will not undo the bars of her cage, or give her anything but hollow victories. She shakes her head. Her hair streams, long and black and uncouth, the color of churned mud. She slides a final invisible bead down, as if finishing the day's tallies, and reaches out to Tam through the mist.

Cam clutches her sister's hand and lets the mist gather them both, dust and sand dancing on the wind—out and out and away, toward the wealth of the world outside.

TẤM CÁM

A Vietnamese Folktale

"Tấm Cám" is one of the most iconic tales in Vietnamese folklore. A story of the escalating rivalry of two sisters, it's been referenced, retold, and readapted countless times in Vietnam in various mediums, from book to movie.

Tấm, a beautiful and kind young woman, is treated as a servant by her stepmother and stepsister after her father's death. With the assistance of a magic fish, she comes to the attention of the king and marries him. After her marriage, her envious stepsister, Cám, repeatedly kills her, and Tấm repeatedly reincarnates in various forms until she escapes the palace. The king, mourning for her, finally finds her and takes her back home. Tấm gets her revenge on her stepsister by suggesting that she take a scalding bath in order to whiten her skin. Cám dies, boiled alive.

I've always been struck by the relationship between the sisters, and how it's always driven by Cám's jealousy of her sister's beauty: there are all sorts of rather nasty undercurrents there, and I wanted to tell a new version that would have sisters who stuck together in spite of all odds. And I kept the bath, too, except in a radically different context!

—Aliette de Bodard

THE LAND OF THE MORNING CALM

E. C. MYERS

It's been five years since my mother died, but I still use the back door when I come home from school. She had always been there to greet me, writing on her laptop at the kitchen table with her knees pulled up to her chest.

I unlock the door and pause to press two fingers to the pearl choker at my throat, reminding myself she isn't waiting for me anymore. But today someone *is*: Harabeoji and Dad sit at the table, drinking soju together. They turn to look at me when I walk in.

"Hey, guys. What's up?" I ask.

Seeing them both there surprises me for a couple of reasons. My grandfather, a South Korean immigrant, is traditional enough that he thinks preparing meals and washing dishes are a woman's work—that is, mine. Dad knows better, but he's also way busy and his cooking sucks. So the kitchen's pretty much my exclusive domain. I bet Mom used it as her office because it was the one place the menfolk wouldn't disturb her.

Harabeoji and Dad also have barely spoken to each other since Dad started dating Lisa a month ago. I mean, of course it's awkward to bring your new girlfriend home when your dead wife's father still lives with you, but Harabeoji just has to deal with it. We're the only family he has left, and we need to stick together. Plus, it's been five years, and Dad deserves to be happy. At least one of us should be happy.

I count the little green liquor bottles lined up between them. Seven empties. Then I check how Dad's doing. He had used alcohol to deal with Mom's death, but he's finally gotten to a good place. Lisa is helping with that, too.

"Where were you?" Harabeoji demands.

"School?" I toss my backpack onto the floor and lean my elbows on a chair to face them. Cigarette smoke hangs thick in the air. The ashtray next to Harabeoji's glass overflows with ashes and butts. I wrinkle my nose.

"You got my text?" he asks.

"Yes. You only need to send it once, you know."

My phone shows four texts from my grandfather, all identical: hannah's angry!!! come home

Sometimes I wish I'd never shown him how to text.

"What do you think Mom did this time?" I ask.

"She hid my cigarettes," Harabeoji says.

"Right. It can't be that you forgot where you left them. Again." I wave my hand in the air. "Too bad you found them. You blame every weird thing in this house on gwisin." Like when he found his comb somewhere he didn't expect, or tiny pebbles ended up in his slippers, or his tea went cold while he was drinking it. Gwisin, gwisin, gwisin.

Harabeoji says my mother is a gwisin. That's the Korean word for "ghost." Of course that's ridiculous—I'm right there with you—but it's not always so easy to discount, because he knew she had died as soon as it happened, even though she was three thousand miles away. He claims she visited him in a dream.

It was my eleventh birthday, which I'd been looking forward to for ages. I woke up to find a letter from "Horgwats" on my pillow—Mom obviously hadn't committed a typo like that—along with a white owl feather, a small buttercream flower cake, and a pouch of jelly beans, which I immediately discovered were only nasty flavors like vomit and earwax. That was Dad's doing, of course.

Before you think, "Aw, best family ever," you should know that my parents were both in San Diego for the weekend without me. Dad was running focus groups for a new game his company was making, and Mom was at a science-fiction convention. She called it a business trip—she was writing a fantasy novel and needed to "network" to get an agent—but I knew she was really going for fun. She had made a new costume: a kumiho from *The Land of the Morning Calm,* an online video game commonly called *LMC.*

Mom had debuted her costume for us in the family room just a few days before the con. I was amazed at how her body language subtly transformed as she slipped on the brown velvet mask with large slanted eyes, pointed ears, and whiskers. She shook her butt, and the nine orange feathers attached to the back of her red shorts swished behind her, making her look more like a scantily clad peacock than a nine-tailed fox to me.

"Sunny, your mom's a fox!" Dad said.

I groaned, but that was far from the worst pun he'd ever made. No, that one would be my name, Sun Moon. I still can't believe Mom went along with that.

"You look just like Eun-Ha!" I told her. She had modeled her costume after her *LMC* character, a warrior-mage fox spirit. The purple pearl on the leather choker was a perfect match for her in-game "kumiho bead"—a relic that contained the magical fox's knowledge and soul.

"Thanks, flower cake," she said. "You could still come with us. It would be easy to whip together a costume for Isang." Isang was my character, a thief-scholar who could transform into a bear cub.

"Maybe next time," I said. Unlike Mom, I couldn't get away with skipping out on responsibilities to go play pretend with my friends. I had to write a book report on *A Bridge to Terabithia* by Monday, and I still had to read the book.

"If I don't get stuck at work, Bitgaram also will make an appearance at the con. *Rowrrr*!" Dad swiped at Mom's tails with a clawed hand.

"Easy, tiger!" Mom looked around. "Now where's my brush gotten to?"

Dad and I pointed to the computer desk, where she'd left her hairbrush beside the keyboard again.

I miss moments like that.

Anyway, so finding the letter, and even the gross jelly beans, was a nice surprise—almost magical, if I hadn't known that Harabeoji had snuck them into my room during the night. I'd gone to thank him, and found him sobbing and rocking back and forth in bed.

"Harabeoji? What's wrong?"

He waved me over and then grabbed me in a tight hug. He smelled like cigarettes and Tiger Balm. "She's gone. Hannah . . . Your mother is gone."

I pulled away from him. "What?"

"I dreamed about her. She was standing right there." He stabbed an index finger toward the foot of his bed. "She didn't visit you, too?"

"Oh! You had me worried for a second." It was just a dream. Mom was fine. Harabeoji was obsessed with the prophetic meanings behind his dreams. He sometimes bought a bunch of lottery tickets when he had a good "money" dream, but he hasn't won yet.

"You just had a bad dream," I said.

"No. It was Hannah's gwisin."

He'd been telling stories about gwisin since I was little, great stuff for bedtime tales if you want to make a kid wake up screaming in the middle of the night. Gwisin were usually transparent and legless, the spirits of dead people out for revenge or with some unfinished business. Sometimes that unfinished business meant an unmarried woman who is, well—Harabeoji called it "looking for love." Some of them hid underwater and tried to drown you, or haunted forests and killed hapless hikers. But most of them were supposed to be harmless, unless you ignored their attempts to get your attention.

"First of all, ghosts don't exist. Second of all, Mom can't be a ghost because she isn't dead," I said.

"It was her!" He slapped his knee.

"Fine!" I threw up my hands. "What did this ghost look like?"

"She had a fox face and nine tails fanning behind a white hanbok."

I covered my mouth. Harabeoji couldn't have known about her fox mask and tails. He hadn't seen Mom's costume before she left, and she never would have mentioned it since he didn't approve of her "playing dress-up like a child." The white dress didn't match the halter top and shorts from her costume, but Korean ghosts typically wore traditional clothing.

This was starting to freak me out.

"If she was wearing a mask, how did you know it was her?" I asked.

"Not a mask. It was her, but she looked like a kumiho. I felt it. I know my own daughter." He laughed gruffly. "She looked ridiculous, like a cartoon. She always was a foolish girl."

"Look, I'll call her right now," I said. I went back to my room and got my phone, and for some reason I picked up the owl feather from my bedspread and brought it, too. I dialed as I returned to his room. The line rang and rang and rang before it went to voicemail. That was the last time I heard her voice, and it was telling a lie: *Hi, this is Hannah Kim Moon. Sorry you've missed me, but I'll call you right back.*

"Hey, Mom. Just calling to see how you're doing." I twirled the feather around in my fingers. "Call me when you get this?"

Harabeoji was looking at me with pity, like he knew he was

right, and he couldn't even hope that he'd dreamed up her ghost.

An hour later, Dad called. One of Harabeoji's dreams had finally come true.

Dad doesn't believe in ghosts any more than I do, but he's been strangely silent since I walked into the kitchen.

I want to believe the world is bigger and more mysterious than it seems. It would be great to have Mom around, in any form. But when she died, I learned that wanting something with all your heart doesn't make it any more real.

"Dad, you're not buying this, right?" I say.

"Well . . ." Dad drains the last bit of soju in his glass and then stands up. "Come take a look at this and tell me what you think."

He leads me to the desktop PC in the den, Harabeoji trailing behind us a little unsteadily. This used to be the family computer, but only Harabeoji uses it now. Dad and I use our laptops on the couch or in our rooms, together but not together.

It's a goofy horror-movie cliché, but I freeze when I see what's on the monitor: the splash screen for *The Land of the Morning Calm*.

"Wow, we haven't played this since . . ." I swallow. "In a long time." Five years, to be exact.

While Mom was marathoning *LMC* at her convention, she suffered a sudden brain aneurysm and collapsed right at her keyboard. She never woke up. So you see why Dad and I hadn't particularly felt like returning to the lands of the ancient, magical Korea of the game since then.

"This is where we found Harabeoji's cigarettes." Dad points behind the monitor.

"Not surprising to find his cigarettes at his computer."

"I didn't leave them here!" Harabeoji says. "And I didn't turn that damn game on either."

Dad clears his throat. "What makes it even weirder is that today Chasa announced that they're shutting down *LMC* next week."

"Oh, Dad." I give him a fierce hug that takes him—and me—by surprise.

Chasa Entertainment has been running *LMC* since 1998 in one form or another. The massive multiplayer online role-playing game had been a big part of our lives. My parents met in the game. A year later they had an in-game wedding reception for their characters Eun-Ha and Bitgaram in Andong District. (They also had a real-life wedding, but they only ever talked about the virtual one.) I celebrated my eighth birthday party in *LMC*, when they finally let me start playing, under Mom's supervision.

No matter how often we moved, or what else was going on in our lives, *The Land of the Morning Calm* was there. Until it killed my mother.

I shove our fat cat, Muta, off the chair and plop into it. She bats my foot with a paw in irritation before slinking off, tail up in the feline version of flipping me off.

Dad puts a hand on my shoulder, leans into me gently. "It feels like we're losing her again."

"Eun-Ha," I say softly. When the game's servers go offline, Mom's character, Eun-Ha, will be wiped with them, erasing the last remnants of her from the world.

I blink away tears and reach for the fake purple pearl around my neck, the kumiho bead from the costume Mom was wearing when she died. I saw it on her during the viewing, and I took it just before we closed the casket. It was weeks before Dad found out that I had it, but by then he couldn't do anything about it. He could hardly blame me for wanting something to remember her by. Over the years, whenever I would start to forget what Mom was like, I touched the bead and saw her again as clearly as if she were right in front of me.

I nudge the computer mouse and click on the Start Game button. I try to remember my password. Our family has a lifetime subscription to *LMC*—which seems morbid when I think about Mom.

Dad's phone buzzes. He checks it, and the gloom lifts from his face.

"Tell Lisa I say hi," I say.

Harabeoji makes a disapproving sound, and the temporary peace between him and Dad is over.

Dad kisses the top of my head and squeezes my shoulders. "Will do."

I close the program and turn off the computer. The aging machine takes forever to chug along. When the fan switches off, it's suddenly really quiet in the living room. So quiet, I hear Harabeoji's stomach rumble.

"I'll start dinner," I say.

Mom looked over my shoulder while I created my user account for *LMC* on the living-room computer. She reached for the mouse to show me where to click, but I slapped her hand away. "I can do it!"

I was excited because Mom was finally letting me into her world. It seemed like she preferred spending time in a virtual re-creation of ancient Korea with a bunch of strangers to playing board games with her family. We'd never done the things TV tells you mothers and daughters do together: braiding each other's hair, clothes shopping, trying on makeup. Once I'd asked her to help me make a Toph Beifong costume for Halloween, but she stayed up all night to make it herself. It was terrific, much better than anything I could have done, but I hated it.

"Shouldn't you be writing?" I asked.

"I can do that later. You have to pick an animal," Mom said.

"I know." I clicked on the owl. The little animated bird flapped its wings and went, "Whoo, whoo!"

"Why did you pick that?" Mom asked.

I shrugged. "It looks cute."

"This is an important decision! You shouldn't rush it," she said.

"Can't I change it later if I don't like it?" I asked.

"Life doesn't work like that, Sun."

"This is just a game."

She sighed. "You're starting to sound like your grandfather."

"Harabeoji is old and wise," I said. "Oh, I'm going to make my character a venerable shaman!"

"Maybe you aren't ready for this."

Hot tears slipped down my face. "Mom! *Please.* You promised."

She threw up her hands and walked away. "Fine, do whatever you want."

❖❖❖

After dinner, Harabeoji goes out to drink and play hwatu cards with the other Korean old men in the neighborhood. Home alone, I curl up in bed with my laptop and prepare to plow through a mountain of homework.

But I haven't been able to stop thinking about Mom and *LMC* since I got home, so instead of answering discussion questions on *1984*, I open my browser and load thelandofthemorning.com. The site hasn't changed much since the early two thousands, except for the front-page notice about the game ending, with a timer counting down to midnight next Friday, GMT+9. They're planning a big blowout to bring the game to a conclusion, and everyone's invited. For its last week, *LMC* is free-to-play. A download button is right next to the timer.

Before I change my mind, I click the download link. While the game installs, I fiddle with Mom's kumiho bead, and it all rushes back to me: The countless evenings I'd spent watching her play while I read on the couch. The stories she and Dad would tell from their online adventures, as detailed as if they'd really happened—which she had tried and failed to work into her sprawling novel-in-progress. Late nights spent as a family trying to destroy King Yeoma's undead armies. My final visit to the Land, the night before Mom died and my world ended.

It takes three attempts before I remember my password. When I succeed, I'm surprised to see my old character, Isang the Brave Bear Cub. Isang the Naïve. He had waited for me all this time, unchanged. But Isang has a mother, and I don't anymore. Life hasn't been on pause for me, and I'm a different person now. So I create a new character.

I select the gwisin-hunter class, and this time I pick a girl and make her look as close to my actual appearance as I can: glasses, white tank top, black tights, short black hair with a blue streak. Some people, like my mom, put on masks and costumes to feel more like themselves, but I haven't been into cosplaying for a long time. I don't mind adding thick combat boots and a ludicrously large broadsword to my ensemble, though. That's just sensible gear to have.

As a final touch, I give my avatar a necklace with a single purple pearl.

Then I consider for a moment—it's a big decision after all—before choosing an owl spirit again. This choice isn't only fueled by nostalgia, though; wings will let me cover the most territory as quickly as possible. I plan to log in just long enough to fly over the Land's Three Kingdoms one last time. And it doesn't matter anymore, so I enter my real name, Sun_Moon.

I sit up straight in bed when one name in my friends list catches my eye: HannaKimmy. Status: Online.

Mom.

It has to be a bug in the system, a cruel glitch. The last time she could have logged into the game was five years ago. But there's no harm in firing off a private message to her: *"Mom? It's Sunny."*

It's as foolish a hope as buying a Powerball ticket. I wait and wait and wait, but there's no response. Of course there's no response. I don't believe in ghosts in the real world, but that's the joy of the Three Kingdoms. It's a fantasy world where animals can turn into people, people can become gods, and basically anything can happen. The eleven-year-old girl in me who once believed in magic still wishes there was something on the other side of death.

It takes a moment to reorient myself to the game's controls, but I let sense memory take over, and soon it's like I never left. *The Land of the Morning Calm* is just as I remember it, and my heart practically aches at its beauty. I should have come back sooner.

I start the game in the village of Yangdong, in the southeastern part of the peninsula. I don't have a destination in mind, since I was just planning to explore for a little while, so I wander around aimlessly. My first encounter is with a stag walking on his hind legs. The green text floating above his name identifies him as ShaolinSucker: Level 719. Wow, that's really high. I'd only gotten up to around level 73 when I quit, and that was pretty respectable.

"Good morning, Sun_Moon! You're new here?" he types. *"Do you need some help?"*

I type: *"Long-time player, new character. I've been away for a while. Thought I'd take one more look around before they switch off the lights."*

He types: *"Bad news, alright. But hopefully the new server will hold up."*

"New server?!"

A private message pops up, along with a friend request from ShaolinSucker. I accept both. (Still no response from HannaKimmy.) I open his message and see an IP address.

"What's this?" I ask.

"A player named Jeoseung set up his own private server to emulate the game. While he's testing capacity it's invitation only, unless you find an access point in-game to transfer your character over. I hear it's running Underworld source code right now."

I laugh. *"Clever,"* I type. In the Korean myth that *LMC* is loosely based on, Jeoseung Chasa is a kind of grim reaper working to collect souls for death.

"Sure I can't help with anything?" He sends me a smiley face.

I hesitate, but as silly as it is to ask, it's also silly to be afraid to. *"I'm looking for someone who used to play five years ago. If you're Level 719, you must have been around for a while."*

"Since day 1," he types. *"My user ID is 88."*

"Did you know a kumiho named Eun-Ha?"

It isn't that much of a long shot that he would know her. Millions of people play the game, but in her heyday, everyone knew Mom. She was a guild leader and was active both in and out of the game, not to mention she was pretty well known for her *LMC* cosplays.

"Sure," he types. *"I saw her a couple of weeks ago in Hanhoe. I was just passing through, so I didn't stop to chat."*

That isn't possible.

"HannaKimmy?" I type.

"That's her," he responds.

A chilling thought occurs to me: Someone has hacked Mom's account, taken over her identity. *LMC* has a wonderful, supportive community, but like any online group, it also has its share of assholes and opportunists. Mom was in the 500-level club, and everyone knew she possessed a few of the rarest items in the game. Dad and I left a lot of credits on the table by leaving Mom's character untouched, which could have translated into real-world money. Maybe we should have done more with Eun-Ha, tried to secure Mom's legacy somehow. Then we would have discovered that someone had stolen it, or prevented it from happening.

"My guild's planning a raid on the palace later if you want to come," ShaolinSucker types.

"Thanks, but I'm just going to explore a bit."

"Have fun! Be careful out there. Dokkaebi and mul gwisin have been more active in the 3K lately. Stay away from open water."

Not all gwisin are harmless. In Harabeoji's bedtime stories, some of them would try to waylay travelers to eat or drown them, like the mul gwisin—"water ghosts"—ShaolinSucker warned me about. And then there are the dokkaebi, Korean goblins, who might challenge you to a wrestling match. More nightmare-fuel for imaginative little kids.

I turn my character into a giant white owl and get airborne. Thanks to ShaolinSucker's information, I now have a goal: Look for whoever is masquerading as Eun-Ha.

It may just be that I'm running the game on a more powerful computer, or else they've upgraded the graphics engine over the years, but the Three Kingdoms have never looked better. I had read that the number of active accounts was way down from the millions of people who used to play *LMC* daily, but the countryside is clogged with travelers. People cluster in villages and climb the mountains on whatever random quests they've undertaken. News of the game's shutdown must have brought them back, as it has for me.

I land in Hanhoe and shift back into human form. I walk

up and down the village streets, and I realize that most of the travelers I see are computer-controlled characters interacting with players, making the game seem more active and alive. These NPCs, "non-playing characters," typically react according to programmed algorithms meant to simulate human behavior. I marvel at how many there are in one place; practically the whole village is full of fake people.

I try asking a couple of NPCs if they've seen a nine-tailed fox, but they won't diverge from their scripted actions. They aren't programmed to think. Instead, they only comment on the weather or mention items they're looking for, people they've lost track of—offering side missions that I don't have the time or interest for.

Then I see her.

Even without the "Eun-Ha: Level 999" (wow!) above her head, I would know Mom's avatar from all those countless hours of watching and playing beside her, and of course, her outfit resembles her kumiho costume.

My shock and happiness at seeing her again, even as a digital artifact of her former self, is quickly overcome by anger. Her avatar is walking back and forth aimlessly just like all the NPCs around us. Back and forth. Back and forth. I hurry over to her and click the Talk icon.

"Who the hell are you?" I type.

"Greetings, Sun_Moon. Fine day, isn't it?"

"Who are you?" I type again. *"Eun-Ha is my mother's character. You stole it. How did you access her account?"* Then I notice that her kumiho bead is missing. *"Where's her necklace? Did you sell it?"*

"I am Eun-Ha," she says.

"MY MOTHER IS DEAD, ASSHOLE."

Her avatar graphic glitches. *"Have you s-s-seen my hairbrush?"* she asks.

That really unsettles me. I can practically hear Mom's voice: "Have you seen my hairbrush?"

Mom always used to lose her brushes and combs. It got so bad that we bought them in bulk and sprinkled them around the house so that one would always be nearby, and even so, they slowly started to disappear. But here, it's been presented as a mini-mission. This can't be another person behind her character, but maybe someone coded her likeness into the game. Sometimes programmers added little tributes to their players when enough people asked for it. Dad and I never did—we were done with all this.

What would happen if I found or bought a brush in the game and brought it back to her? Would she give me a clue to some kind of treasure or a cryptic hint for defeating Yeoma's hordes?

Then a tiny, hopeful voice in the back of my head wonders whether it *could* be her.

"Mom? Mom, if you're in there, it's me, Sunny," I type.

I try any number of different approaches, but she never responds in anything but a limited, robotic way. Eun-Ha is just like any other NPC, a slave to the game instead of an agent of her own fate. And yet . . . It was like Harabeoji said. I know her. This is more than a mass of glowing pixels on my screen. It's my mother. And I have one more thing to try.

I get up and go to my desk, rummage around, and grab

my old gaming headset. I pull it on and plug the mic into my laptop.

"Mom?" I say. "Hello?"

The word "*Sunny*" appears onscreen. For a moment, I think her character is just remarking on the damn weather again, but then I hear her voice, too. "Sunny," she says. "Sunny."

I start crying.

I have to crank the volume up all the way, and even then it's barely audible, nearly lost in an electronic hiss and crackle. No, it's *composed* of it, noise and air, like very poor audio sampling. Her voice is distant and breathy and strained, but it's her. And while I never forgot what she looked like because we have so many photos of her, I'd forgotten what she sounded like.

"Mom, it's really you in there," I say. "How? What happened? What are you?"

"I don't know what happened, I've forgotten. It's been too long."

"Five years," I say.

"You look good, little flower cake." I don't know if she's referring to my avatar or if she can somehow see me beyond the screen. This is so strange.

"I sort of remember . . . I was in two places at once, in my body, and here," she says. "I see Oppa sometimes." Her father.

"Harabeoji thinks you're a gwisin."

She laughs, a harsh, disharmonious sound in my headphones, like garbled sound effects.

"He says you visit him. You move things around," I say.

"I was try . . . get his attention."

So she'd been trying to communicate with us in the only way she could, just to let us know she was there. But why Harabeoji and not me?

"The computer," I say.

Harabeoji was the only one who used our old computer with *LMC* installed on it. Maybe that is her link to the real world. If Dad and I had continued playing the game, would we have found her in it sooner?

"Mom, we didn't know you were still . . ." Not alive. "Around."

"You left me here," she says.

"I'm sorry, I didn't know! But is it okay there? You used to love it in the 3K."

"It's wonderful, but I miss . . . real . . ." The sound garbles. "How's . . . father?"

"Dad? He's okay." I hesitate. *Should I mention Lisa?* "He met someone. She's nice."

"I think I knew that. Good."

"I should text him to come home. You can talk to him, too!" I pull out my phone, trying to figure out how to get him to believe me. What about Harabeoji? He'd want to see her again while he can.

"No, Sunny. Let your father be. This time . . . It's for us. How are *you*?"

I almost shrug off her question with the same answer I give Dad and Harabeoji and the school counselor when they ask how I'm doing: "I'm fine, really. My classes keep me busy." But this may be the last time I get to speak with her, and I don't want to lie.

"Not good," I say. "I miss you so much." Tears drip down onto my keyboard.

On-screen, her character hugs mine, and I can almost feel her arms around me. I do feel her, I'm certain of it—like a cool breeze wafting over my bare arms. I shiver.

"I miss you, too," she says. "Tell me everything."

"I don't know. I go to school. I come home. I cook dinner. I do homework."

"Is there . . . Are you see . . . anyone?"

"Like I have time for that. Which works out, because no one else has time for me."

"You used to have a lot of friends."

"I used to have—" A mother. I chew my lip. "Never mind. We're wasting our time. Mom, I found your book on your computer. I read it. I hope that's okay."

She's silent for so long, I worry we've lost our fragile connection. "Of course. What do you think?"

"It's not bad. I wish you'd finished it. You should have. Maybe . . ."

"What?"

"If you'd spent less time in the game . . ." I want to take it back as soon as I say it, but it's too late. That's the point, isn't it? All of this—it's too late. She should have been there for me and Dad more often instead of literally losing herself in a game.

"We'd all be better off, huh?" She sighs. "You should finish it for me."

"I've thought about it."

"You should," she repeats.

"Maybe. Maybe we can work on it together." I sit up

straight. "We have to get you out of there. The game—"

"I know. This world is dying," she says. "Maybe when it's over, I'll . . . move on."

I shake my head. I've just gotten her back. "I ran into your friend ShaolinSucker. He told me there's a way out."

I explain about the new server that's supposed to be running a copy of the game. I have to repeat myself because I'm talking too fast for her to follow. "We should go there. It's based on the Underworld, so I bet that's where you can transfer over."

"I don't remember the way," she says.

I don't either, but I'm already Googling for game maps and walkthroughs to get us there. "Follow me."

I lose track of the time while we walk and talk. I do most of the talking, filling Mom in on what's happened in our lives and the real world since she's died. She shares some of the adventures she's had in *LMC* since she died.

She tells me that as time went on, she started to forget she was once a living human person. The more she forgot, the more she became part of the game—she was simply Eun-Ha, the kumiho warrior.

Best I can figure is that the longer she spent in the virtual world, the more she lost of her real self until finally she was just code held together by sheer spirit, a nearly mindless extension of the programming. The only thing keeping her tied to the real world was her connection to me, which allowed her to haunt our home. I suddenly contemplate all the NPCs I've encountered in the game over the years. How many of them began as more than bits of data?

And I notice that we're being followed. As we walk, NPCs

stop what they're doing to trail after us. Their numbers swell as we reach the southern tip of the peninsula, where there's a gate to the Underworld. A small army of gwisin soldiers is lined up in front, with a towering figure at their head: a white tiger in full armor standing on its hind legs. The ghosts pull back to create a narrow path for me and Mom as we approach their leader. I don't need to read the words floating over his head to know who he is.

"King Yeomra." I kneel before him.

"Greetings, Ogushin." His voice booms, a rich sound that expands beyond my headphones and reverberates on the earthly plane. "Ogushin," he called me. In the stories, the Ogushin is the one who leads spirits to the Underworld.

I hear shouting in the distance and lift my head, looking around. It sounds like Harabeoji, calling my name. Mom's eyes are wide, so I know she hears it, too, but no one else reacts.

That's when I realize that I'm not interacting with the game through my keyboard and mouse, looking at pixels on a screen. I'm inside it, in the Three Kingdoms, and it all looks so real. Too real. How much time has passed? What if I'm still in the game when the servers are shut down?

I have to get out of here. But first, I have to get Mom out.

"My lord," I say. "I wish to deliver my mother, Eun-Ha, to your safekeeping."

"That is not her name," Yeomra says.

I look at Mom.

She bows low in supplication. "Hannah Kim Moon."

"Hannah Kim Moon, you must give me something of value before you may enter," Yeomra says.

Hasn't she already given up enough?

"I have many treasures, King Yeomra," she says. "All of them yours."

Yeomra holds up a paw, and I see a readout of Eun-Ha's inventory. "Mere trinkets," he says. "But this—" He highlights one item: Kumiho Bead. "This is interesting."

Wait, he's pulled that from *my* inventory. Mom isn't wearing the pearl that belongs with her kumiho costume because I am.

"No," I say. I've had that bead with me since she died, and I can't let go of it now. Once Mom's spirit departs from this game, it will be all I have left of her.

Mom looks to me. "Who else does my soul belong with but the king of the Underworld?"

"Your soul?" I touch the bead dangling from my neck. I remember the moment she found it. I had gone thrifting with her to find pieces for her costume, but I was more interested in browsing through the fifty-cent books and DVDs than musty racks of clothing.

I had heard a crash and a soft tinkling sound. When I looked for the source, I saw Mom had dropped the plastic tub of costume jewelry, and colorful glass and plastic balls were scattering and bouncing on the tile floor around her. But she ignored it all, slack-jawed as she stared at something cradled in her palm. "This is perfect," she'd said. "It's mine."

A kumiho's bead contains knowledge, and memories are a kind of knowledge. The shape-changing fox spirits also were known for capturing people's energy. Some myths say that the kumihos are the beads themselves. Could this cheap bauble, a sentimental keepsake, have been storing my mother's essence since her death?

I close my hand around the bead, and Mom looks like herself again. Not her game avatar, Eun-Ha, but the woman who used to kick my ass at Scrabble, showed me how to make Dad's favorite seaweed soup, taught me to read, took me to the library whenever I wanted, stayed up all night with me to make a model volcano for school . . .

This is her soul. I've had it with me all along. The bead has been helping me remember, whenever my memories of her start to fade, whenever I need her most. I can't give it up now. I squeeze the bead tighter.

"I don't want to lose you again," I say.

"You never will." She reaches out to stroke my cheek the way she used to when I was small and woke up in the middle of the night with a bad dream. Her touch had always comforted me and helped soothe me back to sleep, but now her hand is cold, not quite substantial. I lean into it anyway and close my eyes. I consider what she means about me never losing her.

If our shared memories had been coming from the bead, they would be hers, not mine—so maybe it has been keeping us connected by holding her in my thoughts. Without it, my own memories of Mom might diminish over time, but whether I recall every detail or not, those moments are part of me. They made me who I am and will always influence who I become.

More important, the bead is Mom's only ticket out of here. Keeping it, trying to hold on to her any way I could, would be selfish, and she's already been stuck here for too long.

I let go of the bead and rest my hand over Mom's on my cheek for a moment. For the last time. I nod and step away from her. She's back to looking like Eun-Ha, but Mom's face is still clear in my mind.

"You may have it, Lord." I unclasp the chain, slide the bead off, and drop it into his outstretched paw. I immediately feel lighter.

King Yeomra pops the kumiho bead into his mouth like a Tic Tac and swallows it. Then he steps aside, and the doors to the Underworld open.

Mom turns toward someone I haven't noticed before, a tall Korean man dressed in twenty-first-century clothing like me, with a black button-down shirt and black jeans. Graying hair pulled into a long, scraggly ponytail. He's in his fifties, and he looks familiar, but I can't place him. The stats displayed over his head say simply "Jeoseung (Chasa), Level ∞."

Mom kneels before him and says, "Thank you for allowing me to see my daughter."

He places a hand on her head in blessing. I kneel before him, too. He clasps my shoulder. His touch is firm and charged with energy.

"The way is open," Jeoseung says. "Where your mother goes, you may follow, Ogushin. But not today, or for forty thousand days."

I hear sirens, far away, as if they're on the other side of the city. The sound washes over me. More voices shouting. Someone sobbing. Harabeoji praying in a soft rush of Korean, words rising and falling.

My mother and I stand up and look at each other. She looks like herself again, in the white hanbok we buried her in. We hug as NPCs swarm from behind us, move around us, and disappear through the open gate.

"Bye, Mom. I love you," I say.

"I love you too."

Jeoseung presses his hands together and bows to *me*. "Go well," he says.

I wake up in a strange bed with a hard mattress and stiff, rough sheets. Something in the room is dripping, beeping. The lights are dimmed and the blinds drawn. A hospital.

I slowly turn my head to the right. Harabeoji sits beside my bed poring over his big Bible with the black leather cover and pages gilded in red. He lifts his head and his eyes widen.

"She's awake! Nurses!" He rushes to me and grabs my hand with trembling fingers. "Sun. Thank God."

Nurses sweep in; a doctor checks me out. They take blood and ask questions until I want to go back to sleep just to make them stop. Then they swirl out again, and when they're gone, Dad is standing in the open door holding two Styrofoam cups. He hasn't been sleeping. His eyes are red.

"Well, look who's back!" He grins. "Here comes the sun."

I groan. "What happened to me?"

"I found you slumped over your computer," Harabeoji says.

"I was playing *LMC*." I don't know how much I should tell them now, or whether I will ever tell them what happened to me, where I really was. "I must have fallen asleep," I say.

"We couldn't wake you." Dad sits on the edge of the bed. He hands a cup to Harabeoji. I eye the other one. I could use coffee. My head feels heavy and my thoughts are muddled. "I was afraid you . . ." He sniffs and shakes his head. "They didn't know what was wrong. Just that you were in a coma. You were someplace else."

"I was." I swallow. My throat's dry. *I saw Mom.*

I reach for the pearl around my neck, but it's gone.

Dad sees the gesture. "I looked all over for your necklace, but I couldn't find it."

"How long have I been here?" I ask.

"Six months," Dad says.

I pull myself up and the room spins. *"Six months?"*

Time in fairylands moves differently, so a day can be a year. But *six months* . . .

Harabeoji sucks in a breath and shakes his head. "Brian," he intones disapprovingly.

Dad chuckles. "I'm kidding! Sorry, I couldn't resist. It's only been eight days."

I collapse back onto my pillows in relief. That's still a long time, but much better than losing six months of my life. I look at the clock. Just after 11 a.m. Which means . . . I do the math. It's just after midnight in Seoul, South Korea, where the makers of *LMC*, Chasa, are based.

"It's Friday?" I ask.

"Yeah. And I know what you're thinking, but I just heard some good news. One of Chasa's developers launched his own private server to keep *LMC* running. It isn't an official release, and there won't be any new content except for fan mods, but eventually it'll be a playable archive of everything that was there. They're opening it to crowdfunding, so as long as there are donations, the game will exist in some form."

"It's based on the Underworld," I say.

He's surprised. "How did you know that? It was just announced this morning."

"Did you bring my computer?" I look around the room.

"Oh. Sorry, your laptop's toast. Your doctor thinks maybe it shocked you somehow. We'll get you a new one."

"You're not going back into that game, are you?" Harabeoji asks sharply.

I give him an odd look, curious about his phrasing.

I'll never log into the Underworld server or visit the Three Kingdoms again. The experience wouldn't ever be the same, and it might even be dangerous for me to go back. It's too easy to get lost in there.

"There's no need, Harabeoji. She's gone," I say.

It takes a moment for my meaning to sink in, but then he smiles. He looks happier than I've seen him since his only daughter died.

"Sun?" Dad asks. "Is there something you want to tell me?"

"A lot. Later on. Hey, instead of a new computer, do you think you can dig up Mom's laptop for me?"

He frowns. "What do you want with that old thing?"

I smile. Mom didn't disappear with the game or the kumiho bead. Part of her has continued on in me and in our memories, and in everything she created in life.

"I'm going to finish her novel," I say. "I finally know how it ends."

The *Chasa Bonpuli*

A Korean Epic

Korean mythology and fables have a robust oral history, but the stories have not been recorded as thoroughly as Greek and Roman mythology or the European fairy tales that many people grow up with in the West. Since I didn't have a lot to work with, "The Land of the Morning Calm" became a kind of mash-up of the greatest hits of Korean mythology and folk literature.

The framework for the story, fittingly, is the *Chasa Bonpuli*, a Korean epic myth that is very well known in South Korea. The tale has several variations, but its key players are King Yeomra, the god of the dead; Jeoseung Chasa, a kind of grim reaper; and the Ogushin, who guides the dead to the underworld.

While there aren't many Korean tales available in English, you only need to read a few to recognize some elements common to all of them, such as spirits, shape-shifters, and magical animals (often tigers). Gwisin, Korean ghosts, can be as mischievous or malevolent as poltergeists and other ghosts common to stories from around the world. Similarly, the kumiho, a nine-tailed fox spirit, is a trickster that usually takes the form of an attractive woman in order to seduce men.

Although my mother didn't tell me any uniquely Korean ghost stories when I was a kid, she did tell me about family members who visited her in their dreams after they died—before she heard the news that they were gone!—so I knew that I wanted to tell a ghost story. From there, an origin myth about the underworld seemed like a perfect match, and once I had that magical version of ancient Korea for my setting, I had to populate it with talking animals and creatures like the kumiho. At its most basic, I wanted to tell a story that followed the conventions of the Korean legends I've read, only with contemporary characters and a thoroughly modern milieu.

—E. C. Myers

THE SMILE

AISHA SAEED

The musicians warmed up their strings, tablas, and lutes in the marble dance hall, steps from the room where my maidservant Simran was finishing lacing the bodice of my silk dress. A sheer curtain separated us from view.

"Almost done?" I asked.

"With minutes to spare." She knelt, clasping gold anklets around my ankles.

"And the emerald earrings?" I studied myself in the mirror, from the white jasmine threaded in my hair to the silk the color of pomegranate blossoms in full bloom that hugged my curves. "Do they complement the dress? They don't, do they?"

"It is perfect, as are you. You will be the only thing they see, anyway."

This was our routine. It had been, since she was presented

to me when I first arrived to be Prince Kareem's courtesan. For two years, she had drawn my bath. She'd prepared my meals. When I fretted, she comforted. Normally she soothed my nerves as predictably as the mustard canaries that perched on my balcony and cooed each morning. But today I frowned at my reflection.

"Is something the matter?" Simran asked.

"No. Nothing."

Simran always kept my secrets, but I didn't want to trouble her with my confused feelings today.

The lights brightened through the sheer curtains. The murmur of arriving guests echoed against the walls. The two kerosene lamps that lit this room were deliberately designed not to draw attention to my preparations behind the stage. They were meant to obscure me until the final moment.

"His guest is back," Simran whispered as she adjusted the flowers in my hair. "I heard earlier today that the prince is quite anxious about him."

I nodded, as I already knew this. Prince Kareem had whispered it to me this morning when we lay entwined beneath his canopy, the velvet curtains closed, shielding us from the world. This was no ordinary visitor, but an influential merchant with ties to trading routes the royal family needed to expand their empire.

"If I don't resolve this matter before my father returns, it will be me he blames. My brothers are already conspiring to take away my place as the rightful heir," he'd said.

I had soothed him, reminded him of his importance. I'd quoted Rumi's words: move within but not the way fear makes you move.

He had smiled and his shoulders had relaxed, the anxiety shifting off his skin like steam.

"You will come with me to greet him?" he'd asked. "It is for you he agreed to come all this way to meet me in the first place."

"Of course." Not all were granted the honor of watching the girl who danced with feet that took flight. I had dressed in my finest silk frock with gold shimmering pajamas, feathered blush against my cheeks, and penciled my eyes before joining him to greet the guest at the palace doors. I'd smiled and bowed. I had shown the guest his room and brought his tea. He had glittering green eyes like Simran's and golden brown hair like my father's, the color of wheat. My stomach had tightened at the memory of my father's broad shoulders and deep belly laugh. I'd poured the man's tea and swirled in the sugar. It did no good to remember the past. It was best to focus on the reality I now lived.

This was not the first time I'd assisted Prince Kareem in charming his guests; it was part of being a courtesan. Nor was it the first time I had felt Prince Kareem's eyes on me from a distance. When I'd glanced up, there he was in his royal-green kurta, his arms crossed, his lips pressed together into a thin, straight line, watching me from the parted door.

"Is something the matter?" I'd asked when I joined him afterward.

"You spoke to him quite comfortably," he said, without meeting my gaze.

"I served him because you asked, my prince."

He said nothing.

"I do what I do to please you." I took a step forward and grasped his hands in mine.

"Do you?" His gaze burned steadily on mine.

"Yes."

"Your heart belongs to me, then? To no other?"

"I belong to you, don't I?"

He'd smiled at this and pulled me to him. The dark clouds that lingered over his expression vanished. I'd tried to push away the darkness settling over me, as well. I'd focused on his jokes, laughed at the right moments. I'd kissed him back when he reached for me. But was this how it would always be between the prince and me? A relationship I navigated with care, catering to his every whim while he stomped about the earth with no thought about how his jealousy affected me?

"I also heard something else." Simran brought me back to the present. "Tarek said the prince is hoping your dance tonight will seal the merchant's decision before his father returns."

It wasn't a boast to say I was the best dancer of my time. It was my dancing, after all, that had brought me to this palace. Just two years earlier I had attended a local festival that King Hamad had thrown to commemorate the birth of his newest child. I'd heard the lutes and the strings and seen the dancing girls in the distance. I'd breathed in the music that day, and as it often did, the music took me. A small crowd had gathered to watch me. They'd clapped and cheered when the music ended. I had laughed and bowed and went about the festival with my friends. I had not known the prince watched me from the alcove of his palace bedroom that day. I had not known he saw me stop at the poetry booth and took in my smile as I traced my hands over the scrolls. "Your smile was like a garden of jasmines in full bloom," he told me later. That is why he named me Yasmine.

He did not force me to live here. I should make that clear. I was invited. The invitation—a gold embossed missive—arrived by messenger the day after the festival. But my parents did not know if one could refuse a prince, and so I came.

The thought of my parents and my sisters still stabbed at my heart. Many times I almost went to see them, but I had heard enough stories from the other courtesans, favorites of other princes in the palace, to know homecoming could be bittersweet. Arriving home to clay houses with gold on your arms and around your neck could make the deepest love waver, tinge the dearest eyes with envy. I was not yet ready to know if my heart would be broken. I belonged to the prince. This was my life. It was better to accept it instead of longing for all the paths that would never be mine.

In truth, I was happy enough. I was desired by a prince. I had dresses of any color I desired in silk, georgette, and chiffon, tailored to suit my body. I strolled through the carefully tended gardens and between marble pillars that seemed to reach for the heavens with diamonds tucked in my earlobes. The guards always heeded my requests because they knew to whom they would answer if I had any reason to complain. The first months after I arrived, Prince Kareem had courted me. He'd given me the keys to his walled library and the pick of any book I chose. He'd lent me scrolls of poetry and we'd walked under the sycamore trees in the palace courtyard, sharing stories and whispering secrets when the night was heavy and the scent of jasmines enveloped us both. It had been I who kissed him first.

Though I missed my old life, Prince Kareem cared for me. He loved me. And of all his brothers, he was the most just and best suited to be the future king. Tonight I would shake off the unsettling feeling pooling in my stomach and do my part for him and this empire. Tonight I would dance for this guest better than I had ever danced in my life. I would leave his heart soaring. He would have no choice but to say yes to anything Prince Kareem wanted.

As I moved to the curtain, Simran trailed behind me, fussing over the veil and then filling my pockets with the jasmine flowers that would flutter out with each pirouette, leaving a scent of jasmine in the air.

"Are you ready?" she asked. "Everyone is seated."

I gazed at her. Simran and I were similar enough that people mistook us for each other when I first arrived. Her mother was one of the maidservants for the Queen. Simran had been raised entirely behind these walls. In the two years since I had arrived, I had never seen her leave. I often felt sorry for her, but we were the same, weren't we? We both served the prince. We both belonged to someone else besides ourselves.

"Simran," I asked her. "Do you ever feel trapped here?"

"Trapped?" she repeated. "But why?"

"Don't you wonder what life would be like if we weren't made to live within these walls?"

"My mother says our lot is a lucky one. The outside world is full of struggle. You fight to find food to eat, clothing to wear, shoes for your feet. Here, we have all our needs taken care of. We're the lucky ones, you and I. And besides," she said. "Tarek is here. I have no reason to leave these walls."

The music rose outside. There was no more time for such thoughts. I stepped through the gauzy curtains and into the dance hall.

Instantly, the voices quieted. The crowd was all men today. They sat on tufted cushions surrounding my dance floor. Prince Kareem sat on his golden throne. His beard was closely trimmed, the golden crown with rubies on his head. Next to him sat the man of honor. The man's eyes bored into me.

I bowed and pressed my hands together in salutation. Then the music began. The sitar first, then the tabla, and then the lute. I exhaled as the music quelled my troubled thoughts—the only thing that ever did. As it built to a crescendo, I began my dance. I swirled and pirouetted. I knelt and raised my hands to the heaven before I rose up again, spinning with the harmony of the lute. I smiled at my prince and regarded the man I needed to impress. He sat with his back straight, his arms crossed. And then I let the music take me. I no longer danced for these men, this guest, or even Prince Kareem. Instead, I soared for myself, for my mother, for the master trainer who had shown me what dance could do.

At last, the music wound down. I bowed, sneaking a glance at the crowd. As expected, the guest's self-satisfied expression had vanished. His eyes were wide with admiration. He thumped the prince on the back and whispered in his ear.

Praise echoed against the walls. I pressed my hands together and bowed. Not one mistake. Not even the smallest sort that no one saw but that I would agonize over for days.

But Prince Kareem's eyes narrowed. Instead of raising his hands in praise, he crossed them against his chest.

Instead of love, I saw hate.

❖ ❖ ❖

And now that story ends and this one begins. Now you find me in this damp tower. Brought here by Tarek, the guard whom Simran loved. The one who yesterday pressed his rough hands around my wrists as he pulled me out of the dressing room and led me across the courtyard, depositing me here in the cold dead of night.

Water trickles against the edges of the tower; green specks of algae blossom along the cracks in the wall. The brick here is so old that every now and then it crumbles like dust from the ceiling onto my hair. The door is made of steel. Twenty-three different latches secure it shut. Where once I had gold bangles clinking against my wrists, I now wear shackles.

The tears have dried since last night; a numbness has taken its stead. I've had plenty of time to think, and all I can think is this: After everything we shared, after every whisper about how much I meant to him, nothing could merit his banishing me without explanation, no matter what misunderstanding took place.

Yet here I am.

The sole window in this tower has thick iron bars, but through them I can glimpse the rose-colored edge of the palace walls and the leaves of a sycamore tree. Sunlight filtered through this morning. Soon the sun will set and it will be dark.

I flinch at a sudden noise outside the tower. The workers are back. They grunt as they scrape and mix their clay. They have been hard at work outside since I arrived. Laying bricks, row after row, growing taller and taller. My father was a bricklayer. I know the sound.

The door creaks open. Tarek steps inside, in his dark armor. He holds a tray of lentils and bread. He places it near my feet and leans down to loosen my chains enough to allow me to eat.

"Tarek," I plead. "Talk to me. Tell me. What have I done?"

He says nothing. He stands up to leave.

"Please!" I beg him. "For Simran's sake, please tell me. What was it? What was my crime?"

"As if you don't know."

"I swear on my mother's life."

He studies me.

"Your smile."

"My smile?"

"You gave him away. The merchant saw your smile and he saw Prince Kareem's response. He read the story. He tried to use it to bargain with Prince Kareem. You know the prince. He never loses." He nods to the window. "Those people outside? They build for you. Prince Kareem intends to bury you alive."

"I see," I say quietly.

"Better not to know, wasn't it?" he asks. His voice softer now.

Tarek's footsteps echo into the distance. A burning sensation splashes like scalding water over my heart. I had slept in Prince Kareem's bed. I had soothed him with poetry. I'd greeted his guest. I had danced for him. The prince always said I belonged to him. I had thought this word protected me and kept me safe, but now I understood. Belonging meant he could place me wherever he liked, whether in his bed or in this dank tower. Belonging is not love. It never was.

I shift in my seat. The cement grows cold as evening

approaches and the sun at last slips away. The bricklayers have finished their work and the iron around my ankles rests heavy. I'm certain, years from now when they recount my story, they will tell you how the other harem girls were envious of my status. How they coveted my silver and gold bracelets, my necklaces made of rubies, my earrings with delicate amethysts. But they will be wrong. Not even Simran envied me. Now I understand why: to be the most beloved means when love turns to hate, the hatred will burn as hot.

The door creaks open.

But it's not Tarek who has returned to take away my uneaten food.

It's Prince Kareem.

He rushes toward me in a royal-blue kamiz with gold embroidered along the edges. Finely tailored pants. His crown, as always, on his head.

"Yasmine." He stares at the chains around my ankles, my arms, and my waist. Wordlessly, he pulls out his ring of keys and kneels before me. He turns the locks, unclenches the metal from around my body until at last it all falls to the floor. Angry red welts line my skin.

"Tarek will pay for this," he says in a low voice. "Are you all right?"

"You did not order this?"

"Well, yes. I suppose I did." He shakes his head. "But the command was for show. He should have understood my meaning." He touches my wrist. I wince from the pain, but he doesn't seem to notice.

"I wanted a chance to explain first, but everyone was

watching. There was no time. He found out, Yasmine."

"The smile."

"Yes." He runs a hand through my hair. "Your smile that leaves me unable to function or think. He saw you smile at me and knew you were not a mere dancing girl. It made him want what he had no business coveting. It made him want those smiles for himself."

"And so for his desires, I die."

"Die?" He stares at me for a moment, and then he laughs. "Let my beloved die? I let him see how far I will go to protect what is mine. He signed the agreement at once when he saw you wrenched away. In the morning I will publicly pardon you. My subjects will cheer my merciful nature, and you will be back in my arms by nightfall."

He watches me. An expectant smile plays on his lips. What does he want me to say? Does he expect gratitude?

He draws me to him, his arm around my waist like a shackle. "The gall of that man's request. I know you would rather be buried alive than to be with anyone other than me."

I stare at the cement blocks of this tower. I say nothing.

"You can't stay angry forever." He kisses my forehead. "You love me too much for that."

I look down at my palms caked with dirt.

"Do I?" I ask quietly.

"What?"

"Do I love you?" I look up at him.

His eyes widen as though I slapped him. I should hasten to apologize—my mother always told me men's attentions are as fleeting as a cool breeze—but the truth is I don't want to say I'm sorry. The truth is that, perhaps, it is only through his removing the gold bangles around my wrists and the anklets around my feet that I can see.

"You are in shock." He shakes his head. "You love me. You do. You know me better than anyone else."

"And you don't know me at all."

"Yasmine—"

"My name isn't Yasmine. It's Naseem Begum. The name my mother gave me when I was born. The name of my grandmother. I live in this palace because you saw me dance and plucked me like a flower for your vase. Everything I've done, every poem we've read, every kiss we've shared, is a result of your choices. I belong to you, yes. But love you? How can I love you when I am not free?"

"What is the matter with you?" He stares at me. "The brick grave outside is for you. Any one of my brothers would have sent their courtesans off without a second thought. I'm promising to pardon you and give you a life of comfort. You will never want for a thing. How many would wish to trade places with you and live the life I give you?"

"I did not say this is a bad life. I said I do not love you."

"Is this about my father and what he would say if he found out about us?" he asks. "I was going to tell him about my feelings for you upon his return this month. I was going to tell him I want to make you my wife. I've never been happier than I have been since you entered my life."

"You don't understand." I shook my head. "Whether you save my life, marry me, or send me into a brick grave while I still breathe, the choices are yours."

"Do you know the risk I'm taking?" His face glows. "My father could threaten to disown me, and now you tell me your heart doesn't belong to me?"

"As long as I live within these walls I am not free. My heart is all I have to freely give."

He takes a step back, but I meet his fiery gaze. As if a rush of wind swept through him, his expression dims. The silence stretches between us. The water drips cold in the distance.

"Then be free," he says flatly. "Tarek will be outside if you come to your senses before dawn."

He turns toward the gated lock and taps on it once. It slides open.

He is gone.

Evening dips into nightfall. The stars glitter through the barred window. The metal door vibrates, the locks turning. Perhaps Tarek brings me a message from the prince. Or perhaps he is here to bring me my last meal.

It would be easy enough to soothe the prince and apologize. I must only say I was frenzied by my circumstances. He would forgive me.

But as the locks turn, I feel strangely at peace. If I am to die, as every living thing must, at least I leave the earth with my dignity.

The door opens.

Tarek steps inside. Behind him is Simran.

She's in her sleeping tunic and hurries toward me.

Before I can say a word, she speaks.

"I'm going to get you out, but we must be quick."

"Simran," Tarek mutters. His arms are crossed, his expression terse. Simran gently presses his arm and smiles before turning toward me.

"Come." She gestures for me to follow her to the far end. She presses the gray wall, and the wall parts— It's a tunnel. A slim gray tunnel.

"The tunnels weave beneath the estate," she says. "But I played in them as a child, and they end into a gully; it will take you out into the world."

"Simran . . ." I trail off.

"You asked me last evening if I would leave if I could." Her voice was gentle. "I can. I stay for my mother and"—she smiles at Tarek—"my life is here. I choose to stay. But you," she looks at me, and her eyes glisten, "you can choose to leave."

"And Tarek?" I glance at him. "Won't you be in trouble?"

"Prince Kareem is the one who unchained you." Tarek shrugs. "You found a tunnel I could not know existed."

I stare into the darkness before me. It is easier to stay. I could simply speak to the prince. It's not too late. Until yesterday I had never imagined leaving. What lies ahead?

What will the future hold?

I embrace Simran. I step into the tunnel.

I smile.

The Story of Anarkali

A South Asian Legend

According to legend, there was once a dancing girl named Anarkali, who was a courtesan for King Akbar of the Mughal Empire in the fifteen hundreds. Little is known of the exact details surrounding Anarkali's life, and there are many different versions of her story. Most concur that she served as a courtesan in the king's harem and that King Akbar's son, Prince Saleem, fell in love with her. When the prince and Anarkali had an affair and the king learned of it—some say from a smile—he sentenced her to be buried alive in a brick tomb. Some say the king carried out the punishment, while others say the prince helped her escape through a series of tunnels connected to the dungeon in which she was held. Today, visitors to Lahore can visit a tomb where Anarkali is believed to have been buried. A large bazaar near the tomb is named after her.

I grew up watching movies about Anarkali and listening to my mother's tales of her, but the older I got, the more I wondered: How could a girl made to be a courtesan enter into an equal and consensual relationship with a prince, illicit or otherwise? What sort of love could this be? That is what prompted me to write this retelling inspired by the legend. I like to imagine the true conclusion to her tale was the one you just read.

—Aisha Saeed

GIRLS WHO TWIRL AND OTHER DANGERS

PREETI CHHIBBER

There are three reasons I know fall is *awesome*: the most anticipated Bollywood movies are always on a fall release schedule, my mom starts practicing her delicious party dishes, *and* it means it's time for Navrātri! One of the absolute best things about Hinduism is that we have hundreds of thousands of gods. That might sound weird, but what it really means is that any given day can be a literal holy day and cause for celebration. And tonight? Tonight was *finally* Navrātri. My favorite. My friends and I were just one short car ride away from dancing until our feet fell off.

"Jaya, remind me again why this is happening in a gym?"

Jessica, Nirali, and I were squished in the backseat of my parents' (very sensible) Toyota on our way to the function. Unlike Diwāli, Navrātri wasn't covered in the average world-history class, and so Jess had a lot of questions.

"I wish there was a more interesting answer, but really that gym is the only space big enough for the entire Indian Association."

"We're actually lucky we don't have to drive an hour. Families come from all over since our IA is so big. But, I'm definitely not into how overcrowded it is." Nirali rolled her eyes.

"What Nirali's *really* saying is that only having one celebration means Dinesh might show up and he is—"

"*The worst*. Pompous, rude, thinks he can dance so much better than everyone." As Nirali's voice got louder and louder, my dad caught my eye in the rearview mirror.

"Sab kuch theek hai, betiya?"

"Everything's fine, Dad! Nirali's just *really* excited." A sharp elbow jabbed in my side. "Hey! Ow! Come on, that story is so old that you've turned him into a mythical beast at this point."

"I was *traumatized*! When we were ten he stepped on my lenghā, and it came off and I did a half turn in my choli and underwear before I realized!"

"And then he never came back, so why would he be there tonight?"

Nirali just rolled her eyes again and turned to look out the window.

Ever the peacemaker, Jess brought the subject back to the matter at hand, "So, Navrātri. Is there a TV movie I can watch that will explain the meaning of the holiday to me using two very attractive, but relatable, leads?"

My mom turned in her seat. "No, but I think there was

a miniseries in the nineteen-eighties." She looked back at my dad. "Rahul, serial thā nā?"

"Woh *Mahābārata* serial ke jaise . . ." My dad was clearly only sort of paying attention. It didn't matter that he'd made this drive four hours earlier to drop off a million pounds of rice that I had helped my mother cook: he still got nervous about missing turns after it got dark.

"Chalo, I can tell you, it starts with the demon tyrant, Mahishāsur, half man, half buffalo. . . ." My mom loved telling these stories, but they had a tendency to go very, very long.

"Falu Auntie, we're going to be there in five minutes. I don't know if we have time to hear the whole story of Mā Durgā before we get there. I wouldn't want Jessica to hear a rushed version." Nirali managed to waylay my mom without being rude about it. I squeezed her hand. If my mom had started telling the story, we'd have been stuck in the parking lot of the school until she was finished. Which would be a travesty. My bangles were *chum-chum*-ing against my wrist as if anticipating the drumbeat inside the gym.

"Acchā, you're right. Jessica, I'll tell you when we get inside."

"Bet you wish there was a made-for-TV movie, now, don't you?" I whispered to her.

"Aa gaye!" my dad exclaimed as he pulled the car into a parking spot. We were out the door and halfway to the entrance before he'd even turned the engine off. Nirali let out a whoop.

"It's time for garbā!"

❖❖❖

For the first time in a long time, Mahishāsur sensed a presence behind him. He'd been in a stance of meditation for years, paying homage to Brahmā ji. He balanced on one foot with the sole of the other pressed against his knee, and his hands clasped over his head. But he was not tired, he was exhilarated.

"Mahishāsur." A thousand voices at once called to him, and he turned. Before him was Lord Brahmā, his four faces looking out and seeing all of the universe. As was told, in his four hands he held a lotus, the holy Vedas, a ladle, and a mālā. An unearthly glow surrounded his head, so bright it was nearly blinding. Mahishāsur couldn't tell if it was coming from within Brahmā or from some other source in the sky, but it made discerning Brahmā's features difficult. "You have performed tapas in my name and I have heard." Mahishāsur waited; his moment was coming. "I grant you one boon." A line of sweat dripped down Mahishāsur's snout. He slowly lowered his leg. The cloth of his dhoti nearly disintegrated at the movement; it had turned threadbare and now hung loose at his hips. He brought his folded hands down to his chest and bowed in pranāma to Brahmā.

"Namaskār, Bhagwān," he greeted the god. "I wish only for one thing."

"Ask." Brahmā minced no words. Mahishāsur had prayed to him for a thousand years, and Brahmā was bound to comply.

"Immortality." Had the god been human, Mahishāsur was sure he would have balked at such an outlandish demand. Instead, Brahmā paused and considered.

"I cannot offer you immortality. All things must end; such is the law of creation. But I will *grant that no man or god will be able to kill you."*

As Brahmā spoke, the power infused Mahishāsur's very blood. He was unkillable. The world would be his.

He turned a sinister eye to Brahmā.

Heaven would be his.

❖❖❖

Jess, Nirali, and I walked through the gym door to a huge pile of sandals and ballet flats, and the gigantic basketball sneakers that were the preferred footwear of Indian boys. Random uncles and aunties milled about, chatting and chaat-ing. The thrum of the dhol and feet hitting the floor in beat with the music drifted through the door to the court.

Nirali and I slipped our sandals off and hid them toward the back of the pile. Jess pulled at the edges of her borrowed salwār, watching us.

"Don't stretch my top!" Nirali said. "Just go with it; your shoes'll be fine." She gave Jess a tiny shove forward. Jess gave us both a major side-eye, but threw her shoes down with ours anyway.

"If anyone takes them, *you* have to tell my mom what happened."

"Jess, in, like, four seconds you're not going to care about your shoes!" I linked arms and pulled her through the doors to the basketball courts.

Inside was a blur of color and sound. Dupatte were flying and lenghe were blooming. The band on the opposite end of the court was still on baa-rhythm, slow enough that all the grandmas could dance a few rounds. The circles of people dancing weren't quite at that so-fast-it's-kind-of-scary-but-in-a-good-way speed I loved. But each ring was just moving a little faster than the one outside it.

Little kids were running around on the outskirts, and along the tucked-in bleachers, folding chairs had been set up in lieu of pulling the seats out. Older men and women sat there watching the makeshift dance floor. My parents joined in with a few of their friends on the far end of the court. At the center of it all was a ceramic statue of the goddess Durgā—the legendary badass we were here to celebrate—on a pedestal, surrounded by prayer accoutrements. I lingered on her face, the kohl-lined eyes and her knowing smile. I had the strangest sensation that she was looking back at me like I was her daughter, telling me to have the night of my life celebrating her victory.

"Wow." Jess had stopped cold. I shook myself and grinned at her.

"Let's hop in!"

We wove our way through other groups to the rim of the outermost ring of dancers, kids from school closer to the center, while their moms (with a few dads now and then) were on the outside.

"Wait for a break in the line. And don't worry if we get separated, it happens."

Just then, an auntie in a green sari danced by, making a space big enough for three people to jump in.

"Go, go, go!"

The beat was starting to pick up, and our turns moved a little bit quicker every couple of rotations. The intricate mirror work along the bottom of my skirt weighed the lenghā down enough that it stayed low while I twirled, a dizzying array of blacks and greens and reds. Nirali led our trio, her dupattā flying behind her. Jessica followed, only slightly awkward. And then me. The auntie behind me fell farther away as the drums sped up and we moved faster. My feet pounded against the floor in rhythm to the band, *dum-dumadum-dum-dumadum,* but I wanted *more*.

I watched for a break in the circle at the center, closest to Mā Durgā's murti. The steps there were far more complicated than what we were doing. And *way* more fun. The dancers turned and jumped and swapped places, with their arms going around and over their heads. The boys and their giant leaps forward, the girls lower to the ground but moving and jumping just as far and just as fast, swirling in tandem under the watchful eye of the goddess.

There! A spot between a girl from school and a boy I'd never seen before. I jumped into the step in the middle of a turn. The rhythm of the band and the energy in the room swept me into a blast of movement. I caught eyes with the boy midturn and grinned. He smiled back. Oh, wow. He was *cute*. Garbā *and* cute boys?

I hopped to the right, turned, and ended up directly in front of him in one of the more complex garbā movements. The lacquered wood floors of the gym gave no traction, and there were blisters forming on my feet, but it didn't matter. Navrātri was about abandoning ourselves to dance in complete and utter elation.

As the music sped up, more people joined in, creating more circles when they didn't find one with the steps they wanted.

Soon seven circles were going at once, all at different speeds, with different steps. The boy behind me got closer every time he bounded forward. My breath came short.

All of a sudden the dupattā hanging down my back snagged. I stumbled and a body crashed into mine. Oh no. No. Please not him. But of course it was.

Before I could say a word, he shouted, "If you don't know the steps, you should move to the slow circle on the outside!"

The irritated sneer made him significantly less attractive and way more monstrous. Face aflame, I looked down. His dupattā had tangled up in mine.

"Your scarf is clearly the reason this happened! Calm down."

Wordlessly, he yanked his scarf out of the tangles and danced around me, pushing me out of the circle. A jerk move from start to finish. I glanced at the statue again, and I swore Mā Durgā's eyes were flashing in indignation.

"Brahmā ji, Vishnu ji, Shivā ji, he has run us from heaven. He has taken over the earth. What do we do?" Indra and several other deities surrounded the trinity. Vishnu was thoughtful. He glanced at the weapons he held in his two left hands: his mace, Kaumodaki, and the Sudarshana disk. The latter was the most powerful weapon on Earth or in the heavens.

"He cannot be killed by god or man, no matter how powerful the weapon, Vishnu ji." Brahmā's voice shook with anger.

"Perhaps not god or man, then." Shivā toyed with the tail of

the snake, Vasuki, wrapped around his neck. "Perhaps someone else." He grinned, a thought forming as he threw his trident from hand to hand. Indra and the other deities stepped back. The crescent in Shiva ji's hair shone against the water of the Ganga, freely flowing from the matted bun at the top of his head down to Earth. Brahmā and Vishnu stood on either side of him. If anyone could find a way to defeat Mahishāsur, it would be these three.

"Mahishāsur's actions are inexcusable." Vishnu's voice echoed in the thousands, and a light poured forth from his mouth. Without prodding, Brahmā and Shivā joined their voices to his and, likewise, light from their mouths joined to create a brilliant force. The devas added their energy to the trinity's, and slowly, the shape of a woman manifested there, in the midst of the three gods: Divine female energy made material. Resplendent in a saffron sari and covered in gleaming gold, she bowed to Brahmā, Vishnu, and Shivā, two of her ten hands clasped in front of her.

"Namaskār."

"Durgā ji, we've called you here to do battle on our behalf. Mahishāsur has taken Earth and Heaven, and he must be stopped."

Durgā quirked a thick black brow and smiled.

"Then give me your weapons. I will see Mahishāsur finished."

◆◆◆

I wove my way through the circles of dancers to the edges of the court and stood on the sidelines, fuming. How dare that cocky trash boy? *He* was the one with the stupid scarf that got caught in my dupattā. Now I looked like one of those little kids who tried to jump into steps they weren't ready for. But really, it wasn't even about being embarrassed. I knew that in the chaos of the dance only maybe seven people had even noticed. But Navrātri was about joy for the *community*, not just for one person. And this *guy* had just spit in the face of that.

"Hey!" As Nirali and Jess wound toward me, I tried to wipe the scowl off my face, but I must not have succeeded. "What's wrong? Did someone eat all the ras malāi already?"

"What? No. I haven't even been to see the food line." I turned back to the melee of dancers. "Do you see that guy? The one in the blue kurtā with the black scarf?" Nirali and Jess both turned in the direction I was pointing. "In the circle closest to the statue? The cute one." I added that last part begrudgingly. "He's a complete butt." That was easier.

"The one with the soft-looking hair?"

"Jess!"

"Sorry, sorry, I mean the one with the awful haircut?"

"Thank you. I know you're lying, but it's the thought that counts." The girls were looking at me like I was speaking another language. I filled them in. "And *then*, he just danced around me, like I wasn't even there."

And I had them.

"Are you *kidding* me? That is *so obnoxious*!" Nirali stood on her tiptoes to find him again.

He went around the circle one more time. How unfair that he was such a great dancer. If only he would trip. Instead, the girl dancing in front of him missed a turn, tripped, and he twirled right into her, landing a blow on her face. It was like Mā Durgā had heard my pleas but then missed by just a hair.

He yelled at the girl, and while his voice didn't carry over the sounds of the music and conversation around us, it was easy to see the same irritated scowl he'd given me earlier.

"Wow. He just ran right into her and then blamed *her* for it. What can we do? Do we tell his mom?" Jess asked, and started looking around, as if she could pick the auntie who spawned the dance demon out of all the women standing in the room. "Are we supposed to tell moms at garbā?"

"Oh my God . . ." Nirali was staring at the boy. "Jaya, that's Dinesh."

"What?"

Nirali had been telling the Dinesh-at-garbā-stepping-on-her-skirt-ending-in-underwear story for so long that to me he was this faceless monster. I always assumed his family had just moved out of the area or something, but that didn't make for as good a story.

"I see he hasn't changed." The way she was staring, I half expected the point of Nirali's eyeliner to turn into an actual spear and head straight toward Dinesh's chest.

"Hmm . . ." The beginnings of an idea were starting to form in my head. "This whole holiday is about good defeating evil, right? Dinesh is not going to magically get what's coming to him. So, it's on us. We can finally teach him a lesson for being a crappy kid and for growing up into a crappy fifteen-year-old." I started walking to the back of the gym, farther away from the dance and the food. Nirali and Jess followed, dodging through the minigroups of people socializing, settling in a quieter spot near the locker rooms. I leaned back against the wall.

"But *how* is the real question." Nirali leaned next to me and knocked my shoulder with hers. "I guess we could try and talk to his mom . . . but if she's anything like I remember, she's not going to believe us. She probably thinks he's literally God's gift, even though it's more like he's a human version of a poop emoji."

"And preferably a 'how' that won't get us in too much trouble, please. I want your parents to let me come to another garbā," Jess added, glancing back at the action on the dance floor behind us.

"I guess somehow having him end up in his underwear in the middle of the court is out of the question?" Nirali sighed wistfully. I laughed at the mental image of Dinesh scrambling to get his pants up and the nada retied around his waist.

"That might be too hard to pull off, but . . ." I played with the end of my braid while I worked a thought out in my head. "Maybe embarrassment is the best way to do it. His mom won't listen to *us*, fine. But if we find a way to make his takedown public so she couldn't ignore it? You know how it goes, desi-image community mein and all."

"That's not a terrible idea."

"Gee, thanks," I responded drily.

"No, no, I *mean* that could work. My mom would murder me if I embarrassed her at Navrātri." Nirali smiled.

I looked back at the crowds in the gym, hoping for inspiration. People dancing, people at stands waiting to hand out dandiyan for raas, people rushing in and out of the foyer for food. Again, Mā Durgā's statue pulled my gaze. She shone in the middle of all the dancers. She stood on a pedestal alongside steel plates filled with incense and diyas, kumkum, sindoor, chandan, and haldi powders, with a bowl of rice grains—all the pieces necessary for pre-raas prayers that everyone would participate in. *Oh.* That was it. "We're going to make sure Dinesh ruins *everything*."

"That sounds hyperbolic."

I ignored Nirali's sass to keep us on topic. "When is everyone guaranteed to be paying attention to the same thing during garbā?" I nodded toward the statue.

"During the pujā before raas." Nirali followed my gaze. "Jaya, you're a genius."

"Wait, I don't get it. Raas is the dance with the sticks, right? What does that have to do with prayer time?" Jess craned her neck to see over the dancers and tried to glean whatever Nirali had seen.

"See the pujā setup, Jess—the big steel plates?" I pointed through the bodies on the court to direct her. "Wouldn't it be a shame if someone ran into it during garbā because they were being too aggressive? And if it all clattered to the ground and covered everything in colored powder and rice? And if that's all our gossipy-as-hell community talked about for the next month?"

"He'll never hear the end of it." Jess was slowly nodding her head.

"Exactly! And his mom will definitely not let him play raas. I bet he won't be able to perform in the competition, because Kiran Auntie is in charge of it this year. She doesn't mess around with kids who can't hack it. Because it has to be better than when my mom was in charge last year." Nirali's grin was getting wider and wider as she counted out the potential results of our plan on her henna'd fingers.

"You guys are scary. And are you sure it's not like . . . disrespectful?"

"Don't worry Jess, it's all in the spirit of Navrātri! Mā Durgā, of all goddesses, would understand." I flung an arm around her shoulders. "Come on, let's get some food while we plan." The three of us headed back to the floor, weaving our way through the chaos like the unstoppable force that we knew we were.

Durgā looked at the gods before her, and felt the power of three inside her, building and amplifying her presence. She could see the thousands of beginnings and endings she had and would endure. She was ready for this story.

"Durgā Devi, we've given you our weapons and have called a lion from the Himalayas to bear you to battle. Do you go?"

She gripped the gods' weapons in her many hands, pulled herself onto the back of the lion, and tangled her fingers into his mane. "I go."

"Might I recommend the ras malāi or a basan ke ladoo?" We were in line for some delicious sweet treats, and I was playing good host for Jess. Vengeance was on the backburner while we waited for the perfect moment. Nirali leaned out to the side to see how many people were ahead of us.

"This line is *long* and I'm not really hungry. I think I'm going to go get some more dancing in before *the plan*." She tapped the side of her nose and bared her teeth. Nirali was really owning the warrior role. "But, so you know, Jess, my vote's for ras malāi." She took one last look at the line of hungry desis ahead of us before scampering back to the dance. Jess leaned out to judge the line for herself. "Actually, I think I'm going to take this chance to use the restroom. If you get to the front before I get back, will you just fill a plate for me?"

"Duh."

"Thank yoooou!" She sang out the last syllable as she headed off. I was left standing behind a group of kids I didn't know, and not for the first time I bemoaned the fact that people still didn't automatically sew pockets into the average lenghā so I'd have my phone to look at. Instead, I was stuck eavesdropping on the group in front of me.

"—so then Arjun told Pooja Auntie that he couldn't be in the competition this year because he had to work at his dad's shop, you know? And he had that big part at the end with Kinna? So, I guess Pooja Auntie told Dinesh's mom—"

Well, this just got more interesting. I sidled forward a little. I bet this story was going to end with Dinesh stealing the spotlight. Jerk.

"And then Dinesh split shifts with him so Arjun could still come to practice enough to be in the show. Which is so necessary. The two of them are how my cousin's team is gonna win for sure."

I started, surprised. That's not how I thought that was going to go.

"Back!"

I jumped again at Jess's sudden reappearance.

"Sorry! I didn't mean to scare you."

"It's okay, we're almost at the front, finally." I gestured for her to get in front of me and tried to push what I'd heard out of my head. I didn't even have all the facts. Dinesh probably only helped that kid, Arjun, out that so that he'd be on the winning team. Still sounded selfish to me. Mā Durgā's ceramic face flashed in my mind. I held on to that image as I filled my plate.

Mahishāsur was sitting on Indra's throne of pure gold. The skulls littering the stone at his feet shook as his minister ran into the room.

"Master! They cannot defeat her—she is too strong." The gods had sent a woman to defeat him, *the most powerful being in the universe. He laughed at the thought. A woman? Too strong for his army? She truly must be a fearsome thing to behold.*

"How can my warriors be so weak as to be defeated by a woman? I will own this Devi. She will be my wife. Let us see her defeat me!*"*

"He helped one kid stay on his garbā team so that he and his team can win the competition . . . and?" Nirali had joined Jess and me on the floor in a corner of the gym while we ate our weight in desserts. I had just finished sharing what I'd overheard in line, and she was dismantling my guilt block by block. "Mahishāsur was nice to Mā Durgā for like five minutes during their battle, too. Remember? Crap people can do good things and still be crap."

I paused, a piece of jalebi halfway to my mouth, and stared at her.

"I can't believe you just compared Dinesh to a shape-shifting demon who literally created hell on earth."

Nirali shrugged.

"Whatever. I still think we should do it. He is a Navrātri terror." She looked past me at the dancers flying by to dhol beats. The toes peeking out from under her lenghā were tapping along.

"Aahw ooo hurr?" Jess attempted to ask around the dense ladoo in her mouth.

"Swallow your food, Jess."

She made a comical effort to swallow and then downed half a glass of water. She grimaced.

"That was like eating a spoonful of peanut butter. Next year, remind me that I should stick to the delicious soft sweet cheese, please. I was *saying* 'are you sure?'" She gestured toward the dance. "We could just have a good time and not take down any ridiculous boys for past evil deeds?"

Nirali focused a very intent stare on our favorite do-gooder.

"Jessica Zhang. He left me. In my underwear. And he hit some girl in the nose. And he was a butthead to Jaya. I need this. I need closure."

Jess put a hand on Nirali's shoulder. "Then that's that. Uteruses before duderuses, as the T-shirt says."

"Yes! You're the best!" Nirali all but tackled Jess in a hug. "Okay, so we just have to get him between us in that fast circle and trip him into the pujā setup. That seems easy enough."

Not going to lie: it felt a little bit like we were devi warriors planning for battle. Nirali's feet were tapping faster, and I could feel the energy building in my core. Even Jess's eyes had taken on a wild glint.

"I *am* the best but, like, I'm not going to do the actual plan. My dancing is nowhere near good enough. We all agree, right?" Jess tucked her hair behind her ears.

"No, Jaya and I can handle that." As Nirali laughed, I caught Dinesh entering the gym floor from the foyer. He cut through the lines of dancers with purposeful disregard. I narrowed my eyes.

He was going down.

"Mahishāsura! I've defeated your fiercest rākshasas. Come and see if you can succeed where they have failed."

Mahishāsur beheld Durgā in her finery: the blood of his demonic Asur marking her sari only made her seem more beautiful. He was not afraid, but intrigued.

"Devi, if you would join me, we could rule as husband and wife. You are magnificent. What better place for such a woman as you than beside me?" Before he'd even finished speaking, he felt the tip of an arrow graze his snout.

"I'll see you dead, Mahishāsur. There is no balance in you."

He growled at the audacity of the goddess. He pulled out his sword and leapt forward. "I'll show you balance. Asur, let your arrows fly!"

❖❖❖

The garbā had nearly reached its last crescendo. The beat was thumping as fast as it would get before the break to do Durgā's prayer. Nirali was already starting a circle closest to the murti in the center of the room. I broke through lines of dancers so I could join in behind her. I turned and jumped and bent low and then did it over and over again. Every time I passed by Dinesh, I could see him eyeing our dance moves, deciding whether our steps would be more fun than his.

Three more dancers joined our group. Then Dinesh jumped in ahead of Nirali. He still couldn't resist showing off. But she matched his leaps and twists and turns, waiting for her chance.

The balls of my feet burned as I slapped them against the wood of the basketball court. Because we were in the inner circle, steps could only go so far. I was right on Nirali's heels and she was on Dinesh's. A well-timed jump would cause him to trip directly into the priest's thalis, and everything would fall to the ground. And every person in the gym would see.

Sweat ran down the back of my neck.

The song would be over soon. Nirali had to act now if she didn't want to miss her chance. I looked at Mā Durgā again to find my resolve. The statue stared back blankly. All those previous flashes of Durgā ji's implicit validation now seemed ridiculous. This was a bad idea! Ahead, Nirali deliberately turned early and missed her next step. I reached out a hand to stop her.

❖❖❖

Durgā lifted Sudarshana to her finger and let it spin. The jagged points on the outer rim could cut through anything. As long as it was her hand that threw it, Mahishāsur was finished. The battle had been going on for nine days and nights. He'd used different forms, different weapons, and she had overcome every obstacle.

His marriage proposal was laughable and his fighting was pure aggression with no thought given to tactics. He would destroy the universe with his hubris. She watched as he ran toward her with his gaping maw on display, teeth ready to tear into her throat, and she let Sudarshana fly.

❖❖❖

Nirali's foot slid right under Dinesh's. I was too late. He twisted to the left and tripped into the pujā thali. Everything clattered to the ground, the steel plates hitting the boards of the court in an explosion of sound, and the floor became a mess of red and yellow and orange powder. Grains of rice scattered *everywhere.*

"Hey, if you don't know the steps, maybe you should start in a slow circle!" Nirali's voice rang out gleefully.

But if she was waiting for Dinesh to respond, she was going to be disappointed. Dinesh couldn't respond because Dinesh couldn't stop. He fell into the statue and rebounded right back into a girl's shoulder as the final notes played. That girl fell into the person in front of her, who in turn hit their friend. It was a domino effect. And it all seemed to happen in slow motion.

I looked on in horror as Durgā's statue wobbled back and forth, and tipped to the side.

❖❖❖

Mahishāsur's head was lying beneath her, and Durgā had a new name to add to an evergrowing list. Mahishāsur Mardini: "Killer of Mahishāsur." She had saved them all.

❖❖❖

"He Bhagwān!" An Auntie muttered behind me as she surveyed the scene. Mā Durgā's murti was cradled in the arms of the priest, who was trying to hold on to the goddess and not slip in the mess at the same time. The priest held the statue so her face was toward us, and her eyes bored into mine. Dinesh was standing off to the side, surrounded by people giving him dirty looks, staring blankly around like he couldn't quite understand how he'd gotten there. I let out a sigh. This wasn't a demon, this was just a stupid guy.

"DINESH!"

A grimace flashed across his face at what could only be the sound of his mom's voice.

"Before you say anything—it wasn't my fau—" But a well-manicured, heavily jeweled hand went up to stop him from talking.

"I told you, nā, that you are too aggressive! Maine kahā thā, slow down?" Dinesh's mom couldn't have been more than five-foot-three, but in that way that all tiny Indian mothers can, she knew how to make herself gigantic when she was angry.

"It's happening, Jaya, it's happening." Nirali stood next to me, rubbing her hands together. I gave her a weak grin.

I couldn't look away. And I wasn't the only one. The people around us were staring. And Jess was in the crowds at the bleachers craning to see what had happened. It was like a train wreck.

"Pandit-ji se māfi maango!"

The priest had placed Mā Durgā back on her pedestal and was dusting excess powder off her feet. I couldn't even look at her face.

"Sorry, Pandit-ji." Dinesh put his palms together and bowed his head. It seemed he could show humility. It was becoming less and less likely that we were the devi warriors in this story.

"Okay, betā, now jā, help clean up the floor before the pujā starts," The priest was barely paying attention. He probably just wanted to get the pujā started. Dinesh's mom pulled him away from the priest and started walking toward us. Probably because we were standing in the path to the closet where all the cleaning supplies were kept and hopefully not because they knew that we actually caused all this.

"No garbā competition this week, Dinesh—that's it." Dinesh's mom was still yelling at him as they walked right by us.

"Mom! No! Someone tripped me and the team *needs* me. I can't bail on them last minute—"

"Dinesh, you always say it's not your fault, but you are always too forceful. Aur sab ne dekhā." She emphasized that last part with a smack to Dinesh's arm. It was clear that what she was really mad about was the fact that everyone had seen the embarrassing debacle. This exchange wasn't giving me the feeling of righteous vindication I imagine Mā Durgā felt after her battle with Mahishāsur, that was for sure.

I couldn't let this happen. I didn't want his entire team to suffer because we were on a vigilante high.

"I don't think this was what I wanted." I mumbled the words, but Nirali heard me anyway. She looked at me and sighed.

"It's possible we went overboard." Nirali let out another deep breath before continuing. "I can't believe that I'm starting to feel bad about this."

I put an arm through hers. "Don't worry, I won't tell." We ran to catch up to Dinesh and his mom. "Auntie!" They stopped short and turned back to see who would be so awkward as to interrupt an I-am-yelling-at-my-child moment.

"Hi, Auntie, I'm Nirali, Sonam Bhatt's daughter, and this is Jaya Shah."

Her eyes narrowed in irritation.

"Haan? What do you need?" Dinesh's mom responded. Dinesh was avoiding looking at both of us.

"We saw what happened, Dinesh just tripped. It was a total accident, Auntie." We'd reached the closet by then. Auntie reached a hand out to pull it open and found that it wouldn't budge.

"See! I told you, Mom!"

"Chee, it's locked." His mom *tsk*ed and sucked air in through her teeth. "Dinesh, we will talk about this later." She turned to us. "Bete, thank you for telling me what you saw. Acchā, I'm going to get the key to the cleaning closet and then, Dinesh, you're going to fix everything up so Pandit-ji can do the pujā. I'll be back ek minute mein."

As soon as she walked away, Dinesh turned on us.

"You're the one who tripped me!"

Nirali was not having *any* of that. She stamped her foot and shoved a finger into his shoulder. There was a manic energy bleeding from the number of people behind us who didn't have enough to do, and it seemed to be fueling my friend.

"You stepped on my lenghā and everyone saw me in my underwear!" She drove her finger in a little bit harder with each word. She moved forward, forcing him backward. He stumbled and caught himself before responding.

"What are you talking about? You're wearing your lenghā, weirdo!"

Nirali drilled her finger deeper.

"Not *tonight*, you dillweed. Five years ago!"

"When I was ten? That was *you*?" He glared at us. "Have you spent . . . five years planning this?"

I stepped back, surprised at how quickly he remembered.

"It was an accident!"

Oh no, he didn't.

"*Please*. We did not spend *five years* planning this! You were a dick to me tonight, too, remember? Maybe you should quit being such a garba gānd," I shot back, throwing my hands up in the air.

"I am not a—" he started to defend himself, but Nirali cut him off.

"Nope. You don't get to talk. Let's go through your screwups." Nirali had pulled her hand back and was counting again. "Starting with leaving me in my *underwear*. Tonight you hit some girl in the face and yelled at *her* like it was her fault you don't know how to handle your own limbs!" Dinesh tried to interject again, but Nirali just kept going. "And *then*, you blamed my *best friend* because you weren't watching your own dupattā?" With every point, a tiny wave of guilt flashed across Dinesh's face. "You are a total gānd!"

"It doesn't sound great when you put it all out there." He rubbed the back of his head. What had started as an angry, defensive expression was melting into a thoughtful one.

I tried picturing him as the demon we'd all thought he was and found that I couldn't anymore. "You should just apologize: you know it was a garbage way to act."

"I'm . . . sorry. For yelling at you." He turned to Nirali. "And I'm sorry for the, ah, underwear thing."

"Thank you." We thanked him in tandem, my voice decidedly less icy than Nirali's.

"And . . ." He paused, waiting.

We stared at him blankly.

"*And* you're also sorry for overdoing it on the revenge?" He dared a small grin that could be defined as rakish. He *was* cute, and it was annoying.

Nirali just groaned while I responded.

"Ha! No."

"Dinesh!" His mother had returned, broom and paper towels in tow. "Challo, stop yeh flirting-*wirting*, let's go!"

She pulled him away, protesting all the way. We watched them walk back to the center of the floor. Dinesh got onto his knees to wipe the floor clean, and slowly his friends joined in to help him. I looked at Mā Durgā in the center, and the statue finally looked pleased again.

"I can't believe that just happened." Nirali was shaking her head in disbelief.

"I can't believe he apologized so quickly. Maybe he's not so bad? I really thought that was going to be harder." I looked at him thoughtfully.

"What. Did. I. *Miss?*" Jess broke through the crowds who were milling about the floor waiting for the prayer to start.

"Dinesh *apologized.*"

"Yes!" We slapped palms in a victorious high-five.

"And then he flirted with Jaya," Nirali deadpanned.

"He did not." Even though he definitely had.

"Ooooh, Jaya. Maybe you can be his redemption arc!" Jess grinned.

"It doesn't matter, because I forbid it." Nirali said, smiling in that evil way that always got us in trouble. I pulled on her ponytail.

"But Nirali, she could *reform* him, she could make him better!" Jess teased.

"Jess don't encourage this! *Ew.* He's my nemesis!" Nirali shuddered.

I looked back to see Dinesh sweeping up around the statue. He glanced up and gave me a tiny shrug. Behind him, the Durgā murti looked on peacefully. *Lesson learned, Durgā ji,* I thought. We shouldn't lose our joy in petty arguments or cockiness. Let the gods have their battles of good and evil. We were here to *dance.*

"He apologized, and I don't think good nemesi apologize? He is pretty cute. . . ." I tapped a finger against my chin and smiled.

"Oh my god, please can we stop talking about this and get our daandiyan?"

I let Nirali drag us toward the tables set up in the back. "Okay, okay, but don't get mad if I ask him to be my raas partner."

"Jaya!"

I laughed at Nirali's sputtering and pushed forward to beat my friends to the daandiyan tables. We grabbed the sticks just as a bell chimed out from the center of the room. The priest was starting the pujā. My friends and I moved closer to Durgā ji's murti. When she came into view, I put my palms together, raised them in namaskār, and found her gaze. All around me, voices rose in song and prayer, but I swear that in that moment her smile was just for me. Hundreds of thousands of gods, and sometimes one sees you.

Navrātri

A Hindu Festival

Navrātri is a holiday that represents a few different myths in Hinduism. But whether it's Mā Durgā and Mahishāsur, or Rāma and Rāvana, at its core, Navrātri is always about good defeating evil. In my story, we see a very Gujarāti celebration of Navrātri. Garbā and Raas are traditionally celebrated in the North Indian state of Gujarāt. In this version of the mythology, a shape-shifting demon named Mahishāsur performs tapas, an intense form of meditation, to the gods for a thousand years, ensuring a god-given boon. When Brahmā appears before him, Mahishāsur asks for immortality. Brahmā, cleverly, allows that no man or god will be able to kill Mahishāsur.

Mahishāsur gains control of Earth and then sets his eyes on Heaven. He drives the deities out of their home, and in despair they go to the holy trinity of Vishnu, Shivā, and Brahmā. The three of them know they cannot defeat Mahishāsur, so they band together to create a physical manifestation of divine female energy. This is Durgā. Durgā battles Mahishāsur for nine days and nine nights (the word "Navrātri" literally means "nine nights") before she kills him.

I chose Navrātri because it is my favorite Hindu holiday. It's about community and being good to one another and accepting people into your space. It's about celebrating the divinely feminine. And it's about dancing into the night until your legs stop working.

—Preeti Chhibber

NOTHING INTO ALL

RENÉE AHDIEH

Many years ago, a girl and a boy lived with their parents in a bark-shingled home near a flowing river's edge. No more than twelve moons separated them in age. The boy was called Chun, and his sister's name was Charan. Though Chun was younger, he grew at almost the same pace as Charan—a fact he frequently noted to all who would listen. And though Charan was elder, she rarely scolded him. For she had learned early on the cost of scolding her brother.

When they were very small, many of the townspeople would comment that it was difficult to tell them apart, for Charan and Chun shared a love of the outdoors. On warm days, the forest's sighing branches would beckon them beneath a canopy of leaves, where the siblings would let entire afternoons be swallowed in mischief and make-believe. Their wanderings bronzed the skin of their faces a similar hue, and—though their mother tried to stop her—Charan had insisted on cutting her hair short to keep it from tangling in the wind.

One crisp morning of Charan's fifth year, she'd begun singing as she ran toward the forest, past her father who was stoking the glowing embers beneath her family's iron rice pot. Chun had followed closely at her heels, nearly causing her to stumble in his exuberance. Annoyance creasing her brow, Charan had spun to face him, words of rebuke flowing past her lips like water from a steaming kettle. Startled, young Chun had stepped backward, only to lose his footing and crash to the ground, his right hand outstretched to brace his fall.

That same small hand had landed among the embers beside the iron rice pot.

On the darkest nights, the sound of her younger brother's screams and the smell of his seared fingertips still ripped Charan from her sleep. And the ever-present reminder of her needless rebuke—the mottled skin on Chun's right hand—ensured that not a day went by in which she forgot what her hasty words had wrought.

The townspeople stopped remarking that the two children looked so similar. The passage of nine years made it all the easier. Though their hair was still shiny and dark, Chun began wearing his shorn near his scalp, while Charan's touched her shoulders in a graceful caress. Charan could often be found singing to the skies, whereas her brother had a smile resembling that of a scheming fox. Only their eyes remained the same mirrors of black.

Though the same townspeople were careful not to make

any undue comparisons, they would ask Chun and Charan's parents what their children did in the forest every year on that late summer day when the sun sat high in the sky. What was it that drove the two siblings to venture beneath the fragrant trees?

Their mother would smile and say Chun was looking for a treasure.

Their father would laugh and say Charan was learning to sing like a songbird.

But in truth the brother and sister were searching for something else entirely. Something they'd sworn to keep secret. Something they'd caught sight of only once, eight years ago:

Goblins.

On a particularly bright summer morning of Charan's fourteenth year, she woke her brother early to help their mother make breakfast. Charan stoked the fire beneath the pot while Chun served the rice, for he still feared the fire, though he tried hard to conceal it. Beyond the courtyard, their father gathered peppers and sweet cucumbers to eat with seasoned bean paste, alongside their bowls of rice. After Chun and Charan finished their morning chores, they returned to the kitchen to pack their doshirak tins so they could have something to eat while wandering through the forest on a sweltering afternoon.

Their mother rolled balls of rice made sticky with sweetened vinegar. Then she passed them to her daughter. Charan took special care to coat all sides of the rice in an even layer of roasted sesame seeds. Though he busied himself with other things, Chun made certain from the corner of his eye that he had been given exactly the same amount of food as his sister. Not a single sesame seed less. He'd become even more watchful of late, especially when he'd learned that Charan intended to audition for a place in the most prestigious music school in the land.

His sister intended to leave them behind. Even though she had caught the eye of Heechal, the best tracker in the village, and the match was an advantageous one for their family.

Once they were done forming the rice balls, their mother packed them into two small doshirak tins before layering the rice with strips of dried seaweed and vegetables. In the past, she'd garnished their lunches with grilled beef marinated in garlic and sweetened soy sauce, but their meals had grown meager in the last few years, just like their coffers. It could not be helped, so instead of lamenting the fact, their mother folded the cuffed sleeves of her jeoguri up even farther and began preparing rolled eggs in place of the meat.

"Umma, why don't I make the gaeran mari this morning?" Charan smiled as she reached for the bowl of speckled eggs.

Chun frowned. "No, Noona," he said to his sister. "Your rolled eggs are always burned. They taste like ash. You'll never make any as good as the ones Umma makes, and no amount of schooling will make a difference."

Charan's smile fell. Annoyance coiled up her throat like an angry viper ready to strike. She took a breath as though she meant to defend herself. Her eyes cut toward her brother, then glanced off the mottled skin of his right hand. Her words disappeared as quickly as they'd collected.

A small smile curved their mother's lips. "Chun, why don't

you help Charan make the gaeran mari? Neither of you will ever get better at preparing food if you're not given the opportunity." While she spoke, she placed a dollop of spicy gochujang on top of the rice, seaweed, and vegetables in the doshirak.

Chun's soured expression softened at his mother's suggestion. He divided the tasks with his sister while their mother offered her patient instruction. When Chun's rolled egg came out slightly misshapen and burned around the edges, he sniffed and frowned, frustrated to have been bested by his older sister. Without a word, Charan replaced his ruined egg with her own well-prepared one.

Their mother squeezed her daughter's shoulder in silent thanks.

Chun noticed, but pretended he did not.

After all, it was his sister's fault his egg had burned. She'd allowed the pan to grow too hot.

Late that afternoon—as they had since they were children—Chun made his way toward the Goblin Tree, his sister following close behind him, her eyes ever watchful. His lanky form skidded to a stop beneath a gnarled branch that looked like outstretched fingers, summoning them closer. Charan and Chun were the only ones to call this oak tree the Goblin Tree. From their childhood, it had been their secret. For on a summer's day eight years ago, they'd seen goblins gather in a circle beneath its swaying branches. For just a moment. And from that day forward, Chun had sworn that if they returned at the exact time the setting sun touched the fifth-closest branch to the sky, on the same day of the year, the goblins would reemerge and share their source of endless wealth with them.

Especially after the lean harvest of the past year, Charan liked the idea of gold. Of making the lines across her father's forehead disappear. But mostly she wanted to meet the goblins and learn a small bit of magic. Just enough to convince the songbirds to teach her how to sing as they did. While Chun began climbing the tree, Charan lay down to rest in its shade, fluffing her hair in a dark fan about her head. Her brother rustled in the branches above, and an acorn fell to the ground beside Charan.

She reached for it. Curled her fingertips around it.

Then brought it closer to her face.

It smelled like an acorn. Of the strangest sort. Different from any she'd seen before. Its dark brown hat was polished. Its meat was the color of faceted amber.

It looked almost like a jewel.

Another acorn fell from the branches into her outstretched palm. It resembled the first.

Charan stood. "Chun-*ah*!" she called to the branches.

Her brother did not answer.

"Did you see these strange acorns up there?" she shouted louder.

Still no answer.

"Chun-*ah*!"

The branches high above rustled once more. But her brother did not reply.

Another acorn fell a stone's throw from where Charan stood. She pocketed it, along with the first two. This last acorn appeared even larger than the first.

Then another acorn fell, even farther this time. She

moved toward it, only to hear yet another acorn *plink* to the ground a few steps in front of her. Charan stepped from beneath the shade of the Goblin Tree, toward a thicket of mugunghwa flowers. The dark centers of the blushing mauve blossoms seemed to wink at her, summoning her nearer.

Another shining acorn fell, just by the thicket.

Charan bent to reach for it.

And the ground swallowed her whole.

When Charan awoke, she found herself in darkness. Hungry and shivering from the cold, she scrabbled her trembling fingers across the floor.

It seemed to be made of earth.

On her hands and knees, she crawled forward, her hair a tangled curtain of dried leaves and soft loam. Just as she was about to call out—to ask if anyone might be nearby—a light flickered into sight, just beyond a bend of nearby earth.

Her heart pounding, Charan crawled closer and peered around the corner.

A circle of goblins gathered around a single lantern. In each of their right hands, they held clubs half their size.

Charan held her breath. If only Chun were here with her! He would stride forward and insist the goblins become his friends, in the same fashion that he dared any and all to challenge him.

Charan wished she could do the same.

But the clubs . . . frightened her. And she had not been invited to this gathering.

The goblins raised their clubs high. A tinny voice from the center began to chant:

As the leaves fall
As the sky turns to night
Summon the magic
To turn nothing
Into all

They began drumming their clubs against the earth. The light in the lantern began to grow brighter. To show the walls of earth around them. A cavern of some sort.

The goblins began chanting even louder.

A strange music filled the air, like the chiming of many distant bells. The space around the lantern shimmered as the goblins stepped back with a final flourish of their clubs.

In the center of their circle gleamed a mound of gold.

Charan almost gasped—just as her stomach rumbled. She clutched her middle, willing her hunger silent.

A goblin along the farthest edges of the circle brought forth a large rock. He placed it near the mound of gold. Again the goblins began the chant:

As the leaves fall
As the sky turns to night
Summon the magic
To turn nothing
Into all

And—just as before—a pile of gold emerged from the place where the goblin had set the rock.

Charan's eyes grew with wonderment. She watched, awestruck, as another goblin with a tilted hat brought forth an old bucket.

Her stomach grumbled again. This time even louder. Fear began winding through her chest at the thought of being discovered.

Just as they raised their clubs once more, Charan reached into her pocket, searching for something she might eat to silence the rumblings of her stomach. The only thing she had were the four acorns she'd collected earlier. She popped two into her mouth and began to chew.

And a gong struck the sides of the cavern. It echoed into her bones, causing Charan's teeth to chatter.

The goblins stopped chanting. Lowered their clubs.

"Who is there?" the goblin with the tilted hat demanded.

Charan trembled, but she knew she had been caught. She stood and began walking toward the gathering of goblins, clearing her throat as many beady eyes glared her way. "My name is Charan. I'm so sorry to disturb you. But the ground swallowed me, and I found myself here." She took a deep breath. "If you would help me find my way home, I would greatly appreciate it."

The goblin with the tilted hat stepped closer, one eye narrowed. "All you want is to be led home?"

"Yes."

"You don't want our gold?"

"I like gold, but it would be rude to ask for something

without earning it, though such riches would benefit my family greatly."

Another goblin leaned closer. "And you don't want to capture us to force us to work for you?"

"I like the idea of working alongside someone, but it is wrong to take a goblin anywhere against his will."

"So you have no interest in our magic?"

At this, Charan paused. She glanced away.

"Ah!" the first goblin with the tilted hat exclaimed. "See? You are not as good as you might think yourself to be. Of course you want something from us. All of you do." He sniffed.

Charan inhaled carefully. "I like the idea of magic."

"And what would you do with magic if you had any?"

She thought back to her wishes from earlier. "Of course it would be nice to turn rocks into gold. But"—she gnawed at her lip—"I think it would be nicer for me if I could ask the songbirds to teach me how to sing so that I can ensure myself a place in music school."

Several goblins grumbled in response. Two taller ones in the corner snickered.

The goblin with the tilted hat canted his head. He looked toward several of his comrades and shared a wordless conversation.

"What do you have as payment, little human?" he demanded gruffly.

Charan winced. "I only have two acorns." She held them out.

He considered the acorns for a moment. Shared another wordless conversation. "Very well." The goblin extended his club her way.

A quizzical expression appeared on Charan's face. "I don't understand."

"Give me your acorns." The goblin rolled his eyes. "In exchange for them, I will give you my magic club. Use it just as we have. Chant the words you undoubtedly overheard. As payment for the two acorns, I grant you two chances to turn nothing into all."

Cold shock flared through her. "Th-thank you—"

"Don't thank me yet." He made the exchange of the two acorns for his magic club. With that, the goblin waved his hand.

From the domed ceiling of the cavern, thousands of tiny fireflies winked into view. They drifted toward Charan—gathering her hair, gathering beneath her shoulders, beneath her feet—lifting her from the ground.

The lantern in the center of the goblin circle sputtered out, and Charan was dropped unceremoniously before the old oak tree. Blue darkness enveloped her as the fireflies mingled with the stars above.

Charan struggled to her feet. She glanced at the oddly weightless goblin club in her hand. Then she ran home.

Her parents did not believe her.

Even though Charan was not prone to telling falsehoods, her tale was far too fanciful. Her parents smiled at each other and told her that she'd simply fallen asleep and had an interesting dream. They reprimanded her for being gone so long and for worrying them so, and then told Charan to eat her dinner and finish her chores.

Only Chun scowled, his features knowing. Hurt. All

afternoon, he'd wandered the woods in a panic, thinking Charan had left him behind. Once he'd learned where his sister had gone, his eyes had narrowed in thought.

After all the lanterns had been extinguished in their bark-shingled home, Chun made his way toward his sister's bed pallet.

"Noona," he whispered.

Charan turned toward him, still wide-awake.

"What are you going to turn into gold?" Chun demanded.

"You believe me?"

He nodded gravely. "You have to be careful what you pick, Noona. It has to be something immense. Something amazing. Something that will make us wealthy beyond our dreams. Then maybe you can stay here and marry Heechul-hyung instead of going to music school."

Her nod was hesitant.

It frustrated Chun. "So what are you going to choose?"

"I don't know."

"It shouldn't be so difficult. Turn the mountain into gold! Turn our home into gold!" His whisper had grown louder with his annoyance.

"But . . . I like our home as it is."

"It could be bigger," Chun insisted.

Charan sat up. "Yes. It could be. But then we would have more chores."

"Then we will pay someone to do our chores!"

"Then what would we do?"

"It doesn't matter!" he nearly shouted. "Don't you see, if we have enough money, we can do anything we please!"

Charan said nothing in response.

Chun's hands balled into fists. "Is there nothing that you want?"

His sister toyed with the ends of her hair.

Chun forced himself to relax. In his sister's hesitation, he caught the glimmer of a truth he'd long suspected: Charan wanted to go to music school for herself, not to provide for her family.

Again his eyes narrowed in consideration before he spoke. "I'm sorry I was rude to you, Noona," Chun said softly. "You didn't deserve it. Tell me what happened again, and maybe we can come up with a plan." He paused. "Together."

As his eyes widened with persuasive innocence, Charan remembered how much her younger brother had loved to hear their mother tell them stories at night.

She smiled. "Of course, Chun-ah."

Her brother smiled back, sly as a charming fox.

Chun ran through the forest, hurtling toward the Goblin Tree. The moon above him was at its highest peak, and the skies were a thick blanket of indigo, spangled with stars.

He crashed to a halt at the base of the Goblin Tree.

Then he raised the magic club he had stolen from his sleeping sister.

As the leaves fall
As the sky turns to night
Summon the magic
To turn nothing
Into all

He pounded the club against the trunk of the Goblin Tree, willing the tree to become gold.

Nothing happened.

Chun felt his cheeks begin to flush. He raised the club once more. If he didn't use the wishes before Charan did, his sister would leave him behind, and his family's coffers would diminish even further.

As the leaves fall
As the sky turns to night
Summon the magic
To turn nothing
Into all

He struck the trunk of the mighty oak tree even harder.

Still nothing happened.

Chun tried a third time. A fourth time. When he smashed the tree trunk a fifth time with no success, he shouted into the night, his cry filled with fury.

"That magic was not given to you, you little thief!" an equally irate voice yelled from behind him.

Chun turned to find a goblin with a tilted hat glaring up at him. It had to be the same goblin from his sister's story.

"Then give me my own wishes!" Chun said, the flush rising into his forehead. "My sister does not know what to do with them."

The goblin harrumphed. "I don't give magic to people I don't trust."

"Then trust me. I would do far more good with magic than my sister would."

"Why would I trust a little thief?"

Chun felt his fingers become bloodless in his fists. "Because I promise to use your magic well."

"Promises from a thief are as useful to me as a pebble in my shoe." The goblin turned away. "Give that club back to its rightful owner."

Anger raced through Chun's veins. The spiteful little creature wanted him to ignore his family and let his sister vanish to the city in search of her own dreams? In a fit of fury, Chun lifted the club as though to strike the goblin.

The goblin spun on his heel and swiped his hand through the air. A loud crack echoed into the night, followed by a flash of green light and a cloud of smoke.

When the smoke began to rise, the goblin waved his sight clear.

Then he sighed before bending to collect the new pebble beside his feet.

When Charan combed the forest in search of Chun the next morning, she found the magic club beside the trunk of the Goblin Tree.

She knew in an instant what her brother had done. Without hesitating, Charan made her way to the thicket of nearby mugunghwa flowers.

Though she did not know how to summon the goblins or fall through the earth into their cavern, Charan held the magic club in both hands, like an offering.

"Please tell me what you have done with my brother," she asked the flowers. "If you return him to me, I will give back the magic club without even using it to turn nothing into all."

The ground did not give way. Nor did anyone offer her a response.

Charan asked again. She knelt before the flowers and rested the club before her. Briefly her mind drifted to thoughts of her parents. Thoughts of her past. A memory of last week, when Heechul had smiled at her and she'd turned away. Visions of a future she should want, yet did not.

She took a careful breath. "I have no doubt what my brother has done. What my ignorance has allowed to happen. But beneath Chun's petty thievery lies his care for our family. Please forgive him."

Neither the flowers nor the trees took any notice of her.

Charan thought about forgiveness. Her father had once said it was an act meant to unburden oneself. She'd failed to understand him then, and still she did not quite grasp his meaning.

The birds twittered through the trees above. A brush of air stirred the purple and mauve petals before her. "I know it is difficult to grant forgiveness. My brother has not yet granted me forgiveness for what happened when we were children, and he is angry that I wish to leave him. I have not unburdened myself either. But perhaps I can try. I forgive Chun for what he did today, and I hope he will forgive me in time." She inhaled slowly. "And I ask you to forgive him as well."

But neither the flowers nor the trees took any notice of her.

Charan swallowed. The morning swelled into noon.

She sat studying the mugunghwa flowers, determined not to leave the forest without her younger brother.

"When Chun lied, I would ignore it. Sometimes I would tell my mother and father I was the one who had done wrong," she said. "And when he made mistakes, we all pretended he had not. But it was not out of love. It was out of pity." Charan recalled the rolled egg from the morning past. "Often I hid my successes so they would not burden him." Her thoughts cleared, just as a ray of sunshine cut through the trees. "I know this is not my fault. It is not my responsibility to make amends for my brother. It is Chun's fault he has become a thief. But please let him have the chance to make it right. Give him the chance to become a great man."

She placed her forehead against the magic club as she bowed low to the ground, her palms on either side of her head.

A bright light flashed to her left.

Beside her hand lay a single shining pebble. As dark as the thick hair she and her brother shared. As dark as their black-mirror eyes.

Charan raised the club into the air.

As the leaves fall
As the sky turns to night
Summon the magic
To turn nothing
Into all

The Goblin Treasure

A Korean Fairy Tale

When I was a child, my mother would often read Korean fairy tales to me from a collection of bright green hardcover books that had been given to us by a family friend. My favorites were ones that involved talking animals and the complicated relationships between siblings. "The Goblin Treasure" has been a favorite of mine because I love the way its two brothers—one a good soul and one a troubled soul—disappear into a world of magic beneath our feet. After they are faced with the chance to gain riches beyond their wildest imaginings, the two brothers' respective treatment of money and each other often gave me pause, even as a child. The idea that good and evil could exist in the same person is intriguing to me even more now.

When Ellen Oh approached me to write a story inspired by the fables of my youth, I knew I wanted to write a tale of a brother and a sister. It was also of utmost importance to me to turn a few fairy-tale tropes on their heads in doing so, and it was such a joy to bring to life a world of fairy-tale Korea.

—Renée Ahdieh

SPEAR CARRIER

RAHUL KANAKIA

During my first day I was in shock. A many-armed demon-thing brought me to this huge field that was full of millions of people and alien creatures and tents and structures. The only normal things around me were the mountains in the distance. The demon took me to a little trench and said, "Hey dude, you're just in time. This is the last day of enrollments. The battle starts tomorrow."

Those were the last English words I heard that day.

A brown-skinned guy in bronze armor came up and corralled me and the other new arrivals—few of us spoke the same language, and most weren't even human beings, as I'd define the term—to show us how to use our new equipment. Then he formed us into rough lines and taught us the rudiments of what I guess was a military formation: when to lower our spears and when to raise them, mostly.

Afterward he passed out jugs of some kind of liquor: moonshine, pretty much. Everybody started quaffing, and the whole place disintegrated into a nightmare of drunkenness. The—er—the things next to me tried to talk to me by making little drawings, but I shied away. Which sounds cowardly I know, but you would've too if you could've seen them. They were twice my height and had the body of a man and the head of a lion.

I didn't drink. I didn't speak. I went circling around, looking for somebody, anybody, who could tell me who we were gonna fight and why. I guess a part of me figured that the strange man—the one who'd appeared to me in my car and brought me here—had to be around somewhere. When I'd agreed to his offer, it was because I had thought I'd be a hero. But a hero wouldn't be so lonely and so afraid. A hero wouldn't shout for help, and then, hearing only silence, go back to his trench and cry.

When the sun rose, a hand shoved me over, and I stood, groggily. The man from last night—our sergeant? drillmaster?—mimed for us to get rid of all the random crap we'd come with and put on our armor over the bodysuits they'd given us. I collected all my things: jeans, my T-shirt, notebooks, phone, pens, watch, and class ring. When everything was in a pile, I weighed it all down with a rock and tried to memorize the pattern of the pits and ruts around me, but I think I knew I'd never recover any of it.

Our bodysuits were incredibly warm, and you could piss and shit inside them with no problems. The suits were from somewhere farther in the future than I'm from. Or maybe some other world; I still wasn't too sure about the cosmological underpinnings of this place, and nobody was eager to explain.

The suits were skintight, and I was a little embarrassed—I'm not in the best shape. Maybe I've got a little extra around the middle. And there were plenty of human girls around who, er, well—the suits showed off a lot. . . .

Armored in the stuff they'd given me—a white skirt-thing, a bronze breastplate, and a long spear with a wicked point—I stood in line with everybody else.

Though not everybody here was human, I also didn't think they were aliens. They were too humanoid: They had heads and mouths, and we all ate the same food, whereas if we were actually from different planets, our biologies would've been too radically different to allow for that. (On the other hand, what do I know? Maybe it was all magic.) Sometimes they were weird, chimerical combinations of Earth animals. A few were human, except they had the heads of tigers. Others were tiny as ants, and had as many legs, and the only way you'd know they were people was by looking at the little spears they carried with them. Huge snakes lay still, caked in mud, almost invisible unless they moved. The snakes talked, but of course I couldn't understand them.

Our sergeant did his best to shove us into some kind of order.

The day before yesterday I'd been at school, and now I was in this immense valley, tucked between two sets of mountains, and something electric and awesome was taking place. And maybe it didn't *matter* that I was alone, because I was experiencing something so new. Except . . . this place made me feel so small.

We were shivering, waiting. A scream went up. Two tigers embraced, farther up the rise. I heard grunts, and several elephants came into view. The army had woken up. And all around me camps of people were chatting and arguing and fighting. Some people had come with their families. Or maybe with their friends. The other possibility—perhaps they had made friends here?—was something I didn't like to think about, because it meant maybe I was wrong to be so terribly lonely.

Most weren't sleeping rough like me. I was surrounded by huge tents. Some were familiar: canvas stretched over aluminum poles, held together by cords staked into the ground. Others weren't. Furs and skins draped over wooden poles: a yurt, right? Teepees and covered wagons. And other things: a network of tiny tubes and wires that ran along the ground; a huge glass structure full of blooming vines and flowers; a starship with wicked rocket engines that were always hot. The night had been full of fires and music and shouts, but I'd covered my ears and eyes with my shirt and hidden from all of it.

Cold clouds of visible air blew out of my nose and mouth. I was shivering. My toes were wet with muck. I'd slept all night in mud, but my bodysuit had shielded me from the damp. Now I was exposed. Next to me, a crab thing turned its googly eyes on me. This creature was enormous. It was about as tall as a human being, but many times as wide, and I could easily have fit a tent or a picnic table on its back.

"Hey," I said.

We both looked away at the same time. Its pale fleshy body reddened. The creature said, "Hello."

"What?" I said. "You speak . . . English?"

"It's a language I have access to."

Please believe I don't have the words to convey how goofy this thing looked. Its eyes were as huge and flat as the ones on a teddy bear, and the pupils bopped around inside them just like, well, like googly eyes.

"Okay, wow," I said. "Wow. This is . . . wow."

"You're American?" the creature said. "Perhaps you can tell me . . . I wasn't given that much information about why to come here."

"That's just . . . That's fantastic," I said.

The crab's voice was so human. A baritone, cultured voice that came from a slit somewhere in his stomach. I'll spare you the long line of questions about where he (it? they? the voice was male) came from and how he'd gotten here. It turns out that they'd engineered him, somewhere in the American South, to live and work in the toxic delta of some river. He was from the future, my future, obviously. And he wasn't some combat-soldier supermutant type of deal. He was a farmer: his tiny little legs were to pick their way through the rice paddies without hurting anything, and his claws were designed to bend and twist complex irrigation works.

He'd gotten out. Gone to college. The whole bootstraps story. And then a guy had appeared to him with an offer.

"Yeah," I said. "That happened to me too."

"I took it," the crab said. "But now . . . I don't know."

He gestured over my shoulder toward the enemy army. I didn't like to look in that direction. Strange things were brewing over there, within the mists: flying chariots, massive beasts, and showers of light. We had the same things on our side, I hoped, but I wasn't sure that'd help me much during the battle.

The crab had a spear, too. Did I mention that? The spear lay against his side as we spoke, and now he picked it up. His claws had crushed little grooves into the metal handle. He held out the spear, point forward, then tucked the end behind a leg. Then he tried to march forward (rather than side to side), putting one leg carefully in front of the other. The movement was so ungainly and slow.

"This is what they taught me," the crab said. "This is not good. This is not a good use of my body."

"Yeah . . . ," I said. "Stabbing is gonna be a little hard."

"I'll die here. They've brought me here to die."

Two days before, I'd been sitting in my car, parked at a vista point up on Skyline Boulevard: a place where kids from my school sometimes came after dark to drink. I was there with a bottle of vodka and a bag of pretzels, even though I knew if they showed up, I'd only stare in silence. I had no friends, and sometimes wasn't that sure if I even wanted one. My thoughts were so expansive, and I knew, from experience, that boiling them down into words made them soft and weak.

Night hadn't yet fallen, but the sun was low over the bay. A haze enveloped San Francisco, out on the far side of the water, and closer by, the golden sunlight fell on the rows of houses that ran across the hillside.

The passenger window was down, so it was cool, but there was no cross-breeze. My hand was on the outside of the car, slapping the roof, and I was thinking. That's all. Just thinking.

People pay so little attention to thinking. I mean, I would

come home and my mom would ask me what had happened during the day, and I'd say "nothing" and she'd ask who'd I eaten lunch with and I'd say "Nobody. Just some people." And on and on and on, and she'd act like I was stonewalling her, but really she wasn't asking the right question.

Because, to me, real life wasn't something your body did: it wasn't food and sleep and sweat. And real life also wasn't social. I didn't care about the delicate tangle of relationships: the fights and resentments and jealousies that make up a group of friends. Real life didn't even lie within the flicker of lust and desire and romance that everybody around me pretended were somehow equivalent to love.

No, real life happened in your mind. Real life meant dissecting your sensory experience—the evidence of your eyes and ears—then analyzing the pieces, using knowledge you'd gained from books, and reassembling it all into some semblance of a self. Yes, that was exactly it. Real life was about deciding who you were.

But that wasn't a thing you could tell to someone. If I had come home and said to my mom, "Yeah, I thought for hours today about whether there was anything in life that was worth dying for, and decided, ultimately, that there wasn't," then what would she say?

I thought a lot about that particular topic: heroism, and the nature thereof. Because it'd occurred to me that most of my intellectual and emotional life revolved around fictional depictions of heroism. In *Fallout*, I was the Vault Dweller who went out into the post-apocalyptic wastes in order to preserve life for my people. In *Star Wars*, I risked my life to defeat the

Empire. Even in my doodles of gigantic space battles that sprawled across many pages of my notebooks, I understood exactly what each of my space soldiers was giving up. It was a very simple thing: Heroism = risk + altruism + victory.

A hero risks something very important—often, but not always, their life—in order to help others.

Everybody would agree with this, I think.

But it's the third element that I was obsessed with: victory. Heroes win.

If the Vault Dweller died before bringing back the water chip or the Garden of Eden Creation Kit or whatever else . . . if Frodo hadn't destroyed the ring . . . if Luke hadn't blown up the Death Star: Would they still have been heroes?

The instinct is to say, "Yes, of course."

It doesn't feel good to mock a loser. But what does losing really get you? They say that oftentimes when you jump into the churning ocean to save a drowning person, you're just creating two corpses instead of one. Because if you're not a very strong and careful swimmer, the drowning person will only pull you under with desperate flailing. But doesn't the would-be rescuer deserve to be praised? After all, you risked your life. And yet . . . and yet . . . now two mothers have shattered hearts. Now two lives—the lives of human people who might've lit up the world writing a killer pop song or making friends with that one lonely person or, I don't know, doing some other great stuff—are gone forever, when otherwise the cost might've been just one.

That was my problem. Every day, I read about heroes. And when I wasn't reading about them, I was dreaming about them. I wanted so badly to be one. I looked up astronaut careers, so

I could be like Neil Armstrong and Buzz Aldrin and Sally Ride and John Glenn and Alan Shepard (but not like the astronauts who burned to death in *Apollo 1* or in *Challenger* or *Columbia* . . . other than Christa McAuliffe, do you remember their names? I don't). Or I looked up careers in the military or in spycraft. Again, what about the guy who's so full of guts and honor—the guy who charges forward, determined to save his unit—and immediately gets mowed down by machine-gun fire? Is he a hero?

I would be that guy. I knew it. I would be that fucking guy.

So in my car that day, I was thinking, shit, if someone came up to me and gave me a magical sword and told me I was the chosen one and asked me to defeat some cosmic evil, I'd say, "No thanks," because you know what? Death is real. And death is really the end of everything. And I *know* how insignificant I am, and I know any threat worth fighting is probably way more powerful than me.

My head was still resting on the window. The air was damp, and a caterpillar dropped down suddenly from a tree and swung back and forth in front of me. I stared at the little ridges contracting and expanding along its damp body, and for once my mind was empty.

This was the exact moment the other guy appeared in my passenger seat.

His first words were: "Jump scare."

I screamed, and my hand went for the lock, but I couldn't open it. He grabbed my chin and said, "One two three, no you're not dreaming; four five six, I'm about to make you an offer; seven eight nine, shut up and listen."

His eyes were a deep, warm, molten brown, and his skin was very dark.

"You're ready," he said. "Take my hand. We've gotta go."

"Who the—?" I said. "Are you—?" But I knew—maybe I shouldn't have known, but because my mind was already there—I knew that this was the guy: He was Gandalf, he was Dumbledore, he was Merlin. . . . This was the fucking guy.

"I won't lie to you," he said. "If you take my hand, you *will* die. But I swear it'll mean something. So come on."

My hand jerked back. "Are you fucking kidding me? I'll die? You're not gonna try to sell me harder than that?"

His eyes bored into mine, and then his body went slightly out of focus. The man was very dark-skinned, but he didn't quite have the features of a black or African person, so I can't really say what race he was supposed to be. "Do you understand that I am a god?"

And I knew we weren't going to banter. He wasn't going to answer my questions or lead me around. We were not friends or allies. I'd been chosen, but I was so small and so low that I wasn't worth the ten seconds it'd take to answer my questions.

He didn't hold out his hand again, but I grabbed for it, and once I'd caught hold, he wrenched me sideways and threw me onto the dirt. When I stood up, he was gone, and I was in this valley, surrounded by millions of people.

You know the rest: a many-armed demon grabbed me up, marched me off to get all my equipment, and showed me how to find my place. I went through a day of drill, and I ate the food they gave me, and then I went to my little hole and tried to sleep, and during that day and night, I had a lot of time to think.

And, and, and . . . my life might not've had a lot of meaning. My parents maybe didn't care much about me. I maybe wasn't interested in much or good for very much, but I *enjoyed* life. Death was nothingness; it was a black mass at the edge of my mind.

I mean, okay, the fact that I was here meant magic existed, and if magic existed, then maybe so did Heaven or Nirvana or the Elysian Fields or the Grey Haven or whatever, but . . . Death. I mean . . . that'd be it. My life as I knew it would be over. I guess. Maybe. Or maybe not. I don't know the meaning of death! All I know is that I was terrified of it. Shit, I wish I could explain this stuff. I wish I could tell you what it's like to be alone and sleeping in muck and to not know what is happening or why. What it's like to see a valley covered in monsters and to know that this is real. To test the point of a spear and then to feel this unasked-for pain right in the diaphragm as you imagine it sliding into you.

Hadn't even taken any convincing. I cried that night and berated myself for being so stupid. All my life I'd said I was too smart for this. I was the person who knew that heroism was just a story! And yet I'd come to this place anyway.

Our sergeant motioned for us to march, but even if he hadn't, we'd have gotten the message. Our whole army oozed toward the riverside and carried me with it. We left behind the camp, and we marched across the still-unmarked grass between the armies.

The enemy came into view. They were like us: a mass of tiny

figures, interspersed with chariots and horses and elephants. They moved slowly out of a line of campfires. People ranged over the distance between us. And for the first time I saw *real* heroes.

One of them rode on a chariot that floated above the ground. Another took a shot with his bow, and that one arrow multiplied in midair until the sky was dark with shafts. I was sure the enemy army would be completely destroyed by that one shot, but another flurry of arrows appeared, slicing our guy's arrows into mulch that rained down harmlessly. And that wasn't the end. Another of our guys was a fucking giant: hundreds of feet tall, he soaked up enemy arrows without noticing.

The giant stepped into the enemy lines and began swinging his club. The first rank of our forces detached, striding forward. Arrows flew out in their hundreds of thousands. The fighting was too far away for me to hear the screams, but I am sure that I saw people fall and not get up.

We waited, not talking among ourselves. The sun grew higher, but water was plentiful, passed out in paper satchels that dissolved when we were done drinking. My friend, the crab, rubbed the edge of his claw against my armor.

I was numb. This was it. I would die on this battlefield.

And that's when I caught a glimpse of the dark-skinned man who'd brought me here: the god. He was just a few dozen feet away, driving a huge golden chariot and moving toward the rear lines. The god was bare chested and unarmed, but a man in golden armor stood next to him, holding a bow. The horses neighed, forcing their way forward through our army. I dropped my spear, and I tried to push through the ranks, but the press of people was too strong. All day I'd been looking ahead, but now for the first time I got a good look back, and I saw the millions—literally millions—of people behind me.

Sure there were snakes and giants and rat-men, too, but they were all people. And they had every face you could imagine. Torn-up, weary, fearful, stern. I just—I—I—they were a sea of gold armor and black mud. And the whole valley rippled, like a breeze across a meadow, as they moved.

They seemed so insubstantial from where I was standing, but when I pushed, the nearest guy got a harsh look and shoved me back. I fell, and then a huge bulk appeared above and saved me from being trampled.

"What are you doing?" The tiny mouth was set in a fleshy belly. My crab-friend was standing over me.

"We need answers," I said. "We cannot—absolutely cannot—just rush forward into that shit."

The crab stood there for a long time. So long that I feared he'd given up, but then I heard the clangor above me. Somebody was beating a spear against my friend's hard back.

I scrambled from under him, and then I moved next to him, jabbing one guy in the side to make room. The crab scuttled into the space, and with that wedge drawn up, we managed to slowly make our way through the army.

When I saw the chariot again, conscious thought didn't even come into it: I immediately hopped up onto the sideboard. "Stop!" I yelled. Our sergeant grabbed the back of my armor and grunted at me in some foreign language. I fumbled for the clips holding together my breastplate, trying to detach it, but he yanked back, throwing me into the mud.

The muddy trot of the horses was all I could hear. A foot lashed out, connecting with my stomach. I shouted, "Help! Help!"

Suddenly, a groan. Weapons flashed. I got up, free of my armor, and ran through the crowd. Cries went up around me, and I heard a sharp scream, but I didn't turn.

The man in the golden armor—he was no taller than my sister—was holding a bow whose bottom edge was braced against the floor of the chariot. His torso and face were covered with colored powder; he wore golden earrings and golden necklaces, and I saw for the first time the thin crown of gold that held back his long hair.

The chariot driver didn't notice me, but this guy, the one with the bow, moved faster than I could see, and other arms appeared from behind his back—they were attached to him and yet somehow independent—so that he was in the center of a cyclone of limbs. And each of those arms held an arrow.

That's why my feet were stuck. A forest of arrows rose from the edges of my sandals. They'd pinned me to the wooden sideboard without piercing my feet.

"Wait!" I said, pointing to the god who was driving the chariot. "You know me!"

The charioteer made a motion to knock me to the ground with the butt of his whip, but the man with the bow said something, and the charioteer turned, responding.

"Please," I said. "We don't want to d-die here." I turned back, looked for the crab-guy, who was pinned down beneath the fist of a giant. The chariot had stopped. In fact, the entire army seemed to have gone still.

The archer and charioteer engaged in a heated argument. The archer turned to me, sweeping out an arm, and he said something in his strange liquid-gold language.

"Come on," I said. "What'd he say?" My eyes pleaded with the chariot driver. "You know English. Come on!"

The charioteer turned sharply. "He wants to know what your problem is and such; I'm explaining that you're a coward."

"What?" I said. "Excuse me? That's not true."

Thousands of people were looking at me. Spears rose up methodically, and I felt the sharp clack as they banged against one other.

"I, uh." I looked at the archer. "I just want to know what this is all for. I mean, why are we fighting? What'd we come here for?"

The charioteer rolled his eyes and then focused them on me. They went dark, and the swirling of the cosmos was reflected inside him. His arms unfolded, multiplying, and heads spilled out sideways from his head. This nightmare vision—all swinging limbs and sneering mouths—stared at me from dozens of eyes, and I knew it saw everything I had ever done or thought or seen. Then I fell into them, and I saw, well, I saw the swirling of the cosmos. I saw that everything is fire. All of us, we are just a mass of fire that is moving so fast and so ecstatically that it's come to believe it's alive.

The vision went on for a long time. The fire that was me—the little bit of fire I thought I owned—joined in with everything else in a gigantic conflagration that burned and burned and burned and burned until, I, er, blinked. I mean, I blinked my eyes. And then the vision faded.

I looked around me. All was silent. Every face within visible distance was holding still. As I watched, a tick-tock motion began. Heads lolled as they snapped out of the trance. Behind me, the crab rose shakily to his legs.

"Do you see now?" the charioteer said. "Can you finally see?"

"Er . . . ," I said. "Yes . . . in some sense."

"Good."

He bent over and began to pull the arrows from around my sandals. "Then let us be. We have a war to prosecute."

The archer laughed. He reached out a hand and tapped me on the shoulder.

"But—" I said, "in a more direct and immediate sense, I'm still confused. What is happening? Who are those people over there?"

The charioteer started to—

"No," I said. "Are you the one who's in charge? That guy over there's wearing the crown."

"I am quite literally a god," the charioteer said.

"But are you in charge?" I said. "Wait, can you translate this for your friend? What is happening? I get that the fate of the universe in some way hangs in the balance, but can anybody tell me who those other guys are!"

I thought the charioteer was going to blow me to bits right there, but I'd gambled right. The archer had stopped him before; the archer wore the crown; the archer was clearly giving the orders here. So he spoke to the archer, and the archer chanted some words, sparkled briefly, and nodded at me.

"You had questions?" he said.

"And you speak English?"

"In a sense."

"What is happening? Why are we fighting?"

The archer looked to the charioteer. "I said to you this was not the right way to raise an army. They will come willingly from throughout time and space to die for you: this is what you said. But this one does not seem willing."

"He is willing," the charioteer said. "He prayed for this chance."

Then the archer looked at me. "This is . . . It is complicated. My brothers and I are the rightful heirs to the kingdom of Hastinapura. You are on the side of justice."

"Wait, so we're fighting so you can be king?" I said.

I wanted to make a joke about democracy, but I didn't have quite enough chutzpah.

He pointed across the field of battle at the other army. "My cousins, the Kauravas, stole my kingdom. They insulted my wife. They attempted to murder us in our beds. They aren't worthy to rule."

I waited a bit longer, to see if anything more was gonna come out. I looked back at the crab. He raised his claws. Maybe he was confused as I was, or maybe this explanation was enough for him.

"Is that it?" I said.

"I very much understand these concerns," the archer said. "I too had these same questions. Do you think I wish to kill my cousin-brothers? To kill my uncle Bhishma? To kill my teacher, Dronacharya? I would give my life to save his. Believe me, this is something I do only with the utmost reluctance. But believe me, it is necessary." He looked at the charioteer. "Could you show him the vision? The vision is what truly cleared my head."

"I just did that!" the charioteer said. "We don't have time for this!"

"Well," I said. "It's just . . . Are we really supposed to just, like, *trust* you? This could all be a lie or a trick. . . . The vision was cool and all, but it was a little like you were hypnotizing us, and—"

The charioteer broke in: "Americans." He looked then at the crab. "Both of you. Americans. I knew we'd have trouble . . . Well, okay, fine. You can go back." He snapped the head off an arrow. He tossed it at me, and after some fumbling I caught it. Then he did it again, throwing it to the crab, who was more graceful, cupping his gently between two claws. "Scratch your hand with these if you want to go home."

"I don't . . . ," I said. "Home is not . . . I just . . . I want it to mean something. I mean, we're not fighters. We're not immense giants. Or snake people with what I can only assume is powerful snake venom in their fangs. My friend here can't even *hold* a spear! And you want us to fight for you? Why? Would it even matter?"

The charioteer looked at me. "It would," he said. "If you died here, it would matter more than you can imagine. The fate of the universe, it in some way depends on your choosing to die for this. It's a combining and commingling of energies. Without this expenditure of forces, everything you know and love will dwindle and die. I tried to show you—"

"Maybe you could show me the vision again?" I said.

Then there was a clap of thunder in the distance, and I saw four other chariots race out from our army and pull ahead, right out into the space between the armies. The archer shot a single arrow up into the air, far ahead of us, and then he shouted something.

"No," the charioteer said. "Time to decide."

I looked back. The crab locked his odd googly eyes on me, and then he threw the arrowhead down onto the ground. "Come down," he said. "We will face this battle together."

But I was afraid, and the moment passed. As I waited, the chariot raced ahead. I shrank down, and the battle began to rage around me.

I was only on that chariot for a few moments, but I saw terrible things. Swirls of mystic energy. The crash of powerful forces. Thousands of arrows. Spears. Swords. Screams. Every second, hundreds died. And I knew I'd not survive.

There, crouching down on the sideboard, with my arms locked around the chariot's flagstaff, I very carefully jabbed the arrowhead into the palm of my hand.

When I opened my eyes, I was back in my car.

And, of course, an arrow had stapled my hand to the steering wheel.

At first I screamed, but screaming got me nowhere.

The windshield was covered in leaves, and cold air blew in through the window. I would have died there, maybe, bleeding out slowly, except that my key was still in the ignition. Thank God I had an old beater that still used an actual key in the ignition, or

I would've been trapped here because the fob would've been in my pocket, on that battlefield, along with my other shit.

I broke the shaft of the arrow, and I carefully pulled my hand off of the bloody shard of wood. Then, holding the bleeding appendage clenched in my lap, I reached over, putting the car into reverse.

The road behind me was a big commuter road. Lots of cars, and I had to wait a long time for an opening to pull out. Blood streamed into my lap. The drive to the hospital was long and confused; I had no phone, so I followed my memory and the highway signs, rolling across sparse roads for ten minutes before I finally got it right. Shock faded, and pain sizzled through all my synapses, rising and falling.

I got to the hospital in time, of course, and they bandaged me up just fine.

The doctors didn't believe me, but my parents did, because they believe in mystical stuff like God and karma and fate and the battle of cosmic good versus cosmic evil. Most people do, I've found. After I came home, my parents had lots of questions for me, but I eventually shut them up by saying I didn't like to think about what happened (though of course that's not true).

On the surface, nothing has changed for me: I'm still pretty quiet; I still don't have many friends; and I still sit alone in the afternoon in my car. But whenever something goes wrong with the world—whenever there's a disaster or a bombing or an injustice—I do wonder, sometimes, if one more corpse on that distant battlefield might somehow have changed everything.

The *Mahabharata*

A South Asian Epic

With more than two hundred thousand lines of verse, the *Mahabharata* is the longest poem that's ever been written, and it's all about a conflict between two sets of cousins over who's going to inherit the kingdom of Hastinapura. According to the text, something on the order of five million people participate in the battle that concludes the epic. And of those, only twelve survive. Which as a child was something that struck me very deeply. I was like, *Wut? Huh? What happened to all those people? What did they die for?*

It's very easy to be cynical and say, "Well, they died for nothing. This is a story about hereditary nobles who're engaged in a dynastic squabble." But great stories, like the *Mahabharata* (or the *Iliad* or *Gilgamesh*), endure because of their complexities, and this exact question, "Why are we fighting?" is one that the *Mahabharata* engages with very deeply.

In fact, on the eve of this battle the hero of the whole epic, Arjuna, says to his charioteer, the god Krishna: "Honor forbids us to kill our cousins" and "How can we know happiness if we kill our own kinsmen?"

Krishna's answer to this question forms the bulk of the most famous book in the *Mahabharata*, the "Bhagavad Gita," which is basically Hinduism's answer to a timeless question: What's the point?

I'm no guru, and I can't explicate an entire religion for you, but basically, Krishna says: "He who thinks the self is a killer / and he who thinks it killed / both fail to understand / [the self] does not kill, nor is it killed."

Arjuna's anguish, Krishna explains, is built on a false understanding of the universe. He sees individual people arrayed in battle against one other, but that's not the reality of the situation. This universe is so complex, and we are only a part of it. These bodies are forms that we take up or cast off, but the spirit inside is eternal. And war might seem like pain and suffering and violence, but really it's only a process that the spirit is going through.

That explanation was enough for Arjuna, as it would've been for me (I mean, Krishna also throws in some magical razzle-dazzle). But "Spear Carrier" was inspired by the other five million people on that battlefield. I wondered where they'd come from, and why they fought, and whether anyone had ever stopped to explain to them the purpose of the lives they were about to lose.

—Rahul Kanakia

CODE OF HONOR

MELISSA DE LA CRUZ

I almost murdered a girl yesterday.

Literally.

When I opened my locker between periods, I discovered that my diary had gone missing. I knew exactly who had stolen it, but I couldn't say anything. Lilah Samson, the most feared and envied girl at the Duchesne School, hates me. I wanted to tear out her shiny hair with my bare hands. I wanted to claw at her porcelain skin. Thinking about someone trying to read the pages spilling with all my secrets made my skin burn.

No one can know who I really am.

Too bad for her. It's charmed shut. No human can read it. But that doesn't make me any less angry. Ever since I started at Duchesne, Lilah has been trying to nose her way into my personal life. Why does she even care? I'm just an outsider.

Muttering her name under my breath, I slammed my locker shut. A younger girl named Constance was walking by and overheard, and she stopped in the middle of the hallway. "You should really watch out for her, Aida," she said. "Lilah's a piece of work."

"Tell me about it," I said, my veins throbbing with fury. "Does she always act like this toward new students? Or am I just a special case?"

I'm already prone to attacks of rage, and having to deal with her hazing ever since I arrived at Duchesne hasn't made controlling them any easier. I've only been here a couple of months, and Lilah already knows exactly how to push my buttons.

"It's not that Lilah stabs people in the back," Constance said. "She just has a reputation for making people earn their place. You can't earn her trust fast."

"You mean she stabs them in the front," I replied.

Lilah and her group of friends are stylish, confident, and beautiful. Rich beyond imagining, their families have ruled New York forever. They're nothing like me, a loner from nowhere.

Standing in the hallway, I thought about leaving Duchesne, but I've run from so many things in my life already. I need to stand my ground, not let my anger over some girl's immature behavior drive me to fly away. If I leave, I may never discover my destiny. I'm up for her challenge. Life isn't easy for people like me. Not that there are many like me. . . . I might be immortal and feed on blood, but I'm not the usual vampire. I'm also a shape-shifter and a daywalker. Where I come from, they call us aswangs. Vampire witches. The sun doesn't burn my skin. I can go about by day like any other normal sixteen-year-old girl, but once the sun dips down below the horizon, I fly around the city hunting for my prey.

My mother was also an aswang. We lived in a small village on the island of Mindanao, in the southernmost part of the Philippines, and she raised me by herself. She refused to tell me about our family, thinking that keeping our identity a secret would keep us safe. She would kill chickens and any other animal she could find for me at night and bring the flesh home, until one night the villagers caught her stealing a hog and murdered her. Burned with the white fire. The only way to kill one of us. I realized that whether the villagers discovered my identity or not, I would never be safe on the island again.

My magical blood bound me to secrecy. I had to leave Mindanao before I could be discovered. I flew away that night to Vietnam and slowly made my way to New Delhi, where I tried to settle down. But soon I realized that I was forever destined to be a wanderer, an orphan; to never know my family, my bloodline, or my true origins.

My anger at my mother for keeping our family's past a secret burned inside as the years slowly passed. Though I stopped aging at sixteen, I felt old. I grew weary of feeding on human flesh, leaving a blood trail of friends and lovers behind. It's lonely to be a person—a creature—like me.

That's why I developed a code of honor. I used to feed on people, but I couldn't help myself from killing those I loved most. It's only one rule, the golden one: what you wish upon others, you wish upon yourself—which is a lot easier said than done. I only eat animals now, and only as much as I need to survive. I try not to let myself get angry because that's when I most desire human flesh. You can see why I need to keep myself under control. If not for my code of honor, I actually might have murdered Lilah.

After discovering the diary was missing, I couldn't get myself to calm down, which could have been dangerous for me—and for anyone nearby. It's difficult to be honorable at your worst moment and to forgive those who do you wrong, to have to battle what comes naturally to you. But that's what it takes to be a monster living among mortals.

If I was going to stick to my code, I had to remove myself from the situation, so I told a teacher that my aunt Girlie was sick and that I needed to leave school to take care of her. Everyone at Duchesne thinks my parents passed away in a tragic boating accident and that I live with my old spinster aunt. The truth is, Aunt Girlie doesn't actually exist. I have no one, nobody.

I left the school still in a rage. I waited until night fell, shifted into my bird form, and flew around the city, trying to get my pulse under control. There are six flocks of sheep just outside the city. I dropped by for a newborn's liver. It's cruel to rip one out, but better little lambs than Duchesne's most popular girls.

Perspective, you know?

Standing on the front porch of the mansion, I open the door to the Duchesne School. I'm feeling better now that I've had a night to cool down, but I have to arm myself for the day with a mantra. I take a deep breath. *Don't let those girls get to you. Don't give in.*

When I first arrived, I thought life in New York City was going to be perfect. I've traveled all over the world—New Delhi, Tokyo, Milan, London, Cairo, Manila—searching for a place I would truly belong, but none of them ever felt right. Last year, I was living in a shabby little room near Oxford University that I adored, but I was getting restless again. I was preparing to leave for Morocco the next week when I overheard two professors speaking to each other about a theory that an American colleague from New York had presented at a conference.

They said that the American's paper featured recently discovered documents revealing that a coven of supernatural creatures—who were rumored to drink human blood—had settled in New York before the Revolutionary War. Afraid of tarnished reputations, and wanting to avoid persecution, they'd kept their ancestry completely secret for hundreds of years.

The professors dismissed the discovery as a tall tale made up by Protestants to keep their parishioners in line, but their conversation had sparked something inside me. My intuition told me that I needed to change my plans—that there was a hint of truth behind that tale. Early America was a place where those who felt they had been persecuted for their religious beliefs had gone to seek freedom. It wouldn't be a stretch to think that maybe some people like me had ended up there for similar reasons. Maybe I could find some of them. New York, the mysterious city of dreamers and misfits, was calling me.

I had been a nomad for a long time, but my heart began to yearn for America. The same way it had told me to leave behind the Philippines, the place of my birth, in order to find my true home. But here I was, and I'd had no luck finding anyone like me yet. I have to accept that I may never find anyone like me. And that's why I need to keep my code of honor and work on making actual human friends. They might be the only chance I'll ever have to feel like I belong.

I walk toward the marble staircase that leads up to the humanities classrooms. The Duchesne School once belonged to Captain Armstrong Flood, an oil magnate, whose widow bequeathed their home to Mademoiselle Duchesne to open up the school. While some modern concessions have been made for the students, including rows of metal lockers lining the hallways, the original furnishings of the mansion are still here, which makes entering the building seem like stepping back into a slice of history. Honor, however, is in short supply at Duchesne, despite the fact so many students can trace their bloodlines all the way back to the founding of America. They are a closed circle; no one gets in.

A few paintings hang along the staircase wall. Three girls gossip beneath the life-size portrait of the Flood heiresses, their lips sparkling with gloss and sarcasm. Gemma Browne, the school's resident exposé-a-la-Instagram-photog, whispers something to Marnie Wilder, a senior girl who can't leave her house without wearing a pair of sky-high stilettos. They're both standing next to none other than Lilah, who, judging from the poorly veiled glare on her icy porcelain face, still hates me. Just my luck.

"You're back." Gemma snaps a pic. "For my Insta."

"Do you have to?" I grumble.

Gemma's eyes widen long enough for me to know I'm

under her skin. She ignores my comment anyway. "We sort of thought you might have transferred after . . ." She trails off, realizing she's about to stick her foot right into her mouth. She has to at least keep up the pretense of having manners. "We're glad you're back."

"Yeah. We're glad," Marnie adds. "Where were you? Bobby Livingston was looking for you. He had your diary. He said he found it in the art room."

I'm not dumb. I know already that they stole it. Once she discovered that the diary wouldn't open, Lilah must have discarded it for someone else to find and return. What's she after? Maybe she senses I have a double life, but there's no way she could suspect anything close to the truth. Before I knew what I really was, I didn't even think the superstitions of the villagers in my town were true. Lilah probably thinks I'm lying about my parents being dead and wants to figure out what I'm hiding so she can blackmail me.

"Thanks. I'll find him. You know I'd never think of leaving," I say. "My aunt is sick. I had to go home to take care of her."

Gemma nods unconvincingly. If she knew how much I love gorging on raw liver, she would probably puke all over her Chanel purse. What a sight that would be.

Lilah rolls her eyes. "Your aunt seems to get sick a lot," she says. "Didn't you use that excuse a couple weeks ago when she didn't come to back-to-school night?"

"She's old," I said. "Like you care about my aunt."

"If you really have an aunt," Lilah says with a raised eyebrow.

I hate her. I wish I could pop her eyeballs out of her head

and lick the blood in those sclera vessels clean. I'm about to give up the conversation and head upstairs for class when Mrs. Stratemeyer, one of the teachers, opens the front door.

"Aida." She says my name like I'm in trouble as she shakes the water off her umbrella. She's a stout woman with a strict demeanor. "Is your aunt feeling better?"

"Yes. Much better," I reply. "She's a fighter."

"That's nice to hear." Mrs. Stratemeyer takes a step up the stairs. "I'd love to meet her sometime. You should bring her to the next open house."

I nod. I'm not naturally a quiet person, but providing as little information as possible is the best way to keep a low profile. I'm beginning to doubt the feeling in my blood that I needed to come to New York City to stop running and settle down. This doesn't feel like home. Maybe I used the conversation I overheard at the library as an excuse, as a way to justify getting even farther away from the Philippines, the source of my anguish. Was I just running away from my grief over my mother's death and my anger at her for keeping secrets about our origins?

Mrs. Stratemeyer disappears up the stairs.

I breathe a sigh of relief, but Marnie is back in my face again. "Where were you, actually?" She's so close I can almost taste the blood being filtered through her kidneys.

"You're so mysterious," Gemma adds with enough sarcasm to make my veins throb.

Marnie pulls her purse up onto her shoulder and shifts her weight onto her left stiletto. "Everyone makes up stories about you," she says.

"What stories?" I ask.

"Just that you're probably one of . . ." Marnie trails off.

"You're obviously supersmart," Lilah says, picking up her cue to take over the conversation. "That's why you got into this school, but you don't really fit in. You disappear all the time. Where do you go, Aida? Are you hiding a secret life from us?"

"I'm a private person," I say. I'm almost not listening as I look at her leather miniskirt, the coffee spot on her suede ankle boots, and the mother-of-pearl buttons on her gauzy blouse that she actually buttoned all the way up to the collar for once.

"I just want to be one of the girls," I add.

"I've been meaning to ask," she says, her superwhite teeth flashing between burgundy lips. "Why don't you come out to the club tonight? We can get to know each other better. Maybe you won't seem so mysterious then."

Gemma and Marnie cringe. They definitely don't want me to hang out with them. Why's Lilah asking me to go out with her? Just to snoop on me? Is she trying to humiliate me? Anger surges through my blood. Why is she so interested in my life? I can sense something about her, but I can't figure out her motivation. It has to be something more than simply wanting to get dirt on me. These girls have no idea who I really am.

Or what I can do.

They should want to pet me like a kitty instead of cattle-prodding me with their snark. They wouldn't sass me if they knew I could deplete their blood supply. There's surprisingly little in the human body, even if you think there are rivers of the stuff flowing inside you. I can feel blood boiling inside of me, I need to burst, to fly, to take, to squeeze, to charm.

I have to get this under control. My heart pounds in my chest. I fantasize about ripping something apart. But I can't. I have a code to follow. I can't alienate myself again. Whatever my fate might be, I have to stay and figure out the course of my destiny this time. I can feel in my blood that this is my last chance to find my place.

"Yeah, I'll go," I say. "Where should I meet you?"

I love the night. I sometimes hover above clubs and wandering teens. I usually fly in the shadows like a great horned owl, spreading my wings, breathing the mist, tasting the scents. My senses are at their best right after a feeding. The blood kicks in and I can feel the city bustling with a kaleidoscopic variety of humanity.

I'm meeting Lilah at a nightclub called The Bank, on Houston Street, where the East Village turns into the Lower East Side, so I have to walk tonight. As I approach the decrepit stone building, I watch the clubbers prowl the streets in their slinky clothes and dark makeup like night crawlers. The desperate. The strange. The weird. So many types of blood coursing through the youth of this city. Now here I am darting through the streets after a feeding, a bloodletting, and I'm furious all over again, and alone.

I shake my head as I walk toward the entrance of the club, knowing Lilah and her friends are probably in there talking about me. I try to convince myself that the night won't be so bad. Maybe I can actually become friends with those girls. If things go poorly tonight, I can at least feed Lilah some lies about my past and throw her off my trail.

But then I look down.

There's a streak of blood on my clothes. I curse myself because I'm always so careful. So clean in my kills. Even as I gorge, I do so delicately. But this little sow, she struggled. She had a furious life in her, and I struck an artery that shot into my mouth with the rage of survival. That's what I love about life, about real blood-borne life, that every once in a while the fury, even from a pig, is strikingly surprising. I must not have been able to swallow fast enough.

Folding my arms in front of the bloodstain on my blouse, I walk toward the entrance. Two guys slam out of the front door onto the sidewalk and start punching each other. When the bouncer moves toward them to break up the fight, I take my chance and slip inside the club unnoticed. Trance music pulses as couples dance all around me.

As I rush through the dance floor toward the women's bathroom to wash the fresh blood off my shirt, I spot Lilah sitting at a table in the corner of the club. She's, strangely, not with Marnie or Gemma. Some seniors from Duchesne that I don't know well surround the table. I don't remember seeing Lilah hang out with them at school, but she seems pretty close to them now. They're leaning over the table, their heads close, talking to each other. Why did she invite these people? Who are they? Is she setting me up for something terrible?

Whatever her plans are for me, I have to get this stain out of my shirt. I finally reach the bathroom and open the door. I look around, hoping I won't have to explain myself. The coast is clear so I dart in and start washing the blood out of my blouse.

The rust-colored water is swirling down the drain when the door opens. It's Lilah. I think about hiding in the bathroom stall, but she's already standing next to me, and I realize there's no way I can avoid her. "Aida," she says. "Is that blood?"

"I cut myself," I say lamely.

"You cut your stomach? On the way to the club?" She raises a perfectly groomed eyebrow. It's a terrible lie, and she knows it. "Something's wrong with you."

"Clearly," I say, scrubbing the stain. "You don't need to point it out."

"It's so obvious," Lilah says, goading me. "I read your diary. It confirmed what I suspected the moment you walked in the door at Duchesne. You've been lying about who you are ever since you moved to New York. Haven't you?"

She must be bluffing. How could she have read my diary? No human could have possibly have broken the spell. I rear up, startled, and my eyes redden. I hate that her words have control over me, but I can't stop myself. I feel my fangs and claws taking shape as I lunge at her.

"I'd hurt you," I growl. "But I have a code of honor."

As I put my lips up to her neck to scare her, Lilah throws me off with a swipe of her arm. Me. An aswang with superhuman strength. She flings me aside like a rag.

I stumble into the edge of the sink.

"A code?" Lilah laughs. Her laughter sounds like a shriek, only not one of fear. "You think you're the only one with a code?" Is she mocking me?

"What are you talking about?" I ask.

Lilah walks toward me, her eyes flashing. "Pitiful creature."

I step farther away. "Stay there," I say. "You don't want me to get angry."

"I suppose not," Lilah says, looking at me in the mirror. "I've been watching you, wondering about you. And now I know the truth."

"What's that?" I grab my side, groaning in pain.

"That you're just like me," she says, revealing sharp fangs behind her burgundy lips, her eyes red and pink. "As soon as you arrived at Duchesne, I knew. You're one of us. A Blue Blood."

Staring at Lilah in disbelief, I take a moment to consider what she has just revealed. I had been searching for so long, following every rumor, reading every obscure document I could find about them, not that there were many to find. Just whispers here and there. But if she is telling the truth, then I had found the Blue Bloods, the once loyal army of angels who betrayed Lucifer during his epic war with God. Was she telling the truth? But how else could she have opened my diary? Or thrown me against the sink?

She is smiling, and in that smile, I recognize myself.

This is the moment I've been waiting for my entire life. This is my destiny. This is why my heart was leading me to New York. I had been lost to the bloodline all these years, but now I am home. There were stories that they'd been killed off by the Croatan long ago. But no, they are still here. The famed Blue Bloods of Manhattan.

Lilah notes the blood still on my shirt. "Use cold water, otherwise it'll stain," she says. "You have so much to learn. Welcome to the coven."

Aswangs

A Filipino Folktale

Growing up in the Philippines, I used to have nightmares about aswangs—scary vampire-like beings who flew around at night, their torsos separated from the rest of their bodies. They were always pictured in folktales as banshee-like beings, with blood frothing at their mouths and wild hair and bare breasts. They were terrifying.

So when I was asked to write a story for this collection based on a myth from a diverse culture, I thought immediately of the Filipino folktales I knew, and knew I had to write about a teenage aswang and connect this folktale to a story I've been telling for a long time, about teenage vampires in New York City.

—Melissa de la Cruz

BULLET, BUTTERFLY

ELSIE CHAPMAN

The latest illness and its slow recovery left them all bored and restless, and Liang ended up losing the bet.

He adjusted the cloak around his shoulders, the hooded scarf with its thick, fringed edging so that it covered more of his face. Raided from the ward's communal lost and found, both pieces had once belonged to a girl, making them perfect for his disguise.

"If I'm caught, you're all going down with me," he said as he headed for the door. He hoped his walk alone did not give him away—he moved about as gracefully as the city of Shangyu's old war tanks, the ones its army no longer used for good reason.

Propped up against pillows in his bunk across the room, Wei grinned. "You won't be caught, not with your build. And not with your face—too pretty by a long shot, you bastard."

Everyone they knew was thin, the product of a country at war with itself for decades, all its cities perpetually famished. But it was true that the lay of Liang's bones gave him a look more delicate than drawn. And it was both chance and laziness that he'd let his black hair grow long enough to wind into a braid so that it draped over his shoulder. His sister, he knew, would approve—she wore hers the same way.

Tao narrowed his eyes at Liang from his bed, considered him, and finally nodded, satisfied. "You might be making history managing to sneak inside, but don't forget to get back here in time for stats check."

"Don't worry," Liang said. They all had to remotely connect with the lab through the health monitors in their room twice each day, in the morning and at night. During the hours in between, patients were expected to rest in their beds and do little else.

"Let's just hope no one comes by to do a surprise visual check," Chen said from his top bunk as he sorted through his daily pills.

Wei scoffed from behind the book he was reading on the bunk below. "The lab's too busy with real patients to worry about now instead of us, considering our symptoms are hardly life threatening."

"True enough," Tao said. "And if someone *does* show—Liang, you'll just have to conveniently be in the washroom dealing with a bad meal."

Liang pulled open the door of their room. "Not hard to believe, considering I'm still physically recovering, right?"

"Also, we want souvenirs." Chen's expression was amused, but there was a challenge in his voice. "To prove you were really there."

Liang stepped out into the hall of the recovery ward. "Okay, I'll be back tonight—with a fresh bullet for each of you."

Outside of the city armory, he caught up with a group of girls headed toward the entrance. The guard on duty slid his eyes over Liang—cloak and scarf, long braid, a medical mask over his mouth—saw nothing unexpected, and motioned him through the metal gates.

The moment should have been profound, should have left him blown away.

After all, no other boy had ever been inside the armory before.

Boys were kept to the open land, to its streets and fields and riversides. They were to guard the great barbed fence that marked the outermost edges of the war-riddled city, rims of territory it refused to concede to its neighbors. Shangyu's army officials had long ago decided that boys, with their larger hands and sturdier builds, were best used for discharging weapons instead of producing them. *The strongest of poisons,* they said, *are made only stronger with efficiency.* They determined that girls—with their slimmer, more supple fingers, their slighter frames a more reasonable fit over the armory's low-moving assembly belts—would be assigned the dull task of production until they, too, were eventually moved onward, stationed as soldiers throughout Shangyu.

But as Liang stood there and absorbed as much of the

armory as he could, as fast as he could—crooked lengths of worktables, cages of black steel shelves and racks and hissing pipes; suspended loudspeakers buzzing with distorted instructions; the air, smelling of endless labor, of greased churning parts, of the dirt floor trodden into utter flatness by hundreds of feet of workers—he realized that, more than anything, he was disappointed.

This was the heart of Shangyu's forces, where the pulse of all its weapons was first set into beating—shouldn't the place have felt more . . . proud, somehow? Overwhelming, awe-inspiring, *majestic*, even? Instead there was a kind of fatigue within its walls, the place tired of its own purpose, a duty turned weary because it was sensing years of war still looming ahead. Liang wondered if Wei and Tao and Chen would even believe him when he returned with his report that night.

The commanders keep telling us we're so close to finishing the war, he thought—more than aware that his own father was one of those commanders—*that it's almost the end—but whose end?*

Just as he muffled a cough, a hand suddenly landed at his elbow, guiding him forward through the room.

"Come with me," a girl's voice said laughingly into his ear, "since you're just standing here, anyway. Which means you're new, and I'm saving you from being assigned to either the melters or the molds, where everyone's fingers always get burned—bullet metal gets so hot it's almost like ice, if you can believe that."

Liang found himself at one of the worktables, watching as the teenaged girl—black hair atop her head in a thick, shiny whorl, freckled gold skin, unmasked mouth rubbed bright with crimson dye—showed him how to roll fire bombs the size of lychee nuts into bundles to be marked for distribution. Her hands in their fingerless gloves were as deft as bird wings, moving so surely that his own felt more than awkward, would feel that way even if his joints weren't still slightly inflamed from his recent illness. Her voice was lilting and smooth and patient. Sharply tilted eyes crinkled at the corners as they roamed over his face, making it even harder for him to concentrate when his nerves were already jumping.

Focus! his group commander had bellowed in his face more than once, spittle a suspended haze between their faces. *Focus marks your target! Lack of it marks you as one!*

Liang already knew one thing—the girl was about a thousand times more pleasant to have standing in front of him than his commander.

"My name is Zhu," she told him as they worked at the table, side by side.

"I'm . . . Lin," he lied. He rolled more bombs, hiding the lingering stiffness of his fingers. Irritation flared—he didn't miss the irony of his hands being the last to recover now that he needed them most of all.

"How long do you have left in here?" she asked. "I'm sixteen, so just one year to go. Then it's the open land for me, or a stretch of fence, armed with bullets I likely poured for myself right here in the armory." Zhu smiled, and Liang felt it somewhere in his chest, a drum starting to find its proper beat.

"I'm sixteen, too," he said. "So the same. One more year." The truth, though: he would be stationed as soon as army doctors deemed him fit to fight.

Another red-lipped grin, and the bomb in his hand nearly tipped to the ground.

"Whoops." Zhu swiftly plucked the bomb from the edge of the table to keep it from rolling off and placed it back in his palm. She blinked her midnight eyes again and Liang cursed his pulse for skipping. Years of training, of being groomed for war, with only these final months of recovery left before they stationed him—the last thing he needed was to want to know this girl.

"If you want to see fire that badly"—she took him by the hand and led him from their table, still full of bombs—"then I was wrong to keep you away."

Liang made his way back to the recovery ward, his braid loosened into messy waves, stolen cloak and scarf pulled tight around him against the early spring evening wind.

The night around him was aglow with distant gunfire, swollen with the stench of smoke.

His mind was filled with Zhu.

His pocket, with death.

Their fingers were scalded red afterward, just as she'd warned. But still they caught the silver bullets as they'd tumbled out of their molds, already smelling of copper and blood.

"The armory's newest design," she told him. "A cocoon, a *disguise*. Shot deep into a soldier, the bullet then unfurls into the shape of a butterfly. Imagine it, Lin—metal wings, shredding apart a heart, or an artery, or a lung, before spinning out of the body in pieces." Zhu's voice lowered to a hush. "It will be beautiful, and at the same time, absolutely terrible." Her words came simply, without feeling or opinion or judgment—war left room for none of those.

"Why a butterfly?" he asked.

"Since a butterfly is supposed to be a symbol of freedom, right?" The bullet in Zhu's fingers glinted as she turned it slowly in the armory's flickering light. "And a symbol of love? *Young* love?"

Liang's face heated as her eyes lifted and met his. "Sure, that."

Her expression dimmed as though she'd wanted a different answer. She shrugged, and for a second, he saw how she would look as an old woman. One weathered by time, by the fortunes and misfortunes of life.

"That's why we chose it, I suppose," she said. "Because what do either of those things—freedom, love—matter when it comes to this war, for us here as its soldiers? They don't, at all."

As he strode into their room at the recovery ward, his friends sat up in their beds, tossing books and letters and cards to the side. Immediately they began to yell at him for details.

Computers?

Robots?

Machines so sleek, there's no way we can lose this war, just as they keep telling us?

Liang recalled the armory's oil-soaked surfaces, the hot stink of flame. He thought of the grim and relentless turning of thousands of gears and cogs, of work-roughened fingers and thumbs.

"Not quite." He fished the bullets from his pocket and tossed one to each of his friends. "But as promised, souvenirs—and proof."

Chen whistled as he held his bullet beneath his lamp, admiring its new, near-liquid shine. "And the girls?" he asked, grinning.

He was already engaged, dealt away to a girl from Keqiao in the southwest, whose family owned large chunks of that district's farmland. The alliance was part of Shangyu's plans to reestablish the import of meat. But Chen had yet to meet her, had no clue what she looked like or *was* like: his loyalty to the arrangement lay in his duty to his family and not much else.

Liang laughed. "They were there."

"And?"

And there was only one girl who mattered, he thought as he flopped down on his bunk, suddenly unmindful of his sore joints and the pieces of his disguise still wound around him. "I'm going back."

Wei lifted a brow, and Tao laughed.

"One more day, then?" Chen tossed his bullet into the empty medicine cup still beside his pillow.

Liang nodded.

But one more day became two, then three. Then a week.

Other illnesses came to the city, their names ugly and unnatural, lapping over Shangyu in relentless waves and lingering behind like poisonous salt leached from a mysterious and dangerous sea: blue fever, numb throat, K3L3. News reached the recovery ward of classrooms where coughing was as incessant as a strong wind, of the pharmacies selling jars and bottles even less than half full now, of doctors who had begun to accept only food as payment, of more and more farms being looted of their crops and animals. It was yet another truth of their at-war world—that as much as China's warring cities were threats to one other, they all shared the enemies of illness and starvation, in the agonizingly slow production of medicine and the constant shortage of healing, nourishing food. *Felled by our own flesh, by our own soil,* Shangyu's officials lamented, *and yet we will continue to fight for both.*

For Liang's family, life went on as it always had. After his mother developed a persistent fever, his little sister was bartered away to a family in the north of Shangyu—two months of her labor in their kitchen in exchange for a tiny basket of medication. His mother recovered in a few days and returned to her medic station in the fields. His father agreed to a temporary truce with Yuecheng in the west—for a year of peace along that stretch of the border, Liang's older brother would marry a daughter of one of Yuecheng's commanders. Children, if they eventually came, would prove useful as future trade goods.

In the ward, Wei recovered first, then Tao, and then Chen. One by one they moved out, handfuls of days apart, until only Liang remained. Without an influx of sufferers fresh to their illness—he and his friends had fallen sick during its last throes—he was left free of new roommates, even as the rest of the ward remained bustling. Good-bye to reading passages out loud from books, card games with rules no one seemed to follow, and conversations that ran on long past lights out, ones as much about nothing as they were about everything; hello to guns and bombs and the rest of their lives as soldiers.

The ache in Liang's joints eased and he had fewer

medications to take. His cough went from stubborn to sporadic, and he stopped wearing a medical mask. He got better at braiding his hair. The clothing raided from the lost and found grew grimy, so he went back and stole more. He continued to fool the armory's guards and security cameras, and aside from Zhu, he was careful to stay away from the girls. His friendlessness kept him a mystery. And safe.

By the time he realized Zhu was as much a danger in her own way, weeks had passed, and it was too late. She didn't question his shyness, only understood that it was him. She'd grab him by the hand and guide him through the workings of each area of the armory until he knew them as well as she did. She'd show him the quietest parts of the whole place, where she liked to eat away from the worst of the fires and heat and metal, in the slivers of space still secret from the guards and cameras. And—as they shared soldier-grade meals of gritty bread, coarse meat, or rice that had the odd stone in it to break a tooth if one didn't notice it in time—she'd slowly reveal to him who she was.

I have a sister, she's the pretty one of the family, and the nicest. I got better grades while we were still in school, though. My mom says I have a bad temper. I used to ask for mandarin oranges for my birthday, until I finally realized I was asking for the impossible.

Liang did the same, as much as he could.

I have a sister and a brother. My parents are both in the fields. Stations along the fence are the most dangerous, but I don't think I'd mind too much—at least you get to see out past the city. Things I haven't tasted since I was little—persimmons, dragon eyes, star fruit.

Eventually it seemed they were speaking of nearly everything—the rumors of Shengzhou in the south secretly bottling illnesses and disease for use as future weapons; that Shangyu's long-fragile truce with Yuyao to the east was on the verge of collapse; how before they died they each wanted to see a star that was naked and unveiled of gun smoke, to eat a handful of real sugar, to fall asleep truly full. And as their fingers worked steadily beneath the armory's soot-stained ceiling—over its endlessly winding belts, beside its fires throwing writhing shadows on their arms—she touched him casually, then trustingly, making his blood sing at her nearness.

She got to him like a fever.

At the end of each workday, Liang would make his way back to the recovery ward, his head full of her thoughts and ideas and scent, his tongue imagining her taste as he drank up the sound of her voice to keep it from fading.

That was how it was. How it happened. How over the pouring and casting and unmolding of thousands of butterfly bullets, over days of their hands working together and around each other, he fell in love with her. And she remained clueless that the girl she declared she loved as her best friend was, in reality, a boy.

So it began to consume him, both the need to let her know and his fear of her reaction, of being discovered by someone else at the armory. Because only one thing rivaled respect for one's family, and that was respect for Shangyu's army—to make fools of its top commanders was punishable by death.

For Liang's deceit, the city would string him up from the great barbed fence and bellow for its street crows to feed, for its citizens to see and remember they were soldiers first and humans last.

And yet.

Liang's heart hurt with wanting Zhu, and it became a game of self-torture—the hints he let drop, the half-truths he told, wanting her to guess who he was, so his being discovered was no longer his choice to make. Did that make him a coward, when he'd been trained to look into the eye of any enemy and smile while shooting?

He sketched for her a pair of mandarin ducks. His ever-scalded finger pulled clumsily through the thick layer of silver dust that had collected on the surfaces of the armory's melters, drew lines in the small, snowlike drifts that formed on the edges of the pots and molds.

"Look, it's us," he said as he finished his drawing. The ducks were the Chinese symbol for lifetime love between a man and woman, when the death of one meant sure impending death for its mate.

"Except we're not a couple that way." Zhu smiled as she rolled just-cooled bullets into packets and sent them down the chute to be distributed. "But find a symbol of forever friendship, and *I'll* draw it for *you*, Lin."

Liang cradled fresh metal so that it singed his palm, but he barely felt the pain. "And if one day I woke up a boy?" His voice was huskier than it should have been, and he cleared it, lifted it. "Because of a magic spell of some kind, maybe? And because I was in love?" *How about that, Zhu? Could you love me, then?*

She hissed, a bullet burning her hand in turn, and tears came to her eyes as the fiery metal fell to the ground. "Boys or girls, friends or lovers," Zhu murmured as she inspected her palm, "it wouldn't matter. Don't forget we're only ever soldiers here in Shangyu, and soldiers never get to be the ones who wake up from a spell, or who even get to *break* a spell. We're just the dragons guarding the gate, ordered to keep breathing the fire of those who cast the spell in the first place."

Before Liang could stop to think, he took her hand and slowly pressed his mouth to the wound. She went still, and he felt questions jolt through her even as her breath caught—*Lin? A kiss? What?*—but before he could make himself release her and step away, she suddenly curled her fingers around his, holding tight.

"Promise me, Lin," she said, "that wherever we end up stationed, we'll stay alive long enough to find each other again, to be friends always."

He nodded. It was all he could do. His throat was full, his skin hot where it touched hers.

"Good." Zhu dropped his hand with the bleakest of smiles, which didn't crinkle up her eyes at all but instead left them hollow and too dark. And they went back to work.

To Liang, it felt as though they were casting strange spells of their own, with each bullet they unmolded and caught and packaged. That with each silver butterfly they encased in a shiny cocoon, they were asking it to sleep forever, and wishing for more time, and begging death to wait.

Then Liang stopped coughing.

It took his mother calling him through the room's old intercom to wake him up since he'd slept through the incoming message on his health monitor. As an army medic, his mother was transmitted the news from the lab at the same time—that he was fully recovered, and that he'd been stationed in the south of the city, guarding a piece of land left vacant by a newly killed soldier. More details would come, but in the meantime, he was to prepare to leave the recovery ward.

Thunder sounded in his ears and turned his pulse uneven as he waited outside the armory for Zhu that evening. He felt raw, exposed—still sick, even—as the late summer wind blew through his old T-shirt and the jeans he was just starting to fill out again; he'd worn neither beyond the walls of the ward during his months of recovery, of lying. And he'd already returned all the raided clothes so they were once again lost, no longer found. Only his long hair in its braid remained, and he planned on cutting it later that night. Still, he hoped it would be enough to let him reveal his secret before it revealed him.

Liang dreaded telling Zhu, yet he wanted nothing more.

She emerged from the armory, her bun a high crown of shadow, lifting her deft bird-wing hands to cover a dusty cough before lowering them to smooth down the front of her shirt.

He met her halfway up the hill. "Zhu." His *heart* felt like a bird, full of flight and air and cautious, suspended things.

Through the dim of late dusk, he watched her eyes skim over his unfamiliar clothing, the clash of it with his braid, the suddenly low boom of his voice. They filled with confusion. "Lin?"

He took a deep breath and stepped closer—Zhu appeared flushed, her breaths coming in light rasps—and slowly he pushed his hair away from his face. "My name isn't Lin; it's really Liang."

"No, you . . ." She wavered, her careful hands clenching as they darted to hide in her trouser pockets. Beneath the flush, he thought her skin pale, the shade of bared bone. "Who are you? Where was Lin today? She's a girl, and you—you're—"

"I'm me," Liang said again, simply, softly. He wondered how she couldn't hear the pounding of his heart as he spoke, so loud it had to be bending the air around them, a land mine going off and carving haloes into the earth. "I'm sorry I lied. I've been sick, and living in the recovery ward. Sneaking into the armory dressed as a girl . . . it was a bet—"

"What?" Zhu shook her head, confusion still in her eyes even as anger began to grow. "A *bet*?"

"I wanted to tell you, but— Zhu, I'm no longer sick. Which means I have to leave. I've been stationed, and—"

"This whole time, a game. You— Why, Lin?" He heard her breathe, her air catching. "*Liang*."

"It was only meant to be for one day, but then I met you, and—I had to come back. Again. And again. Zhu, I love you. I—"

She turned and ran.

And Liang could not blame her.

His mother called back later that evening with the rest of the details, her voice set. As he listened to her read aloud over the intercom the new terms of the alliance, he stared numbly around his nearly emptied room, at the suitcase at the foot of his bunk already packed and ready for departure.

Liang hadn't thought it possible—that his heart, already hurting over Zhu, could hurt even more.

Why did you have to be that dead soldier in the south, Chen? To leave behind the girl who was promised to you?

"Liang, are you still there?" Suddenly his mother sounded exhausted instead of hardened. "It's sudden, I know, with the ceremony still set for next week. But the alliance will prove beneficial for both families, and it needs to take place quickly."

"Of course." He also knew he had no choice, whatever the circumstances—for his family and for Shangyu, his loyalty could never waver. "I'll leave first thing in the morning."

The knock came as soon as he hung up. When he opened the door, there was Zhu, standing in the hall. He was speechless, helpless, his mind gone blank.

"Just so you know, I love you, too," she said in a rush. Her midnight eyes glittered, seeming almost fevered, and she laughed as she stepped closer. She touched his newly shorn hair, the back of his freshly exposed neck, and encircled him with her arms. "Boy or girl, Lin or Liang, it's *you* I love, okay? And like this."

Her kiss went through him, melting him. Liang silently begged for time to stop as he held her mouth with his own.

But time couldn't stop, because the war wouldn't. And he was a soldier.

He slowly pulled away. "Zhu, we can't."

Color bloomed high on her cheeks. "Still a game, Liang?"

"I've been traded away," he said quietly, "to marry the betrothed of a friend just killed in the fields. My father is the commander who oversaw the original alliance, and he's arranged that I marry in my friend's place."

Zhu fell back into the hall. Liang's heart wrenched.

"No," she whispered. "Break the arrangement."

They both knew it was impossible—they were, after all, who they'd been born to be. Soldiers, first and foremost.

"I love you, Zhu." His voice was a husk. "Always, no matter what."

She began to move away, and he wanted to yank her back, wanted what he could not have.

"Liang, I—" Her flushed cheeks were wet as she turned to run. "Good-bye."

Only after she'd been gone for long, long moments could he move again.

Later that week, on the morning of his wedding—as Yuyao declared its truce with Shangyu over and promised immediate invasion, as Liang adjusted the faded silk tie that had once belonged to his father in the mirror and tried not to think or feel—a letter arrived for him at the door.

Zhu, dead.

A new infection. It started with fever and ended with flesh turning to ash at a touch.

The sickness had cut through her as swiftly as a blade.

Her best friend would need to know, her parents had written, relaying their daughter's dying words, so he would never have to wonder. She'd left him a note, they wrote, and Liang tore open the accompanying letter with shaking hands, soaking up her words with eyes that ached.

I love you, Liang.

We'll find each other again, when the war is over.

Butterflies defy gravity, so maybe they can defy death, too.

The world swayed as images of Zhu as he last saw her—pale beneath the flush, eyes too bright—flashed through his mind. The letter fluttered to the floor as Liang staggered out of his house and down the road, toward the city's long-plundered depths. His heart went to tinder and splintered into shards; his mind wrapped into a knot of grief.

He did not feel the thunder of careening war tanks—*Sleek, silver, so much faster than the old ones!* his commander had screamed in delight at seeing them for the first time—shaking the ground beneath his father's old shoes that Liang had done his best to polish; he did not hear the sharp crack of gunfire closing in from the east, from just beyond Shangyu's border; he did not understand that his tears were also from the fresh smoke that blanketed the air and blocked the sight of the land's mountains. People ran along the sidewalks, medical masks over their faces tinged a dull gray from the grit in the air. The city smelled sour and unwell and lost.

Liang wondered, vaguely, if he'd fallen sick, too. If his and Zhu's final kiss had held more than love and desperation and the wish for what could not be. Wouldn't that explain why his chest ached as though choked with fever? Why his eyes hurt as they combed the streets and saw nothing but her?

Zhu, I love you! Please tell me this is just a deception of your own!

He reached the old temple—war-ravaged, its roof half gone, walls and windows punctured through—and staggered inside. With hands that were once again clumsy—*her hands, deft as birds*—he began to look through the rows of the dead on the floor awaiting their final restful fire. Those of the order would arrive soon to strike their matches, to utter their last prayers.

When Liang found her, his low cry rippled through the air, an ugly parody of the wedding bells for which he had dressed in his worn suit and old silk tie. He slowly and carefully crawled into the hollow formed by her long-stiffened arms.

Zhu's lips dissolved into ash beneath his. Flakes drifted down Liang's throat and covered his heart, stopping its beating as it, too, became ash.

Outside, a group of children ran home to hide from Yuyao's attack. They halted in their tracks as something like smoke began to billow from the temple's gaping roof. The children were silent in their awe as they watched the gray climb and twist, their hands lifting so they could point. *Look.*

A pair of silver butterflies, their shapes formed by two swirls of ash, dancing upward into the sky.

The Butterfly Lovers

A Chinese Folktale

One of China's four great folktales, "Liang Zhu"—"The Butterfly Lovers," in English—is the tragic tale of two young lovers kept apart by familial duty. Often considered the Chinese *Romeo and Juliet* since both stories feature star-crossed lovers, "The Butterfly Lovers" takes place during the Eastern Jin Dynasty (265–420 CE) and grows into legend mostly through the ancient art of oral storytelling. At nearly two thousand years old, it has inspired other forms of art such as operas, plays, movies, and music.

The only daughter of a wealthy family, Zhu Yingtai disguises herself as a boy in order to be allowed to attend school. There she meets Liang Shanbo, and the two classmates quickly become best friends. As the years pass, Zhu falls in love with Liang, and only after she leaves school to attend her ailing father does Liang discover the secret of his friend's disguise. Realizing he loves her in return, he goes to seek her hand in marriage and is devastated to find out her family has already promised her to another. Liang soon dies of a broken heart, and Zhu mourns her lost love. On the morning of her wedding, there is a terrible storm, and as she weeps at Liang's grave, thunder shakes open the ground where her dead lover rests. Determined to once again be with Liang, Zhu jumps inside his grave. When the storm subsides, the earth opens to reveal the lovers transformed into butterflies, flying away to be together forever.

Just how deep can loyalty run when it comes to family or one's land? What if an army and war make the rules instead of wealth and class? When does love go from forbidden to dangerous?

"Bullet, Butterfly" is my retelling of "The Butterfly Lovers."

—Elsie Chapman

DAUGHTER OF THE SUN

SHVETA THAKRAR

For the enchanted Sisterhood of the Moon,
glowing ever bright, growing ever bold

Savitri Mehta's parents had named her for light. For sunshine and ingots and all things gold. Above all, for the sun god Savitr, or Surya, whose blessing marked Savitri at the moment of her birth: behind her rib cage, she carried not a beating heart but a ball of Surya's own blazing yellow light.

The Mehtas served as caretakers for a museum on a former rana's secluded estate, palatial in its wealth of flourishing trees, rain-summoning peacocks, and even a lake surrounded by a pine needle–sprinkled sandy shore, and it was there they retired with their unusual child. Though they and their small staff strove to keep her from sight, the occasional visitor caught

Savitri slipping around corners, clothed all in black. Child-sized onyx chaniya choli, frilly frocks, and little bows. Later, when she grew, charcoal minidresses with locks of purple streaking her inky hair. Black with dragon's-blood-red lipstick against her rich brown skin. Black with silver studs lining her earlobes and a bindi to match.

Black, always black—surely, whispered those adult patrons year after year, she was troubled, despairing, in need. Why else would any girl be so consistently drawn to shadows? The visitors her age were more candid, more cruel: *Oh, look, a baby goth. She just wants to be sad. What a drama queen.*

Year after year, her parents laughed these comments off. Without black, they reminded her, how could she disguise her glow? In reply, Savitri's merry laugh, too, rang out. Yet once she was alone in the forest, her chuckles faded. Even a radiant heart could not burn away loneliness.

She spent her days far from the secured tourist walkways, tucked instead beneath the bowers of branches where she had once discovered a curtain of honeysuckle vines in perennial bloom. With dessert spoon and jar of homemade honeysuckle syrup in hand, she roamed, listening always to the buzzing of the honeybees.

Yellow and black like her, they droned profound secrets for those who knew how to hear them, and Savitri did. She learned all manner of things this way, such as how to be loyal for the greater good, that the sky changed color because its attendants continually traded out the different silk saris it wore, and, best of all, how to sing.

She sang for her parents, for the hue-switching heavens,

for herself. She read fairy tales, epics, and legends and imagined performing them on a stage draped in velvet. But it wasn't enough. She longed for a friend.

"What makes my heart so scary?" Savitri asked the bees one summer afternoon. She was now old enough to know the way she lived wasn't normal, that most people had companions who spoke in words, and that most people's parents didn't isolate them from what they insisted was a harsh, intolerant world.

Few nowadays care for magic, daughter of the sun. The bees paused in their inspection of the honeysuckle vines to flit around her. *Your kind often fears what it does not understand.*

The miniature sun in Savitri's chest ached. It flared, sending warm golden beams out her collar and along the straps of her ebony top. She crossed her arms, but still the luminescence spilled out.

Sensing her distress, the bees gathered around in a halo. Hers, they promised, was a heart meant to be shared with one who could not only bear her light but would even reflect it back at her.

One day, whispered the fairy tales, the epics, the legends all, one day, there would be such a person.

In gold, added an eavesdropping dragonfly. *Everything in gold, in silver.*

Before Savitri could press it for details, it had flown away, a burst of blue-green stained glass on the wind.

Years passed, and Savitri's well of patience had run dry. She was tired: tired of hiding, tired of only ever witnessing the outside world through movies and television and snatches of tourists' conversations. She dreamed of birthday parties with girls her age, of trading confessions like clothes, of dancing on a stage. What would it be like to sing her way down a crowded, mica-speckled city street, to wear black only because she chose to?

She yearned for someone who didn't fear her brilliance. She yearned, she yearned, oh, how she yearned.

Even the gardens with their bowers of honeysuckle and their bees grew smaller and smaller, overfamiliar, until Savitri could barely breathe. Her sun heart threatened to break through her skin and limn the entire estate if nothing changed. No amount of black, whether pitch or raven, would be able to suppress it.

On the night before her seventeenth birthday, when the yearning had grown too strong to dismiss, she resolved to sneak out and sample the world for herself.

Once her parents were asleep, Savitri packed a small bag with a shawl, some cash, and a jar of syrup with a spoon. A small section of the former rana's manor was available for rent to visiting historians, yet all the rooms but one sat vacant. She checked to make sure the visitors, a family of travel-weary researchers and their teenage son she'd only seen from afar, were snugly settled in. They seemed to be. That left only the evening receptionist at his desk in the lobby, where an ancient fan whirred overhead almost loudly enough to cover the clatter of his keyboard. The back door it would have to be.

But just as she reached the exit, the door clicked shut.

Had someone else been there? Savitri shivered as she

murmured a quick prayer to the marble murti of Lord Ganesh, remover of obstacles. Then she followed on tiptoe.

Outside, the sky had donned its sari of smoke and stars, the bees and dragonflies slumbered, and the crickets' choir had begun its nocturnal serenade. Savitri's skin tingled with the thrill of being alive, of surveilling a stranger in the dark, and of course she needed no flashlight to make her way through the gloom, not when all she had to do was unbutton her collar.

Feeling dangerous, she stripped down to her tank top, tied her shirt about her waist, and ran.

The rush of sunlight dazzled even her own eyes, so it took her a minute to notice the surface of the lake. It twinkled with stars and with swans. Swans? She'd never seen them here before.

The swans shimmered in the darkness, as if lit by their own inner radiance. Graceful necks arched high, they formed a semicircle. Savitri crept closer. They were singing!

And at the edge of the water, his attention on the swans, knelt a boy.

Savitri very nearly missed him at first, for he blended into the night. He even sported a scrap of it, a beautiful black sherwani trimmed with silver that set off the warm brown of his cheeks.

"Satyavan," sang the swans, the words like the dulcet strum of sitar strings. "Satyavan, come home."

Satyavan. Savitri caught her breath at the name. She shouldn't have unveiled her sunshine. Any second now, he would turn and spot her.

Any second. This was foolish. She should run.

Yet she stayed put and studied him, trapped in an eternity of anticipation, as the swans sang on, their voices melodic and enchanting, summoning him.

Satyavan slipped the tunic over his head and tossed it to the ground. Savitri must have made a sound, because in the next moment, he spun around.

The boy from the manor! The boy she'd thought asleep in his room.

His stare met hers, fitting together like a riddle and its answer.

Something opened between them, a bejeweled path. The future glittered there, mapped out in brilliant-cut gemstones, green and purple, orange and blue, and soldered in promise. This boy. She saw him there, in that future where she knew the taste of his mouth, the shape of his soul. He was hers, and she, his.

Who *was* he? This boy with eyes so dark they were almost black. Black like kajal. Black like mystery. Why was he here? Her heart flashed, highlighting the lake and the handsome boy standing before it.

"Satyavan," called the swans once more, "Satyavan, come home." One left the water and gleamed, and where a bird had been, on the sand now glided an apsara. The celestial dancer's lovely face twisted in irritation. "Leave us, foolish girl. This is not for you."

"What's not for me?" Savitri asked, more intrigued than insulted. Not even the apsara's otherworldly, beguiling beauty could wrench her gaze from Satyavan's.

Instead of answering, the apsara glared at Satyavan. "Come

now. My tolerance for this game runs low."

But Satyavan smiled at Savitri. "Your light," he said.

Her heart beat fiercely, sending golden rays over the lake until it was bright as day. A breath later, his bare chest began to glow, too—a soft silver like moonbeams.

The winged creatures' prophecy: When the time was right, she would find the one who would reflect her light back at her, in gold and in silver. As if, she realized now, the moon harnessed the heat of the sun and returned it as a cool caress.

By the combined glint of moon and sun and the stars above, she saw confusion, then recollection, cross his features.

The apsara grabbed Satyavan's shoulders and shook him. "Fool! I'm trying to free you!" She turned a pleading face to Savitri. "Enough. Time grows short. Let us go."

Satyavan extricated himself from her hold. "Just a minute, Rambha."

"You do not understand!" Rambha cried. "There is no time." She gestured wildly toward the water. "Come now, or your brothers and I must leave without you."

Satyavan's face contorted as frustration, dread, and excitement all warred there. "You're right," he said at length, his voice oddly detached. As Savitri watched, he swam out into the lake—and vanished beneath the dark surface.

Her curiosity corroded into panic when he failed to reappear. One minute passed, two, then three. He was drowning! Why was the apsara just sitting there on the shore, calm as the lake that had swallowed him?

Savitri flung off her shoes, dropped her bag, and sprinted after Satyavan.

"Stop!" cried the apsara. "This boy is no boy but a devata, one of eight divine sons of Chandra, our lunar lord, cursed by a rishi to be reborn as a mortal to a family who cannot properly care for him."

But it was too late. Savitri held her breath and dove into the lake, tracking the silver trail of light through the murky waters until she located Satyavan's suspended form. The apsara's words registered only as she emerged into the air, Satyavan safely in her grasp.

The apsara herself loomed over the water, hands fisted at her sides, her ethereal splendor no less seductive for her ire. "I begged to soften the curse," she hissed. "At last the sage compromised: After seventeen years, each devata might drown, thus giving up this mortal form, and find his way home. The others ride with my sisters now; this one was prepared to join them." Her spite coiled like a snake into her next sentence. "Until *you* ruined it."

The remaining swans had already ascended into the clouds, and now the shades of the seven devata brothers could be seen mounted on their sleek, feathered backs. They melted as one into the moonlight.

"I was to bring him back," the apsara spat, each word a bitter barb. "He cannot survive in this world of tears and tragedy. He will last perhaps a year, his suffering growing each day, and then expire. I hope you are pleased." She raised both arms, feathers sprouting down their lengths, and once fully bird, took flight.

Savitri dragged Satyavan's dripping form to the shore, where she let the warmth of her sun heart dry them both. Soon he opened his eyes. "You saved me."

In that moment, she forgot her dreams of performing onstage. She forgot her urge to flee. She forgot everything but an end to her loneliness. A son of the moon for a daughter of the sun. Surely it was no coincidence.

"Stay," said Savitri, and the single syllable sounded of longing, curiosity, and wonder. Now she would learn the taste of his mouth, the shape of his soul. She fed him dollops of her honeysuckle syrup. "You can't die. I won't let you."

"Keep feeding me whatever that is," agreed Satyavan, licking the spoon clean, "and I'll stay here forever!"

When he gazed at her, humor giving way to something deeper, the moon in his black eyes illuminated the bejeweled path they would walk together.

They spent the remainder of the night talking and passing the jar of syrup back and forth, until the spoon became their fingers, and licking their fingers became feeding each other. They spoke of stories, of favorite movies, of fashion. They argued and agreed and argued again, until the sky changed its clothes once more, and then they hurried back onto the estate.

Satyavan, it turned out, remembered nothing about the apsaras who had come to claim him and his brother devatas or even why he'd gone to the lake in the first place; he knew only that Savitri, who lived in the former rana's manor, had rescued him from a lethal midnight swim.

Savitri, however, hadn't forgotten anything—certainly not the apsara's warning—but she kept it to herself. After all, she had a year to find an answer.

And a year to get to know this boy she'd instantly recognized.

❖❖❖

After breakfast had been served and cleared away, Savitri took Satyavan to her private arbor and read him fairy tales and illustrated volumes of myth. In return, he recited bawdy ballads and built her a sword out of twigs. At last, even adrenaline wasn't enough to keep them up, and so they napped, curled around each other, heads cradled on a bed of moss, and watched over by the nectar-hunting bees, who continued to buzz confidences for those with the ears to hear.

A week passed in this way. It took little to convince Satyavan's parents to extend their trip another fortnight. The shift in his mood from gloomy to gregarious was all the impetus they needed. When at last they left, they made arrangements for Satyavan to stay on as a guest of the estate, provided he study for his board exams while there. "I don't know what you did," Satyavan's mother said to Savitri, "what magic you used, but I've never seen him so happy."

Savitri only smiled. *I chose him*, she thought. It was what she'd told her own parents.

They'd exchanged a frown. "Are you sure that's wise? This stranger? Does he know—"

"Yes," she said firmly. She didn't add how once she turned eighteen, board exams or no, Satyavan and she would run away to the city and wear gold and silver and sing for their suppers. How they had already begun to compose their own show. She didn't want to think about her birthday. There was time for that yet.

And so the months passed, made bright and sweet with lighted diyas, rainbow rangoli, and silver leaf–topped treats for

Deepavali; tossed colors and mischief for Holi; and parties and songs and picnics and horror-movie marathons for everything else. Savitri strung fairy lights in their bower, where they shared honeysuckle kisses and debated philosophy and nibbled on the savory snacks Satyavan made in the kitchen.

"I never met anyone I could fight with like you," he said wonderingly one sunny afternoon as they sat in the bower, notepads in hand, honeybees humming above, and debated adding an extra line to a song in their show. "It's fun! It makes me think about what I really believe and not just what I thought I did."

"I like it, too," Savitri admitted. "But Himanshu still doesn't need that extra line, sorry." She nestled against Satyavan's side.

"Yes, he does. If he doesn't say anything, it sounds like he doesn't care Anjali's just leaving him behind."

"No, it doesn't. He's so shocked that she would abandon him, he can't speak. His heart's breaking." Savitri wrinkled her nose at him. "It's pathos."

Satyavan mirrored the gesture. "Extra line. Let me have it, and you can have Anjali's bonus solo."

"Fine," said Savitri, and pouted. But her heart shone, belying her grumpiness.

"I was so bored before you came along; you have no idea." Satyavan put down his notepad and stroked her hair. "I just wanted to disappear."

Guilt slid between Savitri's ribs like a sharp blade. She should tell him the real reason he'd felt that way. But what if once he knew, he left?

She couldn't stand to be alone again, not after she'd

found the person who both reflected her *and* whose silly jokes never failed to make her laugh and her parents groan, whose knowledge of everything from medieval banana-tree harvesting techniques to obscure regional-cooking lore astounded her, whose intuitive understanding of music stirred her own inner melody.

Not when she still yearned to kiss Satyavan in the rain, the droplets drenching their clothes and making them huddle closer. To accompany him on a butterfly walk at the estate's newly installed conservatory and choose their favorites. To perform their completed show in public while shining like the sun, while glowing like the moon—to be magic, unfettered, unmasked, for the whole world to see.

Yes, she should tell him. She knew that.

Instead, she watched the calendar and reassured herself there was still time.

The apsara's warning never came to pass; month after month, Satyavan remained in perfect health. He even maintained his studies as promised. Savitri never saw Rambha again, either. Maybe, she thought, she'd been worried for nothing.

She began to relax. To focus on the last few songs left in their show. To dream again about the bejeweled path.

But one day, while Savitri began chopping onions for lunch, Satyavan, humming a few bars from Anjali's unfinished lament, went out to the garden to dig up some carrots and cut a handful of cilantro. It should only have taken minutes.

When he didn't come back, Savitri set aside her knife, rinsed her hands, and went outside to call for him. No one answered, and when she reached the garden, it was deserted.

Just in case, she checked the bower. The bees swarmed, busily gathering the delicate drops of nectar within each honeysuckle blossom. Satyavan had not been there, they informed her, but did she know some wild lilacs had sprung up nearby?

Savitri's heart flared with fear and pain. The sky shared her sentiment, dressed as it was in a sari gray as mourning doves. She knew exactly where he'd gone. The lake.

She ran as hard and fast as she could, certain she was already too late. Praying, feet pounding on the earth, she ran and ran and ran, hurtling past the trees and onto the sandy beach.

He came into view, pensive, searching as he stared out at the water. The longing in the tilt of his head, the pale cast to his cheeks, scared her most of all. Even his black shirt and pants were dull against the dreary horizon. It was as if he had already gone away, and soon his body would follow.

The sun in her heaving chest nearly scalded her at the sight. She wanted to throw herself at him, yank him back, drag him home to the estate where he belonged. He stood so close to the water, as if waiting for a signal. The flutter of a swan's wing, perhaps, the fall of a single feather.

The call of his former existence. The one she had kept him from.

Savitri almost let him go then. Almost.

Yet she wasn't sorry she'd saved him that night, and she refused to pretend otherwise. Moving slowly, deliberately, she strode up to him and produced a jelly jar from her pocket.

She'd forgotten a spoon, but with a syrup-daubed fingertip, she painted his mouth.

Then she held his hand and waited.

Instinctively, Satyavan licked his lips. His gaze cleared, and he smiled, surprised. "Savitri!"

Relief broke over her, forceful as a tidal wave. She leaned in to kiss him, to remind him of what he would be leaving behind. To distract him. Could a kiss truly break a curse? Could devotion? "I came to find you. We're so close to finishing Anjali's lament."

His eyes widened, and the moon in his chest lit up, singing to the sun in hers. "What am I doing here? We have songs to write! Dance numbers to plan." Still gripping her hand, he loped off. "Entire theaters full of audiences depend on us!"

"I don't think we have enough people to fill a theater yet," Savitri said, laughing. "Or even one seat." In the event that Rambha might be watching, she mouthed, *You can't have him. He's meant for me.*

She dearly hoped it was true.

A year to the night Savitri first found Satyavan with the apsara-turned-swans, she woke with the dawn to pluck pink roses and purple lilacs. Once back in the kitchen, she stripped a handful of their petals, which she then rinsed and set aside.

All she had left to do was slice the pistachios, but Savitri allowed herself a moment just to bask in the quiet. Outside the window, the sky wore its crispest, most vivid cerulean silk, trimmed here and there with a lace of puffy clouds.

Something cracked open in her, fragile as an eggshell—

hope. It was her first anniversary with Satyavan. It was the day before her eighteenth birthday, when she would tell her parents she was leaving for the city, Satyavan at her side.

Even Satyavan wasn't up yet; he had taken the day off from studying. Savitri greeted the sun for whom she was named, then set about decorating the rasmalai she'd made the day before. The discs of sweet cheese in thickened cardamom milk had turned out wonderfully soft. Pleased, she ladled two portions onto cut-crystal plates and garnished both servings with sliced pistachio and the fragrant flower petals.

Rambha had said Satyavan wouldn't survive past a year. Savitri would prove her wrong.

By the time he arrived, hair damp from the shower, she had set the breakfast on the patio. "What's all this?" he asked, taking in the edges of the plates ringed with the remaining blossoms.

Savitri hugged him, drinking in his fresh smell, his warm presence. "It's been a year since we met. I thought we could celebrate. Comics, video games, puzzles, karaoke! Oh, and finish our last song."

"Sounds like you've got the whole day planned!" He kissed her cheek, then clasped her hands. "Savitri, there's something I've been meaning to tell you: I owe you everything for saving me. Everything." He shuddered. "I still don't know what was wrong with me that night."

"I'd been planning to go for a swim, anyway," teased Savitri, refusing to acknowledge the bite of guilt. "Dig in."

They ate, and Satyavan lifted a lilac flower to his nose. As he inhaled, a bee emerged from its depths and stung him in the hollow beneath his chin. "Ow!"

"Bee!" cried Savitri, appalled. She ran around the table and knelt by Satyavan, whose breathing had already grown labored. "Why? You said I would find the person who reflected me!"

And so you did, but no one told you for how long, said the bee, and ripped itself free. Its stinger remained behind, pumping venom through Satyavan. Silver light pulsed wildly from his torso, and Savitri clung to him. She couldn't lose him. She wouldn't.

Seconds tumbled into one another. Just as she decided to run for help, someone spoke.

"I told you to let him go," Rambha said, though not ungently. She wore a sari the pink and purple of the flowers Savitri had gathered. "I would have spared you this."

"But—but there's no water. He's still here," Savitri insisted. She cradled Satyavan's slumped form against her chest. The fading flickers of his moon heart merged into the golden flames of her sun heart. "See?"

Yet she knew he was about to die. Otherwise, Rambha wouldn't be here.

"Even so." Rambha cocked her head and listened. "There. He drew his last breath."

Savitri felt as much as saw Satyavan's heartbeat cease. He had gone dark, been extinguished. Her grip slackened, and she put up no resistance when Rambha extracted Satyavan's shade from his body.

"Be content," urged Rambha over her shoulder. "You enjoyed far more time with him than he was ever allotted in this world. Indeed, rejoice in the knowledge that the curse is finally broken, and that he will resume his place in the lunar court."

Alone, thought Savitri, her sun heart squeezing in her chest. Even with all the sunshine inside her, all the heat, she, too, was going dark and cold. She pushed aside Satyavan's dish and tenderly rested his head on the table. Her arms went around herself, but no matter how tightly she pressed, it came nowhere near a hug.

There was no point in fighting. She couldn't save him again. She'd never even given him a choice the first time.

The guilt stung like bee venom. Maybe she deserved to be alone. He'd tried to leave twice, and she'd stopped him both times.

She dropped out of her chair and onto the ground. When she closed her eyes, something glimmered. The bejeweled path! It should have broken off with Satyavan's death, yet it continued to stretch out before her. She saw herself onstage, alone. She saw herself in the bower, all dressed in black, swathed in blankets and books. She saw herself with others, without—with choices.

She wanted Satyavan, but he, too, deserved a chance to choose.

"Wait!" called Savitri, opening her eyes, and raced after Rambha and Satyavan's shade. When she passed the arbor, a ring of bees joined her. *No one told you for how long*, they said again, and this time, she understood their message: It was not destiny but another choice.

She caught up to Rambha at the lake's edge. "Wait! Let him go."

Rambha's elegant features brightened with amusement. "Your determination and foolhardy belief that you can shape any of this charms me. For that, I would give you a boon. Ask anything but Satyavan's life, and it is yours."

"Grant me . . ." Savitri considered. "Grant my parents solace when I leave. Grant them peace and assurance that whatever struggles I have, I'll be fine. Let them know there's no need to hide anymore."

Rambha snapped her slender fingers. Minute bells on her rings tinkled sweetly. "Most would have chosen wealth or fame. But it is done. Now be off, mortal child. Go back to your life and leave us to our affairs." She stepped into the clear water, which somehow did not penetrate the fabric of her sari.

Savitri didn't hesitate before going in, too. Though it wouldn't surprise her in the least if Rambha transformed into her swan self and swam until Savitri grew too tired to continue, leaving her to drown.

The water, warm and tranquil, had reached their waists before Rambha turned to face her. "Oh, but you are a pest, aren't you? Yet I suppose such loyalty should be rewarded. Ask anything but Satyavan's life, and it is yours—and then you must go. I am hardly your nanny."

"Let him remember everything that happened. All of it."

"Even if he blames you?"

Savitri nodded.

Satyavan's gaze, which had been blank and distant, now grew sharp with comprehension. "You kept me here," he said. "Because I matched you, and you didn't want to be alone."

Savitri held her chin high. "Yes." Whatever happened now, at least he knew.

Satyavan said nothing. She couldn't tell what he was

thinking, and her heart dimmed. It was too much to hope for. Too much to imagine that he would be glad she had kept his true identity from him—and so, his choice—a full year longer than necessary.

Yet she didn't look away.

Rambha took Satyavan's arm and continued swimming. Now Savitri could see the semicircle of swans. She should heed Rambha's advice and go home. She knew that.

Instead, she plunged after Rambha. After Satyavan, who looked back with an inscrutable expression.

The mud beneath her feet had long fallen since away, and Savitri swam and swam. She was already exhausted, but the bees surged above her, buzzing their encouragement. And Satyavan hadn't told her to leave.

Rambha halted just outside the semicircle. "You are a tiresome thing," she said. "You have entertained me, but now I grow irritated. Name your final boon and swim home. It is past time for us to do the same. And once more, you may ask anything but Satyavan's life."

The swans flapped their wings, clearly impatient for Savitri to be on her way. She needed a sign.

She met Satyavan's black gaze, trying to ask with her eyes what he wanted. If he still felt anything for her. If he remembered their kisses beneath the bower with ardor rather than anger. If he still wanted to join her on the bejeweled path soldered with promise.

He frowned and looked away.

No, she thought. *No, please.* She couldn't have lost him. Not now.

"Name your boon," ordered Rambha, "or lose it altogether."

A minute passed, and Savitri despaired of being able to tread water for much longer. Still, she waited. *I know you can hear me.*

Just as she lowered her head in surrender, Satyavan turned back. His face had softened, and he pointed to his heart, to hers. When he smiled, his moon heart flared silver bright.

"Grant me that our completed show will be a success. I've worked so hard on my songs," Savitri said, her fatigued muscles loosening, letting the lake support her.

"Done," said Rambha. "Now come, Satyavan. Your father awaits."

"But Satyavan never finished writing Anjali's lament." Savitri grinned, her delight brushing everything with a patina of gold. "How can our completed show be successful if he's not here to complete it?"

Rambha gaped. Then she tossed back her head and laughed. "I suppose it can't. Satyavan? What do you say?"

Satyavan's silvery shade moved to where Savitri bobbed on the water's surface. "I choose her."

"Have him back, then, mortal girl." Rambha nodded at him. "But Satyavan, know the burden is on you to explain your absence to Lord Chandra."

The swans and Rambha disappeared, and suddenly Savitri and Satyavan sat on the lakeshore, tucked into each other's arms, with a sealed jar of honeysuckle syrup at their feet.

The next evening, for her birthday, Savitri and Satyavan wove honeysuckle vines into crowns, borrowed her parents' car, and drove to a nightclub in the city. There, dressed in gold and silver, amid the glitzy décor and throaty growls of the hired vocalists—and after a hefty bribe to the club's manager—they claimed the stage, crooning songs of bee secrets and cunning swans. Together, her voice sparkling like diamond dust, his smooth as clove smoke, they ensorcelled the audience as they had ensorcelled each other.

Once they stepped down into the cheering blue-lit crowd, just before she relearned the taste and feel of Satyavan's lips, just before she ran her fingers through his hair and forgot the rest of the club around them, Savitri thought she glimpsed Rambha in the audience.

Then his hands made their way to her hips, and her mouth found his, and everything else dissolved as the sun sought the moon.

The *Mahabharata*

A South Asian Epic

The *Mahabharata*, the longest epic poem in recorded history and one of South Asia's two greatest epics, consists of stories upon stories upon stories, all intricate and often woven together. One of these is the tale of Princess Savitri and Prince Satyavan; another that of goddess Ganga and King Shantanu. As I brainstormed "Daughter of the Sun," I realized I would need the second story in order to properly retell the first, and soon these two age-old narratives fused into something both contemporary and new.

In "Savitri and Satyavan," Savitri chooses Satyavan as her husband despite learning he is fated to die in a year's time. When Lord Yama, God of Death, comes to claim Satyavan's shade, clever Savitri tricks him into restoring Satyavan to life—along with Satyavan's parents' failed eyesight and lost kingdom.

In "Ganga and Shantanu," King Shantanu weds a mysterious woman on the stipulation that he question nothing about her—not even when she drowns their first seven sons in the river Ganga. But once the eighth is born, Shantanu confronts his queen on the riverbank, where she reveals she is the goddess Ganga herself, tasked with bearing and immediately liberating eight demigods cursed to be born into human suffering. Since Shantanu broke his promise and pried, Ganga entrusts the eighth son to his care and leaves.

I love the feminist aspects of both these stories (though of course that's me viewing ancient legends through a modern lens): Not only do Savitri's parents allow *her* to decide who she marries, but her husband is the one in need of rescue, and she, with her equanimity and ingenuity, is the one to do it. Ganga, meanwhile, knows her own mind. She sets her conditions and sticks to her purpose, no matter how it might appear to others.

"Daughter of the Sun" is my love letter to two heroines I deeply admire and to the myriad ways girls and women can be self-possessed and powerful in a world that so often tells them otherwise.

—Shveta Thakrar

THE CRIMSON CLOAK

CINDY PON

All the storytellers get it wrong.

Despite how the legend goes, the truth of the matter is, Dear Reader, I saw him first.

Countless years have passed, but I can recall that morning so well. The sun had not yet risen, and the colors of the forest were muted. I loved that time within the earthly realm, when all living creatures seemed to hold one collective breath, waiting for the day to begin. I had escaped my duty, fleeing the opulent quarters I shared with my six older sisters. My mother, the Heavenly Queen, had made a surprise visit, and I left them, bickering, complaining and gossiping—all vying for her attention. It was the perfect time to slip into our heavenly gardens and out a side gate.

As the seventh and youngest daughter of the Jade Emperor,

I wear the crimson cloak of feathers. It grants me the power of flight and allows me to weave my colors into the earth's skies: from rose to vermillion, from the lightest blush to the deepest crimson. My six older sisters all bear a cloak and color of their own, but if you ask me, the best was saved for last. I might be the youngest, but I weave the most brilliant colors in the skies for mortal eyes—no dawn or dusk is truly magnificent unless I choose to work that day.

That morning's sunrise was a pallid, anemic thing without me. I lay in my favorite meadow hidden among silver birch trees overlooking an oblong lake below. Eventually, a gentle lapping stirred me from my daydreaming. I rose to my knees and peered over some wild ferns, curious what creature had wandered over to the waters.

A young man with his hair pulled into a topknot stood by the lake; his companion, an old ox with majestic horns and a golden-yellow coat drank at the water's edge. Humans did not often visit this meadow, and it was rare that I came this close to a mortal boy. He had a tanned face and pleasing features. From his coloring and the way he filled out his faded blue tunic, he was no scholar or son from a rich family. The young man was speaking, but I was too far away to catch what he was saying. No one else was about—was he talking to his ox?

The old ox lowered its horns and its owner stroked the top of its head, continuing to talk. Intrigued, I leaned forward and crashed into the thick fern, the rustling of the leaves as loud as thunder in the morning quiet. I squatted in a most unladylike manner in the plants, unmoving as a statue. The young man glanced up and seemed to look directly at me, although it was impossible he could see me through the dense brush. He tilted his head and listened.

I didn't breathe—not difficult for an immortal—and not one strand of my hair stirred in the breeze. You can never outwait a goddess, Dear Reader. I have all the time in the world. But this young man held still and listened for longer than I thought most mortals had the patience for. What was he doing out here alone, so far from the nearest village? I had been restless and bored for over a season. . . . What would it be like to talk to him? My sisters had flirted with mortals before—perhaps it was my turn. It'd certainly make for more interesting days.

It felt like fate, an opportunity presented on a gilded platter.

Finally, the old ox shifted, pawing one hoof at the lake's muddied shore, and the young man seemed to nod in agreement. He took the ox's worn leather leash, and they ambled away from the water, disappearing into the forest, beyond even my vision.

Yet I knew our paths would cross again.

My sisters berated me for neglecting my duties that morning. But if every sunrise and sunset were awash in my beautiful colors, would you not be bored by it soon enough? Wouldn't you *expect* my crimson hues instead of appreciating them? It never ceases to amaze me how easily mortals take nature's beauty—and so many things, really—for granted. But that particular dusk, I made it up to my sisters and to the mortals who had gotten nothing that morning but a pale yellow dawn that faded away in the span of a long yawn. Tying the silk sash of my crimson feather cloak, I leaped into the sky and wove a fluffy cloud at my feet, threading the faintest pink blush into it until it grew to the size of a comfortable divan. Settling into its soft depths, I streaked gorgeous red across the sky, as deftly as a calligrapher with her brush.

When I arrived home, weary from creating the magnificent display, my sisters enveloped me, a cocoon of silken sleeves and floral perfumes. "You have outdone yourself, xiao mei!" my fifth eldest sister said, stroking my cheek. "We do get cross with you, little one, but you redeem yourself every time." My eldest sister, da jie, added emphasis with a pinch of my arm.

I feigned annoyance, and pouted, as was expected from the littlest sister. Do you know what it's like to be the youngest among six strong-willed sisters? I learned very young how to get my way with each one of them, whether it was to act the insolent brat, the sweet one with sugar-coated words, or the naive innocent who could do no wrong.

But that night as I disentangled myself from their petting and cuddles, pinches and kisses, I was thinking only of the young man by the lake who spoke to his ox.

I know my story, Dear Reader, or how the mortals prefer to tell it.

Legend says that my young man's magical, wise old ox told him where to find me, bathing in the lake with my beautiful sisters. How he should look for the crimson cloak cast on the ground at the lake's shore, so I could not fly away from him when I was discovered. How in this way, he could coerce me to be his wife.

Well, that wasn't how it happened.

I escaped from our heavenly palace even earlier the next day, when the stars still winked across the dark velvet skies. Floating down, I landed beside the lake where I had seen the young man the previous morning. And waited. I didn't know the ways of mortals as much as I would like. He might have just been passing through.

But I wished for the young man and his ox to return that morning. And immortals often get what they wish for.

Soon enough, the crunch of footsteps and the tread of the ox's hooves sounded from the wood's depths. Shrugging off my cloak, I ran a hand over its crimson feathers, cool and sleek as the finest silk, and let it float to the muddied ground. The magical cloak was always pristine, no matter how poorly I treated it. I stripped off my pale blue dress, casting it behind a tree, and waded into the lake.

The water was very cold, but temperature does not affect me. I splashed around, making some noise, and swam farther into the lake. When the young man and his ox broke through the trees and he saw me, his stunned silence was louder than any shout of surprise. This time, I could see his features more clearly: the wide set of his dark brown eyes and the strong lines of his jaw. The woods were dense with fog, and mist swirled like phantoms on the lake's surface. He brought a sun-tanned hand to his brow, shielding his eyes, as if unable to believe I was real.

His stance reminded me of the fawn I'd come across in the forests, ears flicked forward in fear, one leg poised as if ready to bound off in a breath. I worried that if I spoke I would scare him away. So I resorted to what I did best—I tricked him. The old ox lowered its noble head to drink from the lake. When it finished, I put words into the ox's mouth.

"The young maiden has left her feathered cloak on the shore." The ox's speech came in a low rumble. "Fetch it for her, boy."

The young man startled, taking a step back from his companion, and gaped at the ox. The animal shook its head, its magnificent horns arcing through the air, then lowed—a deep sound that reverberated in the still morning. "Don't just stand there," the ox reprimanded, still speaking the words I cast. "The water is cold."

For a long moment, the young man didn't move, but then he glanced at me again, and I let my mouth lift at the corners just a touch and nodded. I wrapped my bare arms around myself to emphasize the chill of the water.

"It is as your wise ox says." I tilted my chin toward the crimson cloak pooled like spilled ink on the ground. "Could you get my cloak for me?"

My words seemed to stun him more than his old ox speaking. But he sprinted to my cloak and lifted it from the damp mud. I shivered, but not from the cold. No mortal had ever laid hands on my cloak before. Granted to me by my father the Jade Emperor himself, only the heavens know what he would have done if he came across this scene. Probably fling me to the farthest star in exile. Luckily, Father's attention was occupied by too many important responsibilities. His youngest daughter pursuing a dalliance with some insignificant mortal boy would not even register.

I swam toward the shore, then waded out, feeling the thick mud between my toes. The water slid off my skin in rivulets, and the young man froze, his expression something akin to fear, yet he never looked away. I was not shy with my body, not like I had observed most humans to be, awkward in their own skins, as if their flesh owned them, and not the other way around. His dark eyes skimmed over my figure, then my face; but he was unable to meet my gaze. A deep flush bloomed across his cheeks, spreading down his neck and all the way to the tips of his ears.

The old ox lowed again—impatient. But I sensed an underlying amusement there, too. Ox knew more of what I was about than its naive owner did.

The young man's blush decided it for me. I feigned shyness, too, covering myself with my arms, my eyes downcast, peering up at him through my thick lashes. I willed a blush to my cheeks, the faintest touch of pink.

"Thank you," I breathed. "I wasn't expecting anyone to come this way."

He jerked his face to the side, so he could not look at me, and thrust my cloak forward. I took it from him, drawing it over my shoulders, the material drying my skin the moment I wrapped it around myself. I tied the sash securely at my waist, making certain the opening was drawn closed.

"Are you lost?" I asked. "Not many pass through here."

He drew a long breath before he spoke, as if unsure of his voice. "I was here yesterday morning." He stood as rigid as a strong bamboo stalk and dared at last to meet my gaze. "I thought I heard a noise in the brush there." He pointed uphill, where I had been hiding the previous day. "But I couldn't see anything."

"How odd," I replied. "The forest can be filled with such strange noises."

He nodded once; then after a too long silence asked, "What is a maiden like you doing alone in the woods?"

I laughed softly. How little he knew of maidens like me. "I escaped from my six older sisters this morning."

His dark eyes widened, perhaps stunned by the notion of six other maidens like myself wandering somewhere near, or that I would have the gall to run away from what he'd guess to be a rich manor, I didn't know.

"I enjoy the solitude and quiet," I said.

His expression softened. This he could relate to and understand. "What's your name?"

"You can call me Hongyun," I replied. It was not my given name, which I would never share with a mortal boy. But "red cloud" felt right in this earthly realm. "What are you called?"

"Cowherd," he said.

"That is your true name?" No one loved him well enough, it seemed.

"I lost my parents when I was very young," he said. "So, I never learned my given name. I'm known as 'Cowherd' for the company I keep." As if the old ox heard us, it shambled over, head lowered, seeking a pat from its owner. Cowherd smiled at the ox and obliged by stroking its strong neck. "Ox has been my constant companion and friend since I was a child."

"Your ox has a glorious coat," I said. At closer range, the gold sheen of its pelt gleamed.

Cowherd straightened with pride.

I pretended to shiver again and wound my arms tight

around myself, letting my teeth chatter. It worked.

"You must be freezing!" Cowherd exclaimed. "Why did you go into the lake so early in the morning?"

"The water was colder than I expected," I said. "I can be foolishly spontaneous." An understatement.

He extended a hand, then let it fall. It would not be proper for him to touch me, to wrap his arms around me. That much I knew about mortal interactions: all rules and decorum, at least at first.

So instead, I leaned against his ox, feeling its solid warmth against my arm and side. The ox lowed again, but it was a satisfied noise, not a complaint.

Cowherd grinned, then laughed. "He likes you."

"And I like him," I replied.

"Will I see you here again tomorrow?" he asked.

I smiled up at him.

It was, Dear Reader, as simple as that.

I did not go back to the lake again the morning after we met. I would get too much grief from my sisters if I neglected the dawn a third morning, and one of them might tattle to my mother if she was feeling particularly vengeful. More importantly, I didn't want to do what was expected. Would Cowherd show up another morning if I failed to appear as he had hoped?

He did not disappoint me.

When I returned two days later, he was already by the lake, his ox grazing on some wild grass closer to the woods. "I waited for you yesterday," Cowherd said. "But you didn't come." The disappointment tingeing his voice was clear.

"It was impossible for me to get away," I replied, pursing my mouth. "I'm so glad you returned."

Cowherd grinned, and it made him appear even more boyish. "Me, too," he said. "I've brought a surprise."

I clasped my hands together in delight. "I love surprises!"

He rummaged through the worn leather rucksack he carried, withdrawing a faded quilt, which he spread gallantly on the ground, some distance from the water. "It's dryer here," he said. Then he reached into the bag again and pulled out small packages wrapped in paper. He carefully unfolded each, as if they were precious gifts. "Walnuts and dried dates," he announced, placing the packets onto the blanket and flourishing a hand. "I bought them in a small town yesterday for us"—he cleared his throat—"a gift for you, truly, Hongyun, to make up for our rather . . . awkward first meeting."

We settled down on the blanket and I took my time choosing a dark red date, a color I knew well, but did not often weave into the skies. I popped it into my mouth and closed my eyes, enjoying the full, sweet flavor. Though immortals do not have to eat, it is a delightfully sensory experience. When I opened my eyes again, Cowherd was staring at my lips.

"They're delicious," I said. He blinked. I laughed and picked a date for him. "Here, open your mouth."

His black brows lifted, and then he parted his lips. I fed him the date, caressing his cheek like a butterfly's kiss before I dropped my hand. He blushed as red as an autumn apple, and I claimed him as mine in my heart. I let a rose blush spread across my own cheeks and lowered my chin in feigned shyness. Too bold, and he might bolt.

But this peasant boy, this mortal in his dust-stained tunic with no true name and only an ox for a friend, surprised me. He grabbed for my hand and kissed my fingertips. My head snapped up, eyes wide. Perhaps I had read him entirely wrong.

My whole body flushed, but not from magical manipulation or an immortal trick. I tugged him to me, and we kissed.

He tasted as sweet as I had imagined. Sweeter than that date.

I know how the legend goes for Cowherd and me, Dear Reader.

We married, I was the perfect wife, I birthed him healthy and beautiful twins, and we lived a blissful life together until my enraged mother called me back to the heavens, separating us forever. We were only allowed to meet on the seventh day of the seventh moon each year, crossing the river of stars formed by a bridge of magpies.

But this was what really happened:

That particular spring we spent together stands apart in my memories, like a painting carefully rendered with the smallest brush. We could not spend every day together, but I flew down from the heavens as often as I could, and Cowherd was always there, waiting for me, Ox standing patiently at his side.

He was poor and lived off the earth, eating what he could cultivate, forage, or capture. I gave him small gifts: jade figurines and a gold ring, worth more than he could ever imagine. But I was foolish to think he would pawn them for coin, as he was too romantic and sentimental. He kept them as treasured mementos, so I began bringing lavish picnics instead.

He was eighteen years and at his prime, all lean muscle

from working the fields, chopping wood, and hauling heavy baskets of fruit and vegetables for farmers for coin when he needed it. Truth be told, he always needed it. But I knew he was willing to go hungry to meet with me.

I revealed my true identity to Cowherd a month after we met, and he took the news as well as any mortal could: with skepticism at first, then incredulity and awe when I showed him my powers. After two more moons, I thought I knew him as well as every red-streaked sunrise I had created.

Oh, how wrong I was.

One morning, we were twined together on a bed of cloud I had woven for us, the sunshine warm on my skin. We were tucked in my favorite meadow among the birch trees, our nest floating just below the tree line. It was almost summer, and I could sense the change of season in the air.

Cowherd suddenly shifted onto his side and propped himself up on one arm. "I will be nineteen years in the fall," he said.

"Mmm," I replied. Mortals are so strange in the ways they obsessively mark the time, the passing of days, the anniversary of years. But I suppose I might be, too, if I could only live as many decades as I can count on two hands. "Is this your hint that you'd like a birthday gift?" I smiled, eyes half-lidded against the sunlight.

He laughed softly. "To be with you is gift enough, Hongyun. I wonder every day how I got so lucky." His voice dropped to a hoarse whisper. "I love you, you know that?"

I jerked upward and almost smacked Cowherd in his nose. My cloud billowed behind me, boosting me into a sitting position. "What does that mean?"

He stared at me, a mixture of fear and amusement on his face. "It means that you have my heart, Hongyun. I am yours."

I furrowed my eyebrows. Never once had I wondered what I meant to Cowherd or what he might desire. "And you want something from me in return?" I asked.

Cowherd cleared his throat. "It's soon time for me to marry and start a family. It's all I've dreamed of since I lost my own family so young . . . but . . . " He trailed off.

"Oh," I said with sudden understanding.

"Is that something"—he faltered—"would you—"

"I can't have children." An unfamiliar tightness constricted my chest at the raw emotion in his face. "And I can never marry a mortal."

He clamped his mouth shut, swallowing hard.

It was a half-truth. I could have children if my father, the Jade Emperor, granted it. But I had never desired it. What would it mean to have children with a man, creating half-immortals? Even if I wanted children with Cowherd, my father would never agree to it. I had hidden my dalliance from my entire family.

"I'm sorry," I finally said, breaking the long silence.

He nodded and lay back down on his stomach, folding his arms and hiding his face from me. Sunlight and shadow dappled across his broad back, skimmed over his strong, toned legs. If a mortal were to look like a god, I imagined Cowherd was as near as you could get.

I didn't know if I loved him in the same way that he loved me: wholly and without reservation. But I cared for him tremendously.

Enough to let him go.

❖❖❖

The next day I remember as clearly as a detailed etching carved in a favorite piece of jade.

I descended on a ragged cloud limned in the same red as mortal eyes when they have cried too long. Cowherd tried to sweep me into his arms in greeting as he always did, but I flew backward, away from his reach. He followed, palms open and lifted heavenward, like a man beseeching the gods.

I raised my own hand, and he stopped short, his beautiful suntanned face suddenly leached of color. "My mother has discovered our affair," I lied, my words never wavering. "She has forbidden me from ever seeing you again."

He fisted his hands. "Hongyun, no. Please." Ox, as if sensing its owner's distress, came to stand beside Cowherd.

My heart was heavy, but I did not falter. "Find yourself a nice mortal girl and settle down, make your own home and family."

"I never would have dreamed of loving you, marrying you"—there was a fierce edge in his voice—"if I didn't think you felt the same way." Cowherd thrust his chin forward.

"I'm sorry," I replied. "But I can never give you what you want." I spoke without any divine amplification, and my throat felt bruised. I did not want to give him up. With graceless motions, I gathered dark clouds at my feet and rose into the air, as if I rode on a thunderstorm. "Good-bye, Cowherd," I whispered, knowing he would not hear me.

I surged into the clear morning, the deeper indigo sky just easing into a light blue. Within a breath, the earth was already a league beneath me. Not only did I wield the most gorgeous colors among my sisters, I was the fastest, too. A light breeze swept over my face, tingling my skin. I brought a hand to my cheek, and it came away wet. Astonished, I watched my teardrops rise from my fingers, shooting heavenward, streaking silver behind them. I had never cried before that fateful day, Dear Reader, and the tears kept coming, as delicate as dewdrops, turning silver and blue and red and gold as they lifted into the skies, disappearing from sight.

"Hongyun!"

Cowherd's shout startled me. I was high above the earth. How could I possibly be hearing his voice?

Then I looked back and my heart stopped. He was sitting astride Ox's strong back as the animal galloped up through the air. My thundercloud slowed.

They drew up beside me, the beast treading in place, its hooves moving gracefully, like a bovine dancer. The sight was so ludicrous I burst into laughter. "What?" I said. "How?"

Grinning, Cowherd replied, "Ox is magical. He speaks to me and can fly." He patted Ox's thick neck.

"But you were so shocked when I put words into his mouth the morning we met," I said.

Cowherd laughed. "I was surprised because that sounded nothing like Ox!"

Ox lowed, then said, "It is true. I did not know what to make of it when I said words I did not intend in a voice not my own." While I had made Ox's fake voice a low rumble, the beast's true tone was a rich tenor.

"Why didn't you ever tell me?" I asked.

Cowherd's features turned serious. "Because I had always

kept his magic a secret. I was going to, eventually . . ." His dark eyes narrowed a touch. "You've been crying." He reached out and caressed my face; I closed my eyes, resting my cheek against his palm. "Won't you reconsider?" he asked, his voice gone rough.

I opened my eyes, and we both watched as my tears rose from his palm, leaving a shimmering trail in their wake. "I only want you to be happy," I whispered.

"Hongyun, whatever I might make for myself in this life—hearth, home, or family—they would mean nothing without you." He grasped my hand and kissed my inner wrist. "I know that we can be happy together."

I stroked his dark head, then trailed my fingertips down the nape of his neck. "But my mother . . ."

He lifted his gaze to me and smiled. "I can't imagine you ever not getting your way."

In the end, Cowherd was right.

We were happy together. We bought land a few leagues from the lake where we had met, with fertile ground surrounded by terraced fields. Cowherd spent half a year building a house for us, hiring workers and managing the entire project. He asked me what I desired in our home, and I told him I wished for nothing but a small garden to plant flowers and a deep stone tub to soak in. I got both.

The farm thrived as only a farm under a goddess's benevolence could. But truth be told, Cowherd worked so hard, it would have flourished on its own. Four years after we built our home together, we adopted a little girl who we named

Rose. Then two years after that, we adopted a baby boy into our family who we called Hailan.

I did not live always with my mortal family, but visited as often as I could. By the time we were blessed with our children, Cowherd had hired enough hands to help with running the farm and took care of Rose and Hailan the majority of the time.

As for my parents, my father, the Jade Emperor, never noticed my long absences, and my mother, the Heavenly Queen, might never have as well, if my fourth sister hadn't ratted me out. But I refused to give in, and I got my way. After our third and final argument, my mother said in exasperation, "Do as you like, youngest daughter. Besides, mortal lives are as short to us as a flower's bloom." She lifted her arms in a swirl of silken sleeves and disappeared.

My mother, too, was right.

I do not know how it seems from a mortal's eyes, Dear Reader, but it felt like one day my children were fat and chortling in delight at everything they saw or picked up in their dimpled hands, and in the blink of an eye, they were sixteen and eighteen years, willful and believing they knew everything about the world. I glanced away another moment, and they had left us to make their own homes and families. Then, suddenly, one day, Cowherd's hair had gone white, and although he would be strong well into old age, the years had marked deep grooves in his face and filmed his beautiful dark brown eyes. He lived eighty-six years, a long life by mortal standards, full and happy—or whatever nonsensical platitudes people say when someone you love dies.

Only Ox could console me in the centuries that followed.

Ox missed Cowherd as much as I did. It was so easy to love, but no one had ever warned me of loss. My immortal family knew nothing of it, as our lives were infinite.

It has been two thousand years since my time with Cowherd, and memory is strange. I cannot remember his face any longer. What I do recall are fragments in time: the crinkling of his eyes against the sunshine or when he smiled, the ghost of his unrestrained laughter if I said something goddesslike when I wasn't trying to be amusing, the feel of that callus on his palm beneath the finger where he wore my gold ring. I am left with pieces of remembering though I loved him whole.

So the river of stars in the night sky was formed by the tears I have shed through all the centuries since that first time I cried, in pain or sorrow, but also from joy and love—even in the reminiscing.

This, Dear Reader, is the true story of Cowherd and me.

And I swear upon my crimson cloak, I saw him first.

The Cowherd and the Weaver Girl

A Chinese Legend

There are several variations of this story, but the one that is probably best known and that I used for inspiration is this: Cowherd was an orphan, cast out by a cruel sister-in-law who disliked him. His only possession and friend was a golden-coated ox. Cowherd grew and survived on his own, but one day lamented that he would never be able to find a wife. To his surprise, the ox spoke, and told him to travel to a lake where the fairy maidens often bathed. If Cowherd stole the crimson cloak, which belonged to the youngest fairy maiden, she would agree to marry Cowherd. Cowherd did exactly that, and the youngest fairy maiden was obliged to marry him. They moved into a village, and she had two babies with Cowherd and they were happy together. Everyone loved the beautiful fairy maiden and admired her skills in weaving. But one year on earth was only one day in the heavens, and on the third day in the heavens, the Heavenly Mother noticed that her youngest daughter had disappeared. When she discovered her daughter had married a mere mortal, she was furious and sent heavenly soldiers to seize her daughter and force her to return to the heavens. Thus, the fairy maiden was once again ripped away from the life she had been living. Cowherd chased after his wife (different versions have him riding the magical ox or wearing ox's magical pelt, which he keeps after the ox had died from old age), and when the Heavenly Mother saw this, she let a river of stars spill forth, separating the two lovers, thus creating our Milky Way. Legend says that each year, on the seventh day of the seventh moon, Cowherd and Weaver Girl are reunited. A bridge of magpies forms so that the lovers can cross the Milky Way to be together again. In all the versions of this tale I came across, even Ox spoke more than the fairy weaver girl ever did. I wanted to give her her voice in this retelling.

—Cindy Pon

EYES LIKE CANDLELIGHT

JULIE KAGAWA

Takeo stood at the top of the rice terraces watching his mother and sisters wade through the ankle-high water, shoving green rice-seedlings into the mud in neat rows. From his vantage point, he could see the whole village, its thatched-roof huts scattered haphazardly along both sides of the stream that wound lazily through the valley, sheltered on three sides by mountains and dark pine forest. The summer sun beat down on his head, cicadas droned in his ears, and while the rest of the village planted the rice necessary for their survival, Takeo swung his bamboo stick at imaginary enemies and dreamed that he was a samurai.

A distant bark interrupted him. Pausing, the boy turned, gazing down the hill as a streak of orange darted across the paddy bank, heading for the storehouse at the edge of the forest. Two village dogs, lean and mangy with curly tails, followed at its heels. The orange-and-white creature reached the storehouse and squeezed into the narrow gap between the floor and the ground, barely outpacing the dogs, who howled and dug frantically at the spot where their quarry had vanished.

Takeo sprinted down the hill, crossed the narrow berm between two paddies, and jogged toward the storehouse. The dogs were still worrying the same spot when he approached, bamboo stick held in both hands like a sword.

"Hey!" he shouted, over the din of snarls and scrabbling claws. "Stop it!"

The smaller dog put its ears back and slunk off without hesitation. The larger one, a big brown-and-white cur with a blocky muzzle, lowered its head and growled, showing sharp yellow teeth. Takeo stood his ground. Meeting the creature's flat glare, he stepped forward, raising his bamboo sword over his head. The dog's growls grew louder. Its lean body tensed, either to attack or flee. Takeo took a deep breath, tightening his grip on his weapon.

"Get out of here!" he bellowed, and lunged forward, sweeping the rod down like he was slicing something's head from its body. The dog leaped backward, and with a last defiant snarl, turned and fled, vanishing around the storeroom wall and out of sight.

Triumphant, Takeo lowered his stick, then walked to the hole the dogs had been pawing at. Dropping to his knees, he put his head to the dirt and peered inside.

In the shadows beneath the storehouse, two golden eyes stared back. Takeo could just make out the pointed muzzle and lean orange body of a fox, white-tipped tail curled around itself in fear. When it saw him, it trembled and pushed itself farther back into the hole, making itself as small as it could.

Takeo smiled. "Hello," he said softly, and the fox's long black ears twitched at the sound of his voice. "You don't have to be scared of me; I won't tell anyone." He glanced over his shoulder, making sure no grown-up would see him and wonder what he was doing. If anyone discovered the fox, they would kill it. Takeo knew the stories. He knew what kitsune, the wild foxes of the forest, were capable of. Kitsune could possess the weak, slipping under someone's fingernails to take control of their body. They could make you see things that weren't there. Sometimes, if the fox was strong enough, it could change its shape and become human, appearing as a beautiful mortal in order to lead the faithful astray.

But the creature cringing in the dirt under the storehouse didn't look evil or malicious or conniving. It just looked scared. "It's all right," the boy murmured. "A dog bit me when I was a baby, so I don't like them, either."

The fox tilted its head, an eerie intelligence shining from its amber gaze, as if it were trying to understand. Takeo smiled and scooted back on his knees. "You don't have to come out," he said to the hole. "I'll make sure the dogs don't come sniffing around again. You can leave when it's safe. But if you want to go now, I won't stop you."

He backed up a safe distance and watched the storehouse. For a few heartbeats, nothing happened. Then a narrow muzzle peeked out of the opening, gazing warily around. As the fox looked at him and froze, Takeo held himself very still, trying to be as unthreatening as possible. For just a moment, their gazes met, child and kitsune. Then, in a streak of orange and white, the fox zipped out of the hole, darting across the field to the edge the forest.

At the edge of the woods, it paused, looking back once. Takeo saw the flash of golden eyes as the kitsune's gaze found him again. With a faint smile, he put his arms to his sides and bowed, like a samurai would when saying farewell to a guest.

The fox blinked, cocking its head again in that surreally intelligent fashion. Then, with a twitch of its tail, it turned and ghosted into the trees, vanishing as if it had never been there at all.

Takeo never saw the fox again. But sometimes, on warm evenings when he was outside, he could almost imagine he was being watched.

The seasons passed. Summer turned to autumn, which faded to winter, which eventually gave way to spring. The cycle of planting, harvest, and death continued, as it had for hundreds of years. Takeo grew into a young man, broad shouldered and tall, hands calloused from years of work in the field. Childhood fantasies of becoming a samurai were replaced by the daily struggles of farming: tending the fields, nurturing the seedlings, and most importantly, making sure the village had enough food to live on after the daimyo's men arrived for the rice tax every fall. As the only son of the village headman, he knew that the responsibility of protecting and providing for the village would soon fall to him.

The autumn of Takeo's seventeenth year was brutal.

Drought took the valley; the rains of the wet season stubbornly refused to come. The rice withered in the fields, bright green shoots turning an ominous yellow, until the villagers worried that not only would they be unable to pay the rice tax at the end of the season, but that they all might starve the following winter.

In desperation, Takeo decided that he should take an offering to the shrine of Inari, the god of rice, at the top of the mountain and beseech the great kami to save his village. He had nothing of value himself, so for three nights, he went without rice to save enough of the precious resource to make an offering. On the morning of his third day without food, he accepted a bag of uncooked rice from his little sister, Hitomi, and entered the forest.

The climb to the top of the mountain was steep and unforgiving, and by the time Takeo reached the small wooden shrine at the top of the steps, flanked by mossy statues of Inari's kitsune messengers, he was trembling. Setting the little bag of rice beneath the prayer rope across the entrance, he fell to his knees and pressed his face to the ground in supplication.

"Great Inari," he murmured, feeling the eyes of the stone foxes on his back, "please forgive this intrusion into your affairs. My name is Takeo, and I am nothing—a humble farmer who does not deserve your thoughts or compassion. But I beg that you hear this plea: my village is in danger of starving. With the drought, we will not have enough rice for the daimyo's men when they come to collect it. My father, the headman, will be severely punished if we cannot pay the tax. If you can hear this worthless man's plea, please take pity on us. I would offer my own life for my village, if that is what you desire."

The forest around him was silent. The kitsune statues gazed at him with empty stone eyes, unmoving and impassive. But Takeo, with his face still pressed to the cold steps, suddenly felt like he was being watched. It was not unlike those times when, as a child, he could sense he was not alone. For a moment, he was certain that Inari had heard his request and had come for him, to take his life as he had offered. *If that is what it takes*, he thought. *If it will save my village, I am willing to exchange my life for theirs.*

But several heartbeats passed, and nothing happened. No kami stepped out of the shrine in a blaze of light and thunder, demanding his life. The feeling of being watched faded away, leaving Takeo kneeling on the steps, alone.

Shivering, he sat up, feeling the ground sway beneath him as he raised his head. Three days with almost no food, combined with the long hike up the mountain, was finally taking its toll. Forcing himself upright, Takeo staggered from the shrine, but a wave of dizziness struck him as he was walking down the steps, and the last thing he remembered was falling.

He awoke to darkness, except for a soft orange glow somewhere to his left: a brazier that flickered with dying coals. He was warm, lying on his back on something soft, and there was a blanket draped over him that smelled faintly of leaves. Turning his head, he met the concerned gaze of a young woman kneeling beside his mattress, and he drew in a sharp breath.

The girl blinked at him. She was, Takeo noticed after his initial shock, beautiful, with luminous dark eyes and straight black hair cascading down her back like a waterfall of ink. Her robes were very fine: deep red patterned with threads of silver, with tiny leaves flitting playfully across the fabric. They were perhaps the same age, but there the similarities ended. She looked poised and elegant and lovely, and Takeo was suddenly all too aware of his grubby appearance, his simple farmer's clothing, and work-calloused hands.

"Forgive me." Her voice was a caress, the murmur of wind through the branches. "I didn't mean to startle you." She tilted her head, and for a split second, to Takeo's sleep-addled mind, her eyes seemed to flash gold in the darkness. "How are you feeling?"

"I . . ." Takeo pressed a palm to his forehead, trying to recall what had happened. "Where am I?" he muttered.

"My family's home." The girl shifted closer, gazing down at him like she would at a curious bug. "We found you lying on the steps to the Inari shrine and brought you here. Are you all right? Are you sick?"

Carefully, Takeo sat up, wincing as the room spun a bit. "No, I'm fine. Thank you, my lady." He avoided looking at her face, keeping his gaze on the blankets beneath him. He had never seen this girl and had no knowledge of any family living in the mountains close to the shrine, but from her appearance she was obviously the daughter of an important house. Perhaps even a samurai or noble family. He was unfit to gaze at such loveliness.

The door panel slid open, and a woman entered the room. Like the girl, she was poised and elegant, her raven-wing hair styled atop her head, speared in place with sticks of ivory.

Her robe was the green of pine forests with blood-red berries climbing up the sleeves.

"Ah, you're awake." Takeo shivered as her voice rippled over him like a cool mountain spring. "Welcome, stranger, to our home. I am Miyazawa Atsuko, and this is my daughter, Yuki." She waved an elegant hand at the girl, who was still watching Takeo with a curious, bright-eyed stare. "Please make yourself comfortable. You are welcome to stay as long as you wish."

"I . . ." Takeo had no clue what to say in return. He had no business being a guest in such an important household. "I thank you for your kindness," he finally managed "But I wouldn't want to trouble you." *Or soil your lovely home with my presence. Why would they bother with one such as I?*

"It is no trouble," the lady said calmly, and inclined her head toward the girl. "Yuki insisted upon bringing you here, and our home is large, but we don't get many visitors." She drew back a step, and the light from the brazier flickered orange through her eyes. "Dinner will be served in the main hall. Consider this an invitation to join us. Yuki can show you the way."

She drew back a few more steps and slid the panel shut, leaving Takeo alone again with the girl.

Takeo squeezed his eyes shut for a moment, feeling like cobwebs had settled in his brain. Thoughts came sluggishly, and with a faint, underlying sense of unease: a feeling that something wasn't right, that he was missing something important. But when he opened his eyes and met Yuki's lovely smile, everything else faded away. She could charm bears with that smile, Takeo thought. If he were a bear, he would lie down with his head in her lap and not move until the hunters came for him.

Abruptly, he realized he was staring, and dropped his gaze, angry that he could be thinking such things. "Is it . . . really all right that I'm here?" he asked. "I truly do not wish to trouble your family—"

A soft brush on his arm almost made his heart stop. For a moment, he stared at the delicate white fingers on his wrist, hardly believing they were there, that someone of her beauty would deign to touch someone like him. "Of course, Takeo-san," Yuki said, as warmth spread up his arm and settled in his stomach. "You are always welcome here. Never doubt that. Now, come on." She rose with an easy grace and grinned down at him. "Let's go get dinner, before my rude, insufferable brothers start without us."

As Takeo stood and followed the girl into the long, dimly lit halls beyond his room, he had the faint, passing realization that he had never told her his name.

The Miyazawa home was indeed very fine: passageways of dark, polished wood flanked by painted shoji panels depicting a variety of beautiful scenes—bamboo groves in the moonlight, tiny ponds with jeweled dragonflies on the water, giant maple trees mottled by the sun. Takeo tried very hard not to gape as Yuki led him into a massive hall of polished wood, the entrance guarded by two unsmiling statues. The ceiling soared above them, lit with thousands upon thousands of tiny paper lanterns, so many that it resembled the night sky.

A lacquered table sat in the center of the room, surrounded by cushions and a trio of seated nobility. Lady Miyazawa resided at the head of the table with her hands in her lap, looking serene. Two young men, both around Yuki and Takeo's age, sat beside her at the corners. They glanced up as Takeo and Yuki came in, sharp eyes narrowed and appraising.

"This is him, Yuki-chan?" one of them said as Yuki knelt primly on a cushion. Takeo hovered behind her, uncertain of what to do, where to sit. The other young noble looked him up and down, before breaking into a wicked smile. "He looks like they all do. Just another bumbling, clueless hum . . . er, peasant. What's so special about him?"

"Aki-kun." Yuki scowled at her sibling. "We talked about this. Be polite." Turning to Takeo, she smiled and gestured to the cushion beside her. "Please excuse my brother, Takeo-san," she said. "As I mentioned before, they're rude and boorish and unfit for civilized company. Feel free to ignore anything they say. Please"—she patted the cushion again—"please, sit."

In a daze, Takeo sat, feeling like a stray dog sniffing around the table for scraps. But then Yuki gave him that smile that turned his stomach inside out, and everything else was forgotten.

The meal was excellent, though later that evening, Takeo would be hard-pressed to remember exactly what he'd eaten. Servants delivered steaming, colorful dishes to the table and vanished without a sound. Yuki's brothers had almost seemed to fight over the food, snatching dishes away from each other, on the verge of an all-out brawl until a sharp word from Lady Miyazawa stopped them. If Takeo had been paying more attention, he might have thought it strange, but his mind was not on food or Yuki's brothers, or even the dark gaze of Lady Miyazawa, who watched him across the table. It was only on

Yuki. She was beautiful, gracious, and extremely curious about him and his life in the village.

"What about family?" Yuki asked, after a quick, somewhat disgusted glare at her brothers, who appeared to be in an argument over the last fish. "Do you have any siblings, Takeo-san? "

He nodded. "Two older sisters," he replied. "They're both married now. I don't have any brothers, but I do have a younger sister, Hitomi. She'll be five this . . ."

Hitomi. Memories flooded in, breaking the surreal, dreamlike haze of the moment. He remembered his little sister that morning, solemnly handing him the precious bag of rice to take to the shrine. The grave look of his father as he stared out over the dying fields. *The daimyo's men will be coming soon. Perhaps they are already there. My village is still in danger.*

"I'm sorry." Swiftly, Takeo rose, causing all four nobles to glance up at him. "Please forgive my rudeness," he said, bowing as Lady Miyazawa's gaze fixed on him. "Your kindness has been overwhelming, but I must go home, back to the village. My family needs me."

"No," Yuki said, standing up as well. Her dark eyes were wide with alarm. "Takeo-san, don't leave. Stay here, just a little longer."

"I'm sorry, Yuki-san," Takeo said again, though a stab of pain went through him as he met her eyes. "I wish I could stay, I really do. But this year has been bad for my village. With the drought, we'll be unable to pay the rice tax when the daimyo's men come. My father is the headman, so he and my family will be punished if we can't produce the rice. I must return; the tax collector will arrive any day now."

Yuki looked stricken. She cast a desperate gaze toward Lady Miyazawa, but the lady of the house simply nodded and raised a hand to Takeo. "We understand, Takeo-san. Of course family should come first. Safe travels home."

Yuki shook her head. "But—"

"Daughter." The lady's dark eyes fixed on the girl. "We cannot keep him here if he does not wish to stay." Yuki started to protest, but Lady Miyazawa raised her voice. "Would you have him pine and worry for his village, and eventually come to resent us?"

Yuki slumped and dropped her gaze in defeat. Her shoulders trembled as she bowed her head, dark hair hiding her face.

"It was an honor to have you here, Takeo-san," Lady Miyazawa continued, ignoring her daughter. "Safe travels to you on your way home. Yuki will show you out."

Takeo trailed Yuki down the dim corridors in silence, looking up only when she pushed back a pair of magnificent red doors and stepped into a courtyard surrounded by bamboo. By the position of the moon overhead, it was late indeed. Cicadas hummed and fireflies bobbed past his head as the girl led him toward the gates. A pond with a stone lantern sat nearby, fat red-and-white fish swirling lazily beneath the waters.

At the gate, Yuki hesitated. The moonlight blazed down on her, making her glow like a yurei-ghost, beautiful and otherworldly. "Takeo-san . . . ," she began, and stopped. For a moment, she stood there, gazing at her hands, as if struggling with herself. Finally, she took a deep breath and looked up again, her eyes shining like dark mirrors in the night.

"Do you—do you remember the day you saved a fox from a pair of village dogs?"

The question was so unexpected that at first Takeo could only blink at her. "I—I think so, Yuki-san," he stammered. It had been such a long time ago, back when he was young and carefree, when the weight of the village and his family didn't rest so heavily on his shoulders. Back when he could still pretend he could become a samurai.

And then, the real implications of the question hit him hard, and a cold chill crept up his spine, raising the hairs on his neck. He'd told no one of that day or his actions. The only ones who knew he had rescued a fox from a gruesome death were himself, the dogs . . . and the fox itself.

Chilled, he looked at Yuki again, seeing her for the first time. He remembered, suddenly, the stories. Of kitsune, and what they could do: Change their shape. Appear human. Weave illusions until they blended so perfectly with reality that it was impossible to tell them apart. Yuki met his gaze, eyes glowing a subtle gold in the candlelight, the tip of a bushy tail peeking behind her robes.

"Don't be afraid," Yuki said quietly as Takeo stood there, frozen in shock. "I would never hurt you, Takeo-san. After you saved me that day, I wanted to repay your kindness, to thank you, but there was never a good time. Your people would have chased me off or killed me if I got too close. So, I waited, and watched you from afar. I watched you grow from a cub into the man you are now, and . . ." She paused, and Takeo thought he saw a faint pink glow touch her cheeks. "My feelings for you grew, as well."

"Yuki-san." Takeo breathed, feeling like he was balanced on the edge of a cliff; he could choose to step back, to safety, or take the plunge. She was a fox, his brain told him. A kitsune. Not human. But gazing into her face, he saw no trace of the guile, deceit, or craftiness attributed to her kind. What he did see was an emotion so pure and genuine it made his breath catch and nearly stopped his heart.

"I know you have to go back," Yuki said softly. "I know how much you care for your family. But . . . I can help you, Takeo-san. I can save your village. If you'll let me."

Accepting help from a kitsune was a fool's errand. He knew this. But, his family . . . "How?" he whispered.

"You need rice for the . . . tax collector, yes?" The girl tilted her head, her smooth brow furrowed. "I've seen them: men on horseback come every season, and they take baskets of rice with them when they leave. This is something you must let them do?"

"Yes," Takeo answered. "The land isn't ours; we simply farm it for the daimyo, our ruling lord. If we don't pay the tax, the whole village will be punished."

Yuki blinked slowly, as if such a concept was completely foreign to her, but asked: "How much do you need?"

"How—how much rice?" Takeo stammered, and Yuki nodded gravely. "At least five hundred koku, more if we had an exceptional harvest." Yuki looked faintly confused, so he hurried to explain. "Sixty percent of our crops go to the daimyo every year, but we have to at least produce the five hundred koku to meet the minimum quota. But this year we're short by nearly two hundred koku, and that's if we give them everything and have nothing left to get us through the winter."

The girl pondered this for a moment. Finally, she raised her head, a dark, determined look in her eyes. "I can give you what you need," she said.

Takeo's heart leaped in his chest. "You—you can? How?"

"I am kitsune, Takeo-san." Yuki's lips quirked slightly. "We have our ways. My family and I built an estate from nothing in the middle of nowhere. Two hundred koku of rice should not be difficult to produce.

"But," she added as Takeo contemplated throwing himself to the ground at her feet, "if you wish my help, there is one condition I fear I must ask."

"Anything," Takeo husked. "I don't have much, but if you can save my village, anything in my power to give is yours. What is it you want, Yuki-san?"

"A promise." The kitsune stared at him, and for a moment, he saw the shadow of a fox, gold-eyed and intelligent, in her gaze. "After the rice is delivered and the daimyo's men are gone, you must return and live with us for one year. That is the price for a kitsune's intervention. I want you to promise me that you'll come back, that you'll see me again."

Takeo's stomach dropped. *Live with foxes? For a year?* Some of his anguish must have shown on his face, for Yuki's eyes darkened and she regarded him solemnly. "Would it really be that bad, Takeo-san?" she asked quietly. "You would be an honored guest here. I promise you will want for nothing. You can leave behind the toil and hardships of a mortal life." Her voice softened as she dropped her gaze to the floor. "And perhaps, in time, you will come to see me as more than just a fox."

"I already do," Takeo whispered, surprising himself as well as Yuki. She raised her head, eyes shining with hope, and he swallowed hard. "Yuki-san, you've shown me kindness when most would've seen a worthless farmer. You took me into your home and treated me not as a peasant, but as a guest. I can't promise I'll be able to—to return your feelings, but I can agree to return. After the rice is delivered and my village is safe, I'll come back. I promise."

Yuki smiled then, and it seemed to banish the shadows from the forest. "One more night," she whispered, holding out her hand. "Stay with me for one more night. Return to your village tomorrow; the rice will be ready when you wake up."

The bamboo around them seemed to sway, the fireflies blurring and becoming hazy balls of light. Takeo nodded, stepped forward, and placed his palm in hers.

The night passed in a fluttering of memories, like the fragile beat of a moth's wing. The dim glow of brazier. The feel of silk, sliding over bare skin. Being wrapped in a cocoon of warmth and darkness, the taste of *sake* and sweat on his lips, and the glow of a fire in the pit of his stomach. Gazing into the eyes of a girl and wishing that, be it illusion or fantasy, he would never wake, and the night would go on forever.

He awoke cold and shivering on a bare wood floor, a ratty blanket draped over him. Confused, he raised his head, gazing around the abandoned shell of a tiny wooden hut. Rotting beams and timbers leaned precariously against the walls, and weeds poked up through the floorboards, eating away at the wood. Takeo saw the bones of many small animals lying in corners or scattered among leaves and refuse, and tufts of reddish fur clung to everything.

In a daze, he staggered from the ruin, finding a game trail that snaked through the forest. Staggering from the trees, he blinked in shock. He was back on the road that led to the shrine, and a horse and wagon stood waiting for him at the edge, the back of the cart laden with reed baskets. A quick peek inside revealed they were full to bursting with gleaming white grains. Takeo felt his heart swell, the tension in his stomach releasing in a rush.

Thank you, Yuki-san, he thought, closing his eyes. *I'll see you again soon, I promise.*

But when he arrived at the village late that afternoon, he knew something was wrong. A group of samurai on horseback clustered in front of his hut, their kimono bearing the *mon*-crest of the daimyo. The villagers stood silently nearby as one man, who Takeo recognized as the chief tax collector, loomed over the hunched form of his father, who knelt before him with his face pressed to the ground. An icy spear lanced through Takeo, and he urged the horse to move faster.

"A disgrace!" the tax collector was shouting, his high, shrill voice carrying over the wind. He held a bamboo rod in one hand and was waving it as though he might strike any who got too close. "Lazy, undisciplined, good-for-nothing peasants! How dare you offer this pitiful bounty to your most gracious lord! This insult will not go unpunished."

"Wait!" Takeo called, driving the wagon up to the startled tax collector. Leaping from the cart, he hurried over and prostrated himself beside his father. "Please forgive me," he said, feeling cold dirt pressing against his forehead. "But I have the rest. Of the rice. It's all there."

"What trickery is this?" The chief tax collector eyed him suspiciously, then turned his gaze to the wagon. "What have you worthless peasants been doing? Search the cart," he ordered, and one of the waiting samurai immediately strode up to the wagon, tearing off basket lids. Takeo waited, heart pounding, until the samurai grunted and stepped back.

"It's all here, sir," the warrior confirmed.

"I see." Far from being pleased, the tax collector's voice was ugly. He took a step toward Takeo, his fine *hakama*-trousers swishing over the dirt. "I know what is going on here," he continued harshly. "I've seen it before. You farmers have another field, don't you? A hidden field, where you grow rice on the side. Denying your lord his fair share, you worthless, ungrateful thieves."

Takeo's blood ran cold. "No," he protested, forgetting himself and glancing up at the collector. "That's not true!"

"Really?" The man bent down, glaring at him with cold black eyes. "Then where did you get this rice, peasant? It obviously did not come from these fields."

"I— It was given to me," Takeo stammered, not knowing what else to say. "In the forest. A gift from Inari himself."

A resounding blow rocked his head to the side, laying him out in the dirt. "Liar!" the collector snarled, striking him again with his bamboo rod. "Ungrateful wretch. You peasants have been lying to us, hiding a portion of the crops for yourselves. That is a crime against your benevolent lord. I should execute the lot of you for treason!"

Takeo's head was spinning, and something warm was trickling into his ear. He was vaguely aware of his father, pleading with the collector, begging for mercy. "He is but a boy," he heard him say. "He didn't know what he was doing. Forgive him. Punish me for this transgression."

No, Takeo thought, trying to struggle upright. The ground swayed beneath him, and he gritted his teeth to keep from falling. *Not my family. This isn't their fault.*

The collector sneered. "Get him up," he ordered, and two samurai grabbed Takeo under the arms, yanking him upright, and setting him on his knees. Shivering, Takeo looked up and met the pitiless glare of the other man, who handed his bamboo rod to a samurai before drawing his sword. It hissed as it was unsheathed, a curved ribbon of gleaming metal that caught the sunlight.

"We will take the rice," the collector said, speaking to Takeo's father, who still knelt in the dirt, his shoulders trembling with quiet sobs. "But this crime against the daimyo will not go unpunished. Let this be a lesson to you. The next time, this whole disgusting village will be razed and burned to the ground. Be grateful for that mercy, or you will all end up like this."

Takeo blinked blood from his eyes and looked past the collector to where his mother and Hitomi stood in the doorway of their home. His mother wept loudly, and Hitomi stared out at him with huge, tear-filled eyes. He tried to smile at her. She, at least, was safe, he tried to tell himself. His family and his village were safe. That was all that mattered.

Yuki, he thought, remembering the warm glow of a brazier, the hiss of silk over skin. *I'm sorry. I wish I could have returned, to see you one more time.*

Then the blade sliced down across his neck, and the keening cry of a fox echoed over the trees.

Hironobu Ichiro, official tax collector for the daimyo of the Hida province, was feeling rather smug as he rode back through the forest. True, the drought that year had been hard, but he had still been able to procure more than half the expected taxes for the daimyo. This was more rice than his lord had estimated he would receive, and he would surely reward Hironobu for his efforts.

A breeze rustled the branches of the trees, and Hironobu's mount snorted and half reared, almost throwing him from the saddle. The rest of the samurai's horses, too, began to buck, and the men struggled to calm them. Hironobu cursed and yanked on the reins, bringing the beast to a shuddering halt.

A girl stood in the middle of the trail, long hair rippling in the dying wind. Her eyes flickered in the shadows of the forest, glowing like twin candles. As Hironobu straightened, ready to demand what she was doing, the branches of the trees began to shake. The sunlight disappeared, vanishing behind clouds, and the shadows of the forest began to lengthen, closing around men and horses like the talons of a monstrous beast.

Hironobu's party never returned to the daimyo. A search party found them weeks later, lying stiff and broken at the base of a cliff, entangled with their mounts as if their horses had fled in blind terror. The rice cart had also been smashed in the fall, and grains were scattered everywhere, mixed with the blood of the samurai.

Hironobu Ichiro's body was not among them.

One year later, a man stumbled out of the forest near the base of the mountains. He was naked, filthy, and utterly, raving mad. When he spoke, he screamed and cried about demons in the forest, ghosts and spirits and all manner of terrible beasts, and a girl. A girl who haunted his steps, who followed him wherever he went, her eyes the yellow of candlelight. He was put to death, more out of pity than anything else, but the story of the girl in the forest spread throughout the province. Finally, the daimyo himself sent a unit of men to investigate, and only one returned, babbling of ghosts, a cursed forest, and a girl with glowing eyes watching them through the trees. Unwilling to risk more samurai and further insult to whatever vengeful ghosts haunted the woods, the daimyo forbade travel through that part of the forest and posted signs at the entrance, proclaiming the area cursed. The village at the base of the mountain was given up for lost and didn't see the shadow of a samurai or tax collector for years after the daimyo's death.

The son of the headman was buried without ceremony in the graveyard at the edge of the village. On clear, full nights, if one happens to look in that direction, one might glimpse a figure standing at the headstone. Some have seen a girl. Others have seen a small orange fox. And, on rare occasions, a small boy has been seen at the gravesite as well, his eyes the yellow gold of candlelight.

Kitsune

A Japanese Myth

Kitsune are perhaps Japan's most beloved and popular creatures of myth. They appear in countless stories, books, poems, and illustrations, as well as in modern movies, manga, and anime. In all tales, kitsune possess magical powers, but the most common is their ability to shape-shift into human form. They are also known for their illusions, and for creating floating balls of ghostly luminescence, called kitsune-bi or "foxfire." Their stories are as varied as the kitsune themselves: they can be malevolent tricksters, dutiful protectors, beings of ancient wisdom, even wives and lovers. Kitsune falling in love with and marrying a human is a common tale. Though it usually ends with the man discovering his wife's true nature, often after she has lived with him for years and borne him several children, and the wife reverting to a fox and fleeing into the woods, never to be seen again. With Takeo and Yuki, I wanted to highlight the kitsune's world, but also show the emotions and complexities of Japan's most infamous trickster.

—Julie Kagawa

CARP, CALCULUS, AND THE LEAP OF FAITH

ELLEN OH

It's Saturday in June, and I should be enjoying my summer vacation. Instead, I'm stuck at home with lousy air conditioning, sweating my face off. My mom bought me a bunch of study guides, because she was furious with me for getting a C in calculus. Thing is, I loathe calculus with every anger-filled atom of my physical being.

My first year at NYU was rough. I had loaded up on pre-med courses, which were all science and math and horrible. The only class I managed to get an A in was my literature class. Neither of my parents had been happy about my grades but my mom had been especially angry. My mom was a physics major in college and got her master's in mechanical engineering. She finds calculus fun. I'm pretty sure she isn't really my mother. My latest working theory is that she is a robot that eats only ramen and kimchee, like noodles and cabbage are some kind of super robot fuel.

"Focus, Ellen!" My mom pokes me with the sharp end of her pencil. "You need to do well in math in order to get into a good medical school."

I don't want to go to medical school.

I don't want to do math.

I want to burn my calculus book.

But my mom always just tells me to focus. I'm stuck going around and around in this circle and I'll never get out. I'm trapped in pre-med purgatory.

My dad shoots a sympathetic look at me where I sit at the kitchen table with my mom, clutching my pencil tightly to avoid stabbing my eyes out. He shuffles past and hustles off when my mom starts speaking in tongues about integrals and derivatives. If only he would stand up to her and save me from this torturous hell. He knows that I'd rather eat mud than work on math equations. But neither my father nor I are brave enough to face off my mother. She has determined that one of her children will become a medical doctor. She is one scary lady. I glare at my dad's fast-retreating back as my mother pokes me again and yells at my sister to lower the TV. Janet is watching Saturday morning cartoons, and she lowers the volume by a mere fraction of a decibel. What a little jerk!

After two hours of mind-numbing equations that have killed off a million of my brain cells, my mother declares that she is taking my sister to the store. With her attention now solely focused on the whining one, I sneak off to my room, where I nurse a pounding headache with my hidden stash of

Cheez Doodles and Kit Kats. Junk food is my salvation.

A few minutes later, Dad pops in to check up on me.

"You'd better not let your mom catch you," he says.

"She won't, cause I'm gonna eat it all and dump the wrappers in the incinerator room before she comes home."

"She's still going to find out," he says.

"Nuh-uh." I wipe my mouth on my bare arm, which I realize feels kind of disgusting.

"Oh yes, she will," Dad says adamantly.

"How?"

"Because you've been wiping your fingers on your white shirt and your blanket. Nothing makes that special orange color like Cheez Doodles."

I jump to my feet and look down at the incriminating mess on my shirt and bed and scream out an extremely bad word that gets me a hard smack on the back of my head.

"Ya!" Dad curses me out in Korean for cursing in English, then he shakes his head and humphs his way out of my room. Oh, the irony.

I change my shirt and scrub at the orange stains on my comforter. My mom hates junk food as much as I hate calculus. There can be no trace of my indiscretion. Finally nothing is left but the faint memory of fake cheese odor in my room and the dry mouth my panic left me with. Relief makes me very thirsty, and I head to the kitchen for water and find my dad looking at the calculus books I've left on the dining table.

"Huh," he says as he looks at all the red cross-outs on my worksheet. "Why aren't you better at math?"

"I must take after you."

My dad chuckles. "You're right."

He goes to the living room and turns on the TV. He grabs a bag of pistachios and a big bowl and starts cracking the shells open.

I follow him and plop onto the sofa. "Dad, why do I have to do math? I hate it so much."

"It is your duty to listen to your mother."

"But you can override Mom. After all, I'm just like you."

"And if my mother pushed me to do better in calculus, perhaps I wouldn't be so bad at math, and you couldn't use that as an excuse to get out of it."

He gives me a half-chiding, half-sympathetic look over the top of his glasses. It's the sympathy that hits me hard.

"I don't want to be a doctor," I whisper.

My father wipes his hands of pistachio residue and leans over to peer into my face.

"What is it you want to do?"

I'm quiet for a long moment and then I shrug. "Do I have to know right now? Why can't I figure that out later?"

My father tilts his head to the side and furrows his brows. "How do you know that you don't want to be a doctor? How are you so sure?"

"All my life Mom's been telling me I have to be a doctor. That she wants me to be a doctor," I answer. "Not once has she ever asked me if *I* want to be one. Because if she did, I'd tell her that I'd rather go to the dentist every day for a year than be a doctor for the rest of my life."

It is well known in the family that I believe all dentists are servants of Satan and actual demons from hell.

My dad lets out a deep "Ummmm," which means he's taking my words seriously.

"You are certain?" he asks.

"Absolutely," I say, as I cross my arms for emphasis. This I know from deep within my soul. Med school is not for me. I can't stand the sight of blood, and I don't like most people enough to want to deal with their myriad issues of disgusting bodily functions.

"Then you must face your mother and tell her the truth."

Ha! Easy for him to say. He's not terrified of her. Actually, that's not true. I've seen them argue. He almost never wins. I kick the fringe of the rug in front of me.

"What are you so afraid of? Don't be afraid to tell the truth. She will not kill you."

"You wanna bet?" I mutter. Mom does cold better than anyone I know. She doesn't yell at you, she just stares until you crumble into a little pile of dust specks that she sweeps into the garbage.

My dad turns in his seat to face me squarely.

"You don't want to be a doctor. You don't want to study calculus. But you are too afraid of your mother to tell her these truths, am I right?"

I nod. That's exactly right.

"And this is your mother's fault because she is making you do something you don't want to do, yes?"

I nod even harder. He gets it!

"Well, I think it is your fault for not telling her the truth," he said.

Wait—what? He is blaming me for the hell my mom is

putting me through? I open my mouth to yell, and he cuts me off.

"You cannot live your life in fear. You must figure out how to conquer it or else be ready to accept your fate."

With that, my father goes back to the kitchen to start making coffee. I stare after him for a few moments, then heave a sigh and sulkily slide into a chair by the kitchen table. He boils water in the kettle and pulls out his jar of instant coffee. That stuff is pretty gross even if you add lots of milk and sugar.

"Dad, how do I tell her? Whenever I try, she just tells me I don't know anything and that she knows what's best for my future. How do I fight that?"

My father is silent as he pours the boiling water into his oversized mug and then stirs in cold milk. To be honest, he is drinking more milk than coffee. What I didn't realize was that he had also made me a cup of hot cocoa. He brings over the hot drinks and then a bag of Oreo cookies and that bag of pistachios. He really loves those nuts.

"Here, have this before your mom comes home," he says.

I dunk my cookies and shovel them into my mouth two at a time while my dad slowly and methodically eats one.

"Let me tell you a story . . ." he says.

"True story?"

"It's a famous legend of the Ha clan."

My dad is a great storyteller, and there is always a reason for him telling me a particular story at any given time. I don't always understand it right away, but he is the wisest person I know. So I sit back and listen.

Long, long ago, when tigers roamed freely across the entire peninsula, the Ha clan lived off the coast of the Yellow Sea, hardy fishermen who knew the oceans better than the forests. They lived a simple but happy life in their seaside village. But it was dangerous, living so close to the ocean. Marauding pirates terrorized the coastal villages. Most villages close to shore erected large iron bells that sentries could ring in warning. Whenever the bell's toll rang out, all the villagers ran up into the mountains to hide before the invaders landed on their shore. It became something of an annual curse. The toll of the bell, the run for the mountains, the looting by the invaders. Until one year, very early on a cool autumn morning, the invaders coasted in through heavy mist and the bell never rang. The sentry had fallen asleep and failed to see the invaders until it was too late. The pirates had made it to the village gates.

"That guy is so fired," I cut in. "He had one job . . ."

My father shrugs. "He was probably the first to die."

"Good."

"You are very ruthless."

"No 'falling asleep on the job' allowed when death is on the line. That's what I always say." I am channeling my inner Vizzini from *The Princess Bride,* which is my all-time favorite movie. I even let out a loud Vizzini-esque cackle,but my dad is not having any of it.

"Hmmmmmm," he says. "Your mother would say that falling asleep at church is just as bad."

"That's totally different. Nobody's salvation but mine is in danger. I don't do anyone dirty like that." I glare at my dad. "You're one to talk! I've seen you sleeping many times in church."

"I'm not sleeping, I'm resting my eyes." He closes his eyes and leans back in his chair as if to make his point.

"What about the time I heard you snore."

"That wasn't a snore, it was a chant, a meditation prayer in Korean. From being a Buddhist before your mother converted me."

"Uh-huh, Buddhist chant."

"That's why I always tell you to learn Korean."

My dad reaches over for his coffee and slurps it loudly before he continues.

The invaders arrived at the village gates as the sentry finally rang the bell, but it was too late. All was chaos. The Ha clan lived on the outskirts of town, and when the bell rang, the father quickly gathered all his family members to run for safety. He carried the grandmother on his back and guided everyone else up the mountain path. They ran as fast as they could, but they could hear the pirates behind them, gaining on them. The father led his family farther into the mountains than they'd ever had to go before. They were all exhausted, and the little ones were crying in fear and pain. When they finally reached a large lake, the family collapsed. The father knew that they could not run anymore. The pirates' shouts grew closer and closer. In desperation, he looked up to the heavens and prayed for help. Anything to save his family.

A great shining light appeared directly above the lake. And as the Ha clan stared up in wonder, they began to change one by one into beautiful, colorful carp that leaped into the waters. When the father was the only one left, he bowed to the heavens and gave thanks to the ancestral spirits who had intervened to save them all. And then he too transformed into the largest carp of them all and leaped into the water just as the invaders appeared.

"And that is why no Ha-shi—that is us—can ever eat carp," my father finishes with a flourish. "It will taste terrible because carp are our long-lost ancestors."

I blink.

"So you're saying, we are related to fish," I say slowly.

My father nods. "Specifically the big, beautiful carp."

"They are still fish."

"What's wrong with fish?"

"I don't want to be related to fish! Can't this story be about how they turned into a pack of man-eating tigers and ate all the invaders?"

My dad shakes his head. "You must accept your past in order to fulfill your future."

"What the heck does that mean?"

"Beats me! I saw it in a fortune cookie once. I kind of like it. Did you know fortune cookies aren't really Chinese? They were originally from Japan."

That makes me laugh, but still, the story offends me.

"Don't change the subject. That's the worst story you've ever told me," I say.

"About the fortune cookies?"

I let out an exasperated sigh. "No, about the magic fish."

"That story is your heritage."

"Nope, nope, nope. I denounce that magic-fish heritage." The more I think about the story, the madder I get. I'm trying to figure out why it bothers me so much, other than fish being slimy and stinky.

"Just because you don't like something . . ."

"No, it's a dumb story. I think the truth is, the clan dad got really, really drunk and made up the whole entire thing."

"Probably," my dad agrees with a smile. "But it makes a great legend, right?"

"It's a terrible legend," I complain. "I hate it. The family escapes the invaders by turning into fish. How do we know the invaders didn't go fishing afterward and eat all the family members? What if they didn't want to be fish anymore? Could they turn back? And who wants to be related to fish?"

We are both quiet for a long moment. I'm angry and he is just gazing at me with this look on his face that's both amused and pitying. My father's eyes are the most expressive part of his face. They tell me that he sees me and he gets me.

"Why are you so angry?" he asks.

"Because fish are stupid! They're stuck in a lake, unable to go anywhere else. Just swimming in circles. Trapped forever in water."

"Ah," my father says. He is back to cracking open pistachios again. Crack, unshell, eat, dust off. Repeat. I shift in my seat as if I am the carp with nowhere to go, when all I want is to be free to travel the world and never do calculus again.

"Ah, what?" I ask.

"When you were little, you could never sit still. Always

curious, always moving around. Always opening doors and exploring," he said. "You've never been satisfied with what is in front of you. You always want to see what else is out there."

The statement rings true to me. I'm someone who always wants to know what's happening around me. Whether or not I want to be a part of it, I want the ability to choose. Whether I do something or not, it has to be my decision, my desire.

"Would the story be less offensive if the carp were in the ocean or river leading to the ocean?"

I furrow my eyebrows. I still don't like the story, but that sensation of feeling trapped is lessened.

"Carp are not so bad. Because once in a rare moment, a brave and resourceful carp can transform into a dragon."

I perk up. Dragons are far more interesting than fish. "So that's the rest of the legend? We have dragons in our ancestry?"

"Don't be ridiculous! Dragons aren't real."

"People turning into fish aren't real either!" I sputter.

"Ah . . . So will you accept the Ha magic-fish past if there are also dragons in the legend?" my dad asks.

"Yes?" I ask hopefully. Dragons can fly. They aren't stuck in a sea of pre-med courses.

"Yes," he replies.

"So, is there a dragon in that legend or not?"

My father grabs my hand and pours a bunch of shelled pistachios into my open palm. He closes my fist around them and pats my hand.

"Don't be so hard on carp," he says. His eyes twinkle as he sits back in his seat. "There is a very famous Chinese legend about the Dragon's Gate."

"I hope it's better than the Ha family legend."

My dad ignores me.

"It starts with an ancient Chinese proverb. 'The carp has leapt through the dragon's gate.' It means someone has succeeded in doing something very difficult through diligence and lots of hard work."

"What does that have to do with dragons?" I'm getting a little testy. So far nothing my dad has said has given me a solution to my pre-med problem.

My dad pauses to eat his nuts. He eats them one at a time, chewing slowly and deliberately, not looking at me. This is on purpose to make me even more antsy. But I swallow my words and wait. After a long minute he continues.

There was once a terrible flood in China. The great godlike emperor had to save his people. He receded the waters and brought back the land. He began to create the Yellow River for the flood to empty into, but as he did, he encountered a large mountain blocking the course of his river. He split the mountain, causing a waterfall, and he called the formation on the top of the cliff Dragon's Gate. Legend has it that if a carp is strong enough and determined enough to leap up the waterfall and through the Dragon's Gate, it will become a dragon.

One day hundreds of the strongest carp congregated at the bottom of the waterfall. One after the other they leaped higher and higher into the air, desperate to reach the Dragon's Gate. None made it . . . until one golden carp finally soared through the gate and transformed into a large, glorious dragon.

❖ ❖ ❖

"That's the entire legend?" I slump in my chair, back to swimming in a lake full of derivatives and integrals.

"Carp symbolize endurance, strength, and perseverance," Dad says. "They can become dragons through their own hard work. I would say the same thing about you. You are strong, you never give up, you keep fighting. How many times have I gone to school because you had another fight?"

I slink down even further in my chair. "I have anger issues," I mutter.

"No, you fight injustice," he says. "Remember the time the principal was mad and said you were a troublemaker, that you started a fight and broke the other kid's front tooth? What happened that day on the way out of school?"

I remembered—another parent had stopped us to give me a big hug—but I didn't want to talk about it. There was this kid named Mary who was the smallest kid in sixth grade. She had crooked front teeth and freckles that covered every inch of her pale white face. She was a constant target for the bullies in our school. The parent who hugged me was Mary's mom.

"She said you always stuck up for Mary. That you would stop the kids who were picking on her every day. And she wanted to thank you for being such a good friend."

I wasn't friends with Mary. I found her annoying—but I hated bullies even more.

"Those kids were bigger than you, but you stood up to them. Fought them, got beaten up, and also hit back hard. I asked you why. Do you remember what you said to me?"

I pull at my ear, embarrassed. "I was a lot bigger than Mary, so I could fight them and she couldn't."

"Even if you feel trapped, you are the carp that fights its way upstream and leaps up waterfalls and transforms into a dragon." My dad reaches over to tap me on the nose. "Don't underestimate yourself or carp."

I'm starting to come to terms with my fishy backstory. It's making me realize how I've been feeling. I am the carp trapped by my mom's expectations. And if I don't make the leap, I will forever be stuck in pre-med purgatory.

"So the whole point of this legend is that I shouldn't be afraid to tell Mom that I don't want to be a doctor?"

My father clasps my hands between his firmly. "Stay strong, in the face of her opposition."

"Be like a carp?" I ask with a smile.

He smiles back. "And become the dragon."

At that moment, the door opens and my mom and sister walk in. I look at my dad and take a deep breath. It's time to leap through the dragon's gate.

"Mom, we need to talk."

The Magic Fish

The Ha Family Legend

When people ask what made me want to be a writer, I immediately think of my dad. He was a writer also. He wrote several books that were published in Korea, but which I have never read because I am shockingly illiterate in Korean. My dad was a consummate storyteller. He was the reason I learned all the myths and legends of Korea. Well, mostly the scary stuff. Like ghosts and goblins and demon foxes and monsters that liked to eat bad children named Ellen who didn't listen to their parents and tried to stay up all night reading books until they were so scared they couldn't even go to the bathroom until the first rays of the sun could be seen. Yeah, fun stuff.

He was also the one who would tell me the stories of our clan, of our history, of our family. Like the story of the Ha clan, as the father in this story tells his daughter. And like the daughter, I had questions. But my dad got all cryptic on me—he was like Master Oogway from *Kung Fu Panda*—and said, "You must accept your past in order to fulfill your future." I demanded that he explain himself, but all he did was shake his head at me as if I was the foolish one.

So I found a little Japanese restaurant that served Asian carp. I ordered it. It looked good and smelled great. I took a big bite and . . . spit it out immediately. I looked down at my fish and I said, "I'm so sorry, great ancestors!"

That carp was the most awful-tasting thing I have ever eaten. I tried to scrape the taste off my tongue with a wet napkin, ate ice cream and fruit, and still the horrid taste lingered. I had been justly punished by my fishy ancestors.

The Ha family legend is a part of my heritage and culture that I will pass on to my children. Our very own weird little fairy tale for us to appreciate where we come from. And I'm so grateful to my dad for sharing this legend with me.

My dad passed away in 2015. I miss talking to him and hearing his Oogway-like wisdom. I miss his laughter and his corny jokes. I miss him. But he is always with me as long as I remember his wonderful stories.

—Ellen Oh

Author Biographies

Renée Ahdieh is the author of the #1 *New York Times* bestseller *The Wrath & the Dawn*; its sequel, *The Rose & the Dagger*; and *Flame in the Mist*. She lives in Charlotte, North Carolina, with her husband and their dog, Mushu. You can visit her online at www.reneeahdieh.com.

Elsie Chapman grew up in Prince George, Canada, and has a degree in English literature from the University of British Columbia. She is the author of YA novels *Dualed, Divided,* and *Along the Indigo,* middle grade novel *All the Ways Home,* and co-editor of *Hungry Hearts.* A team member of We Need Diverse Books, she lives in Tokyo, Japan, with her husband and two children. You can visit her online at www.elsiechapman.com.

Sona Charaipotra is the co-author of *Tiny Pretty Things, Shiny Broken Pieces,* and *The Rumor Game* and the author of *Prognosis: Love & Death.* She is also the co-founder of Cake Literary, a boutique book packaging company with a diverse bent, and a journalist. She lives in New York City with her husband and their children. You can visit her online at www.sonacharaipotra.com.

Preeti Chhibber has been published on *BookRiot*, *SYFYWire*, and *The Mary Sue*. She is also the co-host of the podcasts *Desi Geek Girls* and *SYFY's Strong Female Characters*. By day, she works for Scholastic Book Clubs. She lives in New York City. You can visit her online at www.preetichhibber.com or find her on Twitter @runwithskizzers.

Roshani Chokshi is the author of the *New York Times* bestseller *The Star-Touched Queen*, which was a finalist for the Andre Norton Award and a Locus finalist for Best First Novel. She is also the author of *A Crown of Wishes*. You can visit her online at www.roshanichokshi.com.

Aliette de Bodard has won two Nebula Awards, a Locus Award, and three British Science Fiction Association Awards. She has also been a finalist for the Hugo, Sturgeon, and Tiptree Awards. She is the author of several young adult novels, including *The House of Shattered Wings*. She lives in Paris, France. You can visit her online at www.aliettedebodard.com.

Melissa de la Cruz is the #1 *New York Times*–, #1 *Publishers Weekly*–, and #1 IndieBound–bestselling author of many acclaimed novels for readers of all ages, including *Alex and Eliza*, Disney's Descendants series, the Blue Bloods series, the Witches of East End series, and *The Ring and the Crown*, which was also a television drama on Lifetime. Her Christmas movie *Angel Falls* aired on the Hallmark Channel in 2017. You can visit her online at www.melissa-delacruz.com.

Julie Kagawa is the *New York Times*–bestselling author of the Iron Fey series, the Blood of Eden series, and the Talon series. She was born in Sacramento, California, but spent most of her childhood in Hawaii. She now lives in Louisville, Kentucky, with her husband, two dogs, and a cat. You can visit her online at www.juliekagawa.com.

Rahul Kanakia is the author of *Enter Title Here*. His short stories have appeared in *Apex*, *Clarkesworld*, *Lightspeed*, the *Indiana Review*, and *Nature*. He has a degree in creative writing from Johns Hopkins and a degree in economics from Stanford. Originally from Washington, D.C., he now lives in Berkeley, California. You can visit him online at www.thewaronloneliness.com.

Lori M. Lee is the author of the Gates of Thread and Stone series. She was born in Laos and immigrated to the United States when she was three. She has a degree in creative writing (and sarcasm). She currently lives in Wisconsin with her husband, children, and an overly excited shih tzu. You can visit her online at www.lorimlee.com.

E. C. Myers is the author of four young adult novels, including *The Silence of Six* and its sequel, *Against All Silence*, and numerous short stories. He grew up in Yonkers, New York, and has a degree in visual arts from Columbia University. He lives with his wife, son, two cats, and an Australian shepherd in Pennsylvania. You can find him online at www.ecmyers.net.

Ellen Oh is the president and co-founder of We Need Diverse Books. She is the author of the Prophecy trilogy and a former adjunct college instructor and lawyer with an insatiable curiosity about ancient Asian history. Originally from Brooklyn, she now lives with her family in Bethesda, Maryland. You can visit her online at www.ellenoh.com.

Cindy Pon is the acclaimed author of five novels for teens, including *Want*, *Serpentine*, and *Silver Phoenix*. She is the cofounder of Diversity in YA and has been a Chinese brush painting student for more than a decade. You can visit her online at www.cindypon.com.

Aisha Saeed is an author, lawyer, educator, and a founding member of We Need Diverse Books. She is the author of *Written in the Stars*. She lives in Atlanta, Georgia, with her husband and their two sons. You can visit her online at www.aishasaeed.com.

Shveta Thakrar is a writer of South Asian–flavored fantasy, a social justice activist, and a part-time nagini. Her short stories have been published in a variety of magazines, including *Flash Fiction Online*, *Interfictions Online*, *Uncanny*, *Faerie*, and *Strange Horizons*. She has also been published in several anthologies, including *Clockwork Phoenix*, *Beyond the Woods: Fairy Tales Retold*, and *Kaleidoscope*. You can visit her online at www.shvetathakrar.com.

Alyssa Wong is a writer whose work has appeared in the *Magazine of Fantasy & Science Fiction, Strange Horizons, Nightmare Magazine, Black Static,* and *Tor.com,* among others. Her story "Hungry Daughters of Starving Mothers" won the 2015 Nebula Award for Best Short Story and the 2016 World Fantasy Award for Short Fiction, and her story "You'll Surely Drown Here If You Stay" won the 2017 Locus Award for Best Novelette. She was a finalist for the John W. Campbell Award for Best New Writer, and her fiction has been shortlisted for the Pushcart Prize, the Bram Stoker Award, the Hugo Award, and the Shirley Jackson Award. She lives in Chapel Hill, North Carolina. You can visit her online at www.crashwong.net.

Grateful acknowledgment is made to the authors listed below for permission to print their copyrighted material:

Renée Ahdieh, "Nothing into All"
Elsie Chapman, "Bullet, Butterfly"
Sona Charaipotra, "Still Star-Crossed"
Preeti Chhibber, "Girls Who Twirl and Other Dangers"
Roshani Chokshi, "Forbidden Fruit"
Aliette de Bodard, "The Counting of Vermillion Beads"
Melissa de la Cruz, "Code of Honor"
Julie Kagawa, "Eyes like Candlelight"
Rahul Kanakia, "Spear Carrier"
Lori M. Lee, "Steel Skin"
E. C. Myers, "The Land of the Morning Calm"
Ellen Oh, "Carp, Calculus, and the Leap of Faith"
Cindy Pon, "The Crimson Cloak"
Aisha Saeed, "The Smile"
Shveta Thakrar, "Daughter of the Sun"
Alyssa Wong, "Olivia's Table"